NEON GREEN

A NOVEL

MARGARET WAPPLER

The Unnamed Press
Los Angeles, CA

For David

PART ONE:
FOR ENTERTAINMENT PURPOSES ONLY

I

The spaceship hovers on a thin black line. Above the spaceship is outer space, the black gone depthless, matter stacked until it has exploded into either too much existence or not enough. The void between glistening planets, static with stardust until punctuated by chaos. To arrive here, the spaceship dodged rock masses, burned-out moons, and light-sucks. But now it waits, parked on the edge of Earth's atmosphere. Below, the land is partially obscured by gauzy layers of chemical haze and creeping cloud covers. In luxuriating patterns, the layers shift and crisscross, surround and dissolve into one another. People, metal, trees, sand, animals, and water occupy the planet. The people spend their time chopping, building, corralling, killing, harvesting, distilling, melting, commuting. In waves, particles, and sheets, pollution regularly sloughs off into the atmosphere, carried up and up. The chemicals appear to dissipate but instead have settled in the upper regions of the sky, where they trap heat. The spaceship has been waiting for days now, occasionally spinning in circles. Waiting, it stares down, taking in everything it sees.

2

August 1994

Prairie Park was a two-mile slice of dream community: moderately affluent, educated, safe, and green. Prized for its quality schools where the kids buried time capsules preserving *Bop* magazine, Depeche Mode cassette tapes, the front page of the *Chicago Tribune*, and a clutch of Jolly Ranchers. This suburban grid, rich and pliant, with Montessori day care and weekly farmers' markets, supported all the spoils of upper-middle-class American life. Between the petitions to keep Prairie Park free of nukes, dutifully signed before entering the library, and the el train shuttling workers in Reeboks they'd exchange for heels and oxfords once they hit the office, it was a thoughtful and efficient almost-utopia, connected to the city but with enough quaint neighborhood parks to pretend otherwise.

Ernest would never leave it—but he was often worried it would leave him. All of it—the people, the parks, the planet—ravaged in a lifetime or two. Standing right here in Aurora Park, a block away from his house, he could envision the time-lapse demise of Earth from millions of miles out. A dead spot would start on one continent and spread to the entire globe, like a lawn plagued by disease. Granted, on his fortieth birthday, stationed at one of the barbecue grills open to the public, there was plenty else to be panicked about—the images of genocide and war in Rwanda and Bosnia were gruesome and atrocious—but the planet, a temperate rock cradled in a gaseous film as moth-eaten as a vintage veil, was the most precarious and central of all causes. It was *the planet*, for god's sake. Without it, what else?

There certainly wouldn't be Andrés Escobar, Ernest thought ruefully, watching three kids playing keep-away with a soccer ball. The Colombian soccer player had been gunned down at a Medellín nightclub last month for the heinous crime of accidentally scoring a goal against his own team during a World Cup match. Chicago had hosted the World Cup in June for the first time ever, painting soccer balls all over the streets downtown, and Ernest, whose interest in sports was casual, to say the least, found himself swept up in the fever. Escobar's murder stunned him—the kid was only twenty-seven years old. Twenty-seven years old! It was 1994 and people were getting fatally shot in the back for sporting errors? The medieval violence galled him.

OK, breathe. It's Saturday. It's your birthday! Ernest tried to tap into the divine relaxation vibes his wife was always urging him to find. Not that she had the road map to them herself. Not that you could just strike the stream of peace and love whenever you wanted to. It was more spontaneous and lucky than that. "When grace goes by the window," she'd say, "you have to grab it fast." Ernest had to admit the day was doing its part to yield the right circumstances. Far away in the summer afternoon sky, Mercury glowed like a hunk of pyrite. Families, teenagers, and working people sunbathed and picnicked on the plush lawn of Aurora Park, relaxed, open, deliciously dazed by the heat.

But there was a problem. Behind him at the picnic table, his wife and their two teenage children waited for their lunch on the verge of riotous impatience. And the grill master upon whom they depended was distracted, big-time.

At a neighboring grill, another chef—a buff guy around his age— was sparing no fanciful gesture with his engorged bottle of lighter fluid, as if fire, the oldest thing ever, needed a haze of poly-whatever to nurture it into being. He doused his charcoal once, twice, three times, zigzagging at the end for a little extra flourish. Then he threw a match in and immediately flames leaped out of the stacked pyramid. His girlfriend or whoever—Ernest estimated she was a good fifteen years younger than him—clapped her hands together, which made a funny squashing noise because she was still holding her can of illicit beer.

"Ernest," Cynthia said to her husband in a warning murmur. "Don't."

Ernest had a kind of environmental Tourette's, where he was compelled to remark if something didn't adhere to his principles. Cynthia and most people who knew him understood that he didn't intend to offend anyone with his comments. He was just as likely to observe his own failings in the exact same tone of voice, beset with a grim acceptance of life's inevitable compromises. For now, he pursed his lips in a grim line.

The fire at his own grill wasn't going nearly as well. In fact, it wasn't going at all. His son, Gabe, kept repeating, also in a low voice, "Just ask that guy for his lighter fluid, what's the big deal?" but Ernest would never poison his charcoal (and their food) with additives. As a result, the light summer wind kept stalling his efforts at ignition. The twists of newspaper he set on fire blew out before the charcoals could catch, time after time after time.

Their neighbor had a surplus of fire, so much so that he was forced to step back for a moment as the flames roared up past his chest, threatening to take his eyebrows with them.

"That's what I'm talking about!" the man announced smugly to his girlfriend, and pumped a fist in the air.

"You know," Ernest called out indignantly. The man and his girlfriend looked over at them. Cynthia put her head in her hands. "You might want to consider skipping the lighter fluid next time. So many terrible chemicals, you probably don't realize. You should let that fire burn off for a while before you throw your burgers on it so you don't eat any of the residue."

The girlfriend cocked an eyebrow and crossed her legs, anklet jingling. The man took a sip of his beer, and as his flexing biceps caught the sunlight, Ernest noticed then that he was muscular to the point of it being nearly a handicap. His arms did not lie smoothly against his torso; they stuck out at angles.

"I'm good," the man said, before adding, "Hey, how long have you been trying to light that fire?"

"Forever," Gabe piped in.

"This is how we do it," Ernest insisted to no one in particular.

"It's my dad's birthday," Alison tried explaining. "He's stubborn but we love him."

At fourteen years old, Alison was eighteen months younger than her brother and therefore more likely to cut her sarcasm with sweetness. The man grinned. "You're so cute," the girlfriend sang to Alison—though she was barely a woman herself—while her boyfriend started toward them, lighter fluid in hand.

"Tell you what: for your birthday, I can get this fire going for you in no time."

They all laughed, except Ernest.

"No, no, thank you. I'll taste it in everything. It'll ruin my whole day, maybe my week."

The man gave him some side-eye. "Seriously?"

"He's impossible," Gabe said. "This is what we live with."

"You're so nice to offer," Cynthia finally spoke up. "Don't worry about us."

"Listen," the man said, "I know you want to do it your way, but I'll just leave this here, in case you change your mind." He handed the lighter fluid directly to Gabe, who hissed, "Yesssss," and clutched the prize to his chest.

As soon as the man returned to his camp, just barely out of earshot, Ernest leaned over to Gabe and scream-whispered, "You think that guy's cool? Please."

"Well, he can start a fire. That's pretty cool."

"He's also drinking beer illegally in the park."

"So are you!"

"It's my birthday! And it's in a red cup. Everyone knows to put it in a red cup. He's being flagrant about it."

Ernest went back to his collection of cold rocks. More determined than ever, he twisted fresh newspaper sections into potential screwdrivers of flame. For a second they burned with promise but then petered into ash, lighting not a single charcoal in their vicinity.

"Um, I'm shedding pounds waiting for this meal," Alison said.

"Have some more baby carrots," Cynthia said.

"Ew, no way," Alison said, looking at her mother as if she were a festering boil.

"Fine," Cynthia said, dragging the plate of limp sticks back over to her side of the table. The rest of what she wanted to say—"you don't have to be such a little brat about it"—was already implied. She wanted to keep the peace, but Alison must've seen the look pass over her face.

"Sorry," she halfheartedly offered. "But they always remind me of skinned fingers."

Cynthia examined one and then popped it in her mouth. "Fingers taste good to me."

The man and his girlfriend were now sitting down to their lunch of succulent Polish sausage slathered in mustard, relish, and hot peppers, accompanied by skewers of perfectly grilled vegetables. They pretended to chat, but Ernest felt the man's eyes drift over, real casual-like but with a clear mission. The fire was still a no-show.

"Just one squirt," the man said, sweeping one arm in the air, "and boom!"

This was all the encouragement Gabe needed to pop up with the bottle. He held it up high, as if he were slam-dunking, and squeezed— "Here we go," he gleefully announced—but Ernest was fast and pushed him out of the way before any of the chemical splashed on the coals. But the victory was only temporary. Gabe moved in again, his bottle poised for re-attack. "What are you doing?" Ernest yelled. Cynthia cried out for them to "stop it right now!" But too late. In the melee, Gabe lost his grip on the bottle and it crashed to the ground. The plastic cracked and the smelly flammable bile gushed out onto the concrete. Their neighbors had stopped eating their sausages and could only stare in amazement at the disaster.

"See what you've done?" Ernest said.

Gabe scuttled to pick it up.

"Step back," Ernest snapped. He approached the bottle with makeshift mitts on his hands, napkins he'd grabbed off the table. Like a surgeon working with a still-beating heart, he carried the bottle at just the right angle so it wouldn't spill more and brought it to the trash. He laid it gingerly on the pile of soggy buns and crushed soda cans, making a mental note to eventually take it to recycling.

"I've got to mop this up," he told the family, looking at the still-damp spot of concrete.

"What?" Alison said, crashing her face into her hands. "Oh my god, we will never eat."

"Dad, are you out of your mind? It's on the concrete."

"Doesn't matter. You can't just leave a chemical spill like that."

"Come on, Dad," Gabe protested. "You make it sound like Exxon."

"Gabe," Cynthia said in a zip-it tone before exhaling with her eyes shut. To Ernest: "Clean it up how?"

"I'll run back home and get some soap and mop it up."

"The field house doesn't have any soap?"

"Nothing natural," Ernest said.

She put her hand to her forehead. "This is totally impractical."

"I don't understand why you're mad about this."

"Because we're all starving, Ernest. Let it go, just this once."

"It'll take ten minutes. You can start the fire while I'm gone."

Cynthia shook her head and closed her eyes. She drew in what Ernest recognized as a cleansing breath, deep and slow. When she looked back at him she appeared radiantly determined. "Be here with your family, Ernest. What about this day? It's your birthday. Be here with us." She lifted her hand into the air and grasped at something and slowly pulled it down with her palm closed. The air outside of himself, the divine stream. "The day is right here," she said.

He took them in: Alison, rooting around in the baby carrots she'd formerly rejected; Gabe, glaring at the ground, ravenous and ordered to silence by his mother, the only parent he sort of listened to; his wife, her figure directed toward him as a block and an anchor, her palm still closed around the air she wanted him to breathe. He found her attractive when she was like this—focused, determined—even if she had let a little extra weight gather around her hips and arms, but his mind was made up. It was his birthday, after all, and this was who he was—a committed environmentalist. The very idea filled him with energy. His life was a fight. He was a fighter, no apologies and no breaks for inconvenience. Of course he knew that mopping up the spill would probably do nothing, that it was an infinitesimal smidgen in the grand scheme of things, but his fight was no less important when it was symbolic. Symbols added up to something.

"Ten minutes," Ernest said, and gave her other hand a squeeze. He crossed the lawn of Aurora Park, where the high school girls rubbed in more tanning oil and talked in bubble script over their radios playing Whitney Houston, her supple voice reduced to a tinny stream. *"No other woman is going to love you more,"* Ernest sang along as he passed by without breaking his stride, purely for the girls' entertainment and delighting in their laughter. At the bleachers, a homeless man sat and repacked his bags, preparing to take the el train back into the city. Three middle-aged women, scrunchies around their stubby ponytails and wearing shapeless dresses in summer fabrics, walked by, subtly checking him out. Everyone seemed like they were posing for some sort of community yearbook yet to exist.

By the time he returned with a bucket of sudsy water and a raggedy mop, most of the spill had evaporated, but still, he sloshed water on the dark stain left behind. Cynthia had gotten the fire going—suspiciously fast, Ernest thought, but he wasn't about to question her methods. She hadn't greeted him upon his return; only a weak smile played on her lips, pitying or almost mocking, he couldn't tell. Sometimes it was easier for Cynthia and Ernest to move in silent, hostile arcs around each other, marking their dissatisfaction with only the distant orbit of their bodies. The kids didn't acknowledge him either. They had picked off everything edible on the table and were now sullen. The man and his girlfriend had long since decided that totally ignoring this scene was the most merciful gesture. Ernest mopped until he felt reassured that he'd done as much as he could.

Later, he'd think about what Cynthia had said: "Be here with your family."

He should've listened to her. A year later, none of this would exist in the same form: the park or his family. What he had built haphazardly and carefully, with equal parts love and mistakes, would be destroyed, and nothing as he knew it would be left.

Back at home, after the picnic where his kids and wife had roused an acceptable amount of obligatory birthday cheer to get through the meal, Ernest sat in the living room with Gabe, who tinkered with his latest obsession, the shortwave radio, which he'd carried down in a box from its usual perch upstairs in his bedroom.

The muggy early evening wasn't exactly scotch weather, but Ernest stationed himself in his armchair and sipped at his generous pour all the same, determined to enjoy this expensive gift from Tom, his close friend and neighbor and an avatar of good taste. Usually Ernest drank beer, preferred it to all else, but he'd decided that he'd tell Tom the scotch was wonderful, despite the fact that it tasted like that lighter fluid if it hadn't evaporated but rather boiled in the sun. He could still see the liquid gushing out of the bottle, the simultaneous evaporation and sinking in. A part of him wanted to dash to the park right now, to see if he could still find the stain—an idea he'd already run by Cynthia, who'd given him a sympathetic pat on the hand and then promptly disappeared into her home office—but he stayed put, sipping at his fire water.

He wanted time with Gabe, who was setting up the shortwave on the carpet. Gabe had promised earlier, before the fight, to give his dad a tour of the different stations for his birthday, to play him something he called "natural radio," but Ernest could tell that Gabe was now halfhearted about the plan. He'd have to warm him back up.

"Was that the best birthday gift ever or what?" Ernest said, nodding toward the black box.

Gabe, not looking at him, said, "Yep."

"We got you one that came very highly recommended."

"I know, Dad, you told me all this two weeks ago," Gabe said. "What do you think of *my* birthday gift to you?"

Ernest wiggled his toes in his brand-new pair of navy-blue New Balance sneakers. "Perfect," he said.

"Don't you ever get tired of the same shoes?"

"Why would I? They're comfortable," he said. Ernest considered himself an unfussy, easygoing man in dress, even though his commitment to such a look was actually quite fussy in practice.

Every morning he strapped on his digital calculator watch within five minutes of waking up, along with his jeans, dutifully replaced from the Land's End catalog whenever the knees got too threadbare, and his braided belt that made a satisfying creak when he pushed the prong into the woven leather, in the same worn spot every day. Then he topped it off with an old T-shirt with cracked lettering celebrating something like 1983's Earth Day, or a Lake Michigan beach cleanup, or a wildlife initiative like Save the Wolves, and an unbuttoned flannel. He finalized it with the New Balance sneakers (or brown boat shoes when he had to dress up).

"What if next year I get you a bright red pair? Would that blow your mind?" Gabe asked.

"I can't live on the edge like that," Ernest said.

Gabe laughed.

"So, how does this radio work?"

"The ionosphere—it's a shell of electrons around the Earth, and the radio waves bounce off of it."

"So who do you hear out there?"

"Everyone, everything," Gabe said. "Anything can be radio. You could have electromagnetic waves hit a rock and that sound would be radio. And in a way, it's going on all the time. I can shut this thing off right now, but all those voices are still there, carrying on without me."

The scotch had warmed Ernest's tongue; his thoughts flowed. "Did you know that in the 1800s people were scared of electricity coming into their houses because they thought ghosts might make their way through the wires?"

"Really? That's crazy."

"Maybe, but it's hard to trust something you don't totally understand. They had no idea what it meant for them except that it happened kind of overnight and it was totally life altering. How can that not be scary?"

Gabe shrugged. "I guess." As he dialed through the stations, garbled voices and snatches of static emitted from the speakers.

"Those voices on the radio, people used to think that was their dead ancestors talking to them."

Gabe shook his head. "I don't want to hear anything from dead people."

"Who *do* you want talking to you?"

"Pretty much anyone else, but wait, I have the perfect show for you, Dad."

The shortwave radio blinked on the living room rug. Wiring from an antenna snaked over the fleur-de-lis pattern as Gabe twisted the dial, then stopped: a series of pops, whistles that bent in the air, and crumbly static.

"What is this?"

"This one guy plays 'natural radio.' Well, technically natural radio would be live from a special receiver, but it's still pretty cool. He makes recordings of the Earth's electromagnetic field all around the world and then he plays it, like, around the clock."

After a particularly fiery crackle, a man's voice cut in and announced, "That's the sound of some massive coronal ejections."

"Wow, this is amazing." Ernest smiled. "Nice find." It felt good to admire his son, and for a moment, he was there with him, in the moment, as Cynthia had urged him to be. Then he noticed Gabe tugging on his earlobe and plunging his finger into the canal.

"What's the matter with your ear?"

"It's ringing."

"For how long?"

"Like, maybe five minutes straight this time."

"You've been listening to the radio too loud."

"It's not like I'm listening to Slayer." Gabe checked his watch. "Oh, it's time!"

Frantically, he dialed in a station that crackled with static and a whining high pitch. After a few moments, a woman's voice cut in and urgently recited, "Anna? Nikolai? Ivan? Tatyana? Roman?" She stopped after each name. After a longer pause during which the static snapped with more fury, she repeated her call: "Anna? Nikolai? Ivan? Tatyana? Roman?" The woman sounded concerned but also resigned to calling these names for every night of her life.

"Is that from Russia?" Ernest asked. "Can't quite tell from the accent."

Alison walked in. "Ooh, look, it's Christian Slater. What's going on in pirate radio land?"

"Not pirate," Gabe corrected. "Shh, listen."

Alison's face fell as she heard the woman's call. Gabe nodded.

"I wonder if she's looking for her kids. Maybe they got separated?" Alison asked.

"Who knows?" Gabe said, then looked at his dad. "I discovered her a week ago, and every night around this time, she repeats those names."

"That's sad," Alison said. "Is she all alone?"

"How would I know?"

"Let's hear another station," Alison said, taking a seat next to Gabe, but they didn't change the dial. They listened to the sad woman repeat the string of names a few more times, until it became just a stream of syllables.

3

They didn't like it, but Cynthia and Ernest owned two cars for necessity's sake—Ernest's battered Jetta and the Volvo station wagon that Cynthia used for commuting to a law firm in the city. Whenever the whole family had to pile in, Ernest drove the wagon.

Three days after Ernest's birthday, they took a field trip to the new mega health-food store, Demeter Foods. After months of advance buzz, Ernest heard about its grand opening during his committee meeting for next year's Earth Day celebration. Prairie Park had just hired him to direct the 1995 efforts. In years prior, the Earth Day festivities had been modest—a few tents slapped up to educate people on the issues, plus some crafts and activities for the kids—but town hall wanted something bigger to celebrate the twenty-fifth anniversary. When his committee got wind that he hadn't yet basked in the splendors of Demeter, they were horrified. "What are you waiting for?" his boss, Jean, had crowed. For all sorts of reasons, he was skeptical of Demeter Foods, but curiosity ultimately won out.

On the way, Ernest insisted on cranking an NPR story that quoted the president's executive order from earlier in the year demanding that "all Americans deserve clean air, pure water, land that is safe to live on, and food that is safe to eat."

"Wow!" Cynthia said. "It really is a new era. Never thought I'd see it."

"Yep, it's a good time to be an environmentalist," Ernest said. "Best time since the early seventies."

"This is Al Gore's influence," Cynthia said. "Don't you think he's cute, Alison?"

"Not to me," Alison said. "He looks like a high school principal."

"I hate to rain on your parade," Gabe piped in from the backseat, "but I think it's just trendy for the moment. I mean, all I see at school all over everyone's notebooks are those panda stickers from World Wildlife, but I bet you none of them really know anything about pandas."

"So what?" Alison said. "Maybe people want to save pandas because they're cute and that's it. You don't have to know what it eats for lunch."

"It's a little poseurish. It's like saying Nirvana's best song is 'Smells Like Teen Spirit.'"

"Well, I'm going to join the Protect the Planet club and I'm not feeling like a fake."

"That's because you're not a fake. You were raised by these people." Gabe flapped his hands toward their parents.

"All you kids ever talk about is who's a poseur," Cynthia said. "It's like we're riding with the authenticity cops or something."

"That's really more Gabe's thing. It's some kind of code he lives by," Alison said, and looked at her brother: "Pearl Jam?"

His answer was immediate: "Poseurs."

"Wrong. What about Jane's Addiction?"

"Legit."

"Live."

He groaned. "Now you've got that terrible song in my head."

"It's appalling." Alison thought for a minute, trying to stump him. "Jason Priestley?"

"Dork. But that's a whole different scale, by the way."

"Home computers!" Alison announced it like a game show host and applauded loudly.

"Awesome! And our parents should get one."

"Not going to happen," Ernest said. "Not now."

"Just to go back for a minute, I don't mind that environmentalism is trendy right now," Cynthia said. "If that gets more people involved, I'm all for it."

"Did you know that seventy-six percent of Americans now consider themselves environmentalists?" Ernest asked, joining a line of cars turning into Demeter's crowded parking lot.

No one answered him. Attention was now focused on the shopping spectacle coming into view.

Attendants waved them into freshly painted diagonal spaces. Newly planted saplings decorated every few spots. In the back of the parking lot, several independent stands seemed to be trying to capitalize on the frenzy Demeter Foods had stirred up, and—unless they had crashed the party uninvited—the new big dog in town was generously allowing them to sell their wares on its grounds. There was a massage stand, a crystals and hand-blended oils stand, and a few other like-minded entrepreneurs alongside activist groups like the No Nukes in Prairie Park guys. Ernest thought these businesses could fit in at Earth Day next year—and made a mental note to give each of them a call—except for one glaring exception:

"Look, it's one of those spaceship sweepstakes!" Gabe said.

He pointed at a folding table covered in neon-green paper. On one side of the table, a miniature flying saucer on stilts with black balloons and purple ribbons tied to it. A blond woman was manning the table alone, her slack expression belying the giddy banner below: WIN A VISIT FROM JUPITER!! SIGN UP TODAY!!

"Nope," Ernest said. "I want nothing to do with it."

"Why not?"

But Ernest didn't answer and instead hustled his family into the new supermarket.

Once they stepped through the automatic sliding glass doors, Demeter Foods unfurled its glory as the gleaming marketplace for an eco-conscious utopia. The poured concrete floors at a high shine. The refrigerated section of probiotics and fish oil pulsating with inventory. Boxes of cereal with every heart-healthy oat, flake, and cluster kissed with only natural sweeteners. Wedges of cheese sourced from livestock free of hormones and free to roam. Other claims on absolute purity abounded: No pesticides. No GMO. No trans fat. No high-fructose corn syrup. What was left in these foods? Just clean goodness from a never-ending, bountiful crop. Ernest found a tower of green apples so pristine they could've all been plucked from the Garden of Eden. He stopped the whole family to admire it.

He whistled. "Anyone have a bottle of Champagne we could pour over the top?"

Demeter Foods should've seemed like a victory to Ernest, but instead, he battled a vague annoyance. Here was the extravagant temple to his religion, yet he had to resist the urge to run around and drill each customer: "Do you belong to the Sierra Club? Have you ever done a trash pickup on the beach? Do you have three different bins for recycling?" If they answered incorrectly, he'd pluck them of their eco-bounty and turn them out as false apostles. Maybe he was just like Gabe—obsessed with legitimacy. But it was more than legitimacy; it was effort and investment—time, not just money. He wanted them to spend real time and thought. He didn't want people thinking changing the world was as easy as buying a bag of non-GMO corn chips for ten dollars.

The kids were dashing off every few minutes, returning with lavish items they'd dump into the cart for Ernest to inspect. A twelve-dollar box of cookies, made with locally milled wheat flour (local to where?). Sun-dried tomato pasta in a package printed with nontoxic ink (who was using toxic ink on a food product?). Elderberry tincture that was $24.95 (for no discernible reason). He rejected all of these, but when Alison dropped in a bottle of suntan oil with no number on it, just the alluring promise of golden-brown skin, Ernest had to take a stronger stand.

"Alison," Ernest said, "you know that there's a hole in the ozone so big that part of Australia, all the little children there, have to wear head-to-toe clothing, these kind of beekeeper outfits with netting over their faces, to protect themselves from the sun?"

Alison folded her arms across her chest. "I do know about that, Dad. I think you've mentioned it once or twice before."

"We've got one month left of summer. That's still plenty of time for you to get a skin lesion."

"Mom," Alison said, "help me out here."

Cynthia suggested they visit the sunscreen aisle together, where they could settle for something in the middle. On their way, Gabe took the opportunity to bring up what had been bothering him since they'd entered.

"Dad?"

"Yes, son?"

"What's your problem with space?"

"Because it's overhyped," Ernest replied without having to think about it. "These spaceships coming from outer space, landing in someone's yard, everyone gawking, but for what? There's no real interaction with the aliens. They never come out! It's just a commercial stunt. It's just another mindless distraction so we don't have to think about the real problems on Earth."

"But isn't it exciting that a spaceship from Jupiter could land in your backyard? And I've heard that some of the aliens do come out."

"Those are just tabloid rumors. It's all a kind of scheme that exploits our curiosity about aliens."

"How is it a scheme? It's not like you don't get anything," Gabe said. "You get a visit from a spaceship! For free!"

Cynthia pushed the cart down the spacious aisle. "Don't you kids remember when we drove to see one in Downers Grove? You guys might've been too little to remember. I have to admit, it was pretty spectacular. Hundreds of people crowding around in some lady's backyard waiting for the lights to spin around. All this chatter and intrigue: 'Are they coming out?' A little part of me thought the spaceship might attack, government-approved or not—"

"It got gimmicky awful fast after that," Ernest said. "Remember that *60 Minutes* when Morley Safer tried to present it as this quirky American experience? He toured all around suburban America, interviewing the families hosting the spaceships, trying so hard to make it seem so quaint. Honestly, Gabe, after you've seen one you've seen them all."

"Really? So you're sick of them?"

"They're just loud and silly. And probably unsafe on some level."

"Unsafe how?" Alison asked. She vaguely remembered the trip to Downers Grove; she wasn't freaked out by the spaceship so much as the people. There was an old woman in the crowd who looked like she hadn't eaten for weeks, clutching prayer beads and crying with her eyes violently squeezed shut.

"Who knows what those things are exposing us to? It's been only ten years. Not long enough to gather a reliable data set."

"Ernest, you know those things were tested for years before they came over, before the government even told us about them," Cynthia said.

"Seriously, Dad, how unsafe can they be?"

"It's just not our style, OK?" Ernest said.

"OK," Gabe said. "Miracles from space—not your style."

"It's not really a miracle from space if they'll land at any old house."

"No, you have to be a *winner*," Gabe said. "It's not just any old house. It's not random."

"By definition, Gabe, random's what a sweepstakes *is*." He knew his voice was inflected with that pedantic tone Gabe hated, but Ernest couldn't help himself.

"Oh, OK." Gabe tossed up his hands. "I guess since the spaceship isn't made out of recycled boxes or hemp or whatever, it doesn't count as an object of interest."

They walked in silence until Gabe sharply veered off into another aisle and disappeared, muttering something about finding more overpriced snacks. The family went on without him. In front of the sunscreen display, Ernest held up a severe white bottle emblazoned with gold numbers.

"How about this?"

"Seventy-five?"

"It's the strongest stuff on the market; it says so right here."

"Dad, it looks terrifying, like some kind of engine oil." Alison snatched the bottle from his hands. "Active ingredients: avobenzone, homosalate, octisalate, octocreylene, triethanolamine. You guys will barely buy lotion with alcohol in it. Why is all this craziness OK?"

Ernest drew in a breath to speak but then stopped. Alison loved when she could stem, if only for a moment, the tide of education from her dad's mouth.

"Forty-five," Ernest said. "You can still get a little bit of color from that."

At the register, Ernest purchased two reusable bags, the same kind his boss, Jean, had brought to the meeting, despite the steep price.

"I've fallen for it," Ernest mumbled to Cynthia. "These are nice bags. But see how they also have plastic? Karen would charge a nickel for each of those, as a deterrent."

"They're *really* nice bags," she said, rubbing the fabric sacks. "And now everyone will know you shop at Demeter Foods. Pretty fancy!" She jabbed him in the back with her finger.

On the way out the door, the heat from the outside blasted their air-conditioned skin. As they loaded the groceries into the car, Gabe waved at the blond woman behind the WIN A VISIT FROM JUPITER! table. She treated him to a sweet wink.

4

The spaceship descends toward the home of the nuclear family, living in one of the psychic detritus clusters of the universe, otherwise known as the suburb. The utopian landscape is precise and ordered, a video-game grid of

school, park, church, houses;
    school, park, church, houses;
        school, park, church, houses . . .

...that gets more focused as the spaceship gets closer. The flying object cuts through layers of atmosphere, as delicate as filigree, made up of natural molecular ephemera and seminoxious particles of clingy waste: the hairspray and the weed killer and the evaporated windshield wash and the fumes from a polyurethane glue used for a children's toy that is not recommended for below age eight.

The top layers of the atmosphere—the mesosphere, the thermosphere, the exosphere—is made up of garbage and noise, signals from appliances cross-hatching into a graphic density, slivers of metal from aircraft flying on the slipstream, burning lava rock and auroras that vibrate and hum. Closer to Earth, the troposphere is ransacked and violated by the phenomenon known as weather—clouds fattening with water that condenses, bursts, and clatters down to the ground. The spaceship lowers through it all, leaving behind the moon—a pink scrape in the sky—to settle in the backyard of the Allen family.

When the spaceship landed in the backyard at exactly 8:57 P.M. on August 18, seven days after the first day of school, Cynthia was the first of the family to see it through the kitchen's picture window. A flying saucer made of silver sheets of bolted metal hovered over the trimmed grass emitting a low humming noise that pained her teeth, like pressing sugar into a cheap metal filling. At just about twenty-five feet across, the spaceship fit snugly between the house and the weeping willow tree in the backyard. Five delicate tentacles shot out of the belly of the spacecraft and pierced the ground, one of them cleaving through the fruit of Ernest's heirloom tomato plant.

"What?" she shrieked, somewhere between delight, disbelief, and dread.

The saucer rooted further into the grass, vrooming its engine. Above the metal portion of the spaceship, separated by a band of lights, a dark glass top. Twirling lights hysterically crawled around the yard, hot white lights that could shrink pupils into black dots.

Cynthia's hands dripped with the hot, soapy dishwater she'd abandoned to come to the window. "Ernest? Come here!" she screamed, planted to her spot. "Ernest, where are you?" The water, now cool, ran down to her elbows as she plugged her ears. The humming reached a semi-excruciating pitch, vibrating her sternum and surging up through her feet. "Oh my god, oh my god," she moaned, but she could hear only the sound of her voice muffled inside of her head.

She remembered then that Ernest was at an Earth Day meeting and wouldn't be home until late. Her relief that he'd snagged a job he enjoyed—finally!—outweighed her admittedly unreasonable irritation that she'd have to parent this disaster alone. What if they were scared? Wasn't she scared? Was that why her muscles twitched, as if she were about to leap into a dark shaft? Unable to stop watching, she waited for the kids to come down. Some strange knowledge swept in, tidal and moonlit: the spaceship, she thought, was meant to be here, but she couldn't tell if it was bringing release or terror.

Upstairs, Gabe played his sister an album that'd been forced upon him by a senior with a Mohawk that sagged from liberty spikes to wisps by three P.M. On school nights, between seven and eleven, Gabe and Alison's world shrank to the confines of their home, and the options for amusement dwindled as well: watch TV, listen to music, play video games, talk to their parents, talk on the phone. At some point, Alison would usually draw for a while in her room. Sometimes, Gabe would read, lately about the Vietnam War. He was glad he wasn't eighteen in 1968 but oddly jealous too. Everything seemed so meaningful back then.

"If I don't like this band," Gabe said, "Todd said that it means I don't like punk, which means I'm basically a stupid, worthless fag who will end up married to that half-retarded girl Tracy who works at TCBY."

"Harsh verdict," Alison said as she painted her thumbnail with a black Sharpie. "Do you even like that guy Todd?"

"No," Gabe said, "but still."

The music sounded sawed-off and gritty. Gabe wasn't so sure he liked it exactly, but it intrigued him, like looking at pictures of Istanbul or Anchorage.

Alison sat listening for several moments and squinting around the room before she finally said, "Who's this again?"

"Fugazi," he answered.

Alison scrunched up her face. "Fooo-gah-zee. Always the ugly names with these punk bands," Alison mocked in a prim voice. "Is it satanic, or just trash?"

Gabe turned it up as a dare. Alison raised him and flicked up the volume knob even more, inspired as the music redrew all the room's features, rendering it debauched and arrogant, but also carefree.

In her baggy jeans and too-big striped sweater, Alison popped up on the bed but then didn't know what to do. After a moment, she jumped around in place, her hands a little off to the side like she might be carrying a guitar or maybe it was just a household saw. Then she flipped her brown hair around in a fit of head-banging, imitating the long-coated metal guys on MTV. For extra snazz, she threw in a plié from her long-abandoned ballet training. Gabe rolled his eyes. He was pretty sure Fugazi weren't headbangers.

The song ended and another crashed into being. Dizzy from the thrashing, Alison collapsed onto Gabe's bed in giggles. She pressed her face into the mattress. The flannel bedspread hadn't been washed in maybe a month or so, and Alison smelled her brother on it—vaguely minty from shaving cream and toothpaste, plus the lavender dandruff shampoo that Cynthia bought him from Karen's that she always handed to him in a covert paper sack, as if it didn't end up in the same shower caddy as everyone else's stuff.

Above Gabe's bed, a pinned poster of the rock star Ziggy Stardust, with his rooster pouf of pink-red hair, posing in darkness onstage. Alison stood on Gabe's bed in her socks so that her face almost touched Ziggy's face, a space of breath between them. As she stared into one of his eyes, a sliver of iris barely perceptible around the dilated pupil, she entertained a thought about her life: that everything she was experiencing—herself, her family, her suburb—could all be happening within Ziggy's eye, all controlled and ultimately created by him. Why not him? Wasn't he as good as any other god? But what if it all got wiped out the second Ziggy's heavily shadowed lid closed over that blue eye?

She routinely had these kinds of thoughts but hoarded them, little secrets never to be shared with her brother. She lay back down on the bed, content with imagining a deity actually from her era, who'd been to the dentist or eaten a burrito. Lit by Gabe's desk lamp, the ceiling appeared warm and splotchy, an ocean of shadowy and then brighter yellows. Gabe sat cross-legged on the carpet flipping through the CD booklet with photos of the band wearing leather jackets and no shirts, finding them gross and compelling at the same time. Then he cocked his head. A loudness, distinct from the music and morphing from lawn mower to helicopter to something with magnitude, overtook the music, and when the song ended and the speakers were silent, the loudness remained—a mighty roar from the outside.

Alison started to say something as a NyQuil hue poured in from the window. One saturated shaft lit up the bed, her arms and shoulders. The two kids ran to the window. "Oh man," Gabe said, laughing. "I—shit."

A flying saucer, dead center in their backyard, lowered into the space, the walls of the house shuddering. The pure green of the lights, switching to white and then back again, overwhelmed their eyes. A number of small birds scattered out of the weeping willow, which now appeared dwarfed by its new neighbor. Somewhere in Alison's amazement, in the awe that ricocheted and collected strength, she registered the look of ecstasy and fear on her brother's face, fighting for dominance. They quickly cut out of the room and banged down the stairs.

In the kitchen, where the view of their new visitor was the best, Cynthia wiped her soapy hands on a dish towel, a frantic look in her eye.

"I didn't know this was coming," she said, shouting to project over the motorized roar of the spaceship. They all stood at the picture window. Something like an airplane takeoff, the spaceship's noise was occasionally punctuated by a musical exclamation point appropriate to 1950s cocktail records with boomerang shapes on the cover. Every three minutes or so, it climaxed with a saccharine pop—effervescent and thunderous—that made the spacecraft vibrate. The hysterical searchlights roiled in the silvery skull of the ship's top. They beamed in through the window every few seconds, lighting up Cynthia and then plunging her figure into darkness again.

"This is amazing," Gabe shouted.

"Can we go outside and see this thing?" Alison asked.

"Let's wait a little bit until it calms down." Cynthia stared out through the glass where she usually watched cardinals hopping from branch to branch, their little speck brains chittering instinctive code. On one occasion, she spotted a lone deer that had wandered far off course standing in the light cast from an outdoor bulb. When they looked at each other—the deer's eyes were soft and beyond fright, almost paralyzed—something passed between them, the mutual acknowledgment of imminent death. It ran out of the yard and then stood gawkily in the center of their suburban street, seemingly confused about which way to go. It was a long journey back to the woods.

Several minutes passed and the spaceship showed no signs of retiring for the night. But it was firmly planted now.

"OK, let's go out there, but I want you kids to hold my hand," Cynthia said. Both kids began to complain. "Hold my hand!"

Gabe and Alison each grabbed a palm. Together they climbed down the back porch steps. They stepped carefully around the machine: Cynthia's loafers, Alison's Mary Janes, Gabe's sneakers. Up close, the sound of the ship was deafening—whirring, vrooming, pop!—so they cupped their hands over their ears. There was so much to look at: the swooping saucer shape, the dark glass windows they couldn't see through, the magnesium noxiousness of the lights. Where it wasn't obscured by the spaceship, the grass appeared phosphorescent and nearly liquid in the light.

The aircraft seemed more familiar than not. In some ways, it appeared to be little more than old airplane parts repurposed into a saucer, the same sharkskin metal bolted together. The material was sturdy and impenetrable but also weathered. In some places, the surface buckled a bit or was scratched. The legs (each one was two tentacles bound together and then jointed in a few places for flexibility) looked like standard tubing from a hardware store, though with a silkier sheen.

On all sides of the Allen house, neighbors appeared at their windows or in their backyards. Mrs. Chang, a quiet widow next door, surveyed the spaceship from her rarely used guest bedroom. Olivia and Tom, good friends who lived on the other side next door, weren't home tonight or surely they'd be coming over right now, knocking at their door for the inside scoop, Tom toting his video recorder. Instead, Ernest walked into the backyard and joined his family. With deep annoyance etched on his face, he craned his head back to take in the whole sight. What was the threshold figure again for hearing loss? Something above 2,000 hertz?

Ten minutes before he entered the backyard, he'd been watching the spaceship from the Aurora Park lawn with the rest of the Earth Day committee. They'd broken from their meeting when one of them noticed the spaceship flying overhead. As it raced across the sky, throwing beams of light, Ernest had a foreboding sense that the flying saucer was headed for his house. Confirming his suspicions, the spaceship first paused behind the dark thumb of his chimney and the slanted roof he'd recently patched, and then lowered itself down.

Ernest wanted to hit the reset button on reality. "Maybe it just *looked* like it landed in my backyard."

The excitement of his peers told him otherwise. After a moment of stunned silence, Jean said: "My god, did you, of all people, just have a spaceship land at your house? You've gotta go, Ernest."

Ernest took off, running in the moonlight until he turned down his driveway. He had to slow down now so that he wouldn't trip on the oak tree roots that were rupturing the concrete slabs. The disk was confounding, impressive, and dinged up all at once. He met Cynthia's eye and said breathlessly: "Told you the things were overrated." For a moment, they both laughed hysterically from shared nerves and shared thoughts: What was this thing doing here? What the hell set of mistakes had conspired to drop this B-movie contraption onto their private property? Ernest fought off the urge to hustle the family inside so they could figure this all out, but of course he understood. Who could tear themselves away from this hypnotizing spectacle?

He left them to walk around. From every angle, he inspected the spaceship until it became like some Picasso contraption, a cubist repeat and not-repeat of the same curves and slopes. No matter where he stood, he could never take in the whole circumference— always a part of it unavailable to the eye. The unknowable magnitude made him uneasy. He knocked on its legs a few times, but the underside was too high to reach without a ladder. Then he noticed Cynthia, who'd snuck back inside, waving him in from the kitchen window.

The kids sat around the table, Gabe almost squirming from elation, Alison still watching the ship with obsessed focus. Cynthia leaned her hip against the counter. Her arms were locked across her chest, her face a rictus of tension. For now, the funny moment had passed and stress had set in. Ernest forged ahead in the only manner that made sense to him: they would talk logistics.

"Do we know how long this is supposed to stay?"

"Approximately nine months," Cynthia said. "Kind of like a really weird pregnancy."

"Nine months?! How do you know that?"

Cynthia handed him a pamphlet. "I just opened it a few minutes ago," she said. "Guess who it was addressed to?"

Too engrossed to answer, Ernest read aloud the print across the front page: "Congratulations, your friends from Jupiter have arrived!" The printing quality was fairly good; the paper stock was glossy and thick, but it still looked tacky. The illustration on the cover bugged him. It was of a much mightier alien ship than the one currently camped in their backyard. A family stood proudly in a line next to it. They represented a crude replica of the Allens: a blond wife in a conservative denim skirt, a husband with spectacles and a V-neck sweater, and two teenage kids. The boy was holding a soccer ball, and the girl smiled with exaggerated dimples. A scruffy brown dog sat at her feet, its pink tongue lolling out. The ship's band of lights reflected on their faces, glowing and warm. They were so *happppppppy* about their friends from Jupiter!

On the back of the pamphlet was the return address:

New World Enterprises
41000 Lexus Lane
Wilmington, Delaware 19880

"Of course it's Delaware-based," Cynthia noted. "Even flying saucers want a good tax deal."

There was also an 800 number—that was a relief. He'd give it a call first thing tomorrow. Also on the back: the fine print of the sweepstakes rules. Ernest scanned them, but his eyes kept coming back to one of the lines in bold: "Any member of the household, age 16 or older, can register to win."

"Here's my big question: How did this thing get here?" Ernest watched Gabe stare down at the table, barely suppressing a smile. "Hmm," Ernest pondered. "There are four members of this family, but only three meet the requirements for enrolling in this sweepstakes. Let's go ahead and go around the room. Cynthia, did you enter a contest to have an alien spaceship land in our backyard?"

"No, I didn't. Let me ask you, Ernest: Did *you* enter a contest to win a visit from aliens?"

"I'm glad you asked, but no, I didn't either. Well, well, who does that leave?"

They waited for Gabe to say something while Alison enjoyed the show. Finally Ernest couldn't wait anymore, staring at the name of his son, Gabriel Allen, printed on the envelope.

He exploded: "What were you thinking?"

"I don't know," Gabe said, his face pitching between thrill and feigned guilt. "Nothing ever happens around here!"

"Something's happening now," Ernest said. "We're really angry with you, that's what's happening."

"Sorry, but"—and here's where Gabe gave up on pretending he felt bad—"I hope it stays forever."

"No, Gabe," Ernest said. "You do not wish that. Wish that it leaves early and peacefully instead."

"What do you think it's going to do, start a war? How can you guys not see how amazing this is? There's a friggin' spaceship back there—from Jupiter!"

"We should go back out there," Alison said, "instead of talking about it all night in the kitchen."

Ernest ignored her. "We're environmentalists, Gabe. This thing isn't right. We have no idea what kind of footprint it's leaving behind, not to mention what it's going to do to us."

"This is part of the environment too. It's from our galaxy!"

"Part of our environment like polluted rivers and landfills?

"These are neighbors from our solar system," Gabe said, "not piles of trash!"

"For starters, it's probably going to kill the lawn."

"The grass? Is that your big worry? The grass dies every winter."

Ernest was pacing now. "What if it does something worse? What if it's toxic?"

"Why would they be allowed here if they were toxic, Dad?"

"You think this country tells us everything? You don't think mistakes are made in the name of progress? There's toxic shit all over the place!"

"All right, everybody." Cynthia held up her hands. "Why don't we all sit down at the table and read the pamphlet together?"

Once they were all seated, the green lights from the spaceship flared up and bathed them in a sickening glow.

"Jesus, is this going to happen every time we sit here now?" Ernest asked.

"Does that mean they're looking at us?" Alison asked. "I am so creeped out right now."

Cynthia yanked down the shade that was rarely used. She started to read aloud: "In 1969, NASA made an advance previously imagined only in science fiction. It discovered another life-form on planet Jupiter and, through extensive development and research, made contact. Carefully, and in cooperation with the United Nations, NASA led a top secret communications effort to foster a healthy relationship with the residents of the fifth planet from the sun."

Cynthia continued reading, despite the distracting green light soaking in through the shade: "The unique relationship between Earth and Jupiter is built on close communication. After the discovery was made public to the citizens of Earth, the U.S. government established a visiting program in 1984 in which the inhabitants of Jupiter landed at the homes of select Americans. New World Enterprises took over the program in 1986, expanding visitation opportunities for ordinary Americans. In exchange for observing your way of life from a pleasant but close vantage point, you will have the amazing opportunity to host another life-form."

"They always have to make it sound so creepy. 'Host another life-form'?" Alison wrapped her arms around herself. "That sounds like a horror movie."

"Don't be so melodramatic." Cynthia flipped ahead, searching for information about the saucer they hadn't already heard a hundred times before. "Hold on, this part is in bold: 'Do not try to force or lure them out. Do not damage their home, tamper with any equipment, or, in any way, create a hostile environment. Any damage to the spaceship could put the occupants in danger, and possibly the host family. It's also imperative that if the aliens do come out—and this particular event cannot be guaranteed—that you keep a respectful distance. Do not attempt to agitate the aliens. For entertainment purposes only.'" Cynthia snorted.

Ernest shook his head ruefully. "You know, thinking of this from their position, I don't see how they could possibly trust ordinary Americans not to do something stupid to the spaceships. I know everyone's used to them by now, but how can they be so sure no one will attack them? Everyone just accepts aliens from outer space with open arms?"

"Maybe something really bad happens if you attack the spaceships," Alison said. "I wouldn't want to mess with them."

Cynthia steered the conversation back. "Besides what this pamphlet says, what else do we know about spaceships?"

"I remember reading an article where they come out," Gabe said.

Cynthia and Ernest exchanged an exasperated but pitying look.

"For the last time, they don't do that, Gabe," Ernest said. "No one's ever seen them."

"No, they did! It was some rich family in New York who paid for them to land, but they couldn't get pictures or videos because the aliens hate that."

"You read that in one of those trashy tabloids," Cynthia said. "There's never been a credible report of the aliens coming out, and there've been thousands of visits now."

"That's what's so suspicious about these things," Ernest said. "I haven't read a serious news story about them in a while, not since the first couple of years when the visits were new. You two don't realize this, but there was real pandemonium at first. I have to admit that Reagan did a pretty good job handling that one."

During that momentous press conference announcing the existence of alien life—one which Ernest and Cynthia watched anxiously, convinced it was the dreaded beginning of nuclear conflict with the USSR—the Skipper spread his lips into that famous cowboy smile of his and said, "I give you my solemn oath, we share values with these beings—the values of liberty, prosperity, and peace."

During the first months, when spaceships were sighted only rarely as they skimmed the air on official ambassadorial missions, the general public screamed, prayed, and quite frequently shot at the saucers; police and fire stations were overwhelmed with calls to respond. Certain lower-level politicians, left out of the security briefings, demanded immediate accountability. The solution was Reagan's apparently. Share the wealth. Let everybody in on it. And the spaceship visitor program was expanded and outsourced. New World Enterprises and a few other companies were formed by giant conglomerate parent entities that could afford the high cost of communicating effectively with Jupiter. Soon they were sending the spaceships to weddings, bar mitzvahs, museum openings—as long as the clients could afford the exorbitant hosting fees. For the rest, a quasi-lottery system existed, a sweepstakes for the regular guy, though it seemed like the lottery system favored residents who lived in safe upper-middle-class neighborhoods with good schools and minimal graffiti problems. Still, people worried. People complained. There were lobbying groups in Washington dedicated to getting rid of them, severing ties. And there were outlier groups who refused to believe, who suspected that like the moonwalk, it was all fake; these ships had never been to space, and were in fact of human manufacture.

"I'm worried they'll do things to us," Alison said. "What if they can read our thoughts? What if they kidnap one of us?"

"Nothing like that is going to happen," Gabe said. "Why can't everyone see that it's going to be an amazing experience?" He turned toward Alison. "So you don't like the spaceship either?"

She weighed her words. "No, I like it. But it's a little sketchy."

"Why?" Gabe asked.

"Well, for one thing, I think I can see someone in there."

"Really?" Ernest said. "I didn't see anyone."

"I'll show you," and with that they bounded down the back steps.

"If you stand right here at this certain angle." Alison picked out a spot on the grass and pointed at the wraparound band of glass.

"Right here, you can see just a shadow of something."

Ernest went over and stood behind her, following her finger. He saw what she saw—the faintest traces of an interior hub with a lever and some sort of figure with a bulbous head sitting close to the glass, but it wasn't moving. Maybe it was an alien, maybe not. It could be a dummy, even a decoy, or a shadow. What was it? They'd been watching it for a moment now, all of them crowded near one another, holding their breath, but it hadn't moved one bit.

"I don't know what's real and what's not in there," Cynthia said at last.

"Maybe none of it is real," Gabe said, and immediately felt silly. He didn't know what he meant.

5

Ernest and Cynthia diligently avoided most chemical cleansers, but fabric softener was her weakness. She kept a bottle stashed behind the washing machine in the garage, like an office drunk with her whiskey pint in the desk drawer. *Quick, while nobody's looking, just a nip!* The top around the spout was gooey with blue paste; the scent was an unmitigated blast of toxins just waiting to twiddle your endocrine system—including alphaterpineol, limonene, and other chemicals that had been declared "problematic" by the EPA—but Cynthia reveled in it. As the water filled the washer, she poured some in the blue ball that would toss around in the cycle and eventually burst open. Cynthia never used it with Ernest's clothes, but sometimes she forgot and threw it in with the linens. If Ernest caught a perfumed gust while making the bed, he'd complain about her secret addiction to "that smiling bear juice," and dramatically cough. Turns out they couldn't hide much of anything from each other.

In the yard, Gabe waited in a lawn chair, ready to observe the spaceship once it started its nightly show. The garage vents were blowing out soapy gusts that swirled around the ship and then dissipated. Cynthia wondered if the smell of the laundry would agitate the occupants. Wait, did they possess anything like a nose? There were no photographs or films to consult regarding what they looked like or how their bodies (if that was an accurate term) worked. Every article ever written about the Jupiter tribe said this kind of information was known by top government departments but couldn't be released. How awful looking were these aliens?

For the first two weeks of the spaceship's backyard occupation, Cynthia kept a cautious distance. She wasn't calling New World every day like Ernest, demanding that it be removed, only to be put on hold for twenty minutes, but she wasn't exactly comfortable around it either. She'd been avoiding the laundry because of its proximity to the ship, but after a fabric mountain formed in all of their closets, she had to take action. For the last few weeks, even a little before the spaceship landed, she'd been experiencing colorful, weird dreams that wouldn't shake off in the daylight: her fingernails melting, all of her teeth falling out of her mouth, the skin peeling off the soles of her feet in calloused sheets. So far, she'd just barely convinced herself that her subconscious was a morbidly imaginative child who shouldn't be encouraged.

From the garage, Cynthia saw Gabe look up just as the spaceship rocked into its first spasm. The twirling lights and the motorized pops that went off every few minutes made the spaceship seem like an abandoned pinball game in the corner of the arcade, beckoning with its jingle. Their neighbor Tom wandered down the driveway and around the side of the house with a few beers hanging from a plastic six-pack ring, the kind Ernest always carefully snipped with his scissors so that no birds would get their beaks caught in it while foraging in a landfill. In his other hand, he carried a telescope attached to a tripod.

"Wow!" Tom exclaimed. "This is fucking fabulous!"

Though Tom was a good friend, the Allens had grown accustomed to finding all sorts of barely recognized neighbors and benevolent trespassers standing in their backyard, watching the ship with expressions that ranged from rapturous to disappointed. Some ran their hands over the legs of the ship and some wouldn't touch it at all. Others listened to the racket and couldn't decide what to think—was it stupid or great? A sign of the universe's staggering magnitude or just another smaller power manipulated by the United States?

"What do you think it's doing?" Tom yelled, even though at the moment the spaceship was in a quiet period between pops. Yelling came naturally to some around the spaceship, as if its size and sheer alienness might swallow voices.

From her folding table, Cynthia could see Gabe's face light up at the chance to explain the spaceship's routine.

"It's some sort of energy test. They're checking all their resources."

"How do you know that?"

"I read about it in the pamphlet."

"I thought it was trying to say something."

"Say something? Like, in a language?"

"Yeah"—Tom shrugged—"like, to communicate something about its mission or why it's here."

Gabe looked strained. He'd made it his purpose to understand as much about the ship as possible and here was something he'd never considered. Was it trying to talk? Was this ecstatic accounting really a message? If so, what was it trying to say?

Tom set up his telescope on the concrete near the back stairs. The spaceship reared up with another series of vibrations, followed by an amphetamine pop, prompting Tom to keep his hands steady on the telescope until it passed.

"I think you offended it," Gabe jabbed, "with the telescope."

"Where's your dad? He's not out here?"

"Nope," Gabe said. "Not interested."

Tom laughed as he centered the long tube on a fixed area of the sky. "He'll come around. Hey, do you need to print out any papers for school? I got the dot matrix all hooked up again. Whole bunch of floppy discs too if you need 'em."

"I'm OK, thanks. What are we looking at in there?" Gabe pointed to the telescope.

"I'll tell you in a minute. I'm going to get your dad."

Tom's enthusiasms were always hard to resist, so Ernest was lured out by the time Gabe had put his eye to the telescope. In the past, Tom had turned Ernest on to hot sauces and mustards he sold at his hip New Orleans–influenced restaurant downtown, along with sun-warped tapes of long-lost jazz players from the 1950s and secret walking paths along the lake ("you gotta go south, past Hyde Park"). In Tom's basement, they often lost themselves in music—Tom at the drums, hitting the hi-hat; Ernest fumbling through guitar chords. They'd loop over patterns that arose from listening to each other. In those moments of rare connection with another man (he usually found women so much more gratifying to talk to), Ernest would think that he'd rather be related to Tom, who happened to have bought the house next to him some ten years ago, than the one distant brother he did have.

The spaceship, as it wound down, shifted its lights from white to green, bathing the yard in the cool tone. Only a few lights around the band and a few underneath the ship, near the legs, were lit. Finally: calm. The hum of the motor ticked a little bit like an air-conditioning unit just turned off. The quietude of the yard, and the suburb beyond it, poured back in. Cynthia hoisted her basket of laundry and headed for the house.

"You cold out here?" she asked Gabe.

"No, it's fine."

Cynthia passed Tom and Ernest on the stairs.

"Where are you going?" Tom said to Cynthia. "We're going to look at a comet."

"What comet?" Cynthia asked.

"There's a small comet passing by. Actually it's been visible for weeks now, but it's supposed to be at its brightest tonight. We also have a rare appearance from Jupiter."

Cynthia docked the laundry basket at the top of the stairs and joined them at the telescope. Through the lens she saw a smattering of chipped stars and, in the corner of the sky, a denser patch of smeary light with a bright white head, static to the eye, yet some luminous energy it gave off suggested that an enormous, dense struggle was going on. She waited for it to move, but instead, she caught tiny pulsations. Micro-dust swelled and then drained away. To the side, Jupiter, an orange-and-smoke-white marble.

"Why isn't the comet moving?"

"Well, you can't really track it with your eye, but it is. Look at it an hour later and it'll be in a different place."

"Can I see?" Gabe crowded at his mother's back. Cynthia fell off-balance and into the telescope. At the last second, Ernest caught the equipment and righted it.

"Watch out, Gabe," Ernest said.

"But I didn't even push that hard."

Gabe waited for his mom to defend him, but she was distracted by a tinge of dizziness that remained.

"You know what, space cowboy? Why are you even out here? You're still grounded."

Gabe shot his dad a dark look. The punishment for his enrollment in the sweepstakes—handed down in large part because of Ernest's ongoing frustrations with New World's supervisors, who kept blowing off his complaints, promising to get back to him and then never calling back—had been erratically enforced, at best, and he was tired of humoring it.

"Why can't I look at the comet? It's educational."

"It's also pleasure, which you're not allowed to experience right now."

Ernest knew he was being a touch unfair, but Gabe's presumptuousness, and subsequent lack of remorse, pissed him off beyond belief.

"Take a quick look," Cynthia said, "and then go back upstairs."

Tom gestured for Gabe to step up to the telescope, but Ernest's cold stare halted him.

"Wait, what exactly am I being punished for? It's just a spaceship, Dad, not the Death Star. Most of the time it's just sitting back here, doing nothing."

"Doing nothing? The noise pollution is offense enough. I barely slept last night—"

"Who cares about your sleep? Take a nap!"

In a flash, the support from his mother and Tom vanished. Ernest seized the power again. "Gabe, are you trying to talk me into letting you off the hook or punishing you more? Work on your strategy, my friend. Go upstairs. No TV, no telephone, no socializing, no looking at comets in space. Sorry, good night, don't order any more spaceships to the house, please."

Tom didn't laugh but Gabe could tell he wanted to, at least a little bit. Adults who weren't your parents were sometimes even worse assholes; they possessed no real empathy, no seeing themselves in you. Gabe left them to gawk at the comet and eat canapés, or whatever adults ate when they bullshitted around with each other, and stormed inside.

Close to midnight, Gabe turned on the shortwave radio, back in his bedroom, anger keeping him awake. He was picking up another broadcast, not the white-out static of the station where the woman mournfully called for her children, but another woman who sounded so clear, minus a few pops and flurries, she could've been sitting at the foot of Gabe's bed. In a quiet but excited voice she said:

"Hello?

"Hi, you don't know me, but I am talking to you. You can't see me, obviously, but here's my voice. Right here. Isn't that weird? I'm a voice. I'm a radio. I'm this electromagnetic tone separated from my body, solitary, traveling to you.

"If you've never heard this voice before, welcome to *The Book of Connections*. I decided I wanted to talk to people but I don't want them to talk back." She laughed self-consciously. "I know that sounds antisocial, but that's exactly it. You can be social but not communicate. Sometimes I try to talk to people and I fail. I fail to say the things I really mean. Which in the end means I was only moving my lips around a series of sounds."

She paused for a moment, long enough for Gabe to sigh with recognition.

"Sometimes I also call this show *The Book of Missed Connections*, because you can't talk about one without the other. You and I are now connected, and I like thinking about that. It does not matter if we would've stopped each other on the street to talk. It does not matter if we went to school or work together. Being born into the same family or town or cult is irrelevant. *I get to talk to you*. It's selfish but pure.

"You can also turn me off. That is your power.

"Would you like to turn me off?"

Pause. Gabe tried to guess her age, her face. She sounded American, serious, and young, but not as young as him. Likely somewhere in the stretch of adulthood that occurred past age twenty-five, the contours of which Gabe couldn't yet distinguish. He tried to picture a physical appearance, but her voice filled his imagination, blotting out any ideas about a face, eyes, skin tone, weight, hair. She was floating, or, as she said, she was a voice, a radio, and that was enough. Her voice: curious, playful, confident, poised; maybe she was an actress.

"OK, good. Glad you're still here. I should warn you: I have no plans tonight. True, I never have plans because I like to wildly roam. I like to discuss whatever's on my mind, with an eye to connection or slippage, to the smallest of occurrences or the biggest of phenomena. Most of the people crawling on this planet I will never get to meet. Neither will you. This is the fact of being human: knowing that a multiplicity of others thrums around you, existing, dying, being born or reborn. There is a beautiful ache in that. But even the people who you are very close to, in proximity or blood, you can also miss them. Missed connection. Missed contact from very close. A part of you or many parts of you may make contact or intersect, but never the whole you. Two shadows will overlap for a time, and I believe that is the closest you can really get to someone: the space and time when your shadows merge. It can happen right before you drift off to sleep or in another moment, usually when you're not talking. It is an understanding and comfort that happens almost without awareness or desire. It is a soft folding into another. Train yourself to revel in it when it happens."

◆

The next night, Ernest again walked down Grove Avenue, on his way to Aurora Park. He listened to the sounds of the neighborhood, which seemed placid and concerned with its own minor business. Someone dragged their rubber garbage pail down the driveway, the wheels crunching over gravel. In the distance, the same dog barked every few seconds. He waved hello to a neighbor who was raking back the drapes on his living room window. The air was warm, like he was walking through his own breath.

Ernest headed for the field house, cutting across the park's lawn, which glowed a darker green in the twilight. A long time ago, the park had been a gas manufacturing plant. After the plant closed in the 1950s, it was gifted to Prairie Park. By the mid-

1960s, the suburb (which liked to call itself a "village" in its self-promotional literature, as if all the roofs were thatched and the women balanced gourds of water on their heads) had converted the area into a small park.

Ernest could smell the cut grass, so clean it seemed edible. He remembered a few years ago when patches of the park's grass inexplicably died. The park district employees fed it with fertilizer, white perlite balls as big as berries, in an effort to revive it. Ernest asked them why they didn't return the park back to its native grasses. They looked at him like he was some possessed dust bowl minister proposing an exorcism. Glorified crabgrass was out of the question.

In the field house, Ernest found the Earth Day committee mingling and sipping coffee. Most of them were businesspeople or fellow environmentalists from the neighborhood volunteering their time, but a few of them were fellow paid consultants, like Ross, who also brought his sharp-faced wife, Marcy, to all the meetings. She was a caterer and usually handled the food and drinks. After Ross poured his coffee at the side table, he turned and gave Ernest a rousing shoulder clap as if Ernest had just told him an uplifting story. It was Ross's way. His love of backslapping—just men, never women— was part of his masculinity recipe, combining equal parts vigor with physical affection.

"How's it going, Ern? I'm almost scared to ask, but how's that spaceship?"

"How much time do you have?"

"At least you don't have this." Ross pulled up his sleeve to reveal an inflamed rash on his forearm and hand. The skin looked freshly burned with oozing red pustules.

"What happened? Poison ivy?"

"Nope, an allergic reaction after visiting my brother at his furniture manufacturing plant. He's working with some family of ours in Indonesia, importing and exporting. Hey, do you know how much glue and chemicals and flame retardant are all over your couch?"

"Ah, yes, flame retardants. I once tried to find a couch that didn't have them. Long story short: they all do."

Ross grimly shook his head as the men pulled out chairs to join the circle. Now that Ernest was here, the meeting could start. He kicked it off on a high note: "So what's on everyone's dream list for next year's party? What would we love to see at the event? Sky's the limit for now."

"Booths from some of the best restaurants in Chicago," Marcy said.

"Good, what else?"

"What about some roller coasters?" another member suggested.

He politely wrote it down in the notebook.

"I know," Ross said with a gleam in his eye. "What about some kick-ass music? Something that could really draw a crowd!"

Some names were tossed out: Chicago, for obvious civic pride reasons; Earth, Wind, and Fire, because someone had seen them at a benefit lately (likely while drunk and highly suggestible). Ernest scribbled down all the suggestions while watching for a reaction from Jean, his prickly boss from Prairie Park's department of cultural affairs, but he couldn't gauge her blank expression.

"The right live band could draw a big crowd," Ernest ventured, "but would it just attract a bunch of party people who don't care about the cause?"

"But if we educate even ten percent on the issues, it'd be worth it."

Jean spoke up: "Let's get a killer live band. Great suggestion, Ross!"

Ernest inwardly grimaced. He should've been more enthusiastic. Why not? What, he didn't like music?

Jean wasn't done. "Let's have a big booth from Demeter Foods. Have we reached out for a sponsorship yet? We should go after them for platinum. Their logo would look great on the banners."

"I don't know," Ernest said.

Jean frowned. Of course she would love Demeter. She had the eco-affluent look down pat: expensive hiking gear worn for everyday life, eighteen-karat gold earrings hammered by indigenous people toiling in a mountainous enclave somewhere, and a short, elegant hairstyle that saved time for more heroic tasks. But he always suspected her convictions were partially rooted in some liberal fashion ideal. If Jean couldn't wear beautiful, expensive things that displayed her magnanimous care for all the world's peoples and its land, would she still be as committed?

"Are we sure this is who we want at platinum?" Ernest said. "They are pretty corporate, after all."

"What do you mean? Don't be thrown off by the nice floors or the decent Pinot Noir selection. It's still the real deal."

"But what about Karen's?" Ernest asked. He'd been a devoted shopper at the tiny health-food store for years now, hunting through the cramped aisles for the latest take on carob—carob carrot buns, carob power nuggets, carob milkshakes, shredded carob, the possibilities were endless.

"Still there," Jean said dismissively, "looking tired as ever." Then remembering herself: "And of course we welcome her involvement as always. But she can't afford platinum level; you know that, Ernest. If we want a big headliner for the music, the platinum sponsor needs to be in place ASAP."

He nodded and took a sip out of his cup. "What is this coffee, by the way?"

"You haven't tried this yet?" Marcy said. "It's from Ghana."

"By way of Demeter," Jean added wryly, winking at the others.

"Ghana? It's delicious," Ernest said, holding out the cup in front of him. "Too bad it had to be served in Styrofoam."

"It's all the field house has," Marcy said, trying to quell any defensiveness in her voice, but it was always so hard with Ernest, the vigilante.

———

Cynthia liked to take walks at dawn. This morning, she was especially motivated to escape her tension-filled house, but she couldn't find her keys. Probably nothing would happen if she left the door unlocked—and she would've done that twenty years ago without hesitation, young and without children and almost defiantly trusting of the world—but she'd long ago trained herself out of recklessness that had no tangible rewards. If it had a reward, different story, which was why she happily justified driving twenty miles over the speed limit whenever she was running late. And speeding gave her a jolt, to thread the needle on the expressway with expert control.

Dressed in a faded fleece pullover, Cynthia wandered across the thick Persian rugs in all the rooms on the first floor, looking for her key chain. She made a note to tell the Polish cleaning lady, who vociferously chewed tiny pellets of sugar-free gum, to take better care vacuuming next Friday. Immediately she knew she wouldn't say anything, because all of their conversations devolved into semi-comic, semi-excruciating exchanges as Ewa pretended to understand what Cynthia was saying and Cynthia pretended that Ewa wasn't faking comprehension. Just as well, Cynthia thought. She always preferred to avoid pointless conflict. She scanned the surfaces of the living room's heavy oak furniture, ran her hands over shelves packed with books and knickknacks, but the keys still eluded her.

In the kitchen, she rifled through the breakfront, the surface piled with yellowing magazines—the *Nation*, the Whole Earth catalog, *Gourmet*—splattered in canola and grape seed oil. The kitchen, and to a lesser degree the entire house, smelled of recipes past—ginger, garlic, rosemary, and the tangy odor of compost from Ernest's specially ordered box from the Sierra Club.

Drifting around some more, she finally found her keys exactly where she always left them: dangling on the arm of a wooden African statue planted on the kitchen counter. How confusing. Hadn't she checked that spot first, and didn't she see it empty? She couldn't remember whether she'd checked it, but she must've, right? When she forgot simple things like this, it made her suspicious that age was stealing in, wiping out her small abilities first before closing in for the big take.

Out the kitchen window, the sun was breaking over the metal of the spaceship; tiny drops of dew clung to the legs. Cynthia glanced at it as she reached for her keys, not bothered by it—not that much anyway—mostly just eager to forget about it for now. "Compartmentalizing," her therapist friend called it. But then she was rooted in place. She wasn't moving.

Why wasn't she moving?

The metal and the dew merged into one substance, as if the spaceship legs had sprouted glistening bumps. She couldn't stop staring at the drops, the sun glinting off the metal and the water, millions of bright pinpoints.

Why wasn't she moving?

An idea blasted in, as if yelled by someone in her ear: the spaceship is here to find something or someone. ·

No: the spaceship is here to get something or someone and go back.

What? she asked herself, or the voice. Was the voice separate from her or was it her self, an all-knowing self? Whoever it was, the line was now dead. The yelling was gone. She could move her legs again.

She snatched her keys and rushed out the door, away from the spaceship, away from Ernest, away from the kids. A rash temptation suddenly occurred to jump in the car and speed off cross-country, but she decided to walk until she felt calm again.

Outside, stringy clouds were paralyzed into place, hanging low behind the houses. A high wind chilled her cheeks and lashed at her eyes, naked in her skull. She tried to shake off the vision—had she just had a vision?—by focusing on the houses painted in Prairie Park's favored colors of twig, mud, and taupe. Her brain ticked off the chemicals in those exterior house paints—toluene, xylene, and other petroleum distillate solvents—but it didn't really work and then she was back to thinking about the voice, which hadn't sounded crazy or alarming, per se, more like a voice delivering urgent and clear information.

She laughed, which she did whenever she felt truly confused, and kept walking in a bubbly kind of trance punctuated by talking to herself. OK, it was true that ideas or sensations visited her from time to time, communicated in blasts of words or vivid pictures. Some of them were wrong, some of them were right, and most fell into the not-applicable category. Did it matter what this one said? It wanted something or someone? She laughed again. Fatigue, stress, or whatever was streaking through her nerves and would run its course eventually. The spaceship had forced in new antagonism between her and Ernest; when they'd talk about it, he'd get so crabby and hint that her permissiveness with Gabe was somehow to blame. Never those words outright but close enough. Forget it. Marital storms blew in and blew out. *Let's concentrate on the present world,* she told herself. *Prairie Park: rosy sun, small businesses yet to open, houses still warm and dark with sleep.*

The fantasy remained intact until she reached Aurora Park. In the middle of the lawn, a man in a drab uniform was digging out clumps with a small hand shovel and dropping them into a white plastic container with measurements on the side. They were the only two people in the park. The man immediately noticed her and issued her a stern glance before returning to his task. He shielded his activity from her sight with a twist of his boxy figure. Cynthia wondered what could be happening in the plain light of day that prompted such covert actions.

Cynthia, eager to have a task to focus on outside herself, resumed walking the park's circumference but kept her eye out for other pieces of information that might clarify the man's mission. In the service driveway near the field house, she noticed a parked van from the local gas utility. She had never noticed one of those here before—typically it was a truck from the department of parks and recreation, if any vehicle at all. It seemed to her that the service people of Prairie Park—the utility workers who appeared in the backyard measuring the amount of electricity used that month or fixing a gas line, with no explanation about what might be wrong with it—were always moving in the background, seemingly directed by a scent cloud like an army of ants to repair and reinforce the infrastructure. Most of the times that she saw them, it was clearly routine maintenance. But this guy's work seemed different, significant in some way.

As she walked out of the park, something shiny in the dirt caught her eye: a trace of gold chain. She bent down and dug it out with her fingers. Once she freed it, the piece was revealed: a long necklace with a magnifying glass on the end, smeared with dirt and some sort of goop, fertilizer maybe. When she got home with the necklace, she washed it under the hot tap with soap, but still the goop tainted the glass with an amber haze. She tried to chip it off with her fingernail but the goop would not budge. She hung the necklace on a hook in the kitchen, to remind herself to bring it to the Aurora Park lost and found.

———

Gazing out the kitchen window at the ship, his lips hovering over a steaming cup of exceptionally delicious morning coffee—the one from Ghana that he'd slipped into Demeter to buy—Ernest watched the panel on the spaceship's underside slide open. He could hear it through the back screen door. The chunky sound of the panel sliding to the side reminded him of a cheap VCR ejecting a tape. Then a torrent of bright green liquid splattered onto the patch of dying grass.

"What the hell was that?" Ernest asked no one in particular.

Alison looked up from her notebook, where she was drawing the spaceship camped in the backyard, just in time to witness the dumping. The panel closed with the slow purpose of an elevator, almost as if to allow for one last expulsion, if the machine decided it must.

"I've seen that happen before."

"When?"

"I don't know, a few days ago?"

"And you didn't say anything?"

"It didn't seem important."

"What could be more important than green sludge dumping on our lawn?"

"It's waste from the ship, Dad," Gabe said as he entered the room. "It's just what it does."

"Oh, this is just what it does? How often is this supposed to happen?"

Gabe rushed in to speak but realized he didn't know the answer.

"See? This is exactly what I was afraid of when you got this dumb thing to land at our house. What kind of waste anyway? These aliens haven't figured out a better way?"

When no one replied—Cynthia was out or she might've tried to calm him—Ernest stood up with intention.

"We're going to start keeping a log. Everything the ship does, we'll record it. Even if it does nothing in particular, we will write down 'stationary.' If it pukes up green liquid on the lawn, we'll write 'dumping noxious green liquid on the lawn.' We'll make it a daily log. We'll keep track of its every movement."

Logging was a ritual intrinsic to Allen family life. Ernest frequently used it to teach his children the importance of conservation. For several weeks last year, when he determined that Alison's showers were exorbitantly long and probably draining Lake Michigan, he made the kids keep track of their water usage. Cynthia tried to dissuade him—"Ernest, don't you think they may need some sort of private time in there?"—but he didn't see what kind of private time required more than fifteen minutes of hot water pressurized at forty pounds per square inch.

Of course, the monitoring was handily manipulated by anyone in the household with a different agenda. Alison and Gabe fabricated inordinately long shower times for the other—an hour and forty minutes! Five days!!—in the wrinkled notebook Ernest nailed to the bathroom wall. So many pranks were executed via the notebook that it was eventually abandoned.

"I don't want to keep a log," Alison said. "It's just a thing back there now, like the weeping willow tree or the garage. Although it's more fun to draw because it's so weird."

"We have to keep track of what it's doing so I can report to the New World people."

"The New World people don't want to talk to you, Dad. They're too busy."

"I'm having your mom the attorney call next time. That pamphlet didn't say anything about dumping waste on the lawn. Might be time to get litigious."

Gabe regarded his sister with scornful curiosity. "Alison, do you just not even care about a spaceship in your backyard? That might even be worse than hating it."

"I care. But it gives me the creeps sometimes."

"The creeps about what?"

"That someone's watching us in there."

"Really? You're still worrying about that? There's no evidence for that."

"Well, there's no evidence against it either. I don't know. One minute it wasn't here, and then the next it is and now everything's totally different. Like what would we be doing right now if it weren't here? I want to go back to that."

Gabe didn't agree aloud, but he admitted to himself that she had a point. The spaceship, on some level, always occupied his mind, never totally forgotten about, its image flashing when he wandered the hallways at school or rode his bike. He'd brought some of his classmates over, including kids he'd barely spoken to before, to gawk at it and ask questions like "What if the aliens are having sex in there right now?" and comments like "My dog would totally pee on its legs." The attention thrilled and exhausted him.

The teachers were curious too. Desperate to capitalize on the excitement, his English teacher turned it into an assignment for the class. "I want you guys to write a paper about how the main characters of *Nineteen Eighty-Four*, Winston and Julia, would react to a spaceship suddenly landing at Airstrip One," Mr. Levin said. "Would it frighten them? Give them hope? What would be their reaction?"

Kerry, a pretty girl in the front row, raised her hand.

"Does the spaceship look exactly like the one at Gabe's house?" she asked, looking at Gabe and smiling.

In the kitchen's junk drawer, beneath a detritus of pens, tape measures, paper clips, and solar calculators, Ernest found an old notebook. He flipped to a fresh page, speaking out loud as he wrote: "September 12: 11:40 A.M., ship pukes out green liquid, approximately 10 gallons, onto the lawn."

He delivered the notebook to Gabe. "I want you to be the primary keeper of the log."

Ernest didn't bother explaining his rationale and Gabe didn't press.

"No problem."

"Daily posts. You can be the one to keep track of how it trashes our lawn and reduces your hearing every night. How's that tinnitus, by the way?"

"It's nothing," Gabe said, before adding in a goofy rapper voice, "I'm going to murder this notebook like it was the SATs."

Alison laughed. "Yeah, dawg."

"You too, Alison," Ernest said. "I have a feeling you might be a less biased witness than Dr. Dre over here. Write down all the creepy things he won't write down."

"That's encouraging sibling rivalry, Dad. Are you and Mom going to contribute too?"

"Of course."

"How about Athena?" Alison pointed to their white cat, resting in a sunny spot on the floor. "We all have to do our part."

"She's off the hook for now. She doesn't like the spaceship either."

Ernest walked to the window. Traces of the neon-green sludge were still visible, but most of it seemed to have already sunk in, working its way through the dirt and the tiny roots that carried nutrients into the central part of the grass. He wondered what would kill the grass first—the sludge or the oncoming winter?

6

"Honey, I'm sorry, but I only have a few minutes."

"I want to run an idea by you."

Cynthia worked in an unglamorous office at a desk that was always buried in sedimentary paperwork. At thirty-nine, she was one of the few lawyers in a small Chicago law firm that specialized in environmental law and civic government cases. She had the phone crunched on her shoulder while her hands dug through an especially unruly file, spilling over with affidavits and reports.

"At last night's meeting, we realized that we're short on budget. Even with what town hall's giving us, we're not going to make our goals. We don't want to pull back on the plans but we've got to raise money in other ways. Creative, homespun ways that aren't going to rely on corporate sponsorship."

"What's wrong with corporate sponsorship?"

"We don't need yet another partner telling us what to do and how to do it. We need money with no strings attached, given from the goodness of one's heart."

"Oh, I see where this is going."

"Do you?"

"You're talking about torturing our children."

"Torture! I'm talking about building character."

"Everyone knows that 'building character' means doing something you don't want to do."

"I want them to go down to the mall and collect money from the small business owners."

"Babe, really? How much money will they get from that? A few hundred bucks, tops?"

"We're always emphasizing to them the importance of working for their values. And who wouldn't *want* to give them money? It's sweet, these two kids collecting donations for an Earth Day celebration."

"I love them, Ernest, but I don't know if they can play the cute card anymore."

"Sure they can."

"How did this come about?"

Ernest recounted that after the budget had been revealed, he quickly volunteered to raise money. Or more specifically, his children. After all, they were old hands at fund-raising. One year, they'd raised a whopping $168 for a beach cleanup—spent on trash bags, recycling bins, and a humble lunch for all the volunteers. They were little kids then—Gabe, barely ten years old, dressed in a suit, and Alison, eight, wiggling a loose eyetooth and smearing the extra blood on her peach dress. Ernest parked them in front of the local bank, where they kicked their legs out underneath a folding card table. From across the street, he kept an eye on them; he knew they'd get more without him there fouling the scene. "Look for people with nice things," he said. "Leather coats and jackets, big jewelry. Call to them, 'Would you like to save the environment?'"

His strategy was all about leading by example. He thought if he volunteered his kids, as the director of the Earth Day committee, then all the other members would follow suit. But his prime targets—Jean, Ross and Marcy, all of whom had children around Gabe and Alison's age—didn't seem to bite. Jean said something about Leigh having too many commitments this year already— debate team, gymnastics. Ernest pushed the issue but was politely stonewalled.

Cynthia said, "Why don't I ask Stephen if he'll contribute?"

"Oh, Stephen. I don't know."

Stephen was the head of Cynthia's law film, a strapping environmentalist whom Ernest always imagined riding a chestnut horse to work instead of a low-emissions car.

"You'll get a sizable sum at once instead of nickels and dimes from people at the mall."

"But he's going to want the firm's name on something."

"Of course he will, but what's wrong with that? Just list the name with Demeter and all the other sponsors."

"The kids are grassroots," Ernest said. "That's what I want."

Cynthia recognized the ragged maw of an argument opening in front of her. She could point out that it wasn't particularly rootsy to use their children as pawns, regardless of the cause, but she had too much to do and it was already a well-worn argument. Cynthia knew Ernest's gripes about corporate sponsorship; he'd fired himself up last night talking about Demeter's involvement. All the same, she made a request:

"Things are so tense in the house right now. Promise me this: keep the peace with Gabe. I don't need a repeat of last night."

"Don't worry, I'll keep things easy. You have my word."

Last night, things had gotten so annoying that Alison and Cynthia fled the house. But first, in the kitchen, Ernest shook the notebook at Gabe:"The log. Where's the log? No entries?"

"You haven't been entering either," Gabe said.

They'd been loading the dishwasher together; the door hung open, slopped with a few bits of food.

"I'm an adult with things to do. I put you in charge, remember?"

"OK, well, I'm a teenager with equally important things to do."

"No, Gabe, the point is that I asked you, the last few days when I saw the ship dumping and vibrating and otherwise being a pain in the ass, to record it diligently in the notebook. And do you know what you said to that, Gabe?"

Gabe's shoulders slumped and he didn't meet his father's eyes.

"You said, 'I'll do it, Dad,' and then I check on it and the thing's blank besides my first entry. How do you explain that?"

As if the dishwasher contained all the answers, Gabe stuck his head down and fiddled with the arrangement of the cups.

"Gabe?"

"I don't know, Dad. I didn't want to record it, OK? Not if it's going to feed your paranoia."

"I'm not paranoid; I just want to document this like a scientist. I just want an orderly, fact-driven document that captures the experience of having a trespassing alien disk pooping on my lawn."

"Oh my god, I get it, OK? Hand me the notebook."

Ernest passed over the notebook.

"First of all, it looks like, well, not a scientific document at all. This notebook is ugly."

"Oh, please. Fine, let Alison draw a spaceship on the cover. Something like she drew for her shoes."

"It needs a title. It's totally random otherwise."

"How about . . ." Ernest found a Sharpie and started to write in bold letters on the cover: THE ACTIVITIES OF THE UNWELCOME VISITORS FROM JUPITER: AN ALLEN FAMILY LOG.

"Speak for yourself! They're not unwelcome by me or anyone with an open mind."

Their voices continued to batter, and Cynthia felt a headache coming on. She gave up on trying to get work done in the den and jogged upstairs to knock on Alison's door.

"Do you hear the beasts feasting on all that testosterone?"

Legs crossed on the bed, Alison looked up from her notebook. "Trying not to but—"

"Do you want to take a walk with me?"

"It's OK, they'll stop soon enough."

"Even if I let you get a soft drink in a color insulting to nature?"

Alison's eyes brightened. "Ooh, like what?"

"A Slurpee or a Pizzee or whatever. Let's walk to 7-Eleven."

"Really? A Slurpee isn't technically a soft drink, but OK!"

"Whatever it is, it's definitely not good for you."

Once inside the convenience store a few blocks away, Cynthia stood mystified in front of the mixing vats, all three churning a different hue of sweet slush. She gripped one of the black levers and started to twist.

"Oh my god, Mom. You have no idea what you're doing, do you?"

"No, I don't." Cynthia quickly retracted her hand. "I've never seen this before. Every time you kids came in with a Slurpee, I never thought about the machine that makes it."

"Watch and learn." Alison grabbed the biggest cup available.

"No, no, no. Smaller size than that. That one." Cynthia pointed to the adult small.

"Is this for me or for you?"

"It's for you. This is a good size."

Alison sighed but accepted her mother's decree. She pulled down on the black knob and looked pointedly at her mother. "See?"

A shoot of cola fuzz rocketed to the bottom of the cup, and then the machine whined and ceased to drip out anything else.

Cynthia jumped back a little bit. "What's wrong with it?"

"It's like you've never seen a machine before. Hold on," Alison said. She pushed the lever back. "It just needs a minute."

"How do you know this?"

"Because I live in the twentieth century in suburban America."

They giggled loudly, enough so that the sour-faced man at the register craned his neck to look at them. He'd had a lot of candy bars walk out the door lately, and he wasn't taking any chances.

Alison pulled on the lever again and a smooth snake of Slurpee emerged. She expertly twisted the cup with her other hand so that it lay in spirals. Close to the rim, she cut it off with a practiced hand.

"Wow," Cynthia said. "A Slurpee pro."

"You want one?"

"Just that baby cup. The red flavor. Cherry, right?"

"No, steak."

They giggled again. "Just fill it up. I'm going to find some Advil."

On the walk home, they sucked in silence on the straws with the little spoons on the bottom end.

"How's everything going with Rebecca?" Alison's best friend from junior high, ever since they'd started high school, had been palling around with an aggressive jock crowd. For friendship-preserving reasons, Alison was forced to pretend that watching them all play grab-ass and call each other fags while drinking Natty Light was an engaging activity.

"It's fine when it's just the two of us."

"But not when other people are around?" Cynthia enjoyed testing her daughter's openness. It shifted for reasons she could only guess at.

"It's just this certain crowd she's into now. This other girl Claire is pretty much her idol because she has a car and knows about all the senior parties."

"Do you like Claire?"

Long pause. "I don't think she really likes me. The minute Rebecca isn't around we kind of just stare at each other, and then she asks me questions about the spaceship, which is, like, the only thing she knows about me. Well, OK, she does like my drawings. She wants me to draw a logo for her scrunchie business."

"Scrunchies?"

"Yeah, she sews buttons on them, dips them in sparkles. They're really puffy."

"Do you like them?"

Alison paused again. "They're kind of cool. She might start making velvet chokers too."

"Does she have a name for her business?"

"Tiny Vampire."

"Well, there's your illustration right there. A cute little vampire wearing a big puffy scrunchie." Cynthia laughed at the vision of it.

"Yeah, whatever. She said she'd give me twenty dollars to draw something, so that's pretty good."

"You should sell more drawings. Look at your shoes. You could sell hand-drawn sneakers for a lot of money."

"Yeah, maybe." Alison tried the idea on. Her stomach panicked a little at the thought of selling something she'd made herself.

"You could do themes, whatever they request."

Alison had already been approached by a few kids to do a copy of the scenario she had drawn on her own white Converse—a crowded sunshine-lit utopia of spaceships flying through the air toward a wild landscape. Lots of yellow and green. But she'd told the other kids that it was one of a kind. Why hadn't she thought to offer them something else? She wrestled with wanting and shunning attention. On one hand, she longed to be the center, to have her talents praised and used as currency, but on the other, she got squeamish and shy talking about it.

As usual, her mother intuited her thoughts, saying, "You shouldn't be so shy about your skills. You should be proud that you can draw like that. I don't know where you got it from."

Alison didn't say anything, but she basked in the odd sensation that she was a rare creature. That for every moment her parents were clueless, they could stare right into her like this with ease and see something that she'd grasped only the corner of herself. She kept drinking the Slurpee, the icy cola numbing her throat.

A couple of blocks from the store, Cynthia pitched her drink into a trash can. "Ugh, I've got a headache and I think that's making it worse." Cynthia wrenched open the Advil bottle, shook out a tablet, and gulped it down.

"No water? Can I have one?"

"You have a headache too?"

"No, I just like the taste."

Her mother frowned. "What do you mean?"

"The coating. I love the taste."

Cynthia stopped walking. "Wait. Do you just pop Advil for the flavor?"

Alison took another long draw from her drink, wondering what answer could still be relatively honest but not get her in too much trouble. "I guess so. Sometimes I swallow them, sometimes I spit them out."

"How often?"

"I don't know. Once a week?"

"Alison, you can't do that. You can't just eat Advil because it tastes good."

"Most of the time I just suck on it and spit it out."

"Jesus, no wonder we're always out of Advil."

Her mom was surprisingly pissed. "What is the big deal? It's not like it gets you high."

"No, but it's not candy. It's medicine. Promise me you'll never do that again."

"OK, I won't. I didn't know it would be such a thing."

"God, why would you do that?"

"It's sweet; it tastes good. There's never any sugar or candy in the house."

Cynthia nodded. "Maybe we've been too strict about that."

"Well, you don't have to jump down my throat about it."

"I just want my girl to be safe." Her mother squeezed her hand.

Coming down the sidewalk was a tall elderly woman with striking orange-and-red pants, the colors in swirls. She held her beehived head down until the last moment before they crossed paths.

"Hello," she greeted Cynthia.

"Hello," Cynthia said. "You're out late tonight."

"It's nice weather for a walk. Is this your daughter?"

"Sure is."

"Love those sneakers. My gosh are those great! Enjoy your evening, ladies."

Cynthia swatted Alison on the arm. "See?"

After the woman walked a distance away, Alison said, "That woman has great style. I could totally draw her some psychedelic sneakers—peace signs, paisleys, oh my god. Whatever she wanted."

"She walks more than anyone I've ever seen. I see her in the mornings usually. She's in amazing shape for her age, or any age. I wouldn't mind being like her."

"Mom, I don't think you'll ever be able to top that lady's look. I mean, no offense or anything."

Cynthia laughed. "None taken, but I'm not totally hopeless, you know."

"Really? What's the craziest thing you've ever worn?"

"When I was in college," Cynthia said, "I mostly sat around in bikini tops—trippy psychedelic ones with tiny strings—and jean shorts. Either my shoulders were bare or my feet were bare—or both."

"Are you telling me to wear as little clothing as possible when I go to college?"

Cynthia smiled. "Only if the climate's right."

When Cynthia first met Ernest in college in California, they were both enterprising, politically active firebrands who argued that environmentalism touched every facet of life, no matter your race, class, or gender. In a discussion about water pollution, she watched Ernest, handsome and volatile, stand in his ragged T-shirt and rattle off several statistics about water. When a classmate offered the idea that water problems in Latin America might be exaggerated, Ernest drew him into a debate, expertly shooting him down with a steely command of the facts. He knew how to channel his rage and passion and, somehow, still maintain a sense of absurdist humor, a rare commodity among activist types. Soon enough, they were cooking dinners together in her tiny apartment shared with three other girls, throwing slices of squash into a sizzling pan from her parents' farm, his arm wrapped around her back as she was cooking, pulling her in as the vegetable caramelized, his breath tracing her ear as he lowered down to kiss her neck.

Later, on the rumpled sheets of her bed, they'd get lost in each other for hours, until they were tired of the taste of their own bodies, but then the pull would be just as intoxicating the next night, and for a long, long time it sustained them that way.

Though they were in agreement politically, their beliefs manifested in different ways: Cynthia wanted something tangible, so she pursued a law degree once the kids were in school, working herself hard late at night over the minutiae of environmental law, as it was the early 1980s, with still-fresh laws passed by Nixon, back when Republicans saw the good of protecting the land, air, and water as much as anyone else (or at least did a decent job of parroting the rhetoric).

Truth be told, Cynthia never quite understood how a man with Ernest's talents couldn't find the right fit. He was so committed to his ideals, quoting Roderick Nash, Denis Hayes, and Rachel Carson. He recalled the Santa Barbara oil spill in 1969 and how it had compelled him to change his life. He alluded to the conditions in Chicago's industrial South Side, where he'd grown up, with bitter intensity. Yet he graduated with a bachelor's degree in biology and promptly stalled out, getting education jobs that let him work outdoors but little else. "Why not law?" she'd asked him. And he'd hemmed and hawed, sometimes agreeing that one could do good that way, other times ripping apart the system as effecting no real change other than holding up a small hand against the tidal wave of destructive corporations.

He settled instead into a pattern of consulting jobs, most of them low paying, to Cynthia's disappointment. These short-term gigs never provided the right situation to contain or sustain his specific brand of environmental fervor. Before directing Earth Day, he had worked as an environmental impact consultant for the state government. Basically, his job entailed following all the condo development projects in the area and making sure none of them infringed upon protected lands or the survival of natural habitats. In one way, the job appealed to Ernest's watchdog nature, but he complained about how little he could do. Sure, he could get a project to move by a few hundred feet sometimes, but it was only a stopgap measure. There was always a sense from him that nothing was good enough or pure enough. This absolutism prompted both affection and exasperation from everyone who knew him. His friends talked about the certain facial expression he had to go along with his speeches: the transfixed look of a righteous monk.

Cynthia, for all her frustrations with Ernest's career path, appreciated his passion and authenticity. And his lack of traditional ambition allowed her more freedom to pursue her career while he took on cooking for the family and other time-consuming household duties. That flexibility in a man of their generation was hard to find.

And somewhere in all his idealism, he did possess a realist's eye. Cynthia filled with relief whenever he acknowledged practicalities, limits, and contradictions, the daily bread of her practice. When she couldn't manage to block the building of a mall on some prairie grasses, Ernest nodded in understanding at the other lawyer's argument that the financial benefits for the depressed town would outweigh the natural harm. "See," Cynthia had pointed out to him, "you would've made a strong lawyer. It's all about seeing the other side so you can plan the appropriate counterarguments, and an appropriate counterargument can lead to finding a working compromise." That was the backbone of her work: negotiation. But then he said that he was just pretending; in actuality, he couldn't see the other side. He could understand it but he could never empathize. And somehow, in all of his contradictions and obvious posturing, she loved him anyway. For all his complaining, Ernest was in touch with the essential playfulness of life. She still brightened every time he burst into a room with some little fact or wry observation that he just had to share with her.

⸻⬥⸻

Ernest's car was a disheveled old beast that hadn't been serviced in years, a maroon Volkswagen Jetta with scrapes of rust rimming the wheel wells. Cynthia teased him sometimes to trade it in, but secretly, she felt a swell of affection for it whenever she heard its motor rasp to a stop in the driveway. In the backseat, torn upholstery and files from his work. Between the front seats, a few banged-up cassette tapes stored in a heavy pottery dish Gabe had made in grade school, along with change and keys to a long-abandoned locker at the YMCA. The tape player wasn't there anymore, just the wiry guts of a deck long ago ripped out by a thief unconcerned with the fastidiousness of his crime.

For months Ernest had driven around in silence, but Gabe had deemed this too depressing, so he outfitted his father's car with his old boom box; it sat on the passenger seat, some kind of stereophonic pet living off D batteries. When the power ran out, Gabe replaced the batteries for him, fetching the frozen alkaline tubes out of the garage refrigerator that Ernest stocked with frozen marinades, soups, Popsicles for the summer, rolls of film, exotic spicy mustards and hot sauces. Some of the foods were stored with a recipe attached or just the aura of a plan. His children thought it was strange that he had plans so far ahead for something as ordinary as dinner, but to him the days clicked by that way, filled with reassuring little details.

He puttered home from work, spent but still nervous from an exhausting afternoon. In what was supposed to be a quickie freelance gig for the state government—he'd taken it on in addition to his Earth Day duties for the extra cash—he met with developers who had condo plans for a prairie area some sixty miles south of the city. His job was to inform them that their project wouldn't work because some bird nests would be in jeopardy. The CEO of the company asked Ernest a series of questions that grew more hostile as they went along.

Ernest didn't mind educating the developer on the new measure; it had been passed only for a year. The brawny businessman was spoiled by a culture where he could build anything, anywhere, and not worry about the problems. Toxic runoffs into water, fine dust from construction materials covering the ground for miles around, destruction of tree groves and bird nests, buying people's land with eminent domain, changing pathways of roads to go around his projects—he never had to be concerned about any of it until recently, so, at first, Ernest was patient with the man's confusion. But then it became clear that the developer wasn't seeking clarification on the measure; he simply opposed its very existence.

Once Ernest recognized the true mission of the developer's questions, his mood shifted. "There aren't any ways around this measure," Ernest repeated. "And it isn't in effect to make your life difficult."

"How about I make your life difficult?" the developer said with a sleazy smile.

Ernest could sense the developer sizing up his shaggy hair and his unassuming sneakers, and he silently returned the same scorn for the developer's ostentatious pinkie ring and starched shirt.

"No one's life has to be difficult," Ernest said. "Birds included."

After the meeting was over, as Ernest drifted home, he reflected more on his self-presentation. Cynthia would've recommended playing a different part, rather than the granola-chomping nature advocate. "It only muddles the true issues," she would have said, "because then they fixate on you and how you must feel superior to them. Or, worse, how you are an incompetent pot-smoking hippie who can't be taken seriously." That's why, for all professional interactions, Cynthia dressed in simple, moderately priced skirts and blouses. She preferred neutrality, but Ernest couldn't situate himself outside his identity, no matter how much he conceded that it might help him.

Through the windshield he spotted a set of white lines on the sky, a little wavy like they were drawn in shaving cream: contrails. He pulled over at Aurora Park and got out of his car to take in the sight of this man-made intrusion on the natural world, somewhat repulsive, somewhat fascinating. He was also in no hurry to go home.

Twilight pink was settling on the fall day, the kind of breezy beauty that the Midwest delivered around this time of year as an early apology for the next five months of meteorological brutality. On the park's corner near the basketball court, a woman stood alone, staring into the sky. Ernest stood at a polite distance from her, watching one of the cottony lines shred till it vanished. The other lines remained.

He released a long sigh. She turned her chin over one shoulder to look at him.

"Did you know that Chinese astronomers in the fourth century thought that the blue of the sky was an illusion?"

"Is that so?" she said.

"They thought it was an optical illusion to cover up the infinite, empty space."

"I guess we know it a little differently now," she said. Then pointing at the contrails: "See those marks in the sky? They come from all the chemicals we're using."

He knew the contrails theory only a little bit. The sharp lines that jets and planes drew in the sky were really remnants of their pollutants, leaked out of their tails as they soared to oases unknown.

"I've been researching it," she said, still not turning around fully, but he caught enough of her face to recognize her.

"Marilyn Fournier," he said. "You write for the city paper. I remember your piece a few years ago on the city's Earth Day debacle. That was a great story."

She turned around to thank him, but he was already continuing.

"I'm always reading environment stories for my work. You know," he said, taking a step forward as the opportunity dawned on him, "I'm organizing Earth Day's twenty-fifth anniversary next year. It'll be held right here in this park. It's going to be quite the blowout." As he spoke about the town politics of getting the event off the ground, and how he had convinced Prairie Park to increase the budget, he thought he noticed Marilyn checking him out. He had ventured out on an arduous hike yesterday; maybe the healthy afterglow hadn't yet faded.

"And you also consult?" she asked. She listened to his explanation about monitoring certain construction projects with a slight smile. "So you're an enviro-cop."

"To serve and protect."

"I bet people don't like when a stranger drops in and enforces the rules."

"Well, I get a little thrill out of it."

He asked her for a card, so that he could alert her now and again on potential stories. He casually slipped in that he wrote the occasional editorial for the *Tuesday Courier*. The last one he wrote a few months ago was on the importance of green space in the town mall, currently shut off to car traffic. Prairie Park's officials wanted to run a street through it to spur business. Ernest thought it was a terrible idea. His editorial had garnered several responses: some from local businesses who said a street would save the flagging mall, some who agreed with him, and one from a seventeen-year-old Marxist who advocated for the entire mall to be destroyed.

Marilyn dug a card out of her purse, an unfashionable but highly functional canvas shoulder bag that gave Ernest a sense of kinship.

"What are you working on now?"

"All sorts of stories," she said in a way that suggested she wouldn't talk any more about them. She had a serious, secretive air about her, even when she was smiling. "Let me ask you something: Do you spend a lot of time in this park?"

"All the time. I live only a block away."

"I see," she said with a bobbing nod.

"In fact, you can see a bit of my house right there." Ernest pointed down the block. They were close enough to see some neon-green light from the spaceship spilling onto the driveway.

"There?" She squinted. "With that green light? What is that?"

"Well," he said with an exhalation, "that's a spaceship from Jupiter."

Her body froze and then a giddy smile spread on her face. "You're kidding me."

"Lucky winner, right here."

"Right, oh right! Someone at the office was telling me that a saucer had landed in this neighborhood—"

"Do you want to come see it?"

She checked her watch. "Sure, I'll take a quick peek."

———◆———

Marilyn Fournier walked around the ship, rubbing her hand on a leg, then knocking on it. She pressed her hand to her sternum and murmured, "Amazing." Then she folded over with a few vigorous sneezes. She laughed. "Is it made out of ragweed?"

"No, but you're not the only one allergic to it." Ernest pointed to two squirrels who'd been on their way into the yard via the driveway but promptly turned around. "All small critters run in the face of the spaceship, including our cat."

"Not surprising."

"You've never heard of these being toxic, have you?"

"No," she said. "Nothing of the sort."

"You should come back in a week," Ernest blurted out. "We're having a party. It's calm right now, but if you're here for a while, it'll make a racket. You've got to see it."

Before she left, they both checked in on the sky. One of the contrails looked like it had been drawn with chalk. That mark would stay the longest, but by nighttime, it blended in with the rest of the clouds, its edges gilded with moonlight.

7

Southern Sierra Nevada, California, 1972

After twisting and nearly doubling back on itself, the ribbon of
highway delivered him into the center of the woods. Already he
longed for what he'd passed: the gas stations that didn't appear
to have anyone manning them and the lumberyards piled with
glistening planks of freshly milled redwood. The liquor store
he'd stopped at played country radio over the speakers. A man
mournfully plucking a guitar, his only companion, would be the
last music Ernest would hear for days. As he wandered the aisles,
dust flew into sunlight. He stocked up on beer, which would make
his pack heavier, but the sacrifice seemed worth it. Getting drunk
in the woods would be one of his few entertainments. Maybe this
meant he was a budding alcoholic, but he couldn't worry about
that now.

His longest camping trip yet. A vision quest, or so he told his
friends. A woods fantasy, he'd told himself, because he wanted to
submerge himself in it but he was scared to. What was this natural
space anyway? Government-protected yet lawless. Empty, in terms
of all the so-called distractions and escape valves—the telephone,
the TV, the emotional involvement with somebody else's life. But
full of trees, animals, rocks, living things. Were these natural things
supposed to fill a void, a hole inside of him created by distracting
technology? Were they supposed to soothe him? Improve him?
And what was the problem, exactly, anyway? Modern devices, the
car that got him here? The way he loved the hum of the car's tires
over the highway? The signs leading into the forest were painted
brown, the lettering white, inviting him into the past—a time when
man lived closer to nature, and himself. The nation still wanted to
preserve this dream about itself, and it wanted it clearly delineated
(and protected) from waking life.

The longest he'd hiked before was for fourteen hours—getting up before dawn, returning to base as the twilight set in—and he had camped with friends and family. But this time he would be solo for a week or as long as he could stand. Anything could happen—madness, visions, clarity even—and these possibilities kept both his spirits up and sent a squirrel of fear skittering across his chest. But it was what he wanted to do. He'd developed strong convictions about the environment, which motivated him to fight with strangers about its deep importance. And yet he'd never been alone, truly on his own, inside of this nature that was at the core of *his* environment. How could the thing he passionately defended be so foreign?

On the third day his food started to run low. Patchy scruff had sprouted on his cheeks, chin, and neck, but instead of giving him a strapping mountain man visage, he looked ignoble (not that he knew this at the time, lacking a mirror or the desire to see himself in one). In his tent, staring at a box of canned food, he struggled with mathematical breakdowns of how many meals he could get from the last three cans. An exact number would emerge from the sine waves in his head, but then it would float away and he'd have to do the accounting all over again.

His focus was fogged, but his mood wasn't bad. In fact, it seemed to be a platonic, default mood. He was just himself, not performing in any kind of way to fulfill expectation. Hours ticked by in this cerebral day slumber. He wandered the woods and watched animals for as long as they didn't realize his presence, and fell into the grass when he was tired. He napped there, level with the horizon.

On the fourth morning, the sky burst open and clattered rain on top of his tent, fortunately protected under a tarp. All the shades of green cast around him—from the tent, the trees, and the stormy light. He huddled inside, recycling the warm carbon of his breath, the flicker of a candle he had lit throwing shadows, the flannel sleeping bag bundled around his legs, and he felt fluttery, his pulse weak and powdery, his stomach up and crawling not where it was supposed to be, charging and exciting him. His hair was aloft with static; his thinking sparkled in the moist cold air, jumping from image to idea to feeling, all of them soft and yet secure. And then he was crawling out of the tent, moving through the rain in the direction of some hot springs he'd read about but hadn't trusted his sense of orientation to find.

The path to the hot springs was long and built of several paths sewn together. Toward the end, he was pawing his way through rain-slick moss and ferns, sticks and bramble. He fell, his hands plunging into mud, but he pulled himself up, carrying on until finally he was at the lip of a steaming pool buttressed against a slick black rock. It had a few sprouts of life growing out of various ledges and caverns, but otherwise was sluiced with water. The liquid ran down in rivulets and floods into the hot bath that smelled like a chemical reaction. On the surface, the water trembled under the assault of steady rain, a dim light reflected in the middle. What was visible of the sky between the trees did not betray a time of day, only a heaving gray mass. The sound of the rain all around him, dropping at his feet.

He stripped down, stuffing his clothes into a plastic sack. He tested the water with his left hand. It was hot, right at the point. He plunged into the water without thinking.

Under the surface, holding his breath, the water enveloped him and poured into his ears, plugged away at his lips and nostrils. His body completely submerged in a temperature close to his own triggered a shutdown of regular physical and mental maintenance. A different kind of synchronization occurred between the automatic parts of his brain that controlled his breathing and heartbeat, and the cognitive parts related to the self and the world around him, even down to the smallest cluster, the neural cells that carried the instructions for how to change a tire or make scrambled eggs. Every stitched-up way of experiencing loosened and then ripped open. He was floating in some primordial goo and then he *became* the primordial goo. He had one long animal thought that was not verbal. It was a ticking *t-t-t-t-t-t-t-t-t-t-t-t-t-t-t-t-t-t-t-t-t-t-t-t-t-t-t-t-t-t-t-t-t-t-t-t-t-t-t-t-t*. It lit up every branch and fissure of his brain.

When he came out, he collapsed on the ground. The battering of the rain. The sting of the water on his eyes. The sharp chill of the air. The sensations were overwhelming him but not in the way they had in the water. He felt vulnerable to them instead of fused with them. Here was the comedown. He was returning to the rascal self, a twitchy mind that absorbed the same setting as before but now with a host of niggling complaints. Here they came again: discomfort and anxiety. He tried to keep them at bay, but they were there, stark as two starfish on a black rock. Pretty soon, he was scrabbling back toward his clothes, cold and shaking. Relief didn't come until he was back in his tent, dressed in dry clothes and tucked into his sleeping bag.

But the memory of what had occurred stayed with him. He'd chase that feeling for the rest of his life. Sometimes he'd brush up against it for a second, like when he saw the northern lights in Michigan's Upper Peninsula: a heaving blot of orange rimmed with a chartreuse spray that rippled and buckled until it was overtaken. The orange mass eventually conquered it, a type of temporary sun charged by solar wind flowing past Earth. It was smeared in the sky, bright enough so that Ernest could clearly read his watch though it was late at night. But even then, he didn't really manage to unhinge the workings of his mind. The tiny pistons continued to fire, momentarily slowed down only by his amazement. He would never really get back to that feeling in California, but he had the memory stored. From time to time, he'd draw it out to linger over the sensations. Hot water. Black rock. *T-t-t-t-t-t-t-t-t-t-t-t-t-t-t-t-t-t-t-t-t-t-t-t-t-t-t-t-t-t-t-t-t.*

8

THE ACTIVITIES OF THE UNWELCOME VISITORS FROM JUPITER: AN ALLEN FAMILY LOG

October 5: *The ship is blowing out some sort of smell today. It smells like perfume, sweet as hell, like the drill team princess I passed in the hallway at school today. P.S.: I changed the kitty litter. —GA*

October 5: *You know who doesn't care about the spaceship whatsoever? This raccoon I've been watching dig a hole in the bushes for the last 20 minutes. Maybe every other animal is scared, but this guy is eating worms or whatever like he's going on a diet tomorrow. —AA*

October 6: *I checked on the green sludge today around 8:30 a.m. and I found a shredded page from a dictionary. The word "precision" was circled. Isn't that weird? The piece of paper's drying in the garage, if anyone wants to look at it. —AA*

October 8: *Not happy about these smells. Came home to start dinner and the ship was blowing out white air that smelled like hot dough. Took me a while to pinpoint the ship—thought Tom or Olivia might be baking bread. The smells ruined my appetite. Started to make marinated pork chops— next thing I know I've eaten nearly a whole bag of chips and a bowl of guacamole. The least it could do, if it's going to make me so hungry, is produce a loaf of bread. Not that I'd eat it. —EA*

October 9: *Today the ship smells like pungent red curry. It's making me wonder if the family wouldn't like to go into the city soon for Indian food. When was the last time we did that? —CA*

A supervisor for New World Enterprises did return Ernest's calls regarding the smells. Stephanie from Nashville said it was "their way" of experimenting with scents they had caught on the wind at some point in their travels. He hadn't thought about this before. He had assumed that the ship came directly from space to his home. But maybe it had flown over Thailand or Israel or upstate New York first. Maybe the ship wasn't so exotic; maybe it was more like an intergalactic Greyhound bus, touring the various dingy stations of Earth. He asked if there was a way to find out the route this particular ship had taken. Stephanie paused and said she wasn't sure. She put him on hold for a long time, and when she returned she said her boss wasn't sure how to find that information out either, but that he could call back tomorrow and maybe that supervisor would know.

He asked her how the aliens replicated the scents. She said she didn't know, but when asked if it was safe, she responded, "Oh, of course. All of the visitors have been briefed about what's poisonous to humans."

"Briefed by whom?"

"Our company instructs them on government regulations passed a few years ago."

Ernest made a mental note to look into those governmental standards. "Well, could it be the case that they're conducting poisonous experiments inside their spaceships but they've been instructed to keep them away from us?"

Silence on the line, then: "No, there's nothing poisonous in the ship either. Everything is completely safe."

Getting ready for bed that night, Ernest told Cynthia, "Wouldn't pleasant smells be the perfect way to leak other toxins into the air? Maybe they've figured out a way to mask pollutants. Imagine it: you're smelling the warm scent of baking bread"—Ernest inhaled mightily—"and then you start choking and coughing because you're actually inhaling benzene fumes. I mean, the jets are doing it with the contrails all day long."

"Come on, no one's coughing up blood here. Let's just try to enjoy the thing."

"Right, everything the spaceship does is magic and goodness. When are you going to call them for me? Come on, flex that lawyerly muscle. You've been putting it off for a week now."

She ignored his comment about her call. "Well, what if it is magic and goodness? It's certainly making Gabe happy."

"Gabe is not allowed to be outside anymore when it's doing its nightly show, by the way. The tinnitus is getting worse."

"Fine, but he was complaining about that before the spaceship arrived."

"Well, he doesn't have to make it worse."

"He can wear earplugs then. He loves it, why take it away from him?"

"Seriously, Cynthia?"

Seriously? He sounded just like Gabe, she realized with amusement.

Ernest continued: "There's nothing about that spaceship that unnerves you?"

On her back in bed, Cynthia blinked at the ceiling. "I don't know. It feels like it wants something. I always feel like standing in front of the spaceship and saying, 'What? What is it?'"

"Interesting," he said. "You mean like it wants one of us?"

"No, not like that, Ernest. Settle down. We're not talking invasion of the body snatchers. It doesn't feel evil or anything like that. It feels familiar. And like I'm supposed to give it something. Or help it, I don't know."

"Sounds maternal almost, your feeling."

Cynthia gave a dismissive hiss. "I'm not just two sacks of breast milk over here."

Ernest surrendered with his hands up. "I didn't say you were."

They let the conversation drop. Sleep called, but in the back of his mind, an itching concern: What if the smells and the raw dumps of green liquid were seeping into their bones, poisoning their land, doing some irreparable harm? He tried to make a bargain with himself as he drifted off. For now, Ernest would enjoy or pretend to enjoy the aromas like everyone else, but he'd also look into those regulations, and if someone from New World didn't call him by tomorrow evening, end of business, Ernest was taking his fight public. As an added bonus, a public scrap completely legitimized the nagging impulse he'd had to call Marilyn Fournier.

9

Fifteen minutes before guests were due, Ernest found Cynthia scrubbing the back of the sink's pedestal, where toothpaste dribble and specks of soap fell. Her white-knuckled fist clutched a raggedy sponge.

"No one ever notices that place, you know. You could tape a hundred-dollar bill back there and no one will find it."

"I'll feel better knowing it's spotless."

"But what about you? You haven't even changed yet."

She continued scrubbing. Ernest waited, the air filling up between them. He heaved an exaggerated sigh into the bathroom.

"OK," she said. She rose in a shuffle of limbs, breathing in the bathroom's antiseptic air. Once up, she wobbled like a stage actor portraying a drunkard. She teetered back and forth on her feet a few times.

"You all right?"

"Head-rush." She clutched the sink's rim. "That was powerful."

"Careful, honey." Ernest went to hug her, but she gently pushed him off.

"I'm OK," she said. She grabbed a headband and pushed her hair back. In the stream of warm tap water, she bowed her head and splashed.

Ernest busied himself in the dining room, rearranging platters of his most prided dishes: a sun-dried tomato and smoked mozzarella tart, deviled eggs, endive lettuce cups with spicy peanut chicken salad, and several loaves of multigrain breads and stinky exotic cheeses. He'd guiltily bought most of the ingredients at Demeter Foods, after shopping at Karen's for some of the basics.

In the master bedroom, Cynthia zipped herself into a cut velvet dress, silently cursing her widespread hips and then resigning herself to them all in one barely registered thought. Ernest came in and rifled through the closet, selecting a different shirt.

"What's wrong with the one you have on?"

"It's just not right," he said, buttoning himself into a cranberry shirt, the most colorful of his wardrobe.

"Unusual to see you so picky."

"Well, when's the last time we had a party?"

During their soiree, the Allens planned to introduce the spaceship as if it were a debutante stepping into the new season. Their guests, mostly neighbors, could pick at and pet the thing, ask them all the obvious questions, and hopefully, the Allens wouldn't have to talk about it so much anymore. At least this was the way Cynthia had initially sold it to Ernest, who at first didn't want to do anything that could be misconstrued as a celebration.

"So is that reporter coming?"

"Marilyn Fournier," Ernest said, combing his hair in the mirror. "She called today to say she'd be here."

"Stephen's going to have a fit. He's always citing her articles."

"I can just see him now, pinning her into a conversation. He'll try to come off like the hero who squashes CFCs with his bare fists."

Cynthia smirked at him from behind. "I'm sure you'll still have room to brag about your own projects." After a minute, she asked, "Is Marilyn Fournier attractive? I can't tell from the picture in the newspaper."

"Well, you're going to meet her yourself. You tell me."

"But what do *you* think?"

Ernest shrugged. "She's all right."

———————————

Cynthia rushed to answer the doorbell's formal ring. "You're using the front door, this is so strange! Come in, come in."

Standing on ceremony on the front steps: Tom, with a tie lumped under his sweater, and his wife, Olivia, a petite and fiery-eyed nurse whom Cynthia had grown closer to over the last couple of years. They were with their twin daughters, seniors in high school, and the latest addition, Cherice, their adopted baby born with HIV. Olivia bounced the infant in her arms, cooing to her, "It's your first party!"

The teenage girls, Dani and Stephanie, wasted no time disappearing into the basement where the other kids were hanging out. Cynthia pushed glasses of wine into Tom's and Olivia's grateful hands. Several people had already arrived, but Cynthia focused on Cherice, who rotated a drool-slick teething ring in her mouth.

"She's gained some weight! How is she adjusting?" The baby's eyes fixed on her eyes, then her pearl necklace. Cynthia offered her a chapped finger.

"It's a process," Olivia said. "It's kicking our asses."

"An arsenal of shots and fluids," Tom said, draining half his glass. "Around the clock."

"But it's really rewarding," Olivia said. "She's showing so much progress."

"She's not really sleeping," Tom said, "and neither are we."

"Hey, I'm the one getting up all the time," Olivia said with a light squeeze to Tom's arm. "I'm giving her the meds, of course."

"Well, she's getting stronger," Cynthia said. "She's got a good grip."

Tom drifted away to join the cluster in the dining room, triggering the women to wander into the kitchen and gather around the warm stove. The kitchen window framed the surreal attraction of the evening, the melting clockface wrecking the once plain pictorial of the Allens' backyard. The lights cast a lime-colored sickness over the clipped grass. Olivia leaned in close, her hand cradling Cherice's head. "And how's that going?"

"I'm sorry again about the noise."

"Don't worry about it," Olivia said. "As long as it doesn't wake Cherice, I don't care. I just wonder how you're adjusting."

"Well, the kids are enjoying the show," Cynthia said.

"But what about you?"

"It's divisive," Cynthia admitted, "which is making me tired. Fielding the same arguments between Ernest and Gabe all the time. And poor Alison, she's creeped out by it, but she's trying to play it cool, especially since it's given her some cache around school."

Cherice started to fuss. Olivia pulled up a chair at the kitchen table and found a bottle in her stuffed bag. Cherice sucked on the bottle for a moment but then waved it away and wailed again.

"Uh-oh, this might be the beginning of the end," Olivia said. "Her fussiness has been off the charts this last week. If I have to leave early, don't hate me."

Cynthia took note of the dark circles under Olivia's eyes, the jerky movements as she rubbed Cherice's back. Olivia was so tough, she'd never ask for anything.

"Do you want help? I could watch her for a couple hours tomorrow."

"Oh god, please." Olivia broke into a relieved smile. "Are you sure?"

"Of course," Cynthia said, her voice full of affection. "I knew you'd never ask for help yourself."

"What can I say? I'm stubborn. Listen, I should go check on Tom. The stress-drinking, you know."

Back in the dining room, Cynthia surveyed the party. Conversation bubbled in every corner. Soft lighting glowed on her guests' faces. With company over, the house was strong and sturdy, the perfect shelter. But the temperature was off—either within Cynthia or the house itself. A few moments ago, she'd pressed a cold glass of water to her flushed cheek, but now she shivered, vulnerable to every draft in the room.

She'd long ago adapted to Ernest's strict 65-degree rule by wearing sweaters and a battered pair of mukluks around the house, but tonight, she couldn't abide. She snuck off to fiddle with the thermostat. If Ernest suddenly came around the corner, she'd tell him she was adjusting the heat at the request of one of the party guests. Nudging up the thermostat, she settled on a subtropical 68 degrees. Then she darted away from it, checking all around her to make sure no one had witnessed her crime.

———

In the basement, an odd assortment of kids (all of their parents were friends with Ernest and Cynthia, but little else united them) argued with one another, about bands, Prairie Park's level of suckitude, and whether a kid had really masturbated into all the copies of *Moby-Dick* at the school library. Most of them sat on the two tweed couches that had been dismissed with good service from the Allen living room a few years ago.

Aubrey, a freshman like Alison, perched at the window that showed a ground-level view of the backyard. He'd contributed little to most of the conversations, but Alison kept noticing him. He was very tall and elegant, like he could easily fold in half—and he was the only black kid in the room. In the school hallways, he'd blend in with the diverse population, but in this basement, he was the only one out of six. Everyone else was white—well, except for Faryn, who was Lebanese, but Alison didn't have much of a concept of what that meant, other than that Faryn possessed very beautiful brown eyes with long lashes, but Faryn wasn't attracting her attention. It was Aubrey's energy, confident and ill at ease, like he was curtailing his words before he spoke them. He kept looking at Alison too.

"Your shoes," he finally said to her. "You made them?"

"Yeah, I drew all of this."

"How long did it take you?"

"Hours," she admitted without meaning to.

"That's it? I was going to guess days."

Alison sized up his yellow Converse. "You want a pair?"

"Really?"

"Of course! I might start a business soon." Alison surprised herself with how comfortable she felt talking to Aubrey. Something about him being a little uncomfortable gave her permission to be a little stronger than most guys encouraged. "What do you want on them?"

Aubrey thought for a minute. "I don't know. You decide!"

She stared at his yellow shoes, now in her lap. "Well, what are you into?"

"I honestly don't know." He paused. "I just joined crew."

"Like, where you build sets for plays?"

"Yeah," he said, breaking into a smile. "I built a whole wall the other day. One of the seniors let me use the table saw and I nearly lost my fucking hand."

"OK, I'm seeing something. I'm only going to use black markers. Do you trust me?"

Gabe, a few feet away in conversation with Faryn, Dani, and Stephanie, overheard his sister's flirtatious tone but tried not to give away his eavesdropping.

Aubrey gave her a playful side-glance. "Yeah, I guess so. Only thing: no peace signs. None of that hippie shit."

"What about yin-yangs?"

"Nope."

"Ankhs?"

He didn't know what that was, so she drew one for him on her hand:

His eyes glowed. "That's Egyptian, right? Definitely add those. Maybe a pyramid too while you're at it."

Alison hunkered over the shoes with a collection of black Sharpies in varying thicknesses, drawing in tiger stripes with total focus. Her brother came over to observe, standing above her shoulder.

"Nice, dude," he said. "Whoa, what is that *thing* in your hair?"

Her concentration broken, her hand drifted to the puffy cream-colored scrunchie holding her bun. "It's a Tiny Vampire."

"It looks like a giant cupcake."

Alison, hot-cheeked, didn't dare look at Aubrey to see if he agreed. She kept her focus on the saw she was drawing near the heel.

"You guys," Aubrey announced, "somebody's sneaking a cigarette around the side of your house."

Most of the kids rushed to where he stood near one of the basement's high windows. Aubrey had been offering dry observations to the room all night ("there goes Mr. F with yet another plate of food"), but an adult smoking a cigarette was real news in Prairie Park. Sure, people smoked—divorced dads and a couple of teachers were suspects, and kids did it all the time—but no parent ever did it in mixed company.

"Will you look at that, puffing away and loving it."

They all watched the woman wave around her cigarette, seemingly inspired by its corrupt authority. The smoke left a milky cataract on the night air as she held some other woman hostage in conversation.

"Who is that?" Alison said.

"Faryn, is that your mom?" Dani asked.

Faryn interrupted her conversation with Stephanie and sighed dramatically. "Is she wearing a long skirt and big earrings?"

"Yeah," Dani said.

"Then I don't even have to get up."

"My dad will freak if he sees her," Gabe said.

"What's he care? She's doing it outside. It's her own lungs," Aubrey noted.

"My dad doesn't give a shit about that," he said, but didn't explain further.

Alison supplied the missing information: "It's that they're bad for the environment. Everything's bad for the environment in his eyes. People, humans, are bad for the environment, just by existing."

"Existing *is* kind of bad," Faryn bemoaned. "Sometimes."

"If your dad hates the human race so much, why doesn't he move you all into the wilderness? Be the only people around for a million miles?" Aubrey asked (genuinely curious, Alison wanted to think).

"Already tried it," Gabe said. "Mission failed."

"When we were babies," Alison said, "we lived in the middle of nowhere for a few months. Off the grid, growing our own vegetables, wild hair down to our asses."

"Whoa," Aubrey said.

"But then my mom's parents died and left money, and they bought this house. It has plumbing and all, so there you go . . ."

Aubrey shook his head. "That's gotta be for the best. What are you going to do, never interact with people your entire life? Pretend you're a caveman?"

"I think my dad would've been perfectly fine with that, actually. Have you met him?"

Aubrey treated Alison to a rare smile and then gazed back through the window. "Those aliens in the spaceship, did they ever imagine they'd be hanging out in your backyard, watching some lady smoke a cancer stick?"

"You're funny," she said because she couldn't think of anything else to say. Luckily her brother cranked up the volume of his mixtape and her inadequacies were drowned out.

———————

Ernest found himself standing next to Marilyn, who picked through a plate of cold *hors d'oeuvres* as the neon lights repeatedly raked over the grass, making it look as fake as Astroturf. They were outside, with everyone else, watching the spaceship for sport. She had arrived late and by herself, wearing a pencil skirt and blouse that suggested she'd type a news story in the corner later. Ernest offered to warm something up for her but she waved him off.

"Your husband couldn't make it?"

"He's not into parties," Marilyn said.

"Well, let me reintroduce you to the ship. Now, the ship's kind of like a newborn baby or falling in love. It slaps you back into life and it also drives you insane." Ernest checked Marilyn for a reaction.

Marilyn cracked a smile. "Is it at least sleep-trained?"

Her smile stirred a simple and childlike feeling in Ernest—encouragement. She emanated serious vibes, as ever, but that only made Ernest want to drive her into laughter all the more.

"Not even close. As you can see, it's getting ready to launch into its nightly show. You can think of it as the witching hour."

"Uh-oh, maybe we should go back to the falling in love idea. Sounds more fun!"

"That's what everyone thinks in the beginning."

A hint of sparkle in Marilyn's eyes—he'd take it.

From a few yards away, Cynthia caught Ernest's jovial tone and wondered what had jacked up his spirits. Suddenly, the unabated crank was showing off the spaceship to the reporter lady with almost as much lavish enthusiasm as Gabe. She heard him say, "All things considered, it's pretty entertaining." *Oh, really? Since when?* Cynthia walked over just as Ernest was saying, "And here's the hatch where the space-poop comes out," which made her snicker, because clearly Ernest wasn't pacing himself. (Tom and Ernest, they egged each other on with the drinking, and Ernest usually came out on the losing end.) But as she shook hands with Marilyn—and she was attractive in the glamorously manly way of a 1970s tennis star—she felt better. Ernest threw his arm around her and cajoled Cynthia into telling the story of how it landed. For all his crabbiness, Ernest always loved parties, loved telling stories, and maybe he'd finally embraced the spaceship as another tale to spin. After a minute of painting the landing scene for Marilyn, who listened intently and marveled in all the right spots, Cynthia floated back to the rest of the party, almost convinced that Ernest was coming around on the spaceship. Maybe he just needed someone cool to care about it first. Or maybe, feeling a subtle wave of nausea run into the pit of her stomach, she was the one not pacing herself.

Marilyn continued: "So I looked into those regulations you mentioned, Ernest, but there's not much to tell. The spaceships aren't allowed to make or disperse anything that hasn't been tested and approved by the FDA or EPA."

"That was more than I could find out," Ernest said, chugging the last portion of a beer. "Guess it takes a reporter to properly dig. What were your methods, may I ask?"

"I made a few phone calls around New World, but I also researched it on the Net."

"The Net?"

"You know, the Internet," she said.

"I'm not really up on all that."

Ross, who had been hovering nearby, stepped into their conversation. "Are you guys talking about the World Wide Web?"

"Otherwise known as the information superhighway? Yes," Marilyn said.

"Is it really all that?" Ernest said. "I thought it was a bunch of half-empty chat rooms. Not that I totally understand what a chat room is."

"It's pretty amazing. Once you get past the half-empty chat rooms."

"I'm not ready for endless amounts of information at my fingertips."

"Well, it's coming for you whether you like it or not," Ross said.

"Wouldn't be a bad idea to make a web page for our Earth Day party."

"Robot invasion," Ernest said. "No, thanks."

"It's not robots at all," Marilyn said. "It's us. Whoever's on there."

A collective restlessness took over the party, as its guests milled on the grass, surveying the visitor. Tom started to circle the spaceship, spilling some of his beer into the grass as he looked up.

"It's a good-looking ship," Jean said, walking closer to Ernest. "It really is."

"It doesn't look a little cheap to you?" Ernest asked. "Like something used for a promotion on a used-car lot?"

"It's an intergalactic visitor and you're criticizing it for looking cheap? What, are you wearing Armani right now?"

Ernest rubbed his flannel sleeve. "It's a few seasons old so you might not recognize it."

Cynthia's boss wandered over. "What's the probability of them coming out?"

Ernest stifled his annoyance. "You have a better chance of Ron Reagan coming out of there, Stephen."

"Well, I'd take that in a heartbeat. I have some questions for that scoundrel. He probably got his own personal saucer as part of the deal."

Reluctantly, Ernest introduced Marilyn to Stephen, who heaped praise upon his "favorite journalist." Marilyn stopped the tide of compliments by answering his original question.

"There's never been a concrete report of a single one of them emerging from the ship. New World won't even say how many aliens are typically in the ship."

"Tell me," Tom asked loudly from a few feet away, "did they say anything about luring them out?"

Tom sashayed up to the weeping willow tree and picked up a frond that had fallen. He quickly spun around and gave the ship a come-hither stare, then pointed at it as if he were calling out a dancing partner. The neighbors whooped in encouragement. He shimmied over to the spaceship and limboed until he was directly under the center. He held the frond in his hand and lightly whipped the ship's belly, wiggling his fingers on his other hand to communicate some sort of perverse glee. Emboldened by the crowd's laughter, he then shoved the frond between his teeth and danced, taking his hands and reaching up toward the underside; his hips writhed to some imaginary sound track of frenzied hand cymbals.

"All right, all right," Ernest called out, feeling suddenly protective of the thing.

As if on cue, the ship pepped up. The green lights rolled and then pitched to the left and then the right. The party oohed and aahed and then took a few steps back. Olivia held tight to Cherice. Tom hastily retracted his arms but stayed underneath the ship. Would there be more?

The party waited but the ship offered nothing. Egged on by neighbors, Tom tried to rev up the ship again. He slapped the bottom with his weeping willow frond and shimmied faster. Cynthia looked at Ernest and was glad to see him laughing, albeit nervously, the lines in his face looser. She moved close to him and grabbed his hand. He squeezed it, feeling the clamminess of her skin and then stealing a glance at her. She looked pale; red wine stained little dry fragments of her lips. Finally embarrassed by Tom's overreaching need for attention, people turned away and started new conversation; Tom got the hint and stopped, but not before giving a little bow. Ernest pulled his hand away from Cynthia's to applaud his friend (he was one of the few to clap).

As if he had been propping her up, she crumpled to the grass, folding into her dress, then lying in a fetal position on the ground. The crowd startled and stepped back. Jean covered her mouth with her hand and Marilyn made room for Olivia bounding through. Ernest dropped down next to his wife; her face was drained, her lips closer to the shade of the vein that was always lightly visible on her temple. Olivia knelt on the other side as Cynthia blinked awake.

"Stay down for now," Olivia said, fingers pressed on Cynthia's wrist, checking her pulse.

At the moment, Cynthia was uninterested in getting up anyway. But she couldn't quite figure out how she'd gotten to the ground.

As Olivia took her pulse, she focused on the few moments of consciousness that occurred before she fell. Blurry photos slid past in the carousel before it went black. She could remember thinking two things: that she was falling, and that something was wrong.

"Don't know why that happened," she said to no one in particular.

Ernest tried to appear reasonably relaxed, but she could see the shock in his eyes. He was trying to stay calm for the guests, for the kids. Likewise, Cynthia felt she should get up now so that no one would worry too much. She didn't want the kids to panic. They had been standing off to the side when it happened, joined by the other kids from the basement as they smirked at Tom's performance, but now they were closer, crouched near Ernest. They scanned the faces of all the adults for clues about the situation. The adults returned poker faces that would've flinched upon further inspection.

She sat on the couch gripping a cup of tea. Sitting upright was taking more effort than she'd ever thought necessary. Olivia and Ernest peppered her with questions, while Gabe and Alison flanked her on both sides. The rest of those present resumed their roles as party guests, but readied themselves to leave. The soiree was over, but they'd attempt to keep it alive for a little while longer, so it didn't look like a stampede out the door.

"What have you had to eat?" Olivia asked.

"Enough."

"What about wine?"

"A glass or two? No more than that." Tom's ridiculous performance came back to her in a rush. What did his daughters think? Were they mortified? What if everyone at school started gossiping that their dad was a lush? Cynthia halted her runaway thoughts and focused on her tea. Was it a new flavor? It tasted funny, a little metallic.

"I think I must be getting the flu," she said. "I've been feeling very tired."

"Any other symptoms?" Olivia asked.

"Not really," Cynthia said. "A headache here and there. I don't know. I was feeling hot and then cold earlier this evening. I couldn't maintain a balanced temperature. I bet it's the flu. Stephen had it two weeks ago."

They wanted to ask her more questions, Cynthia could tell, but with the kids flocking her she was shielded from further inquiry. No one wanted to scare them.

Later, Cynthia and Ernest lay in bed with slack bodies but heads buzzing. Pieces of conversation drifted through their memories, suffused with anxiety and worry about Cynthia's fall. She had her head tilted toward Ernest, the pillow covered in a sheet of her hair.

"Ern," she whispered, seeing if he was asleep. His eyes were closed, his body turned toward her.

"Hmm?"

She stretched out her hand and drifted it lightly down his chest and then farther down.

He opened his eyes. He folded his hand over hers. "I don't know if that's a good idea."

"It's a great idea," she said.

He couldn't really see her. The sliver moon cast a weak glow into the room that stopped short of their bed, but he could see the glistening of her alert eyes. He pulled her on top of him. They kissed, their mouths soaped with leftover toothpaste that still didn't rid their tongues of purple wine stains. Things happened quickly, yet with some sort of hesitation. Ernest kept measuring her energy, checking for signs that she wanted to stop. But he wasn't hitting any sort of wall. In fact, she was invigorated, doing everything with full purpose. They tangled around and she stroked him and then she straddled him and he pushed inside of her. They knew what the other liked; they knew the positions. Even in its routine execution, the sex felt novel, even new, like they were both outside of themselves, watching. Sitting on top of her husband, she felt something and turned and saw the cat idly gazing at them from the floor, and she suspected for a moment that she might be the cat as well as herself. The thought made her laugh just as he reached for her, and then she felt a stabbing pain. She gasped and rolled off Ernest, and then off the bed.

"What happened? Where are you?"

She crouched on the floor, near the cat, clutching her chest, a fold of blanket on her back.

"Cynthia?"

He got down on the ground next to her. The cat, startled by all the activity so close to her, dragged her belly low along the floor and slunk under the dresser. Cynthia's thighs were slick, her mouth still wet from kissing, but the rest of her was dry and tunneling into one part of her body.

"My chest," she said. "I just had the most excruciating pain."

He rubbed her back, but it made her shiver. "Are you OK?"

Ernest couldn't think of another time they'd both been on the floor together like this, crouched and alarmed. He couldn't help but think it marked a new time, a crossing into something. Hovering near the ground was a new and perhaps legitimate way of dealing with emergencies. It was primal and immediate, in case you needed to crawl away or hide.

"Listen, we should take you to the emergency room."

"The ER? No, please, I'll be fine."

"Come on, honey, you just said you're experiencing chest pains. That, combined with fainting? Something's wrong."

"It's not chest pains," she clarified for herself as much as for him. "It's my left breast. Not my heart, not my chest."

After a few more moments where they continued to crouch in silence, Ernest watching her place her hands on her breasts, her stomach, to see if the pain continued, Cynthia said, "I don't know, it was a really weird feeling, but we don't need to go to the ER."

Pills, hospitals, and anything involving medical intervention had always scared Cynthia. Ernest knew it was the one realm in which her neurosis far outscored his. She feared loss of control, possibly given over to pharmaceutical companies feebly checked by the colluding FDA, her body surrendered to doctors forced to comply with insurance companies' bottom lines.

"We can just go to be sure," he said, gently rubbing her back.

She gave him a kiss on the cheek. "I'll be OK. To tell you the truth, I think I drank too much at the party and didn't eat enough either. I just didn't want to say that in front of the kids."

Ernest nodded, but he wasn't convinced.

———————◆———————

Before going to bed, in the bathroom, under the yellow light of the old fixture, Cynthia examined herself in the mirror. There were deep shadows around her eyes and a smear of eyeliner that she hadn't effectively wiped off. She turned her head to the side, keeping eye contact with the eyes in the mirror. She hunted for signs of bad health, but instead she found a rosy glow on her cheeks. Even the signs of age seemed comforting: the toughening of her skin on the cheekbones where the sun hit the most, the firm knot of jaw and muscle, which she rubbed over with her hand. She got out a Q-tip, squirted makeup remover on it, and wiped under her bottom eyelash, coming away with a smoke-gray tip that she pitched toward the trash.

Her left breast, the one that had screamed with pain, was silent now. Was it just something about the way he had touched her? Her uncharacteristic laughter combined with him reaching for her at that very moment? Maybe, she thought, it was a weird cramp. She lay down on the bathmat. Her breasts lolled out a little to their respective sides. With tiny kneading motions, she pushed into her flesh but felt the same thing she always felt—fibrous mass, a million little bumps. Was one or more of these supposed to be suspicious? She sighed into the closeted air.

When she returned to the bedroom, Ernest was still awake. In the dark, she found his worried eyes and smiled. She told him she was feeling better. Then she waited until he became completely submerged in sleep. She listened to the raggedy catch of his breath in his throat and tried to wander into her own lost place.

10

THE ACTIVITIES OF THE UNWELCOME VISITORS FROM JUPITER: AN ALLEN FAMILY LOG

October 18: *Dad thinks the spaceship might be fritzing out the electronics around the house (all because he couldn't get the Jets game the other night— hello, we live outside Chicago, why don't you like the Bears like everyone else? Not that I give a _____ but I just want to say that the shortwave radio still transmits like it always has. In fact, Alison and I listened last night to* The Book of Connections. *The woman was talking about neon this time because she's got kind of a science fetish, and she actually mentioned something about spaceships and their neon lights—weird! In other news: ship was quiet, who cares. —GA*

October 18: *We recorded that lady's radio hour because we're going to use it for a mixtape. I wrote down a few lines she said: "Neon is a vapor dragon. It sleeps on the Earth's atmosphere with no color or scent until it is acted upon. When a jolt of electricity is applied, neon awakens and appears fiery red. Then it changes to chemical blood, lighter than air." —AA*

October 18: *Can we get back to business here? Why are we quoting radio shows? To remind you of how it's done, I will properly log that on October 18 at 8:52 p.m., the ship made a loud sound that sounded like gears shifting inside. It continued for about two minutes, and then it dumped out approximately three gallons of green liquid onto the lawn. —EA*

October 19: *So in other words, the same stuff it always does, Dad.*

October 19: *You forgot to appropriately sign off with your initials, Alison. —EA*

October 19: *Sorry, Dad. OK, I did notice one other thing today. I watched a pigeon take a dump on the spaceship while flying by, and after a few hours, the poop was completely gone. Like, no trace, couldn't even find the spot again. It's like the spaceship absorbed it or something. Maybe it's food for the aliens? Ha! So gross. —AA*

October 19: *No comment on eating bird poop (I'm hoping they're just neat freaks in there?), but the discussion about neon is interesting, actually. I looked it up in the encyclopedia and read that in order for it to appear as green (the color of the spaceship lights), argon and minute particles of mercury are added so that it reads as a cool blue, and then fluorescent powders are painted or baked onto the inside of the glass fixture, which makes the light appear green. Doesn't that seem like an elaborate process? Does that mean the aliens painted the inside of their light fixtures with fluorescent powders? —CA*

October 19: *Don't they have access to anything better on Jupiter? Some kind of light we've never seen? —EA*

October 19: *But I love that they use the same neon we do! You can only work with what the universe gives you, no matter where you are. —CA*

11

It was late October, and Prairie Park had locked into autumn: chilled mornings, the sun falling before dinner, all of summer's frivolity frosted shut. Proper Halloween weather, her dad used to joke when they were kids, perfect for ghosts. Alison walked five blocks to school every day, the last block near the Frank Lloyd Wright house with its dark wood and gingko trees. The architect was one of the few artists Ernest gushed about because Frank Lloyd Wright cared about nature enough to build a whole house around a tree. For the most part, it seemed to Alison, Ernest paid attention to art only when the work squarely connected with his interests, which pretty much killed the spirit of art, as far as she was concerned. One exception: music. Both of her parents lit up around music, more so than anything visual, which talked in angles and colors that delighted and intrigued Alison but they barely noticed. Maybe her mom got music even more than her dad did, especially if it was curious, playful, essentially upbeat. Her mom, for example, had seized on the Smiths' song "Ask," playing it in the wagon again and again. When her mom belted out, *"Nature is a language—can't you read?"* Gabe begged her to stop—somehow a mom singing the Smiths didn't pass muster with the authenticity cop. But for that moment, Alison could forgive her mother the sin of wearing dumpy mom frocks and the always fluffed and then forgotten condition of her wan blond hair.

Alison sang along faintly with her Walkman, observing the white gusts flowing out of her mouth and nose. She regarded the bungalows as she walked past, large art-glass lamps in the living rooms, tuxedo cats in the windows, carved pumpkins on the outdoor steps. Her hands, in knit gloves with pleather palms, were jammed into her pockets. No matter how she tucked and arranged, the gap between her scarf and the top of her jacket always left her throat exposed to the icepick wind. She walked with her chin tucked into her chest, the wires of her headphones grazing her jaw.

The music, in a way that only headphones made possible, seemed to beam straight into the pleasure center in her brain, a tightly wound snare that glowed brighter from interactions with the things she loved. The Pixies, thunderous and wasted and spaced, singing, *"I had me a vision...There wasn't any television... From looking into the sun."* Then she wanted to listen to something prettier, something she could sing along to, so she pressed fast-forward, listening to the soft blur of the tape, until she got to the Velvet Underground, her voice matching Nico's, but she stopped abruptly when she felt a presence and heard footsteps.

A man was walking at her left side, smiling at her, like he knew her from some previous encounter. She yanked the headphones out of her ears.

"No, don't do that," he said. "Enjoy yourself."

She stared at him, trying to keep her walk even. He was cleanly shaven, clutching a leather briefcase, and more or less handsome— signs that he probably wasn't a pervert, maybe?

"Good song. And you've got a good voice," he said. "Thanks for the concert."

And then he picked up speed, the bottom of his wool coat flapping a little behind him. She watched him walk and then nearly run toward the train station. His black hair was combed down, a little gel or something in it.

"And that's all that happened?" Cynthia asked, exchanging a glance with Ernest. "Nothing else?"

They were sitting around the kitchen table. Alison shrugged, busying herself with inking another pair of Aubrey's high-top sneakers, the left shoe cradled in her lap under the table. The right sneaker rested on top of paper towels on the table, so it wouldn't get anything dirty.

"He didn't ask for your phone number? Or offer you a ride?"

"He was just running for the train, Mom."

"Well, perverts take public transportation too."

Ernest put down the newspaper and folded it with a zeal that signaled to Alison that something particularly mortifying would be coming out of his mouth at any moment. "How come I've never heard you sing like that, Alison?"

"I don't know." She kept her focus on the marker darkening the red canvas.

"What were you listening to that made you sing like that?"

"A band."

"A new band?"

"Well, new to me. Never mind, you wouldn't know it. It's not music made by guys named Peter or Don. It's not comb-over rock."

Ernest ignored her taunts. "It wasn't that filthy music you and Gabe were listening to the other day, was it? God, that song was so scandalous. Nothing but 'pimps' and 'hos.' Cynthia, have you heard this yet?"

"Heard what?"

"What's the name of the guy again, Alison? Easy Steve?"

"No, Dad, it wasn't 'Easy Steve.' I won't even bother telling you his correct name."

"Wait a minute," Cynthia interrupted, "can we return to the point? Ernest, you don't find it disconcerting that a strange man tried to chat with our daughter?"

"Sounds innocent," Ernest said. "The only crime here is that we didn't know our daughter has a good enough singing voice to move a stranger to spontaneous compliment."

Cynthia absorbed what he was saying. "We were just talking the other day about your interests, Alison. And I didn't even think to bring up singing."

"I asked you, Mom, about getting singing lessons in the car the other day. Remember?"

Her mother looked blank but quickly recovered. "That's right. We could get you lessons. That's a thought." *That's a thought.* Her mother's stock noncommittal response.

"You could get money that way, being a singer," Ernest said. "But I don't know if it really makes a difference in the world."

"Why does it have to? Music makes people happy. That makes a difference in the world."

"That's true, but it's so hard to make it as a singer."

Alison showed her dad an especially perfect fist she'd drawn smashing into a brick wall on Aubrey's shoe. "Maybe I'll become an artist instead."

"Well, that's not exactly an easy way to make a living either."

Alison sulkily tucked the shoe back into her lap. "You didn't even say it looks nice."

"It does! It looks fantastic! I'm just talking about paying the bills, which is pretty much the worst part about being an adult."

"Look, I'm not really talking about making it a career. I don't know what I want to do. Can't a person just sing on the street or color some sneakers and enjoy life? Without it setting off such a frenzy?"

Her words came out sharper than she'd expected. Her parents exchanged a wounded look, milking it to be sure but still based in real feelings.

"Well, sorry for taking an interest," Ernest said.

"I'm already doing the stupid fund-raising thing for Earth Day. What else do you guys want from me?"

"Why are you so defensive right now? We just want to talk to you," Cynthia said, her injured tone designed to induce guilt.

"Do you?" Alison shook her head and curled closer to the sneaker in her lap, in some sort of attempt to seem suddenly too inspired to take part in this conversation any longer, but the falseness of her gesture paralyzed her, and instead she hovered with her marker for a second and then put the sneaker back on the table. "You know what I want?" she said. "I just want my life to hurry up and get beautiful."

Her parents appeared stricken.

"Jesus, what does *that* mean?" Ernest asked. "Is it horrible now?"

Alison didn't answer because she didn't know what it meant either, only that it was a pressing need, one she couldn't really articulate except in fumbling, halting attempts.

"I'm curious," Ernest said. "Do you think our lives are beautiful?"

Alison looked at him and then her mother and saw all of their desperation for the first time. They really wanted to know what she thought, specifically about them. They were hanging on her answer. Wait, they cared about what she thought *about them*? Was this the dawn of a new era in which her parents actually sought her opinion? And to top it off, she had the power to not even give it to them?

Her mother stood a little behind her father with her hand on his shoulder, waiting for Alison's answer. They were not going to move until they got something from her. Inside both of their eyes, she saw some shadowy ideas flicker; she couldn't be certain what.

She flashed them an enigmatic smile.

Her parents couldn't help but return it with tentative curiosity. They were civilians smiling at the first seemingly friendly gesture from the savage.

"What?" Ernest said between grinning teeth. "What's that smile mean?"

"I gotta go upstairs," Alison said.

"Oh, no, wait a minute," Ernest said.

"Homework," Alison sang.

She swept up the sneakers and rushed out of the room before she could register their reaction. Upstairs, she sat on her bed, drunk on her power, the tableau of comic violence on the left sneaker still incomplete.

Later that night, in bed, Alison thought about the man again. He had been attractive—definitely handsome—younger than her father, and dressed in a slick, formal way that Ernest would never try, not even if someone had died. In fact, at the last funeral the family had attended, the only funeral Alison could remember, for Ernest's ancient, long-senile uncle, Ernest dressed in navy pants, a gray sports coat, and a white button-down with a tiny boat stitched onto one of the breast pockets, some of its threads ragged and hanging out. On the way, driving through a patch of Chicago that resembled a version of their suburb but with the houses shoved closer together and with only scrubby trees instead of glorious oaks, Cynthia commented on her husband's complete adherence to his dress code.

"Not even death can get you in a proper suit," she said, turning the wheel with slow deliberation.

And then her dad had said, "I dress down for death."

An unremarkable exchange; but for whatever reason it came floating up into Alison's mind from time to time. Maybe because it confounded her. She kept trying to solve it, find some hidden meaning in it. "I dress down for death." What does *that* mean? It was one of the rare times her parents talked about death in front of her, yet they had said nothing of any consequence.

12

THE ACTIVITIES OF THE UNWELCOME VISITORS FROM JUPITER: AN ALLEN FAMILY LOG

November 2: *Last night the spaceship kept shining a single neon light into my room. Like, right at my eye. I never felt sick or anything, but was this thing probing me? Is that how it starts? First the eye and then somewhere else?* —AA

November 3: *Um, no, Ms. Paranoia, it wasn't probing you. Probing you through your eye? Never heard of it. The light was also shining into my room and I felt fine, fell asleep within 10 minutes.* —GA

November 4: *Falling asleep quickly doesn't mean you're OK. And for the record, I think you could be probed through your eye. Anyway . . .* —AA

November 5: *Reporter Marilyn Fournier phoned today. She suggested that she have another younger reporter come by and write a little human-interest story on the spaceship, but I said absolutely not. We don't need more attention. But I do think I've convinced her to write about next year's Earth Day celebration. Your dad's going to have his picture in the paper. Isn't that cool?* —EA

13

Cynthia drove her daughter to the Prairie Park mall, passing her doctor's office on the way, the one Ernest pestered her to call. She finally relented; her appointment was in two weeks. No point in rushing there, she felt fine. Well, decent enough, anyway. Just driving by the medical center shot her with anxiety, so she focused on the task at hand: depositing Alison at the mall so that her daughter could perform her father's spiel about saving the environment to assorted store owners. Hopefully they'd be so moved that they'd write modest checks on the spot for the Earth Day celebration. The sum total, of course, even if each shop owner donated a day's earnings, would pale in comparison to Demeter's platinum sponsorship, not officially signed yet but inevitably on the horizon. Alison had agreed to canvass the mall—because she didn't quite know yet that she could refuse—but she was hardly enthusiastic. She slumped against the passenger window.

"I just don't understand why you let him get away with it, Mom."

"Get away with what?"

"Sending us out to do fund-raising."

She shrugged, her hand on the wheel, facing forward.

When her mother didn't make eye contact, Alison knew her mother didn't want to be having the conversation.

"It's not that bad. Maybe slightly embarrassing, but it's for a good cause."

"So what? You do environmental work too, and I don't have to be dragged into it."

"This is what your dad has."

"I don't want to be part of his crusade."

"Crusade? That's too melodramatic, Alison. You're doing a good thing, just leave it at that."

Alison gave up; she knew her mom found her dad's pet projects annoying too, but she rarely spoke out against them, especially if Dad wasn't around to defend himself. They approached the confused outskirts of the mall. Prairie Park's center of commerce had never quite figured itself out. For instance, two drugstores, Walgreens and Woolworths, were built right across the street from each other, canceling each other out. In addition to necessities like prescription drugs and toothpaste, they both trafficked in dollar toys made in Taiwan, Wet 'n' Wild lipstick in unearthly pinks, and tiny pets that ran on squeaky metal wheels. Woolworths' sole advantage was its long diner counter where the elderly oddities of Prairie Park perched for lunch, their rubbery lips wrapping around spoons full of boiling soup.

"Let me ask you something," Alison said. "Why aren't we living in California, where they probably celebrate Earth Day every day by law? I mean, Illinois? What nature are you guys even talking about?"

"This is beautiful prairie, you just can't see it everywhere. It's not grandiose like California, but that's why we wanted to work out here. It's just as important as anywhere else." And at the time, Cynthia thought but didn't say, Ernest's father needed them. Someone had to take care of him before he died. But she still dreamed of what their life would've been like if they'd gone back to California. Would Ernest have found a job he loved out there?

"Do you ever get the feeling, though, that Dad is, like, too involved or something? He gets some sort of ego boost out of saving the environment, like he's Superman for the planet or something."

Her mother smiled, but directed it toward the windshield. "The Earth is a damsel in distress."

"Yes!" Alison said. "You know what I'm talking about then. It's not normal."

"Listen," her mother said, turning to look her in the eye. "I have my work, my job, and I can effect change there. But your father has never had something like that. He's kind of"—she searched for the right word—"bounced around, but now he has something that he's really excited about. This Earth Day project means a lot to him. So let's just let him have this, OK?"

"I'm not saying he can't have it, but why does it have to involve us?"

Cynthia thought for a moment. "It's about proving himself, proving his commitment in everything he does. Being an eco-conscious parent. Being in charge of Earth Day. It's all tied together..." She trailed off, choosing to distract herself with a busy intersection.

In that time, the conversation flew out the window like an errant tissue on the dash. Alison saw her mother's face close.

They were approaching the drop-off point. "I don't want to do this." Alison knew she was whining but didn't care.

Cynthia gave her the "tough luck" look she'd perfected over the years. "It'll be over before you know it."

Now that Alison was in high school, her mother would coddle her only so much. More and more, their conversations sounded like two adults, one with more experience leading the other one, patiently but forcefully, into a mostly unsympathetic world. But sometimes Alison missed the comforting gesture. When she was a little girl and upset, her mother would walk over to the rocking chair, calling Alison to her by patting one of her hands on her thigh. She didn't have to say, "Come here, Alison," or anything else, the soft pat of her hand on her thigh was enough, and they'd rock in an embrace until she calmed down. As she got older and longer, her tawny legs would stick out of the side of the chair, tangled up in the woodwork. When had they stopped those kinds of embraces? When she was ten, maybe that was the last time it had happened.

"Over here," Alison reminded her mother.

They pulled in front of the third-rate movie theater with one of the letters missing from its blinking art deco neon sign. She unbuckled her seat belt and her mom gazed at her. "I'll see you at five. Good luck!"

Cynthia impulsively reached out and smoothed her daughter's hair, feeling sorry for her and having nothing else to offer. Alison grabbed her hand out of her hair and play-bit it, and they laughed in a way that acknowledged the ridiculous quality of their interaction and the hapless conversation from before.

"And Gabe's out here doing the same thing?"

"Dad's dropping him off in half an hour after soccer practice."

Alison jumped out of the car and then lingered on the street in front of the movie theater for a minute. Prairie Park was firmly upper middle class, but no one could tell from the battered Vista Three. It ran movies two months late. It suffered many indignities. Teenagers threw full cups of Coca-Cola at the screen whenever a character did something stupid, like walk into a room where a murderer lurked with a bloody knife. But Alison and Gabe loved the Vista because they could always sneak into R-rated movies there.

She checked her watch. In two hours, she'd meet Gabe for a milkshake. Last night, they shook hands on a dare/bet. They would approach the weirdest stores in the mall first to get money, just to entertain themselves at the outset of this dreaded task. Whoever squeezed the most out of the wig store (Alison's challenge) or the magic shop (Gabe's) would win. It would also set the tone for the afternoon. If they could solicit funds from these freaky entities, then surely every other business would surrender a donation.

The magic shop was marooned next to an alley in a shoddy corner of the mall, away from any decent foot traffic. Pushing through the front door, Gabe immediately encountered floor-to-ceiling trickster merchandise plastic-wrapped and hanging from pegs: a deck of cards with duplicate aces; a squirting flower for the lapel; ice cubes with spiders trapped inside; itching powder the color of mustard; bloodshot eyeballs meant to pop up in someone's soup. The place was empty. Still.

After a moment, the heavy velvet curtain that protected the back area from prying eyes was raked aside. The tall, burly proprietor smoothed his hand over his flyaway hair and cast a grim slash of a smile toward Gabe as he rested his hands gently on the countertop.

"Hey, Vince," Gabe said.

Vince was one of two brothers, both in their midthirties, who co-owned the shop. As always, he wore an outfit that must've been pilfered from retired Halloween costumes—a red vest plucked from a pirate getup and cheap tuxedo pants once sold with the Old

Hollywood glamour look. Over the years, Gabe had been a loyal customer, buying throwaway tricks to perform on his unsuspecting friends, but neither Vince nor his brother ever let on that they recognized him. Gabe was a little disappointed not to be greeted as a regular, but he figured maybe anonymity was good for magic. Just as Gabe was about to launch into his sales pitch, Vince asked, "Do you want to see a trick?"

Without waiting for an answer, Vince pulled over a velvet mat carrying a few items from the side of the counter. He held a plastic liter bottle with remnants of a soda label still clinging to the side and a pack of matches.

"See how the bottom is filled with some water?" Vince set the bottle on its side.

Gabe saw that the longer lashes around Vince's eyes were tangled with the longer hairs on his brow. Every time Vince blinked, the eyelash hairs had to tear themselves out of the thicket. Fleetingly, Gabe wondered if he'd have the same issues once he became a man.

Vince struck a match, quickly extinguished it, and stuck it inside the bottle, where the match head smoldered. He capped the bottle and waited for the plastic cylinder to fill up with smoke, his expectant eyes flitting to Gabe's every few seconds. Once it was full, he gave it an enthusiastic shake over his shoulder and then presented it to the counter with a fanciful sweep of his hand. Inside the bottle, water vapor clung together and formed a miniature cloud, with striations of foggy matter twisting and then ending in ghostly dispersals. It lightly moved in parts and folded back on itself, limited as it was by the plastic container. Had it more landscape to roam, it would've dragged across the sky, blown by the wind.

"That's Cloud in a Bottle. Not as grand as the cumulonimbus," Vince said, "but it's something."

"Cumulonimbus—that's a cloud?"

"Type of storm cloud."

"What's it look like?"

Vince reached below the cash register and produced a yellow legal pad, the first several pages dense with notes, scribbles, and columns of numbers. On a clean sheet, he drew with a black felt-tip pen a fluffy, vertical tower, shading in parts of it to convey darkness. He pushed it over to Gabe for closer examination.

"They create lightning in the center of the cloud," Vince said. He grabbed the notepad back. "Bam," he said, as he drew a jagged bolt shooting out of the cloud's bottom. Then he quickly drew an oak tree below it getting blasted apart by the lightning, as he continued to enact the storm with a multitude of mouth sounds.

"Nature," he said, "is a badass." He wrote the word "badass" in block form at the top of the lightning cloud. Then he sketched out a lopsided Camaro burying its grille into the side of the clouds.

"Wow," Gabe said. "You can draw as fast as my sister."

"That girl who comes in here with the brown hair to here?" He chopped a hand onto his lower neck.

Gabe nodded, surprised that Vince recognized Alison. He puzzled for a moment, trying to recall if he'd ever seen them interact. He could almost picture it: his sister looking uncomfortable but still polite, maybe touching her hair self-consciously while Vince talked at her. But he decided to switch tracks.

"How do you know so much about clouds?"

Gabe was procrastinating. He hadn't gotten out his pitch right away, and now he had no idea how to bring it up.

"I wanted to be a scientist, like my dad. He was the weatherman in Indianapolis. He knew every cloud, would point up and name them, the way some people do with stars."

Gabe, of course, knew the type. His dad would sometimes walk through a park and point to various plants, pronouncing the names with a musical lilt to his voice that threatened to break out into song at any time. Gabe moved through the world differently, had different impulses. He appreciated plants, but he didn't need to know their names. But clouds, those seemed more appealing, more mysterious and exotic. Maybe he'd get to know clouds too.

He saw his opening, cheesy as it was. "Well, if you love clouds, maybe you'd be willing to give money to protect them."

Gabe's face burned instantly hot. What was he talking about? How could you "protect" abstract cotton puffs forty thousand feet above you?

But Vince was already extolling the beauty of clouds and his strong feelings toward the noctilucent type in particular ("deep twilight cloud, thin and marbled looking"). So Gabe closed in: "Would you be willing then to donate money to the Earth Day celebration Prairie Park is having at Aurora Park next April? There will be dozens of educational stands, activities . . ."

His voice dwindled off at Vince's dead-eyed look. A silence baked between them.

Vince's hands curled into fists. "I get it now. You want money. You're soliciting. You didn't see the sign on the door, 'No Solicitors'?"

"I didn't notice that, no."

Vince hastily pushed aside the bottle with its miniature cloud and placed his meaty forearms on the counter, gripping his hands as if he was praying for patience. "Will there be any stands about clouds there? Any educational information?"

"I'm not sure. Actually, maybe you could run one if there isn't. My dad is organizing the whole thing. I'm sure he'd love a cloud stand."

Vince squeezed his tangled eyes shut for a moment and then threw them back open. "How much do you want?"

At the wig store, the wigs' names were etched into placards at the base of the mannequin necks, fantasies twisted around a sliver of practicality. Downtown Edge: a long chocolate-brown shag cut. Mod Madness: a short style with pieces near the ears rendered in a strawberry-pink color that might spontaneously catch fire if exposed to bright light. Pixie Princess: a wan-looking blond with peltish bangs. The mannequins' softly parted lips, painted in dabs of coral or pink, suggested they were all murmuring something a little sexy.

The heavy glass closed behind Alison, sealing her into a warm room carpeted in plush mauve. "Hello," Alison said, guilt pervading her tone.

The shopkeeper, age indeterminate but somewhere north of fifty, smiled at her with worn friendliness; the idea that Alison was too young and full-headed to be in the store never seemed to dawn on her. The woman's own head was heavy with hair that could've been fake or real, but it was perfect, whatever it was. Brown and dense and shiny, it hung down in piles on her shoulders, with an artfully arranged set of bangs above her sharply plucked eyebrows. The woman looked genuinely happy to see Alison, which made no sense to her at all.

"Is there something I can help you with?" The woman kept her hands, thin and veined and weighed down with a voluminous diamond wedding band, folded on the glass case in front of her. Alison imagined that her hands would have patches of warmth and coolness, if Alison were to grab them. She considered doing it, just as a means of stalling. Now that she was in the store and the woman was asking to help her, she felt like she was obligated to answer, to seem like she wasn't wasting the woman's time.

"Who buys these wigs?" Alison blurted out.

The woman laughed a dry little laugh, and Alison thought she saw a smidge of her goodwill leave.

"Well, all kinds of people. Mostly women, but I do have male models as well," she said, pointing to a few isolated toupees on the back wall.

"But why?" Alison said. "Why would they need a wig?"

Alison knew her questions were awkward and rude, but she didn't know how to pose her curiosity any other way. She offered the woman a conciliatory smile.

"Some people use it as a way to try out a new style," she said. Then she switched tactics. "You've seen some elderly people who are"—she paused—"uncomfortable with losing their hair, right?"

Alison nodded.

"Some people buy wigs for that reason, and then some other people buy them because they get sick and their hair falls out."

"Sick from what?"

"From chemo or radiation treatments."

Alison nodded with what she hoped was appropriate solemnity.

"If they get a wig," the woman continued, taking down one of the models near her, "it's not as upsetting to them. They can feel like they never lost anything. Feel this," she said, holding out a blond lock attached to a shoulder-length style.

Alison pulled the hair through her fingertips, feeling little synthetic snags on the surface.

"It feels real," the woman stated.

"But it's not real."

"It isn't, but it's very close. I have wigs made of real hair, but they're very expensive."

Alison could tell by the way she said "expensive" that she wouldn't get to see or touch any of those wigs. She stood there rubbing the model's hair a little longer, unsure what to say. The shopkeeper, sometime in their conversation, had started to enjoy teaching Alison about wigs, and she felt like the woman wanted to show her more, though she wasn't sure what.

"Well," Alison said, "thank you."

The woman smiled, her eyes glowing warmly in their pockets of crinkled skin. "You're welcome. Do you have any other questions?"

"Yes, but, um, different topic. Would you be interested in donating to the Earth Day celebration in Aurora Park? Your money will help fund activities and raise awareness for the environment. In the last ten years, our planet has seen a crushing—"

The woman gently held up her hand. "No need to continue," she said. "I read the news."

She disappeared into the back and emerged with a checkbook. "Who should I make this out to?" Alison told her, and with her head bent, writing the amount in ornate cursive, Alison had ample time to stare at the top of the woman's head and glimpse the weaving of strands into nude-colored fabric. The woman tore off the check and handed it to Alison.

"Wow, thank you!" Alison turned and headed for the door. As she pushed the door open, she turned around and said, "Sorry if I seemed weird before," to her instant, face-flushing regret.

The woman gave her a startled smile. "Not at all!"

Alison stepped out, relishing the relief of the cold autumn air.

Later, at the table with half-melted shakes in front of them, Alison and Gabe tallied their donations on lined paper and discovered that the biggest gets were from the wig and magic stores. Both wrote checks for $500.

"Did you tell the Magic Brother about the spaceship?"

"Nope, but maybe that's a good thing," Gabe said. "Our conversation was weird enough. I swear that guy is from another planet. Maybe he came over here on a saucer?"

"If he did, the wig lady was sitting right next to him. Ooh, what if all of the adults of Prairie Park came over on the spaceships and they're just not telling us?"

Gabe and Alison looked around at the occupants of their favorite crummy diner, picturing their harried waitress and the old manager sitting at the cash register with a cigarette tucked behind his ear as aliens.

"That would explain a lot," Gabe said with a laugh.

14

Cynthia held a stack of washed dinner napkins in her hand. She tucked them into a drawer, inhaling the fragrance of Ernest's cooking. The oven clanged as it often did after it'd been on for 20 minutes. She watched her husband's back under his thin, putty-colored T-shirt, the shag of his hair, the bend of his figure as he stood over the stove. She grabbed a kitchen towel and swatted it between Ernest's shoulder blades.

He didn't respond. Sometimes, this was the way it was between them. Distance. But she wondered: What was the big desire to be connected to someone all the time anyway? Affinity, in every single moment, was impossible to sustain. She had learned to make peace with these times when the cord between them was less visible. Sometimes it was dark, and she would just have to grope around on the floor till she felt the line.

"You're ignoring me," she said.

"No, I was waiting for you to speak."

"Do you think Alison should take an art history class downtown?"

He didn't turn around. Instead, he grabbed a handful of chopped herbs and tossed it into the pan. It would be the final touch; he couldn't leave it in there too long or the herbs would be overwhelmed. He lifted the pan off the stovetop, swishing the bubbling sauce around in the cast iron with the mauled handle and pocked surface. The tendons of his forearms twitched under his skin.

"I'm expecting those mushrooms to be amazing, since they're taking up so much of your attention," Cynthia said.

Ernest poured the pan's contents into an old chipped serving platter painted with blue flowers.

After a moment of gazing at it contentedly, he asked, "What made you think art history?"

"Well, she's been looking through that book of prints all the time. Plus she's drawing constantly these days. I think her spaceship sneakers are the hot item around school."

"Last year she really liked ballet."

"Doesn't mean she won't return to it."

"Piano lessons the year before."

"So she's curious."

"I'd really like her to deepen her commitment to doing charitable work. She talked about joining Protect the Planet but then she hasn't really done it."

"She got busy, I guess."

"I should get her involved with more Earth Day projects. God knows we could use the help."

"Well, let her take the initiative on that."

"Of course, but there's nothing wrong with mentioning it to her."

Cynthia knew what Ernest meant by mentioning. By any definition, his mentioning was more like demanding. She tucked into her station at the kitchen table.

"This is going to be amazing," Ernest said, his head tucked in the oven, where he pricked juicy pieces of lamb with a prong.

She smoothed her hand over the wood graining. As always, she used her fingernail to scratch at one ancient spot of jelly that had fused to the surface. Out the window, the spaceship was in full tilt—flashing lights, a soaring noise that intermittently broke into grinding, and sometimes a few moments of vibrating, low but relatively light. *Ho-hum*, she thought, remembering the early days, when they'd wondered: *Is this thing about to blow? Are the aliens coming out? Will the spaceship fly away, leaving a people-sucking lacuna in its place?*

"Do you want to log that racket?" Ernest asked.

"I'll let one of the kids have that pleasure."

Cynthia watched out the window, grateful for the peace and warmth of her kitchen. But then came a great surge through the linoleum. Bright green light bathed the backyard; the plum-colored twilight fought back against it. The front-facing strands of the giant weeping willow pulled toward the spaceship. "What the hell?" Ernest shouted.

The window rattled and shattered, blowing into the kitchen with a crystalline bark. Cynthia screamed and threw up her arm, but it wasn't enough to protect her from the glass that rained over her hair and shoulders. Shards fell around her shoes, flecks embedded in her knit pants. Ernest ran and crouched down to where she had ducked, his eyes on the open window that now blew in chilled air.

"Are you OK?" he said, the sound of his voice tinny in the newly extended space.

Dazed, she nodded, plucking glass out of her sweater. The backyard was now calm, the lights of the ship dimmed to their normal, spotlight intensity. He yanked at her hand to get her to stop touching the glass.

"What the fuck just happened?!" she asked.

"Stay in here," he said. "I'm going to see what the hell's wrong with that thing."

Ernest grabbed the magnetized flashlight off the refrigerator, checked its beam, and headed to the backyard. In the mush of the grass, he stood in front of the machine, not frightened exactly but on defense. He'd raced out here, ready to fight—in some way, somehow—but what if it surged again, stronger this time? The beam of his flashlight licked the bolted metal of the ship, the underside, the windows that betrayed no interior but only reflected the light in return. He rapped the flashlight on one of the legs. "What the hell was that?" he scolded. Stalking around the machine, he searched and listened for something different, some clue as to what had happened, but he didn't see or hear anything out of the ordinary. Not a thing. The same flawless but utilitarian metal; the same band of lights around its smooth domed head. It was just a temperamental freak.

He flashed the light up into the windows, rapidly turning it on and off like a Morse code, and said loudly, angrily, "What. Are. You. Doing? Are you trying to kill us?"

No response, of course, because the spaceship didn't do responses. Ernest curbed the temptation to thwack one of its legs again, harder. "Do not damage their home, tamper with any equipment, or, in any way, create a hostile environment." He thwacked it anyway, the crack rattling his wrist this time but eliciting absolutely nothing from the spaceship. Didn't matter, still felt good, especially when he thought of Cynthia inside, picking glass out of her hair. He looked around. As always, the weeping willow stood nearby in its state of dormant wisdom. The garage, and its small, dirt-spackled side window, remained intact and seemingly undisturbed.

He shut off the flashlight and went inside.

The kids stood in the kitchen now, bewildered. The floor glittered with tiny glass fragments. Cynthia had retreated to the dining room.

"What happened?" Gabe asked. He bent down and lifted a big shard out of a pile of crushed glass.

"Don't touch that, Gabe. Are all the upstairs windows OK?"

"Yeah, it didn't do anything up there."

"We've got to sweep this up right now." He rounded up every functioning broom in the house and distributed them to the kids. Ernest looked at his daughter sweeping, her full lips from her mother, her reddish-walnut hair greasy and darker near the crown. He thought about hugging her but he didn't. He wasn't ready to feel any emotional impact just yet. Now it was time to take care of business, a litany of furious demands repeating in his head. He would call first thing tomorrow. He would not rest until somebody agreed to take the thing away. For the time being, he placed heavy cardboard over the broken window, framing it with black electrical tape.

Cynthia reentered the kitchen, looking flushed and shell-shocked. She'd changed her clothes and put on a jacket, a tough old leather one he hadn't seen her wear in ages.

"Are you OK, my love?"

"I guess."

"You're wearing that old jacket!"

"It makes me feel indestructible. Are we all still hungry?"

On the counter, four plates of meat and mushrooms: a couple Ernest had plated himself, a couple more finished by someone else. He eyed the food and then looked around on the floor. Some specks of glass had managed to travel this far across the room, but he didn't think anything had gotten on the counter, near the food. The food looked good, still hot, the lamb lightly smoking and leaking tender juices. He lifted two of the plates and directed everyone to come into the dining room, away from the damage and suddenly cold kitchen air. They sat and began to eat.

"Do you know why it did that?" Gabe asked.

"I already said I don't know," Ernest said.

"You didn't say that already. You just didn't answer the question."

"Right, well, I don't really know. Something's clearly wrong with it."

They continued to eat in silence until Ernest noticed that Alison was eating everything but the lamb.

"What's going on over there? You don't like the lamb?"

"I haven't tried it," she said. "I'm just thinking about eating less meat."

"Why?"

Alison hesitated. "I don't know. Maybe it's wrong to eat meat."

"Where did you get this from?" Gabe butted in. "Is this something Rebecca's into now?"

"No. Believe it or not, I've been thinking about this on my own."

"Yeah, right. Someone's feeding it to you. Maybe Aubrey?"

"Because I don't have my own mind?"

"You have your own mind, but you're easily influenced. You're going to want to eat that meat tomorrow, right after the hunger pains set in."

Alison stabbed the lamb with a fork and held the cut up in the air. "Can I go feed this to the cat?"

"Oh, good, choke Jupiter with a giant slab of meat."

"That's not her name. Oh my god, you can't suddenly rename the cat because the spaceship is from there. Her name is Athena."

"Jupiter. It's way cooler. Besides, the cat doesn't care what we call it."

"Why? Why is that cooler?"

"Guys, enough," Ernest said, filling in for Cynthia. She policed their interrelations more vigilantly than he ever did, but she was lost in the task of eating, lifting a spoon to her mouth with deflated but determined energy.

"I'm going to make a few calls about that tomorrow, sweetheart," Ernest said, grabbing her free hand curled on the table. "I think it's officially time to get rid of this thing."

"You can't get rid of it," Gabe said. "It's supposed to stay until May."

Ernest shook his head. "It just shattered the kitchen window. Deal's over. Might be time to get that attorney we've been thinking about," he said, still looking at his wife.

"What do you mean?" Alison asked, perplexed. "Mom's a lawyer. Why would we need another one?"

"Because your mom may not be interested in going after the saucer. We may need to seek outside counsel for this one!"

Cynthia's focus returned. She lifted her wineglass and took a noisy gulp. Her slightly reckless movements had a certain confidence to them, gained from being close to harm. "Can we all just be quiet for a while, please?" She sounded a little hoarse, like she'd just woken up. "We don't have to debate the thing; we don't have to argue about everything all the time. Anyone ever notice that's generally the mode of communication in this family?"

Such a provocative statement would usually spur an argument about whether their argumentative style was truly argumentative, or did they simply enjoy digging a little deeper and pushing past each other's easy assumptions? But not now, not tonight.

They ate in silence until Gabe stopped, placed his fork on his plate, and rubbed his throat. Ernest watched him, pausing mid-chew.

"My throat hurts," Gabe said.

Ernest looked at his son's nearly clean plate and then looked around the table. Alison and Cynthia hadn't eaten as much. "Does yours?" he asked them. They shook their heads.

Ernest tried to remember where Gabe's plate had been in the lineup. Had he given him one that was closer? That didn't matter, he thought; they were all in the same position as far as the window was concerned. He looked at his wife, her jacket sleeve yanked up and exposing her forearm. She was saying something to Gabe: "You probably inhaled some of it."

Ernest felt a disjointed panic undermining his thoughts, but he said, "Drink some water. It's probably just a tickle." To Cynthia: "What's going on with your arm, honey?"

"I don't know."

Gabe swallowed most of his water and said he felt better. After dinner, Ernest reinforced the cover over the window with more tape, making an X across the cardboard. Gabe grabbed the broom to do one final sweep. He kept clearing his throat, Adam's apple bobbing in his neck.

"You don't have to do that," Ernest said.

"I know," Gabe said, getting on his knees and sweeping one of the corners underneath the window with a precision Ernest found unusual. Gabe's long, swooping bangs hung in front of his eyes as he swept. Ernest saw the glitter of the glass getting on his son's hands, his fingernails a bit raggedy from biting them, miscellaneous scratches on his thumb.

"Gabe, let me finish."

"But you're always after me to do more cleaning in the house."

"Get up, I'll do it."

"Am I being punished? I'm the one who shattered the kitchen window?"

"I said I'll finish it."

Gabe stood up and let go of the broom handle so that it fell against the wall. Ernest quickly grabbed it to prevent it from smacking onto the floor. Gabe stormed out of the kitchen. After a moment of contemplating whether he should go after him, Ernest decided against it. He would sweep up every last bit of glass, his mind working and reworking the speech he would give to the New World supervisor.

15

THE ACTIVITIES OF THE UNWELCOME VISITORS FROM JUPITER: AN ALLEN FAMILY LOG

November 15: *After the ship blew out the kitchen window, I had to take Mom to the hospital. A splinter of glass was lodged in her arm; we couldn't get it out. The ship was quiet when we left. A few of the neon spotlights were on, pointed to the ground. While at the hospital they noticed some problems in Mom's blood work. More tests. Probably nothing, but now more than ever, the spaceship needs to go.* —EA

November 16: *The spaceship has been totally calm since the window-breaking episode. It didn't even dump any liquid or make loud noises for the whole day.* —GA

November 16: *You're forgetting the 45 minutes that it vibrated outside of my window. At one point it made this noise kind of like a giant purring cat. So weird.* —AA

November 16: *Called New World Enterprises to lay the groundwork for spaceship departure. Didn't get very far. Increasingly it seems beyond their scope of imagination. I promised them that the next call would be coming from a lawyer. Are you ready to do battle, Cynthia? Let me know! In the meantime, they are faxing us a damage reimbursement form to send back to them. Apparently, this happens occasionally.* —EA

November 17: *No activity so far today. Verrrry quiet spaceship.* —GA

November 17: *Actually, it released another splash of green surprise around the time I got home from school. It looked kind of metallic too, like it reflected the light. But then it soaked into the ground and everything looked OK, I guess.* —AA

16

While driving, Cynthia's fingers flew distractedly to her left breast to knead the three spots, checking for pain or other suspect sensations. She tried not to formulate ideas or assumptions about what she was feeling, as the doctor had advised. Wait for the test results. Don't jump to any conclusions. Don't self-diagnose. Don't assume the worst. Every time a deathly scenario started to materialize, she countered it with something ridiculous. Maybe the bumps were circus peanuts buried in her chest from the time she'd choked on one in college. Or maybe gold was rising in her body, lumps of it that she could fish out and sell. When her imagination failed, she returned to the neutral and factual: three spots on her left breast, knotty, somewhat squishy, more solid than not.

Other than the masses, she felt completely fine. Well, that's what she told herself, but then other sensations reared up. What was "fine" anyway? Don't healthy people feel like collapsing on the floor from time to time? Don't their armpits suddenly feel fuller, as if they'd tucked golf balls in there? She developed a headache from pushing too much on the lumps, a headache that radiated throughout her breast, traveled up the side of her ribs, and planted its most potent rage at her temples. A new varietal of exhaustion also introduced itself, stealing over her with such force that she wondered what chemical warfare was responsible. Her limbs made of sopping wet wool, her throat scratching and burning—she'd have to immediately grab a chair if she wasn't already sitting. Otherwise, the exhaustion clipped her from under her feet.

But when anyone ever caught her spilling herself into a chair, her knuckles white from gripping the arms, she'd answer in the least attention-grabbing way she knew how. "I feel fine," she'd say. "I guess I'm just tired."

17

At close to midnight—her start times always varied by ten, sometimes twenty minutes—Gabe tuned in to *The Book of Connections*, his nightly habit. The woman had still never identified herself, never spoken her name or her location. She spoke in her confident, lightly theatric manner:

"One entire day. Every day you see, or you have the potential to see, the whole process, but you never do, right? Most of the time you never even get to see the beginning or the ending of any given day. Sunrise or sunset, from start to finish. You've probably looked at sunsets portrayed on postcards and paintings longer than you've looked at the real thing. Children, parents, parties, trauma, school, work, sex, books, movies—all get in the way. What is called life is the sticky film that prevents you from seeing sunset from start to finish. I decided this week that I'd try to rub all that away and see every sunset from start to finish. Why sunset? Because getting up at five A.M. is too hard.

"Here's what I discovered about the end of the day. It's like every light on Earth is harvested and sent to the horizon to melt together. It's all in there: the red neon from the alarm clock; the cabin light that spilled out of the car while you pumped gas; the first flicker of fluorescents turned on in the office in the morning; the sunshine pouring through the stained glass near the baptismal. It all pools together, suspended in a vivid turbidity—pink and yellow, bloodred—but there's movement to it. Have you ever noticed that? Sunset is a moving process. The light and chemicals are caught in a chase, but it's very slow. It lasts until a matte scrim lowers down: night, the extinguisher.

"You know what I realized about watching the sunset? It's boring."

Gabe chuckled.

"But it's also magnificent. Both are true because it happens every day. Each day that is birthed eventually dies. Each day dies in more or less the same way. Some sunsets look grizzly; others look peaceful. They are all the last breath of the day."

She finished her piece, but was she still there? Gabe tried to figure out, as he always did: if she was still sitting by the microphone or if she had left the room. He lay on his bed, listening to the slight fuzz. At the faint sound of steps, he bolted up. Three steps. He counted the muffled beats but then he doubted himself. Had he really heard something or did he just want to hear something? The fuzz remained, bearing no evidence one way or another. The room she was in—was it small? A basement, he always pictured, with a plain table pushed against a wall, a hard-backed chair, nondescript lighting—an unfinished space that only she bothered to enter. Back upstairs, the rest of her life, all colored in. A family, a community, and a job, but none of that intersected with her show, which was her private categorization of the world, though she made it public to whoever was listening. Gabe understood this public/private schism. Sometimes it was easier to share your deepest thoughts with people who didn't know you.

Outside his window, the spaceship's green lights tilted up and flooded Gabe's room. He tried to shut his eyes and sleep, but it was impossible to ignore this reverse-sun shining into his room, saturating his bed with ghost-rays. Sometimes, the spaceship reminded him of a kid he knew in grade school who talked too much. He pulled the shade all the way down so that only a small amount of green seeped around the edges and slung a pillow over his head.

18

THE ACTIVITIES OF THE UNWELCOME VISITORS FROM JUPITER: AN ALLEN FAMILY LOG

November 22: *Nothing new to report, but I said I'd record everything so here I am. Around 6 p.m., the ship let out a small gush of liquid. The usual green stuff, a little less than usual.* —GA

November 22: *The most awesome smell came from the spaceship today: syrup and pancakes, I swear. Remember that summer camp you guys used to send me to, Wild Rose, where they forced us to make our own clothes and cook our own food? That place was kind of weird and jail-like, but on Sunday mornings they served us pancakes as a treat. I was so happy to see them it almost made me weep.* —AA

November 22: *OK, nighttime report—of complete and total blandness because the spaceship's not really doing anything new. But check it out: around 10 p.m., the green lights, which had been pointing down, raised up and shone mostly into my bedroom but also Alison's. After about ten minutes of holding there, they went back down, which I will admit was a relief because it's hard to sleep with that neon party going on. But that's it and now I'm going to bed.* —GA

November 23: *Yeah, they did shine into my room too for a minute but not that bad, and earlier today, when Mom and Dad were out, Mrs. Chang stopped by. I actually found her in the corner of the backyard, looking at the spaceship, her hand on her neck, all worried and concerned. She said she hadn't even remembered the thing was back there until recently because she's been avoiding the north side of the house. She said the thing's usually too damn loud. I apologized to her and she seemed to be OK but still kind of crabby about the whole thing. After a couple of minutes of staring at it, she went inside. The spaceship was still the whole time she was here—a* *good thing because I worried she might've had a heart attack if it'd done anything.* —AA

November 23: *Wow, I can't believe she forgot about it. But OK, that must mean the spaceship's not making THAT much noise. That's good, right? It's been totally still so far today, probably because it made the dump yesterday.* —GA

November 24: *Helllooooooo, anyone out there besides Alison? Dad, are you reading this anymore? Mom? Because if not, I won't bother to keep up with this thing.* —GA

November 24: *Yes, we're reading it. But you're the main logger so don't expect to hear from us every day. Write down a report for tonight—I've got to run to a meeting.* —EA

November 24: *Spaceship, tonight as of 9:52 p.m. Still a circle. Still metal. Still with a dome at the top where you can't see anything or anyone (no matter what Alison says). Green lights, low to the ground. Now that my (pointless?) duty is done, I retire upstairs to my shortwave radio.* —GA

19

Alison and Gabe were rooting around in the basement, in a fit of extreme boredom that had turned rambunctious. They'd discovered, behind some old pipes in the back room, a painting in a gilt frame, which they immediately brought upstairs and thrust in front of Ernest and Cynthia, blocking their view of the television and the nature documentary they'd been watching. Cynthia wanted to think about the nearly translucent crabs that lived on the bottom of the ocean floor, not the ominous tone her doctor had used when he'd told her they'd need to order another round of tests.

Ernest and Cynthia stared, perplexed, at the painting. It was very 1970s, and of a woman's face but morphed with a suburban tropical paradise that didn't adhere to any standard of logic or realism. The portrait was painstakingly lush, with her wild brown hair clogged with leaves and twigs, her glowing yellow eyes standing out from the patches of grass that composed her face. Impressively, the painter had managed to create the illusion of cheekbones but only by shading the facial lawn in a certain way. Dandelions dotted the grass, along with big white daisies painted in psychotropic wavering lines; toucans with pelican beaks flew around the trees behind her head. Silverfish swam in the bubbling creek that merged with the curling ends of her hair. Her lips were split-open hunks of cherrywood. It was a thrift-store gem.

"I don't recognize this, do you?" Cynthia asked Ernest.

"It seems familiar, but I can't place it. Is it ours or is it the Paulsons'?"

The Paulsons were the former residents of the Allen home and often blamed for the various oddities around the house. The Paulsons must've put in the ugly raspberry wallpaper in the linen closet. Those Paulsons who had painted over the brick fireplace. Only the Paulsons would've wired the upstairs bathroom so that the on/off switch for the light fixture was reversed. In the 1970s, they moved to Florida to retire. They sold the Allens their house, leaving behind an assortment of unwanted items, including two white vinyl sofas that the Allens donated to Goodwill.

"It doesn't seem their style," Cynthia said, "and I feel like this is a painting you'd remember to take with you."

"It's really cool," Gabe said. "Can we hang it up somewhere?"

"What do you like about it?" Cynthia asked.

"I don't know," Gabe said. "It's an Earth Mama."

"We like her crazy firewood lips," Alison said.

"You know, I wonder if this is a painting from my old friend Susan," Cynthia said.

"I don't think so," Alison said. "Look at the signature in the bottom corner."

The kids held up the painting for the adults to peer at. In the corner, thick yellow initials: "C.M."

"I still wonder if this is Susan's," Cynthia said. "It's exactly like what she painted in college."

"It's not Susan's, honey," Ernest said. "C.M.? Isn't that you?"

Cynthia nodded at Ernest's point, but she still stared at the painting, looking into the soulful, howling eyes of the woman. She traced her finger over the initials and said them out loud. In the crook of her elbow, a Band-Aid from the second round of tests.

"It's not my painting, but I guess it just makes me nostalgic, that's all. Those times are way gone," Cynthia said, flapping her hand in the air, the way that she always did when she said something a little sentimental.

"Then we can hang it up?" Alison asked.

"I don't know about that," Ernest said.

"Why not?"

"Where do you want to hang it?" Cynthia asked.

"In the living room."

Gabe regarded Alison with fresh respect. She'd gone straight for the artistic jugular of the home.

Ernest balked. "But what will our decorator say?"

"Oh, let's hang it in there for a little while," Cynthia said. "Or let's just place it over the fireplace for a bit. That way we don't have to bother with nails. Just for a little while."

Ernest rolled his eyes, but he didn't interfere with the plan. He had to admit that once it was up, he liked the sloppy charm of the old painting on the mantelpiece, tucked behind candles, dusty knickknacks, and family photographs.

This utopian hippie dream of a woman merging with nature eventually turned into a great source of comfort for him. Not the image itself necessarily, but the moment the painting triggered in his memory. Later, as his wife began to slip away from him, he would stare at the painting and think about how she'd been struck by it, how she'd moved her fingers over the initials on the painting, murmuring to herself, "C.M." And he'd think about how he wanted her back among the strong living things, a familiar creature loping around the unexplained wilderness.

PART TWO:
SPRAWL

20

The doctor delivered the news in a near monotone: Cynthia had three large tumors in her left breast, already at stage 4, which meant cancer had spread to her lymph nodes and had settled in other spots, including her brain. The doctor, whom she knew vaguely from an activism group her friend had thrown together for the last election, outlined the paths of treatment before telling her he'd be passing her on to an oncologist, who would explain it all in more detail. The various courses of treatment, to be done alone or in tandem, not exactly as he explained but how she interpreted: chemo (lose your hair); radiation (absorb the toxins approved by Western medicine); homeopathy (wait out your inevitable death while drinking pungent Chinese teas). After discussing at length with the oncologist (a friendly, sporty woman who seemed fresh off a morning run), Cynthia decided to schedule herself for chemo and radiation at the same time. Twenty weeks of treatment. After five weeks, they would assess the results of this medicinal interference and see if it was worth proceeding.

The treatments were to start tomorrow. The only reason they didn't start right then was because Cynthia said she wanted to discuss the course of treatment with Ernest first. He'd offered to come with her to this appointment several times, but he had a lucrative consulting gig and she didn't want him to miss it. And part of her bought into some lone-wolf fantasy that she'd process the information best on her own. She regretted it now, because Ernest would've asked a million highly specific questions, whereas she was so shocked she asked only a handful and then slipped back into the now abjectly blithe world.

But before she would tell him, she drove twenty minutes west, to the suburbs where she didn't know anyone, and she rented a room at a Best Western. She asked to be in a room away from any other guests. For a few hours, she'd walked around, shrieking, crying, fingering the wrapped soaps in stunned, teary silence, looking at her supposedly nearly dead face in the mirror. She wrote a list of questions about her treatment, summoning back her sensible, practical self that could beat anything, *anything*, with enough research and vigilance. Then she wrote a letter to Ernest and stashed it deep in her purse. She showered and checked out.

When Ernest returned home from a construction site a couple of hours away, she told him in their bedroom with the door shut. There was something almost sensuous about the way the news upended his sense of equilibrium. He was on a boat, helpless, watching all the cargo slide off into the sea. The force of it was admirably sickening. He managed to get out the encouraging propaganda he knew needed to be said—"we'll fight it," "it'll be OK"—and to believe it. She believed him too. For a minute, they almost bubbled over with it, trading platitudes of hope that had never sounded more genuine to them, but then the situation kept deteriorating. He'd ask for the facts again, to tease out some strain of positivity, but the facts were brutal. The facts were shutting them out. Low and speechless, they crawled onto the bed, holding each other for the next couple of hours while the sunset wasted away behind them, and the spaceship, in apparent sympathy, remained silent, leaving its lights turned off.

21

Cynthia explained her diagnosis to the kids while focusing intently on the space between their eyes and not their actual pupils. Sitting across from them at the dinner table, she employed the same professionalism she used for breaking bad news to clients. She had seen people mourn a life's cause in her office while she offered genuine but dispassionate reassurance from a safe distance. Part of her couldn't believe she was pulling the same trick on her children while telling them her breast was now rotten with cancer and it had poisoned the rest of her, but what was the alternative? Terrifying them with her sobs?

Arms slack at her sides, Alison sensed some kind of manipulation but didn't know how to articulate it. "So what are you really telling us?"

"What do you mean?" Cynthia said, blinking.

"What are you *not* telling us? What are you *not* saying?"

"I'm telling you everything I know right now."

"That's almost nothing. So you have cancer and you're getting radiation. You're going to have to go to the wig store. But what are your chances?"

Ernest kneaded his eyes with two thumbs.

"I didn't ask."

"You didn't ask or you're just not telling us? Because on TV the person who gets diagnosed with cancer always gets told how long they have to live."

"Well, if that's what happens on TV," Gabe said, "then it must be real."

"Alison," her father said, "your mother's not dying. She's fighting cancer."

"But I know there's something you're not telling us."

"I didn't ask anything about my chances," her mother said. "I told them I didn't want to know any estimates like that."

"But I don't understand why there's not more information."

"That's all the information I have access to at this time," her mother said.

"*Access to?* Are you a robot? A computer? Where are you?"

Without a plan for what she was doing, Alison backed her chair away from the table and stood up. Both of her parents looked at her in fright, her brother with something like admiration. She'd commanded their attention but wasn't sure what to do with it now.

"Mom," she said, but then she couldn't bring herself to say anything else. Part of the reason she couldn't was because Alison saw her mother lightly shaking and looking away from her, from everyone.

"Mom," she said again, and her mother looked at her but right through her, her face still and white, trying to betray no emotion. "Mom, stop being a robot!"

"Alison," her father warned, standing up from his chair.

Alison blinked, not understanding for a moment. Why was he warning her? What was there to be afraid of?

"Mom," she said again with more force, and when she caught her mother's eye, she made the motion to her, the raised eyebrows, the pat on her thigh. The gesture for soothing, for them to sit in the rocking chair together. Then she angled her body toward the living room where the chair was. Alison wasn't sure if she was offering solace or wanting to get it. Her mother stared at her, confused by the gestures or understanding perfectly, Alison couldn't tell. Then her mother's face crumpled and she set it in her hands. There was a horrible moan as Cynthia broke down.

"Alison," Ernest said softly, "you're making this harder."

Everyone listened as the sobs kept on, sinking them all into despair. Ernest rubbed Cynthia's back and murmured, "It's going to be OK, baby." She leaned into him, wrapping her arm around his chest, her teary red eyes squeezing shut.

Alison and Gabe froze. Here now, something they'd rarely seen: an intimate exchange between their parents, nakedly displayed before them; the kind they'd hear only by accident slinking past their parents' bedroom, the door ajar. How many times had they seen their mother cry? Scant few times, and never choking sobs.

For Alison it was a clear sign that life, and her family, would soon be ravaged, burned to a crisp that she would have to sift through in the future, pocketing the few, still-vivid fragments for their talismanic powers. Without another word, she bolted out of the room, sprinting for the stairs, taking them three at a time, past the staggered portraits of her and Gabe when they were babies, past the shots of her parents' 1970s wedding, with cream and ruffles and long hair on both. She swiped her hand across the framed photos until she knocked one off the wall and heard it clang and shatter behind her on the stairs, and she immediately regretted the melodrama of her actions. But she couldn't turn back. Upstairs, the second floor seemed too brightly lit, not yet beset by the bad news—something passed through daily but totally ignorant of personal details, like a train platform.

In the dining room, no one got up to check on the shattered photo. Both Ernest and Cynthia waited for Gabe to react in some other way apart from his sister. He sat there fiddling with his silverware, his eyes moving in tiny darting motions under his bangs, playing tag with his parents' eyes. He swept the bangs away from his face, his motion that he'd soon speak.

"Is it really bad? Are you..." Gabe started to ask but let the question trail off. He didn't want to finish the thought. He shut the words off. And then he did the only thing left to do. He apologized. "I'm sorry, Mom."

They languished in silence until they became aware of noises from outside, from the spaceship, bleeding into the dining room. Its nightly show was in full swing again, the sounds occurring in an ordered and predictable rhythm. They couldn't see the ship from the dining room, but Ernest nodded his head toward the picture window in the kitchen. "Just another polluter," he said, "taking up space on the grid." Earlier that day, in the mail, he'd found New World's reimbursement check to replace the window. Now more than ever, the check seemed like an insult, a pittance for how much trouble the saucer had caused them.

Alison picked up the phone in her room, dialed Aubrey's number. His mother put him on the line.

"Hey, Aubrey, it's Alison."

"Oh, hey!" He sounded enthused. At least there was that. "What's up?"

"Not that much, I just saved my mom from getting electrocuted. She was trying to rewire this old lamp and it shocked the shit out of her."

"She's OK?"

"Yeah, she just forgot to unplug it before she started working on it."

"Whoops. That's scary. Well, my mom has advanced breast cancer, she just told us."

She could hear Aubrey breathing. "That's awful," he finally said. "Is she going to the hospital?" Alison heard a dropping or hitting noise. "I'm sorry, I don't know why I asked that."

Alison breathed out. "It's OK. I think she might, eventually."

Cynthia and Ernest lay in bed under an Irish wedding blanket given to them for an anniversary gift. Between two rows of linked Celtic rings, white horses galloped across an undefined landscape of empty tapestry that stretched on, giving the horses no particular destination to reach. Cynthia couldn't remember when she had actually liked the blanket.

Glasses of red wine kept them company at their bedside tables—a semi-expensive bottle they had opened after remembering it was in the basement's half-assed wine cellar built by Ernest, with Tom's help and encouragement, during a fitful weekend when he fancied himself a potential connoisseur. Despite the wine's slightly off taste, they refilled their glasses without comment.

"Well, that didn't go as planned," Ernest said.

They lay in more silence. A squirrel skittered along the gutter pipe outside their window.

"The animals avoid our backyard now," Cynthia said. "The birds and squirrels but also Mrs. Chang's tabby, she stays away too."

"I think we should be thinking about the ship," Ernest said.

"A spaceship lands in our backyard a few months ago and gives me—only me—stage four cancer? Every doctor I've talked to says it's been festering in there for a while, most likely."

For the moment, Ernest didn't press his point. Everything had become suspicious, a possible source of carcinogenic poison: The cracked knife handle that trapped bacteria. The air conditioner leaking Freon or some other chemical that tastes like candy to children but can shut down their internal organs within hours. The nonstick pots they used only as backups and that long ago lost their protective coating. Where had the protective coating gone, exactly? Were tiny particles of the residue swallowed with every spoonful, and if so, how did it break down in the digestive system? Is there a moment when your guts lightly seize, so lightly you don't notice it, as they react to a foreign, possibly hostile substance in their midst? And is it that seizing in the guts that ultimately gives you cancer—if it happens thousands of times in a year—or is it that the guts don't know how to dispose of the residue? Which one gets people sick?

"I know we're both exhausted right now, but the spaceship, we can't just let it off the hook. It blew a window out over your head. Who knows what else it's done?"

"Who knows how long this thing has been brewing inside me?" Cynthia said. "The doctor said there was no way to tell."

"A thirty-nine-year-old woman with no family history of breast cancer?"

"My mother only made it to fifty-seven, remember? Maybe she would've developed it if a car hadn't plowed into her and Pops." Cynthia rolled over, facing away from Ernest.

"Either way, I'm going to be investigating that ship. I'm going to test everything it does."

"Don't bother," Cynthia said. "The spaceship is my friend. I'm glad it's here, OK?"

A few minutes later she breathed evenly in a pantomime of sleep.

22

THE ACTIVITIES OF THE UNWELCOME VISITORS FROM JUPITER: AN ALLEN FAMILY LOG

November 26: *Important: As I said this morning, DO NOT remove the bucket that is currently placed under the spaceship. It is there to catch the spaceship's discharge. If I am not home to collect it, please place the bucket filled with discharge in the garage. I'll be bottling and labeling accordingly as we collect specimens. WE NEED TO DO THIS FOR THE NEXT TWO WEEKS. It's important that we have a wide sampling range for testing. Just because it doesn't dump anything toxic for 13 days doesn't mean it won't on the 14th day. We need to be sure. —EA*

November 26: *Um, these are very specific directions. Why are we saving the spaceship's dumps? Toxic how? —AA*

———

Cynthia opened the back kitchen door and flicked on the spotlight, startling Ernest in the backyard.

"It's getting late," she said, shivering on the back landing. "What are you doing?"

Standing underneath the spaceship, he held up some jars. "Taking a few soil samples."

"Is that really necessary?"

"Yes, it is."

"It's too cold out here." She pulled her sweater tighter around her waist.

"Then go back inside."

"Ernest," she said, "just—can you do this tomorrow? I don't want to go to bed alone."

"I'm doing this now because the kids are asleep and you asked me not to do this in front of them," he said. "So can you give me a few minutes?"

She stood out there, audibly shivering, while Ernest scooped soil into a glass jar.

"No gloves?"

"No gloves."

"If you really thought you were dealing with contaminated soil there, you wouldn't want to touch it." After watching him for another minute, she said, "You think you should use that old hand shovel? What if that's been treated with some chemical or it has residue on it from some other project? Now you're not taking a clean sample."

"OK, Cynthia, OK. I'm not a pro lab here. I'm a one-man operation. What do you want from me?"

She gripped the railing and hissed over the side. "I want you to drop the jar and come inside with me."

He regretted speaking harshly to her, really the first time he'd allowed himself to since her diagnosis, but why didn't she respect his project? Frustration ate at him, but he tried to push it away.

"In a minute, I promise," he said gently. "I have to finish this."

She went inside, slamming the door behind her.

Ernest flashed the light at the dirt underneath the ship; he'd lost track of where he was digging. Something caught his eye. Did he see a few sprouts? The soil appeared moist, fresh, and alive now in a way that he hadn't noticed before. Was he imagining things? Trying to make himself feel better? He'd check it tomorrow morning, when the sun was bright and the couple of dinner beers had washed out of his system.

In bed, Cynthia lay waiting for Ernest. She was only a few days into her doubleheader of chemotherapy and radiation. Muscles she'd long neglected in her back, thighs, and stomach were now announcing themselves as fragile and taut at the same time, aching and creaking like suspension cables on an old bridge. But worse was the exhaustion, which threatened to smother every living impulse. Somewhere dimly, she raged that Ernest wasn't up here yet, seeing her off to sleep, helping her to fend off the fear. But she didn't have the energy to maintain the emotion; it fell down a dark well in the center of her exhaustion. This was a whole new sensation, outside of compartmentalizing or reasoning something away. In some ways it was a relief to surrender, to nearly collapse. Or at least that's what she told herself, because what else was there to think about it? Exhaustion was the new master; that's just the way it was now.

Cynthia was asleep by the time he crawled into bed. Soon after, he lapsed into a dream. In the black dirt underneath the spaceship, tiny delicate stems burst into mature grasses and shrubs, the growth captured in stop-motion-like animation. Blooming with an almost psychotic urgency, the plants settled after a while, gently wavering in the breeze. There were several native varieties, some that Ernest recognized: little bluestem, panic grass, hairy puccoon, goat's rue, and sand milkweed. All reedy plants, gruff, not beautiful, but possessing a kind of scrawny grace. In the dream, he walked through them, and though he didn't see it happen directly, he knew the ship was responsible for their growth. He felt a great wave of tenderness toward the ship, maternal but awkward in its stiff inability to do anything physically nurturing. He awoke with a twitch, the blanket twisted around his calf like kudzu. He slipped out of bed as quietly as possible—Cynthia turned away from him—and padded down the stairs and into the living room.

He sat on the couch, nearly naked except for a pair of boxers. *Why this dream?* he thought. The spaceship was the invader from outer space, most likely responsible, at least partly, for his wife's cancer, and yet his subconscious just told him it wasn't here to destroy anything. Maybe the spaceship could even be a life-giving force. Tears erupted at the corners of his eyes; he squeezed a couch cushion into his chest as he folded over and cried.

In the morning, he checked underneath the spaceship and didn't find tender shoots of grass poking through the soil. Instead, the bald ground was slick with the latest dump. With gloves this time, he scooped up three jars of soil from different parts of the area. Next step: to get them tested for the carcinogens surely lurking inside. There had to be a reason his healthy wife was spitting up blood.

23

Ernest and Marilyn met for lunch in the suburb next to Prairie Park, the one with cheaper housing and lower-ranking schools. Ernest knew the old pub well, but he was still surprised Marilyn suggested it. Morgan's wasn't the classiest joint. Strings of pepper lights festooned the bar and taped dollar bills were peeling off the top of the brass rack that held the glasses. Pinned to the cash register: a pair of granny-style underwear with signatures in black marker.

The bartender/waitress approached their booth with a dour expression.

"I'll take the bacon and avocado burger," Ernest said, still keeping the stained menu up in front of his face.

"How about you, miss?"

"I'll have a veggie burger with cheddar, please."

"We don't have veggie burgers. Want a grilled cheese?"

"Sure," Marilyn said. "You really don't have veggie burgers as an alternative?"

"No one ever orders them." The waitress shrugged.

"That's because you took them off the menu," Marilyn said.

The waitress shrugged again.

"We're in the nonsmoking section, right?" Ernest asked.

The waitress looked around at the restaurant's permanently smoky air.

"Yeah."

"Well, if you can make sure to seat any smokers as far away from us as possible, that'd be much appreciated."

The waitress blinked at him.

"It's just that if anyone lights up near me, I will ask that person to put it out. I try very hard not to blame the individual—I blame the big corporations for selling this stuff and the government for not exorbitantly taxing—"

She cut him off. "I remember you now. I'll see what I can do."

After the waitress left, Ernest said, "We make a hellish pair for a dive bar like this. We're lucky we weren't chased out of here."

Marilyn chuckled quietly, watching the scowling waitress polish glasses with a rag. "That's the price you pay for going under the radar," she said.

Ernest couldn't help but luxuriate in the idea: "Are we having a covert meeting?"

"Not exactly," she said. "But I didn't feel like seeing anyone from work or my daughter's school."

Ernest nodded, complicit in his understanding. Marilyn seemed looser, flashing him more smiles, the kind you can't really control. The food arrived in red plastic baskets lined with wax paper, accompanied by a set of condiments that the waitress plunked down like they were a pickax, hoe, and shovel.

"We'll never see her again until she drops the check," Ernest said.

The waitress, back behind the bar, started the jukebox. A soul song from the 1970s.

"Ah," Marilyn said, looking around at the air as if the music could be seen there. "This might be my favorite moment of today. This moment right now."

"Rough day at work?"

"Yeah, always, but it's more than that."

"Well, what makes this moment so great?"

"Good food, good company, and I love when music comes on unexpectedly. It's just a thing that always gives me pleasure."

"Oh, that is always nice." Ernest talked and kept talking, knowing what was happening and ignoring the feelings of guilt that were beginning to wash around in the pit of his stomach.

"It makes life seem like a movie somehow, when a song comes on like that. Like maybe the music's coming in because something momentous is going to happen."

Ernest smiled. "So we're watching the lead-up to a big moment then. Well, let me tell you, I'm on the edge of my seat."

"You're not watching, you're *part of* a special moment," Marilyn corrected, tapping his hand with a trimmed fingernail. "You can be a bozo sometimes, you know that?"

"Right." Ernest put down his burger. He needed to bring the conversation back to business. He tried to switch his role in Marilyn's life movie. "So did you get a chance to look into the matter we discussed?"

"Your little friend still sitting back there?"

"Of course. Believe me, if the spaceship had left, we'd be ordering Champagne right now or at least Milwaukee's finest."

Marilyn laughed. "Well, I think you can relax about it. I made some calls to other reporters and had our librarian conduct a thorough search. No reports of a spaceship visitation causing anyone cancer. Ever."

"Not a single lead or a story? Not even a nibble?"

"Not even a nibble. It's possible someone got cancer at the same time as an alien visitation, but no one's ever connected those dots—which makes me think there are no dots to connect."

"Well, this might be the first time someone's connected the dots. I'm about to send samples of the spaceship's waste to a top-notch lab outside Toronto."

"Well, that's great, Ernest. You're really investigating this thing from top to bottom. Of course it'd be huge news if the spaceship is releasing toxins."

Her response was professionally encouraging, no more, no less, but Ernest drank in her validation nonetheless. She obviously saw the importance of his mission.

"I can't shake the feeling that Cynthia's sickness . . ." He didn't let himself finish the sentence.

Ernest was having a hard time saying the word "cancer" in relation to his wife. Once said, it couldn't be taken back; it traumatized, bluntly and inelegantly, everything said after it. Marilyn put down her sandwich, her eyes softening.

"How is she doing?" she said quickly.

"She's OK. I mean, she's actually doing great, considering her treatments. She's not too happy about the tests I'm doing, though. For some reason, she doesn't really get it."

"Well, she's a lawyer, right? Her kind don't see the point in anything unless there's one hundred percent hardline proof that it can hold up in a court of law."

"Cynthia's not a lawyer like that."

"No, of course not," Marilyn said. "I shouldn't have said that."

"She doesn't want me scaring the kids. But I can't passively sit by while Cynthia is . . ." He trailed off again.

"I know what it's like," Marilyn said after a minute. "My mother died of lung cancer four years ago. I had to take care of her at the end. It was incredibly draining and horrible. But listen, none of that will end up happening with your wife because she's so young. Too young. There's no way. She'll beat this thing, Ernest."

Ernest chewed through a moment of uncomfortable silence.

"Stage four," he eventually said. "It's not like we caught it early. Though that's the thing about it. There was no early, it seems. Suddenly it was just there, full-blown."

Marilyn nodded. "Do you have anyone to talk to? Because when it's happening, it's too overwhelming to keep to yourself."

"Sort of. My neighbor Tom. Sometimes I talk to him but it's awkward."

"Look, if you need anyone to talk to, someone who understands, don't hesitate to call. I know how this feels."

She grabbed his hand off the table and squeezed it, before letting it go and sitting back. Nervous pings went off in his stomach. All he could do was eat the last of his burger, but he badly wanted to reach back across the table and grab her hand and feel the exact weight of it and the texture of her skin. Something pinched at him. He shouldn't feel this exhilaration. He shouldn't feel like he was finally being understood by someone, maybe even admired by someone, after so much time under Cynthia's cool, quiet exasperation that she didn't think he noticed. He thought about blotting it all out with another beer, but he didn't want Marilyn to think he was an alcoholic.

24

On his back under the big belly of the spaceship, Gabe stared at the bolted sheets of titanium metal, taking pictures with a battered Pentax camera.

Last night, he'd caught *The Book of Connections* and certain lines kept coming back. Her topic: the eye. "Did you know that the human eye can't really see red? It's more an invention of your brain. Although you possess red, green, and blue color receptors in your retinas, they're pretty lousy. The 'red' receptor only detects yellow green, and the 'green' receptor detects blue green. To make red, your brain combines these signals and voilà."

An interesting coincidence, because he'd been thinking about eyes lately, and camera lenses, all prompted by his philosophical photography teacher. But at the moment he wasn't capturing the spaceship's weird beauty; he was logging spy documents. The photos were for his next class assignment but also for his father's "internal files." Half the reason Gabe was taking pictures now was because one of the sheets of metal, the one that slid back to uncover what his dad bitterly labeled the ship's anus, hadn't closed all the way. There was a tiny sliver where only darkness could be seen, not even thick enough to stick in a screwdriver. His dad had already tried.

But of course a malfunctioning panel wasn't really the deal here. Ernest wanted these photos for evidence that the spaceship poisoned Cynthia. He hadn't said so directly, per se, but Gabe recognized the fiery concentration on Ernest's face as he circled the spaceship or bottled up green liquid in the garage, printing out the dates on black labels with raised lettering.

Twisting the lens, he sharpened the focus and snapped the photo. Possibly, Gabe thought, his camera eye was looking at the spaceship's camera eye, imperceptible but present all the same, watching like the security camera at the mall. His thoughts drifted. *Mom has cancer.* Mostly that fact existed as an abstraction, though he'd noticed her long naps, her bitter mood. And Alison kept mentioning the coming baldness, the dreaded wig. For now, he told himself that her cancer was a nuisance that would retreat, dissipate, or do whatever cancer does when it leaves. That was really the only possibility he let himself entertain. Any time he thought about something worse— flashes of her in a hospital bed, for instance, comatose—the floor of his stomach gave away.

Saturday afternoon. No one around at the moment—his mom sleeping and his dad out running errands. His sister was at a friend's house, maybe, or roaming the mall with her new vagabond stoner friends (Alison had shifted her social circle away from nice, vaguely popular girls in only a few weeks). In this rare private moment, he could talk to the spaceship without risking embarrassment or recrimination—except from himself.

"Hi, I'm Gabe," he said. The introduction felt forced, like something a boy on a sitcom would do while sitting on his bed holding a football and talking about God. Silently he composed his words so that he could speak them with confidence. At first, the words or the desires were coming in stutters—he wasn't in the practice of verbalizing his life plans, not even to himself—but after a while, he managed to cobble together a few wishes.

"Take me somewhere," he said, "away from here, someplace cool and maybe just a little bit fucking scary." He tried to keep the thought there: simple and pure. But then other questions kept dodging in. *What am I supposed to do for a career? Am I supposed to make a lot of money? Or be really powerful? Will I get married and have kids?* Never mind all that. He went back to his initial idea. "I want to see the world. Period."

He stopped, closed his eyes, and thought about what his desire meant. Sometimes his parents would talk about the big actions they'd been a part of in their youth, protesting the Vietnam War. Listening to their stories, Gabe regretted that his particular end of twentieth-century existence was so unremarkable. What was the big passion of this decade? The media had trumped up the 1990s as some sort of second coming of the 1960s, but so far, Kurt Cobain had died too young and that was about it for profound generational experiences. But he wanted to believe that it was still on its way, rocketing in from a distance so that it'd hit with even more force. There had to be more to define his adulthood than his career, or spouse, or what car he drove.

Not that he didn't understand the desire to buy beautiful stuff. Sliding into a slick car—the smell of expensive leather almost obscenely pungent, sexual—could do wonders for some men, he'd noticed. Take his friend Mike's dad, Mr. Streeter, and his new state-of-the-art SUV. On a smoldering day last summer, he asked Gabe—not his son, who'd presumably already seen the show—to sit in the passenger seat while they were parked in the driveway. Mr. Streeter's large hand dangled over the wheel, while the other one turned the ignition. In his starched white shirt, he turned to Gabe, with bug eyes and a sweaty brow, but somehow still meticulous in his appearance.

"I want you to put your hand in front of that vent," he instructed.

Mr. Streeter cranked the A/C, and within a startling amount of seconds, Gabe's fingers curled against an arctic blast.

"Do you feel that?"

Gabe nodded.

"That's a new kind of air-conditioning system they've never put in cars before."

Gabe didn't know what to say, but he nodded again, afraid to pull his hand away from the vent, though it was getting uncomfortable. Mr. Streeter angled his body more toward Gabe. "You, your hand, are the lucky recipient of one of our world's best innovations."

Gabe nodded again, his hand paralyzed before the freezing A/C with Mr. Streeter still waiting for a suitable reaction. Gabe got the feeling that their conversation might take an intense turn. Were they even talking about air-conditioning? Because it felt like something else, like any minute now Mr. Streeter would reveal to him how to fuck women, not girls, or how to make a billion dollars all while thwarting regular tax law, or how to kill powerful people who'd trained themselves to sleep with their eyes open.

As much as Gabe was grossed out, he also wanted the comfort, the luxury, and, maybe most of all, the uncomplicated entitlement so absent from his own dad. Mr. Streeter turned on the A/C without a thought, confident that he *deserved* the best A/C the world had ever known. What would that be like?

"Hey, weirdo," he heard his sister say, "what are you up to down there?"

He jumped a little bit and opened his eyes. She stood under the willow tree, tucked into a navy-blue peacoat.

"Just thinking about the kind of car I'm going to drive when I'm a yuppie."

"Oh, I already know. Silver Jaguar."

"Is that the only fancy car you know?"

"No, it's simply the best one."

He got up to follow her into the kitchen and couldn't help but notice that, at some point, the spaceship's panel had completely closed. How had he missed that? Did it happen while he and Alison chatted for all of two seconds? The panel hadn't made a sound or else he definitely would've noticed. He took one last snapshot of the underside, seamless once again.

In the kitchen, Ernest stood with his jacket still on and a wild look in his eyes. In his hands, a black device resembling a large remote control but with fewer buttons. At the top, a measurement display with a needle sitting in the lower range.

"See this?"

His children nodded.

"It's an EMF meter, used to measure the electromagnetic fields in your house. I've been reading a few articles lately about people with electro-sensitivity, people who get sick from electromagnetic waves that might not bother the rest of us."

"Wait, did you say an EMF meter?" Alison asked.

"Yes."

She and Gabe looked at each other and then burst into laughter.

"What's so funny?"

"That's the tool they use on *Ghost Chaser* to see if there are spooky spirits in the room," Gabe said, launching into a fright-fest voice: "Ooh, spoooooky spirits, come out, come out wherever you are!"

"Of course that silly show would use it in some BS fashion, but this is actually a real tool used by real scientists," Ernest snapped.

"Where'd you get that thing, Dad?" Alison said. "Did it come with a whole ghost-hunter kit?"

"Ha, ha," Ernest said. "Are you guys getting ready for your show at the Yuk Yuk Factory tonight? I bought it at Becker's Electronics, no other supplies necessary. Now I want you guys to walk around with me to see where these fields are the greatest. You're going to see why I keep most of these appliances unplugged when they're not in use."

Ernest stepped toward the toaster, plugged it in, and waved the tool over the appliance. The needle jumped up a bit—"OK," he said, "not bad"—and then he wandered over to the refrigerator, the tool leading the way. "Oooh," he said, "see that? Big jump. Still in the safe range, though."

"Dad," Alison said after they'd measured a few other appliances, including the suspicious microwave, which rated surprisingly low, "I don't get it. Do you really believe the toaster or whatever is, like, killing us or making us sick? Making Mom sick?"

"With satellites and so many appliances, we have more currents and waves around us than ever. Who knows what they're really doing?"

"But it's something that made Mom sick?"

"Electro-smog. A crowding of waves that pound against our bodies and break down DNA and mess with our immune systems."

The kids stayed quiet. Ernest's words were edged with a desperation that wasn't usually there.

"Is Mom still asleep?" Alison asked. "Does she think she's sick from electro-smog?"

"Let's not bother her with this whole thing." Ernest waved toward the back door.

They went outside, where Ernest set up the ladder underneath the spaceship and waved the tool around its underside.

"Right underneath the ship I get twenty-five hundred microteslas. Pretty major juice, considering the fridge was a tiny fraction of that. You writing this down, Gabe?"

"Yep."

THE ACTIVITIES OF THE UNWELCOME VISITORS
FROM JUPITER: AN ALLEN FAMILY LOG

December 9: *We're out here in the painful cold with the sun going down at its hideously early time writing down measurements for the spaceship's ghost factor. Turns out it's a ghoul from some kind of space-crypt! Measuring 2,500 in ghost-wave nuggets! Lock your doors, everyone, though ghosts don't really give a shit about things like locks.* —Ghost Hunter Allen

December 9: *OK, clearly we need to have another talk about responsible logging. Your wisecracking is distracting us from the real task at hand. So let me be the man to correct the record. At 4:30 p.m., the EMF meter gave a reading of 2,500 microteslas near the lowest point of the spaceship's hull. EMF tests included all the regions of the spaceship reachable by ladder. I'm debating climbing to the top of the spaceship to test later in the evening when it subjects us all to its nightly show.* —EA

Later, at dinner:

"Don't do that, Ernest," Cynthia said. "Do not try to climb that spaceship."

Ernest, leaning into his plate, said, "It's just a matter of timing. Gabe will grab Tom's construction ladder and set it up, I'll run up to the top and measure, Alison will record the results, and then we've got it."

No matter how goofy the premise, Alison and Gabe thrilled to the idea of climbing the spaceship. Cynthia, on the other hand, wasn't convinced. She stabbed at the roasted chicken, the chemotherapy damage to her thinning hair more apparent under the dining room lights.

"Why bother? EMF measurements are useless."

"But wouldn't it be good to know?"

"You're going to risk your safety for a useless measurement? What if you fall off the ladder and break your neck?"

"I'm not going to fall off, for god's sake."

"There's never been a court case lost or won by EMFs, not even swayed probably."

Ernest mulled it over before countering. "Well, it's a burgeoning field. Data collecting can never do any harm."

"Mom, does that mean you're not worried about electro-smog?"

Cynthia glared at Ernest. "You told them about that silly term? Not really, Alison. You shouldn't be worried either."

Alison and Gabe had witnessed this type of argument before, but usually from a room away. Cynthia would battle Ernest with legal experience and current data, but Ernest would counter that the law made mistakes or ignored evidence until too late. Look at DDT, look at thalidomide.

Cynthia chewed a bit more on her food. "You can't do this, Ernest."

He laughed a little at the finality of her declaration. She didn't typically put her foot down; they didn't like setting ultimatums or hardline rules. "I don't understand why I shouldn't. I need to check—"

"Check what? You think you're the first person to check all this before?" Cynthia made air quotes around the word "check" and held them there as she kept talking. "We know it's been checked by the government, we know they've been declared safe. But you climbing up there, encouraging the kids with this bullshit—"

"I'm showing them the importance of collecting data," Ernest blurted out. "It's probably a more exciting science experiment than anything they're being taught in school."

"Science experiment? Is this a lab?"

"Cynthia—"

"Fine, do whatever you want," Cynthia said, flinging her fork onto the floor. "I'm half gone anyway, right?"

At first, Ernest's face froze in shock, his mouth open. But then he shook his head vehemently. "No, Cynthia," he said. "That's not what I was suggesting at all!"

The air thickened with Cynthia's brooding. The plate with its pushed-around food took the brunt of her stormy gaze. Cynthia's

ideas—that she was half gone, that her death was already a given—
had to be combatted or they threatened to solidify into something
immovable. But Ernest just sat there, stunned into inadequacy.
Alison looked at each parent, waiting for one of them to say the right
thing, anything. She looked frightened. So did Gabe. Cynthia saw
their faces and shook her head wearily. For them, crawling on the
spaceship was a crazy lark. Who cared what Ernest's motives were,
so long as they got to have fun right now? They had no idea what
would soon be coming their way.

Cynthia mumbled an apology and picked up her fork. Ernest
grabbed her hand as he saw her expression soften.

"Christ," she said. "Just be careful."

"Just so you know," Ernest said, "I'm not going to climb all the
way on top of it. I'm just going to get on the same level as the top
and wave the EMF meter around and see what I can get. The kids
and Tom will spot me."

Gabe, relieved the tension had broken, chimed in: "Don't worry,
Mom, nothing's going to happen. We won't let it happen."

His mother stared at him. "We have no control over anything.
Remember that."

Gabe waited for the warmth to return to his mother's eyes, but
instead she quickly averted her gaze and resumed eating, not to look
up again.

———

Later that night, the spaceship issued an unusually enthusiastic
concert—a tight series of vibrations and pops. "Let's go," Ernest
said, and the kids peeled out behind him, all of them clattering
down the stairs. Tom, waiting on alert, ran into the backyard too.
Quickly the men unfolded the ladder and all its extensions and laid
the metal rungs against the edge of the saucer. The ladder pulsed
with the spaceship's vibrations, but Tom solidly gripped it from one
side, while Gabe and Alison supported the other. Ernest climbed,
aware that Cynthia watched from an upstairs window. Through
his earplugs—a precaution, in case some deafening noise should

suddenly be emitted—he heard the chugging and the musical pops but also the sound of his own breath in his body, drawing in and drawing out. At the top of the ladder, he clung to the last rung as he outstretched his free arm and slowly waved the EMF meter. Through the flashing bright lights, he barely made out the dark glass of the dome. When he brought the tool back to his chest, he couldn't see it. He lowered himself by a rung and looked at the measurement again. He lowered another couple of rungs and looked again.

"Goddamnit!" he yelled, but his voice was lost in the ruckus.

THE ACTIVITIES OF THE UNWELCOME VISITORS FROM JUPITER: AN ALLEN FAMILY LOG

December 9: *Dad insists that the EMF meter was working fine before climbing the ladder, but once he was up there, waving it around, the power of the spaceship broke the meter. The needle got stuck, and now it just wiggles toward the high end no matter what you wave it in front of (microwave, Gabe, cat). Lesson learned from test: don't use the same tools they use on* Ghost Chaser; *they never find ghosts either. —AA*

December 9: *Highly confused by what exactly occurred while I was at the top of the ladder. My eyes were dazed by the powerful spaceship lights, so I can't be certain of this, but I thought I saw the needle push to the high end very distinctly and then possibly, because of the force of what was coming from the spaceship, the tool was hyperstimulated beyond its capacities. I quickly scaled down and ran a series of tests on the meter, but it no longer responded with accurate readings or any reading at all. As Alison wrote (though I'd like to point out that her personal commentary was unnecessary), the needle stayed more or less fixed at the high end. Will return to Becker's tomorrow. Will also call New World and ask if they have typical EMF measurements on file for the spaceships. —EA*

December 9: *Let me, Gabriel Reed Allen, be the one to keep this notebook organized. What happened to just logging the basics, guys? The facts:*

At 9:45 p.m., the spaceship launched into approximately 10 minutes of vibrating, light grinding, and mechanical popping sounds. In other words, its usual thing, but it cycled through the sounds a little faster than usual. It seemed excited. Maybe it knew we were going to measure it? —GA

December 9: *If what Dad's saying is true, about the spaceship blowing electro-smog all over the place, then I'd like to move out of my bedroom right now. Or at least move into the guest bedroom, which is just a dumping ground for Mom and Dad's files anyway. Mom, what do you think? Gabe, in case you're getting any ideas, I thought of it first, I call dibs.* —AA

December 9: *I don't care, Alison. You can have that sorry room filled with newspaper clippings from the 1970s. Remember, I don't believe in electro-dust polluting my brain.* —GA

<hr>

"Do you want to write something in here, Mom?" Alison held up the log.

Cynthia was in the den, watching TV at an exceptionally low volume. She didn't bother to look over, her head resting in her hand, her elbow on the couch arm. "Tomorrow, maybe." Then back to the TV. The dialogue of two characters, chatting in a coffee shop with oversized purple mugs in their hands, was unintelligible except for their cheery tones and the laugh track.

"Mom, I asked you a direct question in my entry," Alison said. "You have to respond or else I'll just assume yes."

"Assume yes then."

"So I can move into the guest bedroom?" Alison's giddy voice was so manufactured, even she felt embarrassed by it.

Her mother shrugged. She wasn't buying any of it.

Alison plodded ahead. "You should really read the last few entries. Have you been keeping track at all?"

"Alison, not now, OK?"

"But we're all doing it. You should be part of it too."

"It's not a game," Cynthia snapped, then she sighed and rubbed her forehead. "For him, it's an obsession."

"Dad?"

"It's not a joke," Cynthia said. Her moods shifted more often like this now—temperamental flashes cracking through the dark firmament. Sometimes they passed within minutes; sometimes they lasted for days.

"I'm sorry, Mom," Alison said, though she was unsure exactly what she was apologizing for. "Do you want a cup of tea?"

"No, thanks, sweetie."

Her mom said the words kindly, but there was something in her tone that didn't beckon a conversation. Without moving or leaving the room, Alison suddenly realized that Cynthia had left her alone.

25

The room where Cynthia had received chemo for the last few weeks was devoid of any discernible purpose. Decoration and furniture, minimal: nothing but a very comfortable reclining bed, an IV stand, and miles of wall, covered in creamy, textured wallpaper, the kind resistant to the agonized scratches from someone's nails, Cynthia imagined.

"You're looking good today, young lady. How's it going?" Her nurse Dia greeted her with an embarrassing (but also comforting) level of enthusiasm. She was the only person left who complimented her on her haggard looks, besides Ernest.

"Oh, you know, just getting some chemo," Cynthia said. "The way I spend my Mondays now. And all my other days."

"Nothing like it, right? How have you been taking it?"

Cynthia pointed to her right eye, the corner aggravated by a sty. "My eye isn't happy."

"Oh," Dia murmured, looking at the inflamed sore closely. "Let's get you a script for that. What about naps?"

"Every day."

"Good," Dia sang as she hooked her up to an IV. Within a minute, subzero cold pumped into her veins. This was always the worst part, but she tried not to complain about the chill anymore. Acknowledging made it worse; crying out made it unbearable. The entry spot in the center vein of her hand furiously itched. The nurse sat next to her in a padded chair.

"Do you want to look at magazines, or should I stay in here with you?"

"How about both?"

Dia handed her old copies of *People* and *Vogue* and settled in herself with a book with a haunted estate on the cover. Cynthia tried to focus on an article about a celebrity's third divorce, but her internal temperature descended. Her teeth locked together; lukewarm clam flesh took over for her tongue. Dia helped Cynthia crawl under the bedcovers, which didn't offer warmth right away, just a heavier version of cold. Cynthia concentrated on generating heat from some internal hollow. For distraction, she asked the nurse about her kids. Dia chatted easily, telling Cynthia about Jason's college applications and Lorell's new baby.

"Tell me again: What exactly is in there?" Cynthia pointed to the draining bag. She liked to hear Dia explain things.

"The chemo? Well, it's a cocktail," Dia explained. "It's got cisplatin—that impairs cell function. Mercaptopurine—that stops cellular development and division—"

"Are all the chemicals lab compounds of some kind?"

"Well, yes, but some of the ingredients come from plants. There's something called vincristine—that comes from the Madagascar periwinkle—and another med called Taxol, which comes from the Pacific yew."

"Wow, a yew tree is pouring into my veins. Whoever thought?"

"Well, it's even stranger because it's actually poisonous to cells. But for what we're doing, that's a good thing."

Dia winked, which Cynthia found strange, but then again, Dia dealt with cancer every day. No need to be reverent anymore. She could wink, sashay, and croon about it.

After the clear liquid ran out, a new red fluid that didn't feel like much of anything at all poured in.

Dia removed her IV. "Where's Ernest? Is he coming to pick you up today?"

"No, he's off playing lawyer."

Dia laughed. "What does that mean?"

"Well, he's trying to get rid of our spaceship, so he's drafting an injunction."

"Aren't you a lawyer?"

"Yes, but I've refused to take on that particular case."

"Well, you can tell that ship to come to our house. My kids would love me forever."

"I don't expect him to get too far with the injunction. He'd have to get a court to sign off that the spaceship is trespassing. But it's making him feel good, so—"

"And what about you? Is it making you feel good, what he's doing?"

"At this very moment," Cynthia said, "I'd just settle for a husband who likes to watch movies with his sick wife."

Ernest and Marilyn were talking just about every day on the phone, discussing the spaceship, Cynthia's cancer, whatever else blew into their thoughts, but always under the auspices that they were like-minded people plotting out the logistics of an investigation. He always called her, every day chipping away a little more at her professionalism and her natural reserve. The conversations kept getting a little longer. He hadn't seen her since Morgan's.

"When I called New World," Ernest said, "they claimed the EMF load is really no worse than having a telephone pole in your backyard."

"That's not exactly reassuring to some people. There have been some interesting legal cases involving cancer and power lines. But nobody can ever make it stick that a high EMF gave someone cancer."

"Not yet, maybe."

"Well, it would be in no one's interest to have poisonous spaceships visit American homes—think of the lawsuits, think of the terrible press written by people like me."

"Whatever I find, you'll be the first to know so you can write your Pulitzer Prize–winning exposé."

"Fantastic," she said. "That's the dream." Ernest could hear her closing her office door. "I need an award if I'm ever going to leave this shitty newspaper."

"You can go wherever you want," he said. "You're the best environmental reporter in Chicago."

"I think you mean the only."

"Exactly. You've got it locked."

"Well, I hope so. Anyway, what's the latest with the samples?"

"In Toronto right now."

"Canada, that's good. They'll test for stuff an American lab would dismiss."

"I hope so—and once I have firm evidence, that should make the injunction easy to back. The problem is that the tests are expensive. When Cynthia sees that a few thousand dollars are missing from our account, I'm going to have to explain."

"Good luck with that," Marilyn said. "See, that's exactly why my husband and I have separate accounts."

Ernest didn't know what to say. Long ago Cynthia and he had merged all funds, though Cynthia was far more involved in managing them. Ernest's income was erratic and less than hers; he didn't like to think about their arrangement too much.

"I should get going, Ernest, but we've got to get you interviewed about Earth Day. What's the latest?"

"Oh, it's just great. Our blowout might even top the city's. Just wait till you hear the band lineup. We have some major surprises in store."

"But you'll share them with me?"

"Only if you can keep a secret until the right time."

"You have my word."

After three weeks of chemo, Cynthia's hair fell out, as presaged by the pamphlet with washed-out illustrations of the suffering patient. First, she pulled out strands that clung to the shower walls, then clumps that couldn't be nudged down the drain with her toe. Bent over, she'd collect the blond hair in her fingers, the water pounding her back and her skull, leaving her to wonder if the water pressure, even at the weak level Ernest insisted on, could pound off more.

On a school night, she let Alison and Gabe shave off her hair in the kitchen, while Ernest busied himself with a complicated marinade. When he wasn't looming around the spaceship (which was thankfully quiet at the moment, on its best behavior this evening) or organizing his test bottles, he threw himself into making an infused-with-something sauce, or overseeing an all-day roast, or pickling. As he stirred tonight's distraction, he drank beer after beer. He chopped and diced piles of cilantro and garlic into near oblivion. The *rat-tat-tat* of the knife made a harsh music with the electric razor taking off the part of his wife he associated most with her: her hair. First, the kids shaped her straggly long bob into a Mohawk. Well, more like a sad flap of hair covering one side of her head, but with a little squinting, she could pass for a skater. Gabe documented her transformation with his Pentax until he felt self-consciously macabre.

But Cynthia insisted. "Take more pictures! This is the side of my personality that never comes out anymore."

Cynthia's mood was buoyant. She couldn't explain it, but chopping off her hair felt like she was switching identities, trading in softness for something more radical. Everyone played along.

"Are we going to hear another story about your wild days?" Alison asked. "Mom, what's the craziest thing you've ever done?"

"Ernest, should I tell them?"

"About the monkeys?"

"About the monkeys." Cynthia paused and roughly eyed them both. "Well, I was almost arrested once."

The kids blinked.

"Arrested?" Gabe said. "Because of monkeys?"

"Just listen. My sophomore year of college, right before I met your dad, I had a big crush on another student—"

"This is the bad part of the story," Ernest yelled from the stove. "When your mother lost her mind and thought some other man could fulfill her."

"Hush up. I didn't even know your dad. Anyway, we were dating, this guy and me, but he was never all that impressed with me. I wasn't serious enough. He was into animal liberation."

"Animal liberation?" Gabe snickered a little. "Was he breaking gorillas out of the zoo, or what?"

"Ever seen the cages they keep veal in?" Alison snapped.

"Whatever."

"Listen to me for once, you little chatterboxes. Jail is exactly how this guy Laird talked about it," Cynthia said. "'All the test animals are living in a prison.' He wanted to free these test monkeys from the medical school. It was common knowledge that about twenty monkeys were housed in the building, and he plotted this great big escape plan for them. But he wasn't just going to unlock their cages and be done with it; he wanted to smuggle them off to a farm nearby that had agreed to take them in. And he asked me if I'd borrow my father's truck to help transport them."

"What your mother's trying to say is that she drove the getaway car."

"OK, that is seriously cool," Alison said. "Please tell me you wore a black ski mask."

"No, but the whole thing was really freaky. Laird and another guy went in there and came out with maybe five or seven cages. He and the other guy were loading them in the truck. The monkeys were screaming and completely panicked. And I couldn't even get off of campus with them." Cynthia recalled that it was three in the morning, some desperate hour. Within minutes, security guards surrounded the truck, shining flashlights at Cynthia and the monkeys, who became more agitated. "I tried to make up something at first, but there was no denying what I was trying to do. But luckily they felt sorry for me."

"Where was Laird?" Gabe asked.

"He'd gone back in, and by this time, I was on the other side of the campus. The cops were coming for Laird. I could hear the reports coming in on their walkie-talkies. The security guards asked me to wait, said the cops were coming to arrest me too, and that's when I drove right over the cones and hightailed it out of there."

"What? Mom, you're a stone-cold criminal!" Alison said.

"Let's arrest her now!" Gabe said. "Citizen's arrest! What's the statute of limitations for monkey thievery?"

"I'm telling you," Cynthia said, a glint in her eye, "you think you know me but you don't. I drove those monkeys to the farm, using these crazy back roads I knew from Gramps all the way. I was constantly looking over my shoulder. But it's like the monkeys knew—after all that screaming, they stayed quiet till I got there."

"Do you think they really knew, Mom?" Alison asked.

"I'd like to think so. They knew they were on their way to something better. I managed to smuggle seven monkeys to freedom, and because those security guards never wrote down my plates or my name, I got away."

"Amazing," Alison said. "That's the best story I've ever heard. Why didn't you ever tell us before?"

"I don't know, you weren't old enough, I guess."

"Did you ever do something like that again?"

"Not like that. I became a courtroom gladiator in nude pantyhose." Cynthia pulled on her rooster hair and laughed. "OK, I think it might be time to shed the last vestige of my rebellious youth."

"No, keep it," Gabe said.

"If you keep your hair this way now, Mom," Alison said, "you're forever that way."

"It's OK," Cynthia said, closing her eyes. "I'm ready."

Gabe watched his mother's tiny Adam's apple bob a little in her throat as she leaned back, her lips pursed. Reluctantly, he turned the razor back on.

Later, at 11:40 P.M., he caught *The Book of Connections*. He'd moved the radio back downstairs because Alison wanted to hear it too. They lay on the rug together, the transmission close to their ears.

"I've been thinking about electricity," the woman said. "The moment you plug into a wall socket, you're plugged into the network. You've touched into the higher power of an interconnected system: sockets, plugs, currents, power lines, the electromagnetic field, the always-buzzing grid. If you've ever been shocked by electricity, then you directly understand the importance of keeping within the right boundaries of this power. Don't cross electricity. She'll fry you."

Ernest hesitated for a spell as he walked by on his way up to bed. "That's funny," he said. "She mentioned the electromagnetic field? So soon after our EMF tests?"

Gabe shrugged.

Ernest stayed in the doorframe for a minute. "Are you recording this?"

Gabe nodded.

"Good, I want to hear it later." Ernest continued on his way upstairs.

———————

Cynthia couldn't stop touching her newly shorn scalp. She was exhausted from her hair makeover, but wired. Tonight, she'd been initiated as an official member of the cancer brigade, but for some reason, it fired up her hope. She would cross through this miserable passage and exit victorious on the other side. Maybe with her hair singed off from chemicals and her body a new kind of flesh pulsing with radiation, she'd come through. She'd transform into a phoenix with ashen wings and fly back into her life, wise and seeing her territory anew. Ernest came in, interrupting the trajectory of her determination.

"Not bad," he said, pointing to her hair, or lack thereof. He set a small wrapped box in her lap.

"What's this?" she said, opening it. Inside, a soft lavender knit cap, mohair, with flecks of other colors. "Thank you, this is so beautiful." She pulled it on. "So warm; it's perfect."

He smiled, and she could smell his beery breath.

"Ernest, I've been thinking," Cynthia said after a minute, "I know I've been surrendering to the darkness lately, but I'm ready to beat this thing. I'm ready to live."

She glowed at him. He grabbed her hand.

"Let's make a deal," Ernest said, "you attack the cancer and I'll attack the spaceship. Then we'll all live happily ever after."

She withdrew her hand and adjusted the new hat. The lavender knit rolled up near her ear lobes, outfitted with copper studs.

"Well, that's not exactly—you understand that the cancer is my own cells, right?"

"Yes, but what does—"

"I'm uncomfortable with 'attacking cancer' because in the end it's only my own body. It's not something else."

"You just said 'beat this thing.'"

"It's an expression."

"Let's not get hung up on semantics," he said, lightly enough, sensing the precariousness of their conversation, feeling himself teetering on the ledge of something familiar, unpleasant.

"The spaceship—did you have to bring it up? It's enemy number one now?"

"The spaceship isn't *human*, Cynthia. It's an *intruder*. It's from *outer space*. An *alien*. We're supposed to attack stuff like it," Ernest said a little wildly. "It's unnatural for us to just sit around and be friends with it."

"According to who?"

"According to every alien movie ever made."

"Do you take all your cues from alien movies?"

"We're never friends with them. They're not our benevolent neighbors. We're not going to toast eggnog glasses with them for the holidays."

"Why am I arguing with somebody who's just polished off a six-pack?"

"Jesus. Why do you do that, Cynthia? You discredit me almost for sport."

"What kind of foreign policy is that anyway, Ernest? Who have you been talking to about this spaceship—Henry Kissinger?"

"Hey, come on now. Ronald Reagan, of all people, embraced them. That's reason enough to be suspicious."

"Give it up, Ernest."

"I was kidding around about that," Ernest defended himself, even as guilt about his clandestine phone calls with Marilyn tweaked his chest. "Just trying to find some solidarity with you. Foreign policy? Christ!"

She studied him sullenly.

"I was trying to make a point, Cynthia. I want to show the kids that this is how we answer a challenge. If we have to fight cancer, we should also fight the thing that caused it."

"That caused it? It's not the spaceship, it's my shitty genes."

"Jesus, Cynthia . . ." He trailed off. "I'm trying to fight for you. Don't you want that?"

"You're not fighting for me. You're fighting for you." She was looking at him, her chin imperiously tilted up. The courtly superiority she could bring to their arguments had always killed him.

"Can you say this without the self-righteousness?"

"Fighting," she said, "doesn't always have to be about opposition. It doesn't always have to be about sides or blame. Sometimes fighting is about lying down. Not giving up but knowing when to accept."

"You can accept something and still want answers."

"What if you never get them? Or what if you get them but they only open up more questions you have no answers for?"

"Do you really want the kids to see that you had no questions about what made you sick? Just no curiosity at all? You get cancer and what? That's it?"

Tears were running down her face now as she turned back to stare at him, all of her energy and enthusiasm draining from her. "Do I look like I don't care?"

"Cynthia," Ernest said, reaching for her hand.

She sobbed.

He shook his head. "I don't know what this is, Cynthia. Why we're fighting like this."

She saw a choice—she could either push her point or she could let it go for now. He didn't seem to understand what she really needed from him. Not a hero, not a vigilante, but a listener, a soother. Ernest had always been obsessed with fixing problems, using direct action, attacking the issue.

Ernest wrapped himself around Cynthia—and she let him lean into her—but an essential warmth was missing. He grasped for it anyway.

26

At the Prairie Park Village Hall, Ernest carried his injunction that he'd drafted from studying some of Cynthia's old forms. Reluctantly she had agreed to polish the last draft. The injunction specifically stated that New World must remove the alien ship, a trespasser on the Allens' property, within the next six weeks. Ernest hoped that the township of Prairie Park would support the injunction and throw some of its weight behind it. He also hoped that his connections as the director of Earth Day might get him somewhere. Through Jean's assistance, he'd gotten an appointment with the head of community building, a woman named Diane Albero. Located at the Village Hall, getting to her office took Ernest several zigzags down a long hall decorated with silvered photos of late nineteenth-century Prairie Park.

At the front of office 270B, a woman in her late twenties perched at the secretary station. A cigarette fumigated in languid curls from the ashtray on her desk. An IBM with green LED blinked behind her. One open drawer of a tall avocado-green file cabinet showed a bulge of white, pink, and yellow papers. A window at the end of the small room showed clouds and a few bare tree branches crawling up the sky.

"I'd like to file a document with the Village of Prairie Park."

"And what's this document concerning?"

Her cigarette smoke wafted directly into his eyes, so he stood at an angle, antisocially tilted away from her. She gave him a strange look.

"It's regarding a certain presence I'd like to leave."

She blinked at him for a moment before something clicked in her eyes. "Oh, this is concerning the alien visitation, right?"

She told him to have a seat, excitement bubbling in her voice. He deposited himself into an orange scoop chair right across from her desk. She took a drag off her cigarette and sumptuously exhaled, which Ernest greeted with a cough. He coughed, wiggled, and slightly waved his hand over the next several minutes, but she blithely puffed on. To still have a smoking office in 1994 was enough of a shock, but to smoke while a stranger sat in there waiting? He struggled to keep his mouth shut, in case he should need this young woman's assistance. She stood up to file papers and Ernest noted her outfit—a baby-doll plaid dress over black tights—and thought it was something Alison might wear. This smoking secretary, he realized, wasn't that much older than his daughter. Probably still in college.

Ernest waited in the smoky room for twenty-three minutes, timing it on his calculator watch.

"Is she coming back soon?"

"One of her meetings must've run over."

To Ernest's horror, she grabbed her pack from the desk, plucked out another stick and lit it.

"Can I wait in the hallway?"

She frowned at him. "She should be here any moment now."

"Well, then would you mind putting out your cigarette?"

She sucked in a gigantic inhale and puffed it back out. "Fine," she said, crushing it out in the ashtray.

A new heaviness settled in the air as the secretary went about the same tasks as before, but with the occasional hostile look at Ernest. Eventually her looks softened into something like empathy, or just a desire to break the boredom with conversation.

"I think those alien ships are kind of trashy," she offered.

"Agreed. I never wanted it," he said.

"It's like when you go downstate and everyone's got those cheap pools in their backyards, instead of the nice in-ground ones." She started to clack away on the IBM, then stopped. "Or," she said, whirling around again, "like those people who leave Christmas decorations up all year. Don't you hate those people?"

"Hate's a strong word," he said.

Finally Diane Albero entered. She looked both smarter and more disheveled than he'd expected.

"Cari, you've been smoking in here again? Jesus, open a window," Diane said, before waving Ernest into her office. As she sat behind her desk, her wrinkled hands folded over her ink blotter, Ernest explained why she should support the injunction. He focused mainly on how the spaceship was an obnoxious, littering presence at a difficult time for the family. She listened with scrutinizing crow-like eyes, saying nothing till he finished.

"You say it's polluting the environment?"

"Absolutely," he said. "It's been regularly dumping this toxic green sludge—"

"How do you know it's toxic? It's my understanding that the ships are thoroughly vetted and completely safe for humans to be around."

"I'm uncomfortable with the materials it's dumping."

"Have you had them tested?"

"They're off at a lab right now, along with soil from below the spaceship where the waste is absorbed."

"Why didn't you wait for the results? That would make your claim much stronger."

"Because I wanted to get this in motion before the holidays. You can understand my situation, I think. With a sick wife, I have a lot on my plate. I want to get this resolved as soon as possible."

"I understand, but the sweepstakes rules are fairly binding. When you sign up for something like this, you are signing a contract. You need to give me a reason to get involved with this."

"I think I've given you several."

"But they're not unusual or pressing for Prairie Park as a whole. Have you asked New World to take it back?"

"Of course. It's all in the injunction."

"Have you ever thought that maybe they can't? Maybe once a ship has arrived at its destination, it's there for the duration. I just want you to think about this. You might be asking for something that's impossible. Maybe the notion of 'uninviting' somebody isn't in the alien lexicon. Let me ask you something: Are you from here?"

"Prairie Park? Not exactly. I grew up in the city near the industrial hellhole known as the Stockyards."

"That's where I grew up," she said, striking the first tone of warmth.

They traded their addresses and realized they'd been raised scant blocks from each other. This, he acknowledged to himself, would not help his cause. She was a hard-nosed South Sider, no bullshit, facts and figures only or get the hell outta here. Like Ernest's dad, who died of lung cancer, yet never blamed the factories for his illness because he didn't want to be "one of those whiners."

"Listen," she said, "obviously I'm much older than you so we didn't cross paths, but I wanted a better life for myself too." Diane paused, clearly switching into speechifying mode. "I wanted to move to Prairie Park because I believed in the ideals. I believed in the promise of a village that nurtures its residents. Prairie Park isn't a suburb—we don't like to call it that, too much baggage. It's a *green village* that offers all the resources of a big city but without the crime, the overpopulation, or the pollution. So if you can tell me that the spaceship is definitively polluting your environs, then we have something here. But I need to see something definitive."

"So you need those test results."

"When you get the results, fax them to my office and we'll see what we can do."

She rose from her desk to show him the door. As he was leaving, he spotted a framed photograph of an old lady standing on a sidewalk, outfitted in a snazzy mod pantsuit, with her white hair in a beehive.

"Isn't that Catharine the Walker?"

"She's my dear old aunt," Diane replied. "Walks Prairie Park from north to south, east to west, every day."

"She's your aunt? My wife chats with her all the time; they crisscross each other on walks."

"She knows everyone. I wish she'd write a book about her life, but she's too busy painting. She went to art school in the forties. She paints and she walks, that's how she spends her days."

"Good life," Ernest said. A silence followed, and Ernest seized the moment to thank Diane Albero for her time.

THE ACTIVITIES OF THE UNWELCOME VISITORS
FROM JUPITER: AN ALLEN FAMILY LOG

December 18: *I don't know what the deal is, but I've noticed the spaceship speeding up during its evening show. The vibrating and pops and gyrating and little whistles—like it's on speed or something. It goes through them reallllly fast. This has been the case for the last three nights, but I didn't really put my finger on it till tonight. Alison, you're the resident pill popper around here: Are you feeding it uppers?* —GA

December 18: *Remember, I've been banned from my beloved Advils. But yeah, I've noticed the same thing. Plus, the ship also does this thing after the shows where it plays dead. Like, possum style. There's no movement, no low hum or vibration, nothing. And then it starts up again. Super weird.* —AA

December 18: *GA, what do you know about speed?* —CA

―――――◆―――――

A few days after meeting with Diane Albero, Ernest got the test results, but for the pretty penny he'd spent, they yielded very little. The soil: normal. The green sludge: comprising chemicals found in a variety of household products and not at excess levels. No smoking guns; no signs of foul subterfuge on a molecular level. The only slightly unusual result, the lab report explained, was a trace amount of tar creosote in the soil. But it wasn't enough to register as ecotoxicity; it was barely worth mentioning.

Ernest faxed the results to Diane's office, including the chemist's signed report that all results fell clearly within the safe range and were not a cause for alarm. He also sent a letter, per Marilyn's suggestion, stating that though the spaceship wasn't measurably toxic, it had proven a great disturbance to his gravely ill wife. "All you have left now," Marilyn advised, "is the emotional plea." The spaceship should be regarded as a trespasser, Ernest wrote, because it was disrupting Cynthia's rest.

"Did you spend three thousand two hundred and fifty dollars at a place called the Environmental Testing Lab?" Cynthia stood over him in the kitchen, clutching a raft of paperwork. The kids were at school; in their absence Cynthia spoke with an immediate rage Ernest wasn't accustomed to.

"Yes. I got the soil and the green waste tested. You knew I was collecting samples." Quickly, Ernest moved from defensive to defiant. "What did you think was happening?"

"I guess I did, but I didn't think you'd blow this kind of money on it. So what came up? What did our three thousand two hundred and fifty dollars get us?"

The coffee cup he fiddled with wasn't going to save him. "Nothing came up, OK?"

"Nothing at all? It's not Chernobyl out there?"

"Just because nothing came up doesn't mean I was wrong to do it."

"Usually we discuss these kinds of expenses with each other. We don't just spend three thousand two hundred and fifty dollars willy-nilly when hospital bills are pouring in."

"Well, I had to do it."

The papers shook in Cynthia's hand, the red pokes from the IV needle inflamed on her vein. "Oh really? Does this mean that you'll back off of it now? Is this obsession over, now that you have no evidence for your theories at all?"

He composed a careful response: "I'm still keeping my eye on it."

"Great! Because that's what we need right now, is hypervigilance on the spaceship. Goddamn it, Ernest!" Cynthia paced the kitchen, gripping her forehead. "I have reasons to worry here."

"About the spaceship?"

"Hello, one-track mind, will you listen? I'm talking about you. Something is happening. You're getting obsessed in a way that's not healthy, that reminds me of Wisconsin," she said, referencing their primitive home when they first married. "Remember how you wouldn't let it go? Wouldn't let go of your fevered nature-boy dreams of living off the grid? Of homesteading? Thank god my parents left us money or we'd probably still be there, trying to live off of a cup of syrup a week from the maple tree."

"Cynthia, we were different people then."

"I see the same pattern, the same look in your eye."

He tossed up his hands. "Apples and oranges. Flying saucers and homesteading."

A calm settled into Cynthia's rage, which signaled to Ernest that something big was about to come. "I've been talking to Stephen about money lately."

"When have you been in to work? And why on earth have you been talking to your boss about our money?"

"Because he's smart, and we've known each other for years. Here's what I'm thinking: the inheritance I got from my parents, I'm considering leaving it in two trusts for the kids."

Ernest shot up from the table, a movement that was an excuse to do something while the shock ricocheted throughout his system. "If you do that, Cynthia, I'll have next to nothing myself."

"That's not true. You'll have the house," she said. "And your own money," she added.

"The house? But none of the liquid savings in our account, our joint account? It's not like it's all yours, you know. I know you put in the lion's share, but . . ." Ernest shook his head almost violently. "Ugh, what are we actually talking about right now? You think I'm not mentally fit to entrust with money? Is that what you're telling me?"

"It's like you're totally frugal until you lock on some crazy idea or scheme. Remember the Salvo geo-dome? What the hell happened there? We spent thousands on that stupid thing, all the tools, and it's now collecting dust in the garage. You didn't even resell it."

"So I'm being punished for the damn geo-dome? Except you're going to exact the punishment in postmortem?"

"I have to make sure they're taken care of before I go."

"What happened to wanting to live? What happened to that? Why are you talking like this?" Suddenly there were tears in Ernest's eyes.

Cynthia's shoulders slumped. She didn't look at him but at a spot to the side of his face.

"I'll let you know what I decide about the money," she said before she left the room.

Emboldened by their fight, Ernest made a quick call from the phone in the kitchen, while Cynthia was upstairs getting ready for her chemo appointment.

"What are you doing these days to take care of yourself?" Marilyn asked.

"What do you mean?"

"You know: fun, relaxation. Remember those things? When was the last time you went on a hike, for instance?"

"Months, I don't know."

"Well, let's meet at Shapley Woods at one P.M."

He balked; he was supposed to take Cynthia to chemotherapy. But Marilyn pressed: "You told me you can't be with her anyway, in the room with the meds. Tell her you need some exercise, she'll understand. You'll be back in an hour to pick her up and take her to a nice late lunch."

"No one can eat after chemo."

"Oh, right. Well, something else nice then."

27

By the time they trekked into the middle of the forest preserve, the sound of the highway had vanished except for a very low hum that could've been wind. Islands of untouched snow lay between the bare trees, like sleeping backs. One bird close to them cried out in sawing screeches over and over again. Relief persisted as best it could, but another part of him, most of him, was scratchy and unsatisfied. Was it the surroundings? The forest preserve was brown and scraggly from winter. Where there wasn't snow, there was brittle mud. Stray bits of litter decorated the path. A plastic shopping bag, crinkled and grimy, fluttered around a tree branch, but none of that was the problem either. He couldn't forget his self, which in this moment was a density, a high-pitched noise, nothing that could recede. Like fleas on a dog's coat, the self seethed in and out of the hairs, sometimes invisible but always sensed. He jogged off from Marilyn into the thickest patch he could find.

"Race you," he said.

She laughed. "Not a chance."

But he didn't slow down. The icy air scraped at his skin, urging him on.

"Should I try to find you?" she called out.

He found a bed of dead pine needles and stretched out on it. The vision of the hospital room where his wife lay as a white shadow, red liquid pumping into her veins, moved in quick as an ocean fog. The best he could do was to see less of it, to keep opening his eyes to the tangle of trees above him. Eventually he approached something that was as close as he could get to freedom, but he was still tense. Where was the simple course of his breath? Where was the *t-t-t-t-t-t-t-t-t-t-t-t-t*?

After a few minutes, he heard Marilyn thrash in after him.

"You're lucky I like you, Ernest. I don't run for anyone." He heard her footsteps stop near him and then her body crunch over the pine and lie beside his. "What's going on?"

"I'm here in the woods," he said, "and I thought I could chase down some kind of peace."

He heard her smile.

"Did it work?"

"A little bit."

"Ernest, what you're doing is brave." She found his hand and held it. "You're following your gut, which is what all people with a vision do. You're one of the few people legitimately questioning the spaceships anymore. Civilian people at least."

They sat up, blinking in the daylight, a smothering gray with wisps of white. They blinked at each other, newly aware. Marilyn was a live conduit, and he wanted to step into her charge. The flushed tone of her face, the glint in her eye that carried her specific blend of intelligence and perception—all of it twitched with life. They drew toward each other.

To feel someone else's lips is always fundamentally jarring. The shape that was neither his nor Cynthia's shocked him and then fascinated him. He didn't let it show in the actual kiss. The feeling— it wasn't desire exactly, this searing, goading insistence—but it was the first thing that had made him course and pulse in a long time, so he kept doing it. She responded too. Clothes were pushed and manipulated to make touching easier; the chilled wind quickly found their skin, but staying warm required only a state of mind. The kissing advanced from alien to familiarly alien, and then he was on top of her. But at the last minute, he pulled away and then rolled to the side.

"I know you have to get back," she said, staring straight into the sky.

He raked his hands through his hair, fixed his clothes, otherwise fidgeted. Softly he spoke: "What am I doing?"

Still on her back, she pinned her fingers over her closed eyes and exhaled. "I'm sorry, Ernest. If it's not already obvious, I haven't been happy in my marriage in a long time."

"I'm not blaming you."

"But you don't want to ...?" She trailed off.

"I didn't say I don't want to. I just don't think I can."

His revelation relieved him for a moment, as if he'd heard it spoken by some other, more authoritative person, but it was a temporary comfort. He was the man who could do it, that was the problem. He was that man because he'd let it get this far. He was that man because he wanted to reach out for more. They put their clothes back together in a silent stupor, occasionally daunting themselves by looking at the other. She walked at a distance from him as they left the woods, until he waited and then walked by her side.

The radio, tuned to wallpaper classical.

The single thing Cynthia said on their way home was "Mind if I turn this off?"

"Everything OK?"

She nodded.

"Almost Christmas. That'll be nice, won't it? I thought about going plastic this year, but they still haven't found a way to responsibly make a good fake tree. You know it's all petroleum and PVC."

He looked over and noticed her eyes were closed. He stopped talking. The car took on the same atmosphere as it did when he drove alone.

"I'll let you rest," he said. But he couldn't abide her silence for long.

"Should I have been waiting right outside the door when you came out? Is that what you're upset about?"

She didn't answer.

"OK, I'll just shut the hell up then."

Once at home, she remained aloof and avoided eye contact. Vacated, her body slumped in a kitchen chair. The lavender knit obscured the fragile skull.

"Do you want some tea? I picked up a bunch of new ones for you: chamomile, peppermint, rooibos—"

"Peppermint, please."

He rummaged for a cup while she occupied the other side of the room. As he moved, flashes of Marilyn beset him: twigs caught in her hair, the dirt of the forest floor on the back of her coat, his hand pushing aside her underwear. A low stab in his stomach hit as he poured hot water, a little splashing onto his hand. "Shit," he said, sucking on his burned thumb while he carried over the cup.

He set it down to no reaction. "OK, Cynthia, I can't take any more of this."

She nodded with a mournful blink and then said, "My five-week cycle of chemo is nearly up, and it's barely done a thing. I'm not going to go for another cycle. I've reached the end of the line."

He started to object.

"No, babe. Those were the doctor's words, not mine. I can't tell the kids."

After a moment, he said softly, "Get up."

They stood and then folded into each other, wrapping arms, stepping into it in such a way that her head craned and tilted onto his shoulder with the smooth, fluid motions of a dancer. This choreography came naturally after years of hugging the same person. Cynthia trusted him to keep her secret; he resolved to bury his own.

◆

Safe under the spaceship, where his dad wouldn't hear the radio and get all bothered, Gabe tuned in to *The Book of Connections*, listening on his headphones.

"Let me ask you a hard question: Are you religious?"

Gabe didn't know how to answer. Maybe the best answer was no, but he wasn't exactly an atheist either.

"Are you spiritual?"

Maybe? But then what was that anyway? Crystals and auras and mind reading? He did have a girl, Lacey, give him a tarot card reading one time. "Pull one," she said, and fanned a deck on the floor between them. They were at his friend's house after school, the parents gone. All the kids were off in corners, drinking one six-pack of Miller Lite between several of them, rationing it into red cups. He pulled and got the Knight of Wands, which Lacey said meant he was an "act first, think later" kind of guy. "You're passionate," she said, assessing him with newfound lust. He agreed to the description, if only to keep Lacey's low-cut dress in his vicinity. Nothing happened, of course. Nothing ever did.

"Sometimes I find myself in a church," the woman said. "But not out of accordance with my own beliefs. It's just a place I have ties to. Tis the season and all that. Sometime soon, I think, I ought to find a religion, or believe in something that feels just as authentic and powerful as God did to the fourteenth-century mystic Eckhart. He said you had to empty yourself to find God. Absolute stillness for as long as possible.

"Are you holding still right now? Let's try it for a minute together."

Gabe tried it. The shortwave fuzz simmered on as he held his limbs still on the ground, a sleeping bag underneath him for warmth. Did his chest rising with breath count? He tried to breathe shallowly, as if he were hiding and didn't want to give himself away. Was the point not to be found or seen by anyone, and then some sort of god poured in? When you were pretending to be dead?

"Did you feel anything?" Pause. "Me neither."

28

Five days before Christmas and the neighborhood glowed and blinked with holiday regalia, all of it wavering slightly under the pressure of maxed-out credit cards. One lawn on the block showcased a hand-carved wooden Santa and sleigh, the cedarwood procured at an eye-popping cost. Most houses opted for the classic white lights strewn on the trees, which would be forgotten till March. Parents hid away purchases in the remote closets of the house, some to be discreetly returned after the holidays.

Unlike most of their neighbors, Cynthia and Ernest eschewed the suburban mega-malls and shopped exclusively in Prairie Park. But none of those semi-floundering shops answered the kids' true desires: Alison wanted art supplies bought from the store across the street from the Art Institute downtown, or clothes from the Limited Express or the Gap. For Gabe, it was photo supplies, not bought from the "dork photo hut" in the mall but the sleek gallery-district loft where professionals stocked up.

Cynthia planned to get the kids what they really wanted, but a trip to the city was beyond her capabilities at this point. In fact, she barely made it to the Prairie Park bookstore, where she opted for $100 gift certificates, which would probably last them throughout high school. She'd never been the type to hand-curl silvery ribbons for every present, but she considered herself an astute gift-giver. Not this year—she had to submit to her illness before everything else. She left the envelopes under the "tree," which was really a life-size felt cutout the kids and Ernest had made ten or so years ago.

That night as they were shedding clothes for bed, she told Ernest that she felt disappointed about the gifts.

"Eh, there's far too much pressure on it all anyway," he said, his back to her as he took off his socks. "You shouldn't have gotten them anything. Certainly not a hundred bucks each."

"I'd never get them nothing, Ernest," she said, trying to keep her voice light. For the past day or so, they'd been trying to be more tender with each other. "How's the Earth Day stuff coming?" she asked.

"Brilliant. We've got big plans but it's all on hold right now."

"Really? Seems like it'd be gearing up."

"It will, after the holidays."

"What still needs to be done?"

"Plenty," he said, shoving his legs into the plaid flannel sheets and flipping away from her. "But it'll get done and done well. Now that we've got Demeter involved"—he heaved an annoyed sigh—"everything has to be shipshape."

"I'm sorry about Demeter. Is there anything I can help with?"

"No, you don't need to concern yourself with it."

"Surely there's something—"

"When it gets closer, I'm sure we'll need it, but right now, everyone's on the case."

"I'm not going to steal your thunder, if that's what you're worried about. I know this is your big masterpiece."

"Don't make fun of me," Ernest said.

"No, seriously, I could help with paperwork. I know no one ever likes to do that."

"Marcy's on it."

"I'll be around, you know. I'll still be here in April," Cynthia blurted out.

Ernest rolled over to face her. Around her head, the lavender knit cap. He had already forgotten what her old hair had looked like.

"In January, I'll put you to work, don't you worry." Ernest shimmied in the bed so that his head was in her lap. "In fact," he said, looking up at her, "never mind paperwork. I'll give you our most important task. Would you like to be the point person for the crazy guy who runs the pottery stand? Maybe you can explain to him why no one's interested in buying clay busts of his wife's breasts."

"Well, are they shapely? If so, they should be flying off the shelves."

"I know; it's a mystery. Or you know what? Here's another choice position: Want to be in charge of getting all the used grease out of the deep fryers?"

"There's nothing I love more than pouring hot oil into stinky grease traps. Anything else?"

"Let's wait to see what else plays into your skill sets."

———

Early on the morning of Christmas Eve, Cynthia and Ernest came down to the kitchen to discover that the spaceship had plugged itself into their house. After some investigation, they discovered that a long orange extension cord had, as if by magic, snaked out from its place in a box in the garage, slipped in between two folds of metal, and disappeared into the ship's guts. When it had first plugged in, no one knew, but it had happened sometime overnight. Exactly how was also a mystery.

"Was there a midnight escapade?" Ernest stormed around the kitchen while Cynthia shushed him. "How did they get out to plug it in—by ladder? By sliding down a big yellow inner tube? And why didn't we hear anything?"

Cynthia shrugged.

"Did the kids have anything to do with this?"

"Don't be ridiculous. Maybe the kids heard something, but I doubt it."

"Why plug in now? The ship has been sitting there for months, living off its own supply of energy, but now it's mooching from us—on Christmas. Great timing. The whole grid is already stressed with the Christmas lights. Maybe it's trying to shut down the whole neighborhood."

"OK, Ernest." She sighed. "What nefarious events are going on in there? You think some alien's huffing energy off of the power cord like some demented space trucker doing whippets out of an aerosol can?"

"If they're getting high, and not poisoning us, I'm relieved."

Ernest called the electricity company and asked it to check his meter. Within a couple of hours, the utility informed Ernest that his household's output had tripled in the last several hours.

"It's guzzling our electricity, Cynthia. I'm telling you, this is a new level."

"So unplug it."

Ernest and Cynthia stood in the weak morning sun, unsure of their next move. They watched the outlet, formerly hidden behind a trash can where Alison had once found a squirming mass of maggots beneath the black rubber, which she used as an excuse to never handle the garbage again. The orange cord was slack, slightly swaying in the wind, offering no clues as to how it got there. "Well, I can promise you Alison did not help plug this cord in," Cynthia muttered.

"I don't think we should unplug it," he said.

"Why not?" Cynthia asked.

"We don't know the consequences."

There was a quiet moment of mutual contemplation, and then Cynthia reached down and jerked it out.

Immediately there was a jolt, a vibration in the ground.

Cynthia yelped, blinking wildly into the cold air that bit at her eyes.

Ernest glared at her. "Jesus, Cynthia! So much for discussing our next move."

"I have cancer—what can they possibly do to hurt me?" Out of the corner of her left eye, tears leaked out, not from sadness but pure exertion. This was something that happened to her now, the involuntary tears resulting from the smallest of tasks. Bending down. Pulling on a cord. She swallowed hard and swiped away the tears. They scanned around. Nothing seemed amiss, just a temperamental wind rattling through the trees, the sound of a car door shutting a few doors down. Ernest turned toward the ship—which the ground resolutely refused to swallow, which the sky no longer welcomed, which the whole suburb had grown indifferent to—and waited for it to do something. Nothing happened.

"What do you think is happening in there?" Cynthia whispered.

The ship's windows were dark, as always.

"What if it's exactly like our house in there?" Cynthia asked.

"What do you mean? An exact replica?"

"Not exactly. What if there's nothing futuristic in there beyond the hardware it takes to fly that thing around? What if there's a couch, a TV, a rug? A tacky painting above the mantelpiece? A junk drawer?"

Ernest laughed. "Is this supposed to comfort me right now?"

Cynthia didn't seem to hear what he said; she was caught in her vision. "They wanted to escape their ordinary lives to look into ours. Are we their fantasy? Do they want to be us?"

A shadow passed across the window of the saucer—Cynthia's breath caught in her throat, Ernest's neck stiffened—but it was only a passing of clouds overhead.

"What if it's some wacko psychological experiment, to see how humans react to the potential possibility of alien life?"

"So humans are in there? Or robots?"

"Do we really have any idea? Why don't they come out? If they're willing to fly all the way out here and park in our backyard, why not make themselves visible?"

Ernest had no answer but he saw her point. But did it make it any less scary if there were humans in there after all? What kind of humans would be in there for months at a time? Ones remunerated handsomely? Ones desperate for cash? Spies? Scientists? Reagan?

"I can't be bothered with this thing right now," she said after a moment, their reveries broken. She reached down and plugged the thing back in. "Merry Christmas, spaceship. Have all the electricity you want. Let's go inside and give the kids their stockings. It's early but we need the distraction."

"Stockings?" Ernest asked in disbelief. "Right now?"

"What else are we supposed to do? Ernest, look at this thing. It's never looked so defeated."

She had a point. Without the electricity from their house, the spaceship wasn't running its lights or otherwise signaling that it had any energy at all.

"I'm going to rest first," she said. "But when I get up, I want to have a normal goddamn Christmas." As Cynthia trudged upstairs, the full import of what the ship had done hit her. How did it move the cable? And if it could do that, what else could it do? Could it erase her tumors? She marveled to herself about its powers, picturing it shining its light into her, resetting her system back to good health.

"We still on for the twenty-ninth?"

"Of course," Marilyn said. "Is everything OK?"

He pulled the phone into the pantry, as he'd seen the kids do. "The spaceship plugged into the side of the garage. Into an outlet with a long cord."

"Really? They're taking electricity? Wow, never heard of that." Ernest heard her put her hand over the phone and say, "Coming, one sec," then even quieter, "It's a source, OK? For Aurora Park."

When she returned to the line, he asked, "What do you mean, Aurora Park? Are you talking about Earth Day?"

"Basically. So what's up, Ernest?"

"I'm sorry for calling you right now, but I feel rattled."

"I'm sure it's nothing, some glitch. Listen, today's a joyous day. Put that spaceship out of your mind. Nothing you do today will make a difference. You will get to the bottom of the matter eventually, but not today."

He listened, trying to use her words to neutralize the acid in his stomach. "But how did they do it? If they didn't get out, how did they do it?"

"Merry Christmas, Ernest. I'm looking forward to seeing you. We'll make some plans about the story on you and Earth Day."

"Yeah?" He smiled. "I can't wait."

With the motion of setting the phone back into the cradle, he split into two. One version of himself tended a potentially exciting new persona: newspaper star, Earth Day hero, Marilyn's lover, the man who exposed the spaceship scheme for the noxious force that it was. The other walked back into his living room, 100 percent focused on turning in a fine performance as a more or less decent family man.

Cynthia dangled woolly stockings in front of the kids on the couch. A steady stream of Christmas music emanated from the shortwave radio. Ernest, who had been busy tending to a roaring fire, spoke up: "Wait a minute, it's stocking time? I need to see those stockings. Santa forgot a few things."

Cynthia handed Ernest the lumpy socks and he stormed out of the room on a mission.

"This should be good," Alison said. "Is he going to come back with those safety plugs for all the outlets? You know, so the spaceship can't plug in anywhere else?"

From her rocking chair, her mother shot her a disapproving look. Alison might've shot her a cranky look right back, but instead she was consumed with how her mother's eyelashes looked like little spider legs found on old paper, like some ghost lady from a Victorian horror story. Alison looked away. On the mantel, still tucked behind a litter of family photos and knickknacks, was the painting of the Earth Mama with the firewood lips, a red candle in front of it, shadow and flame flickering on the paint.

Her father returned and laid the stockings back in their laps. Then he stood ceremoniously with his hands clutched behind his back.

"Dad, stop standing like that. You look so dorky," Alison said.

Her brother dumped out his stocking on the couch, so she did too. They were careful not to cross piles. Alison pawed through the usual stuff from Cynthia: vitamins, natural perfume samples, hand-milled bath soaps, a few healthy chocolates and mints, some pink barrettes she'd never wear unless called upon to play some girl-child who still slept with stuffed animals. She eyed a tube of toothpaste.

"Mom," she said, "I hate this kind."

"What kind?" Cynthia said. "That's what I always get you."

"No, it's the kind that tastes like black licorice. It's gross."

"Let me see." Cynthia was getting out of her chair.

"Sit down, Cynthia," Ernest said sharply. "Conserve your energy." Cynthia, halfway up, stretched to pick up the blanket that had fallen to the floor, her breath coming out in a forced *guh* with the effort, but she didn't get up from her seat. Ernest changed the topic. "What else do you have in there, Gabe?"

Both kids returned to unpacking the bottom of their stockings. Gabe pulled out a box of film. Not Kodak for amateur vacationers, but a fancy brand in a green box.

"Whoa," Gabe said. "Fuji. This is totally pro."

"Top of the line for nature photography," Ernest said. "Can handle a superlong shutter speed."

Alison watched her dad watching Gabe, who was too busy reading the tiny script on the box to notice anything. Dad seemed like he was thinking of something else, definitely not Christmas. What a bunch of man-bots they were. She plunged her hand deeper into her stocking, wriggling a box out from the bottom. It was a set of Sharpies, a selection that Ernest had put together himself, tied together with ribbon.

"Ooh," Alison said, immediately using one to color her thumbnail. "I just ran out of royal blue."

"I got you all primary colors," Ernest said.

"Listen to you, Dad," Alison said proudly. "Primary colors, all right!"

Later that night, when they were plodding around their bedroom before bed, Cynthia brought up the presents. "Well, well, look who spent money on frivolous things."

"Cynthia, you're going to lay into me about money now?"

She smiled. "No. You got those kids what they wanted."

"Those kids have no idea how lucky they are. I got used tools for Christmas."

The lights browned out, all the lamps issuing a low buzz.

"Goddamn it." Ernest looked around. "They've plugged back in."

After a moment, the lights resumed their regular glow.

"Ernest, it's midnight. I know you've had a lot of beer. Just get into bed and forget about it."

To her relief, he collapsed onto the bed, flipping off his slippers so that they thunked on the ground. In the back of his mind, he knew the plug had snuggled right back in there, but he was drunk enough to convince himself he'd tackle the issue in the morning, or sometime soon.

Resistance was futile—a cliché of some alien movie or another, but nevertheless, at 7 A.M., before they unwrapped their Christmas gifts,

Ernest yanked out the cord. He bent both of the prongs with a pair of pliers, then flung it across the yard. Noble defiance, but wasted.

———

THE ACTIVITIES OF THE UNWELCOME VISITORS FROM JUPITER: AN ALLEN FAMILY LOG

December 26: *Due to the selfish and gross usage of our electricity by our "guests" at this time, the family will need to tighten up the usage of utilities. This is mandatory family action until further notice. Thermostat: 63 degrees. Brushing teeth: NO WASTED WATER. SHUT OFF THE FAUCET. Should be basic practice by now but crucially important at this juncture. DON'T leave lights on in rooms that aren't occupied. To make up for the cold temperatures, we'll have fires most nights. We'll make it cozy instead of unpleasant. —EA*

December 26: *Dad, chill out a little bit? —AA*

December 26: *Maybe the ship needs the electricity. Maybe it's not such a bad thing. Maybe it's trying to leave. It's important to keep an open mind, right? Haven't you guys always told us that? Actually, I think only Mom has said that a few times, so maybe it's only important to HER and not the OTHER parental force of the family. —GA*

December 26: *"Chilling out" was taken off the table when the alien bandits from outer space resorted to pure thievery. Sorry to put a damper on the holidays, but this is important. Will be policing for egregious mismanagement of resources, and rewarding for conservational diligence, thusly. —EA*

29

Last summer Tom nestled speakers into the arms of the giant oak tree that overlooked both of their yards. He hooked the speakers to his stereo so that he could listen to music outside. Mostly he played classical, but if he was in a rambunctious mood, drum-heavy jazz erupted from the tree limbs, chosen to enrich Tom's ongoing education in percussive studies. Now, as Gabe wandered around the spaceship with his camera, flurries drifted down. It was hard to believe that the spaceship had landed while it was still muggy outside. Gabe took more pictures, listening to a chaotic drum solo that seemed to have no conclusion in sight—just endless fills, rolls, and the clinking, brushing, and rattling of the snare and cymbals. In a puffy vest over a flannel, Tom wandered down the driveway, ardently air-drumming. He nodded to Gabe before disappearing through the back door.

In the kitchen, Tom found Ernest rereading the New World pamphlet.

"You rang?"

Ernest nodded but kept reading the pamphlet.

"You looking up where the off button is?"

"Ha, no, but I've got an idea."

Within an hour, Ernest was spotting Tom while he climbed high on a ladder and secured a video camera to the tree with wire and bungee cords. Tom cleverly nested the video camera into the tree's natural cavity so that it was barely noticeable, just a lens peeking out from the wood, trained in the direction of the ship.

"Now we can catch it in the act," Tom said.

A four-hour tape was loaded, and Tom pressed record with a flourish. They walked to Ernest's yard, checking out the camera from the vantage of the ship. It could barely be detected, save for the crimson pupil.

"Prepare," Tom said with a grin, "to have your mind blown."

Regrettably, their minds remained intact. The ship plugged in again, but not on film. The camera recorded for only about an hour and then it blasted to white for the last several seconds. One of the spaceship's bright lights trained itself on the lens until it blotted out the entire picture. The second night, the camera filmed for another couple of hours before the battery drained of life. Tom ran some wires so that the camera was plugged into an outlet in his house, but even then, it went back to the first day's results.

Intervention time. Ernest, Tom, and Gabe agreed to stay up and watch for how exactly the spaceship managed to thwart documentation. In the meantime, Ernest got the call center on the line. First, the representative (Fran of Wilmington, Delaware) told him that she was sorry to hear about the drain on his electricity. "It is unusual for a ship to borrow resources like this." She paused. "There might be something wrong. The ships are designed to be self-sufficient units."

The fact that she copped to anything less than an extraordinary miracle taking place seemed like an encouraging step. She must be new, Ernest thought.

"Well, if it's going haywire," Ernest said, "shouldn't it be forced to leave?"

"It's not scheduled to leave for another few months, Mr. Allen."

"Are you listening to me? If this is unusual behavior, isn't that grounds for it to leave early? To be forced to leave? It's already shattered a window and dumped thousands of gallons of waste into my backyard."

"We don't force them to do anything, sir. That's not the agreement."

"OK," Ernest said, trying another tack. "Who's going to pay for all this electricity? Can you fax me another reimbursement claim?"

"I'm not sure how we'd go about settling on a fair price, Mr. Allen. How can we really determine the amount of energy the spaceship is using?"

"Easy, compare last month's bill to this month's, which is going to be double the amount."

Fran fell quiet, apparently thinking about the logic of his claim. "Let me see what my supervisor says."

Fran was definitely new. Never had anyone volunteered their supervisor. After a few moments, Fran's superior came on the line and asked Ernest to photocopy the bills and order statements from the power company and all sorts of other tedious data-fetchings designed to wear him out.

"I've got to fax in all that crap while I'm taking care of my sick wife?"

"Well, how else would we do it?"

"Why don't you just shorten the order," Ernest said, "and tell me directly to fuck myself?"

Long pause. "That's not my intention," the supervisor said. And then he offered to make things better by sending Ernest some tapes of other visitations, some documentaries that might shed some light on the history of the program.

Ernest recognized the bribe that was being offered: as long as the customer is still taking it, the customer is satisfied. He refused the tapes and hung up the phone.

———

Waiting outside on one of the last fragmentary days of 1994, Tom, Ernest, and Gabe wore scarves around their mouths, wool hats that flapped over the ears, and puffy down jackets. Their gloved hands were converted to woolen bear paws that made it tricky to grip their beverages. They arranged their lawn chairs in a loose half-moon, sipping whiskey toddies out of Thermoses (except for Gabe, who was drinking hot caffeinated tea). The plan was to stay up and see the video camera get scrambled and to also witness when (and how) the plug snaked its way back in. At the moment, it was on the ground, close to the outlet but still several feet away. The prongs were once again straight.

At midnight, Tom turned the camera on and returned to his chair. Nothing to do now but wait and see.

"Want some whiskey, Gabe?" Tom shook a half-empty bottle at him.

Ernest looked at Tom with raised eyebrows.

"I know, the law," Tom said. "But no one's here to see it."

Ernest scrutinized Gabe's ability to handle booze. His son had one glove off, to better hold his Thermos. Long and slender, Gabe's fingers gave away his peculiar state between adolescence and manhood.

"What are you drinking?" Ernest asked.

"Lapsang souchong," Gabe said.

"That'll keep you up for three days straight," Tom said.

"That's why I like it."

"Whiskey would go well with that," Ernest said in a neutral tone.

Tom let a stream of amber liquid gurgle out of the bottle and into the steamy bath of Gabe's tea.

"Wow," Gabe said softly after taking a sip, though it was largely theater. Of course he'd tried whiskey before. He couldn't be sure, but he was pretty certain he'd snuck a shot out of the very bottle they were drinking from.

Tom eyed him. "Like you haven't taken a nip before."

Ernest and Tom laughed, clapping their thighs. They waited for him to confirm their suspicions, but Gabe didn't say anything, just shrugged and looked away with a small smile.

In the night sky, a few stars plucked out of the dim twinkled; the air barely moved, though it carried pleasant wafts of the fire Ernest built for Cynthia, who had fallen asleep in front of it. She had meant to usher Gabe out of this silly night watch around midnight, but she figured he might be having fun. Why fight it? Beyond the performance of mother for the Christmas season, she barely had energy for anything—worry, anger, fear. She tried to focus on the only unit of time that was real: the present. She'd kicked up the meditation lately so that when the white roar of death whispered in her ear, she could say that it was still not here—not yet, not yet—and instead look around her at the obvious, tangible objects: the specific quality of light, the exact expression Alison wore when pulling on her gloves and fitting it around her fingers just so. She'd try to carry these things with her, wherever she was going.

"Is the eye still blazing?" Tom asked.

Gabe turned around to check. "Yeah. You don't see it?"

"Sort of," Tom said. "I'm color-blind. Red's a tough one."

"Really?" Gabe said. "How does that work?"

"Certain colors just read as gray, like different tones of it. So that camera eye just looks like a gray glow to me."

"Then how did you know it was red at all?"

"Because it's the certain shade of gray that red is."

"What about the spaceship light? Can you see that?"

Tom looked out at it. Ever since it had started sucking energy, it was keeping only two lamps on in the front.

"I know that it is green because it's the color of gray that means green."

"Do you know what a tetrachromat is?" Gabe asked. The men were blank. "It's someone who can see four ranges of color instead of three."

"Sounds like a cyborg or something," Ernest said. "I don't think I'm one of those."

"You can't be anyway. It's only women," Gabe said. "Something to do with the X chromosome. Alison's obsessed with it. She thinks she might be one."

"Well, she does like paint chips a lot," Ernest said. "It's like she sees something extra in them." Alison had little squares from the hardware store tacked all over her bedroom walls. She also kept a stash in a drawer by her bed, sometimes getting them out to examine a hundred shades of beige: eggshell, Navajo white, chalk, whitewash, sourdough, cotton, ecru, sand, cream, oyster.

The men drank slowly, the night starting to unfold its deeper layers, the houses around them no longer glowing with lights or vibrating with sounds or the sense that people were awake inside. True night.

"If you could travel anywhere," Gabe asked, "where would you go?"

"Alaska," Tom said. "Denali Park."

"That's a good one," Ernest said. "I'd go there too, or the Amazon."

"I'd go to Tokyo," Gabe said.

"Why there?" Tom asked.

"Because it's not here; it's nothing like here."

"What do you mean?"

"It just seems as far away from America as you can get." Gabe waved his hand in the air in front of them. "Far away from all this."

"Seems like it's the same," Tom said. "But they're more tightly packed in than us. They built up instead of out with their suburbs."

"But even that," Gabe said. "Building up, not out. It's different."

"What would you do there?" Ernest asked.

"I don't know. See the sights, get to know people, take pictures," Gabe said, his voice tremulous, embarrassed that he'd never thought firmly of a plan. After a pause, he offered, "I mean, I heard there's an exchange program. You can spend a year in Japan learning the language."

Ernest frowned. "What would you do with knowing Japanese afterward? Spanish is much more practical. Now that's the language to learn."

"Well, my history teacher says that Japan is kicking our ass right now in all kinds of things, cars and technology and stuff. He says it may pay off to know Japanese."

Tom nodded. "I wouldn't buy an American car at this point, not when you could get a Honda."

They fell silent again for a while, returning to their drinks. It hadn't been commented on, but Gabe was getting as many refills of the whiskey as Ernest and Tom, though Tom was the bartender and, without making a big fuss over it, he was pouring far less into Gabe's Thermos.

As 2 A.M. came and went, the conversation turned to the things people talked about at 2 A.M., namely other times in their lives when they were up at 2 A.M. Tom told most of the stories, Ernest a few. Gabe just listened. Another hour scattered past; momentum lagged. Tom had fallen asleep with his head back, the muscles in his neck twitching, and snapped himself awake every now and again, mumbling an apology and sitting slit-eyed for a minute before falling asleep again. Ernest and Gabe were left to keep vigil, which they did with little conversation between them. By 3:30, they were ready to surrender. Maybe the spaceship had harvested enough electricity the night before. Maybe it was self-conscious from being watched so closely.

"This is starting to feel dumb," Tom said, his words warped by a barely suppressed yawn.

"Let's give it another half an hour," Ernest said. "Aren't we almost to the end of the tape?"

They waited, and the tape eventually ran out, leaving the men with a four-hour documentary that was all talk and no action.

"Gentlemen," Tom said, "this has been thrilling." And with that, they stood up to retire. Just as Ernest folded his chair, there was a crisp and metallic snapping noise behind him. All of them whipped around in time to see the end of the extension cord hovering in the air, like a snake's head rising up, charmed, or maybe preparing to strike. Quickly it swooped toward the outlet with unerring precision and plugged in, neatly and securely. An elegant movement, flawless.

"Magnets," Tom said, "that's the only way."

A hum started up from within the ship, as if a large meat cooler had been turned on.

"Is that recorded?" Gabe asked. In his excitement, he had splashed some of his open Thermos on himself, a tonic of Lapsang souchong and whiskey.

"It didn't record it," Ernest said. "But there's always tomorrow night."

As soon as he said it, he realized they could stay up again but they still wouldn't get any action on tape. The spaceship always waited until the tape ran out before making its big move. But why? Why couldn't the plugging in be caught on tape? What didn't the spaceship want to be recorded, exactly? It actually seemed pretty simple, what happened. Like Tom said, it was magnets inside the cord, activated to find the plug. But were the magnets sitting in the plug all the time, normally dormant, and activated only when the spaceship needed it? Who the hell knew what was going on in the duplicitous mind of the spaceship?

"We could unplug it now," Tom said. "See if it does it again."

"Don't bother," Ernest said.

"Listen," Tom said, "if you want to get rid of the spaceship, we've got to do it right. Remember? You talked about a plan. We'll figure it out when we've had a good night's sleep."

30

For her final dose of chemo, they gave Cynthia the strongest shot yet, loosening her insides. Her gut muscles hauled out the last few hours of gastric production: half-digested stew coated in yellow bile, floating in the toilet water. Her mind went blank with every heave, only a raw focus on the jettisoning of nutritive matter. Once the vomiting passed, she leaned back against the bathtub, the chill of the porcelain penetrating through her shirt.

The cancer was now a distinct presence dominating her body, a governing system she involuntarily sheltered. She told herself she was used to this—her body had harbored other beings before. Pregnant with Gabe, she'd known he was there in her body before the blood tests confirmed it. While reading in bed, a wave of nausea bowled into her and she clutched at her stomach. A picture emerged in her mind: a suburban street at night with a starless sky above. She strolled past house after house, all of them dark, vacated, but at the end of what turned out to be a cul-de-sac was one bungalow with a light on in an upstairs bedroom, one glowing light in the entire house. The features of the interior couldn't be made out, only the light emanating from a lamp near the window, the particles released into the night air. Somebody was present, a new person. Nascent and unformed, but a friendly force.

Soon the street and the house disappeared and it was just the light. The shine from a primordial being, forged in the core of herself. It was the big bang in the body. Combustion. Light. White-blue light but not cold. A series of cellular replications exploding again and again. She loved to close her eyes and look at this image, this density made from her but still totally separate. Eventually as the fetus grew inside of her, the light poured into the physical creature, which changed what she saw when she closed her eyes—she imagined the curl of his fist, his fresh tiny lungs—but she never lost track of the way it felt in the beginning. Like a secret between her and Gabe.

For the moment, she was stable enough to drag herself to the bathroom window. Looking through the dusty glass, she caught the alien ship with one neon-green light pointed downward, blanching a spot of grass.

She waited for the nausea to build up again, and wondered what kind of light was in her now. Was cancer a light or was it an absence of light? Maybe it was a black light, picking up little white flecks in her system and highlighting them as ultraviolet. Was it a searchlight, sweeping back and forth over her insides, looking for more vulnerable tissue? Did it permeate the cancer cells themselves so that they radiated a bitter white, like burning magnesium, which she remembered from college chemistry class? Or was the color more like the neon green of the spaceship, shining out on the green of the grass? The two greens were nearly indistinguishable—one alien, one natural, but nearly the same. The cancer cells were almost like her other cells, with one catastrophic shift in code.

Another wave of nausea came so strongly that she nearly blacked out—but then it passed and she was OK again.

Diane Albero phoned at last. The township of Prairie Park, she informed Ernest in a kindly tone, had decided not to support the injunction. "We don't believe it's negatively impacting the community," she said. "It's an unfortunate issue for your family, but there is no indication there is any threat to anybody. I'm sorry, but it simply doesn't warrant our involvement." He told her how the saucer had stolen his electricity but she remained steadfast in her position. "Perhaps that's an issue you can bring up with New World Enterprises."

"I have."

"I wish you the best of luck with it," she said.

"It's disappointing that my service as the Earth Day director couldn't make more of a difference in this matter."

She paused. "And what did you have in mind?"

"I-I'm not sure," Ernest stammered. "Some kind of special consideration regarding my case? I mean, Prairie Park has enough faith in my abilities as an environmental leader to hire me to direct one of the biggest cultural events on their calendar, but not enough to back me against this toxic trespassing spaceship?"

"It's not trespassing, and there is no indication that it is toxic," she said bluntly. "Thanks in large part to your own tests, Mr. Allen. It's as simple as that."

"I have proof that the spaceship is causing my sick wife unnecessary grief." He knew this was a lie but didn't care.

"I'm sorry for that. A member of your family voluntarily registered to win a visit."

"Right, my sixteen-year-old son. When my wife was healthy. I wish you trusted my word enough to get involved."

"I trust that you think the spaceship is a nuisance, Mr. Allen. Look, it'll be gone soon enough, and then you'll forget about it. You'll be in the thick of celebrating Earth Day at your wonderful festival. Is it true that you might get Joni Mitchell to play?"

Ernest ignored her question and let a little South Side come into his voice. "So much for being from the same neighborhood, huh?"

There was a long pause. "This isn't Chicago." Her tone was hard. "There's no cronyism here."

"I know that," Ernest said. "Look, I was just hoping for better."

She wished him happy holidays and hung up the phone. Happy holidays! She couldn't even be bothered to zero in on the one secular holiday that was left: New Year's.

He brooded at the living room window. There was 1995, lurking around the bend, and his most powerful option was sunk. The truth of the sentiment weighed on his spirit. At last, the situation had truly become desperate. No one was coming to help him, and the spaceship could do whatever it wanted—squeal, puke, dump, and steal—and no one cared. It had shattered windows, destroyed lawns, and possibly poisoned his wife, even if he couldn't catch it yet, and no one cared because it was legal and not obviously toxic, which equaled "just fine" in America. Previously some pop-eyed optimism would've offered itself by this point, but only a black pool of certainty remained. He'd been soft-shoeing this investigation so far, but he was about to strap on his combat boots.

Ernest and Marilyn met again at Morgan's. The waitress sized them up, flapped her arm toward the tables, and said, "Whatever tickles your fancy." Only one table had yet to be claimed; the rest were jammed with manager types working on their lunch buzz.

Once tucked into their booth, Ernest started in: "What if they're playing the long game? What if they've waited all this time to establish trust, to get everyone to let their guard down, only to start the mission they had all along: to kill us all off slowly but in a way that looks happenstance or coincidental. What if all the spaceships that land from now on do the same thing?" Ernest knocked his fists on the table's surface and then shook his head. "I know I sound crazy but these are my thoughts."

Marilyn looked at him with glittering intensity. "Look, Ernest, you do sound like a crazy person, but if you could prove even a scrap of this, you'd have a huge story on your hands."

"I know, I know," he said. "But I have nothing except my gut feelings."

"Ernest, let me ask you this: Do you *believe* what you're saying? Like, take away for a second that you feel angry about your wife's cancer. Do you believe what you're actually saying?"

The food landed on the table, giving him a chance to sort out his answer. Did he believe what he was saying? He couldn't figure out how to explain it. On one hand, he'd never been more certain of anything in his life: the spaceship was wrong. It had poisoned his house and was attacking it, leeching from it. The evidence pointed that way, yes, but also his intuition. In his surest moments, the certainty chased around inside him, in his blood, until he felt it pumping through his racing heart. But then there were other kinds of moments that complicated his belief. Sometimes he caught himself worrying for the sake of it, feeding on the worry, like a zealot handling a crucifix. He rubbed and rubbed and rubbed until it was stone-smooth. He had no idea where the time went, what his actual thoughts had been, only that he'd been fixated.

"I believe it, yes," he answered, "but it's probably not good for me. It's all kinds of embarrassing and insane."

Marilyn's smile was wry and familiar. "Well, all you can do in those situations is push it, Ernest. Push the whole situation till it breaks and yields something conclusive."

"What do you mean?"

She shrugged. "That's for you to figure out. But sometimes to get any clear-cut answers, you have to force the other party's hand. Back it into a corner."

"Back it into a corner."

"Yes."

"What would that mean here? Blow it up?" Ernest was past the point of keeping ridiculous ideas to himself.

"What would wrecking your number one piece of evidence get you?"

"What if I just want it to leave, pure and simple? What if I don't care about proving it's toxic, so long as it leaves?"

"Wouldn't you want to know that? I mean, if it's toxic here, who's to say it's not hurting other families?"

He stared at her. Sometimes, during their conversations, he got the impression he was being interviewed. Ernest dropped his face into his hands. "Let me ask you something," he said, looking back up. "Do you believe me about the spaceship or do you think I'm just an entertaining nut?"

After a few contemplative chews, Marilyn answered. "You are definitely entertaining. But you're also inspiring. You're really following your gut with this and I really believe there's no other way to live when you have those feelings. You have to pursue it."

Ernest leaned back in the booth, the old leather releasing a not unpleasant waft of dried beer.

"You're smiling at me," Marilyn said.

"Thank you for not treating me like an insane old kook."

"Oh, you're a kook all right, but I'm excited by the way you think. And you're not *that* old."

Later, when they said good-bye in her car, he'd express his appreciation again, his breath fogging in the interior.

"It gives me great relief to know that you believe me, Marilyn." She gave him a dubious look. "OK, maybe 'believe' isn't the right word, but you understand that I have to follow it through."

"I do, that's true." She gave his hand a squeeze.

Leaning over the stick shift, Ernest kissed her, his palm curving around her face. Puncturing the cloudiness of his mind was the sharpness of his impulses. There was a crisp thrill in unshackling himself from his morals. They floated above him, distant trinkets.

"Sorry," Ernest said when they finished.

"I didn't think . . ." she said softly, while trying to suppress a pleased look.

They sat for a moment, watching a busboy swing full bags of trash into the dumpster.

"I'm not really clear on things right now," Ernest said.

"Let's just let it be for now. Let's not worry about anything." She grabbed his hand, but Ernest was already onto something else.

"What if whatever they're doing can't be detected with our tests? What if that little bit of tar creosote meant something?"

Marilyn turned to him in her seat. "Tar creosote?"

"Yeah, a little teeny bit showed up in the test from the soil. It's barely anything. It certainly didn't matter to Diane Albero, one of our fine civic leaders."

"Why didn't you mention that earlier?"

"Why? What does it matter? Marilyn?"

She turned back to the windshield with a set expression. "Get your soil tested, Ernest, but go deeper this time. Go a couple of feet at least. Take a number of samples from all over the yard. Don't"—she turned to point at him—"use anyone in Prairie Park. Use someone in the Chicago area, just not Prairie Park. If the test turns up more tar creosote than it's already shown, let me know."

"What is going on? Are you telling me that you have heard something about the spaceships and tar creosote? But you said nothing has ever—"

"I know, Ernest. Just do it, and I'll tell you later what I'm looking for. I can't right now."

Right when he got home, he called a lab he found in the phonebook: Suburban Analytics, based a few suburbs over. It was closing for New Year's, but shortly afterward, lab technicians would come to collect the soil samples from six feet under.

31

"Come on, Tom," Ernest said, gripping the ax. "Take your best swing."

Twenty minutes before midnight on New Year's Eve, and the neighborhood was awake and antsy. Blaring TVs tuned in to the ball drop. Clumsy holiday sex occurred in carpeted master bedrooms. A few loud revelers out on the street whooped in the distance. Tom and Ernest had been stationed at the kitchen table drinking beer since the late afternoon, swapping outlandish spaceship-extraction methods, when the idea hit Ernest with imposing clarity. They would chop down the alien spaceship like a tree. Simple.

Before they went outside, Ernest checked on Cynthia. She'd been sitting with them in the kitchen, one moment laughing at their haphazard plans and the next moment gone. He found her asleep in a fetal position. When Ernest sat down next to her, she stirred awake.

"Did you do it?"

"What?"

"Get the spaceship to leave."

"In a minute."

A faint smile curled at her lips, and she fell back asleep. For a minute, he watched her, the injustice of her illness tearing through him, her figure smaller and unfairly broken. He rubbed her back, his fingers bumping into her protruding ribs and vertebrae.

Each man stood near a leg of the ship, lumberjack axes in hand. Slowly they walked around the silver disk, sizing up their prey. Ernest was drunk with a sense of mission and drunk in the regular sense of the word too. Why had it taken him this long to decide to destroy the spaceship himself? OK, maybe not destroy it, but to scare it away. If New World refused to move it, then all bets were off. He had a right to defend his property. Why had he allowed it so much opportunity to wreck his life?

"I think it's best," Ernest said, "if we strike at the same time."

His son appeared on the back porch, staring at the men holding axes low in front of their pelvises with a slack grip. "What are you doing? Dad, are you crazy?"

"It's a solid plan. We're cutting down the alien ship."

"You can't do that." Gabe ran down the stairs. "You can't just destroy it. They'll arrest you."

"Arrest me?"

"Or something."

They were at a standstill in the backyard when Alison and her friend Rebecca arrived. The girls had bailed on a lame-ass party that Claire had forced on them, even though Claire barely liked Alison anymore, now that Alison was making spaceship sneakers for everyone in school, obliterating the Tiny Vampire scrunchie business. Alison had tried to talk Rebecca into going to another party, but Rebecca didn't want to hang with "stoner weirdos," so hitting up the 7-Eleven turned into the odd compromise. Both of them were pretty buzzed from drinking Slurpees with cheap vodka poured in, the liquor nearly burning through the cups' bottoms.

Alison observed her dad, shirtless, holding an ax beneath the ship. It wasn't the ax that bothered her; it was his bare chest. Her father had this annoying tendency to take off his shirt for the slightest physical task. When he changed the car oil every six months, he'd crank open the hood and tuck his shirt into his waistband.

"Dad, it's freezing out here," she said. "Get a shirt on."

"Dad and Tom are trying to kill the ship," her brother complained.

"Kill it?" She was drunk enough that her words—at least to her— sounded abstract, as if they were in a cartoon bubble above her head.

"Destroy it. Hack it down. Whatever. It's the stupidest idea ever."

"We're not going to destroy it. We're sending a message," Ernest said.

Now that they had an audience, it was time to strike. Ernest wound up, Tom followed, and they whacked at the legs of the ship. Alison noticed that at the last second, Tom held back a little, hitting with considerably less force than Ernest. The sound of the axes on metal was surreal and silly, like someone attempting to imitate the sounds of a Detroit car plant with a few pots and pans. Ernest cursed as the blow rang through his spinal cord, and both men dropped their axes.

No one, including Ernest, was impressed with the result. Looking down at the leg, he couldn't see a ding in the metal. He rubbed his fingers over the spot, but he couldn't feel any evidence of the hit by touch either. The leg was still smooth.

"Dad, seriously, it's, like, thirty degrees out here. You have to put your flannel back on."

"I can't move that well with it on, Alison. I need to have the full torque of my body."

"Dad," Gabe said, "you're not going to be able to do anything to that ship."

Ernest wouldn't surrender yet. He looked at Tom, who was staring off into space and scratching his elbow. Ernest loosely waved his ax and Tom snapped back to attention.

"One more time?"

"No, not one more time! Dad, Tom, what are you guys doing? This isn't going to do anything but piss off the aliens." Gabe scrambled for ideas. "Dad, would you do this if those were native owls in there? Would you hack down their big, beautiful oak tree?"

"This is not a big, beautiful oak tree. This is a toxic intruder. Besides, I've never seen an owl around Chicago."

"Cardinals then! Whatever!"

"The native birds avoid this thing like the plague—that should tell you something."

"Toxic how?" Alison interrupted. "I didn't think any of those tests came back with anything."

Alison enjoyed letting her father know she was up on the score. She'd heard him discussing the tests with someone—who, she had no idea—on the phone.

Ernest ignored her. "Are you ready, Tom?"

Tom officiously nodded. Alison and Rebecca were riveted, mostly because this was the craziest thing Alison had ever seen her father do, her formerly sensible, logic-heeding father. He had his fair share of passionate outbursts but rarely did they manifest into action, much less of a violent nature.

The men wound up again, and this time they hit with blunt but collective force. Ernest's shoulder sockets vibrated with the symphonic crack of metal on metal, but this time he didn't drop the ax. The ring of it, several seconds after it had actually occurred, continued to clang in his ears. Alas, it was obvious that once again, their blows brooked no difference. Ernest checked; the legs remained silken.

He sighed and shifted around, overcome with an aching back and twitching biceps from so much concentrated effort. He yanked his flannel back on. This was what it was like to be old, to have nothing yield to your will—physical, mental, or spiritual. But then he remembered Cynthia, how he could track the strength wasting out of her with each passing hour. He blinked away tears in the blowing wind, aware of his children watching him with something approaching boredom.

"OK, we're going to go reheat some pizza," Alison said. For a moment, Alison and Rebecca remained rooted, waiting for a reaction. When none came, they shuffled up the back steps. The kitchen was frigid, the heat in the house set low, in keeping with Ernest's latest policies. Alison hunted around in the refrigerator for the leftover pizza; the experimental braid-bun she'd tried for the party sagged on the top of her head. Ernest slipped into the kitchen, with Tom and Gabe trailing behind. Tom propped his ax against the cabinet, blade side on the floor, and stood next to it rubbing his hands. He covertly peeked at his watch.

"Listen, I should go back to the house for the final countdown," Tom said. "Olivia's there, the girls . . ."

Ernest nodded, but then Tom didn't leave. They were bound in some sort of failure cocoon together.

"Maybe I'll stay," Tom offered a moment later. "They've probably all fallen asleep on the couch."

"Of course they have," Ernest said. "Stay here."

In the microwave, one of Cynthia's antique plates slowly rotated, sparks flying off the gold-painted rim, the pizza slices a glistening, gooey center. The appliance produced a fuzzy monotone of minor chemical reactions.

"Alison," Ernest yelled, "what have I told you about using the microwave? How do I stop this thing?"

He leaped at the machine and bent down with his finger, ready to avert catastrophe, but he couldn't locate the off button. His finger waggled helplessly. He didn't want to just open the door; what if that somehow resulted in a surge of electromagnetic radiation?

"What the hell are all these other buttons? Pizza, popcorn, leftovers? Where is off?"

"Dad, your face is practically inside the oven," Alison said.

The microwave triumphantly chimed the end of its cooking time.

"Give me that plate," Ernest said. He dumped Alison's pizza and the antique porcelain into the trash. The room erupted in audacious laughter.

"What are you doing, Dad?" Alison said.

"I always hated those plates anyway. Why don't you guys use the glass ones?"

"You're not letting us run the dishwasher right now, remember? So barely anything's clean around here."

"You could've washed one, with your hands." To Tom, he said, "They don't know how to do anything that isn't machine associated."

"What time is it?" Gabe asked.

"Oh my god, it's eleven fifty-eight," Rebecca said. She was the only person in the room who still cared that it was about to be 1995.

Ernest tore off a few paper towels and laid out the slices. "Kids, allow me to prepare your first meal of the new year."

"Wow," Gabe said. "You going to pop those in the radiation box?"

"Nope, you're eating it cold. Tomorrow I'm getting rid of the radiation box."

Gabe started to argue but stopped himself. His dad didn't always remember these threats the next day.

"It's 1995," Rebecca cheered.

Upstairs, Cynthia slept through the turn of the year with a cool washcloth pressed into the corner of her eyelid where another sty festered.

Three nights into the new year, Cynthia knocked on Alison's door.

"What do you think?" She bounced her hand under the end curl of a new shoulder-length wig. It resembled her natural color, an ash blond. The wig was close to Cynthia's real hair, yet drained of some essential live quality.

"Um, it's nice."

"What's the matter with it?"

"Where'd you get it?"

"At the mall. I can return it. What, it looks tacky?"

"No, it doesn't." Alison could say that much. The wig looked expensive. The hair lay in the right ways, not too starchy or fake.

"So what don't you like about it?"

"I said it was nice."

"But you don't like it?"

"I like it. It just took me a minute to get used to it."

A nervous smile. "I know it's more glamorous than anything I ever tried with my real hair . . ."

"Well, exactly. It doesn't really look like you. You know, you don't *have* to wear a wig."

"I know that but I want to." Her mother self-consciously touched the manufactured strands around her head.

"OK, well, just know that it's fine if you don't."

"I'm not sure what you're trying to get at but—"

"I'm just saying we can handle it, OK? Gabe and I are both in high school. We're practically adults."

Her mother raised her now-sparse eyebrows and kept them there for heightened effect.

"Never mind," Alison said. "You look good, Mom."

"Thanks."

Cynthia never wore the wig again, not around anyone else. She hid it in her closet and every once in a while she'd slip it back on. If she squinted in the mirror, it looked close enough to her real hair, but as if she'd styled it for a wedding. Now that her hair was gone, she regretted how little she'd paid attention to it. Not that she didn't shampoo and condition every time she showered or indulge in subtle highlights when she felt especially dumpy, but she had never taken full advantage of it. She had never manipulated it to grand effect, the way some women did. Now she longed to wear a crown braid, grow it to her shoulder blades, beat and tease it into a 1940s movie-star twist—anything that announced she was still fresh and vital. Not the woman who swallowed pills every night that starved her body of estrogen, one of the hormones that paradoxically fed her tumors but also her entire system. The pill, tamoxifen, shut down the hormonal lines. Her body, once alive with supply tracks carrying in resources to a booming town, now resembled a war-ravaged collection of buildings that everyone had fled.

A trio of workers, utilizing a small backhoe, tore the guts out of Cynthia's backyard and then transferred the dirt into smooth, clear compartments. She watched from the kitchen window, freezing despite her sweater and robe combination.

When Ernest came back inside she asked, "So when were you planning to tell me that men would be digging graves in our backyard? I hope they're doing mine first."

"They're not graves. It's a few test sites for collecting soil. It's necessary to go deep into the ground."

"I see," Cynthia said, her annoyance blunted by exhaustion. "And why is this necessary?"

"Because the spaceship might have deposited tar creosote way down there."

"How? How would that be possible?"

"Through its tentacles in the ground, or through its waste dumps seeping down there. It's hard to say, but I've been told I should have it tested."

"Really? Who told you?"

"It's my money, OK, Cynthia? I used my earnings." Ernest's voice came out with more force than he meant to. He recollected his calm. "So don't worry about it right now. You don't need to bother yourself with all this."

He took to her shoulders and started to knead them, anger, guilt, and sympathy fusing into his movements.

She shrugged him off. "I'm sitting here, dying of cancer, and you want to launch a battery of tests? Is this the time?"

"You are so excited to disregard my theories. What if I'm right?"

"So you're right, and I'm still dying. I'm jealous that a fucking spaceship gets more attention than me. But I guess it makes sense. I wouldn't want to focus on me either."

Ernest threw his hands in the air. "All I'm doing is worrying about you, fussing over you. I make you food, I give you massages, I drive you to nearly every doctor's appointment you have. What am I not doing?"

"Just listening to me. Being here without a task or an assignment."

"I'm trying my best, I really am."

She believed him but it hardly helped. "OK, but I want to know who recommended these tests to you. This person must have a lot of say."

"Doesn't matter. It's quality advice."

"Let me guess: Ms. Marilyn Fournier, ace investigative reporter."

"OK, you're right. Is it wrong of me to want to take her advice? She knows some things about tar creosote." Ernest worked hard to keep his voice level.

"Well, so do you and so do I, but what *she* says, that's what matters."

"She's an environmental reporter; I think her instincts in this case are really helpful."

Cynthia sputtered. "You said that like she's some sort of hero, exposing corruption with each squiggle from her pen."

"Right," Ernest shot back, "idealism is so stupid, isn't it?"

"What's that supposed to mean? Like I'm not trying my best? Sorry if I'm not particularly optimistic these days."

"Forget I said it." Ernest crawled with shame but he couldn't stop himself from lashing out again. "So when am I cut off for good? Any more secret money plots with Stephen I should know about?"

Cynthia drew in a breath and calmly stated: "The trusts are set up for the kids, and you should be happy about that."

"So what do I have access to?"

"The joint account still has plenty of money. I'm not leaving you high and dry, Ernest. You're an adult with a capacity to work, for one thing. We should probably talk a little more about—"

"We probably should," he snapped. "To do this alone. I never expected—"

To be a single dad, Ernest was going to say, but it seemed pointlessly cruel to go on about it. He hadn't talked about what would happen after Cynthia's death, though she'd prodded a couple of times. Beyond telling her that it would all be OK, he didn't want to linger on his anxiety about parenting alone; he didn't want to make her feel guilty. But he also hated her for not intuiting that money was a huge part of his worry. For making him say that he needed her money. Couldn't she have left the money first to him, and then ask that he set up the trusts later? And then there was always the outside chance that she could survive. One dry reed of hope, but he clutched to it almost as fiercely as she did.

"OK, Ernest," she said gently. "We'll figure it all out."

He held her hand in a truce. After a few minutes of silence between them, she left the room. He thought about going after her, but he had to wait for the ugliness to recede.

The living room lamps dimmed, the spaceship leeching off the power. Olivia glanced up from folding washcloths in the Allen family's living room. She'd been spending more time at her neighbors' house in the last couple of weeks, helping with housework and keeping an eye on Cynthia while Ernest disappeared on inexplicable errands. Her baby, Cherice, was there too, dragging a felt book across the floor of her portable playpen. Olivia was proud that she'd fattened Cherice up, gotten her strong through formulas and medicines, so that she was now able to sit up on her own and smile in that gleeful way that seemed to involve her whole body.

The lights returned to a robust gold. From the top of the stairs, Cynthia's creaky steps as she descended in her quilted robe.

"Cherice was wondering when you'd come down," Olivia said. "How are you feeling?"

Cynthia jiggled Cherice's hand, looking into her alert eyes. Cherice cracked a smile and giggled. "Looking good, little lady," Cynthia said. Then to Olivia: "I miss the way I used to walk."

Olivia nodded, but it was clear she didn't understand what Cynthia meant.

"The way I walked all around here"—Cynthia flapped her hand toward the window—"so that I knew everything that was going on. I've barely seen anyone for ages."

"Well, as long as you don't venture out for too long and you really bundle up, you could do it."

Cynthia sunk into a seat across from Olivia and pensively watched Cherice in her playpen between them. "I think Ernest is up to something."

Olivia sighed. "He's just trying to kill a spaceship, that's all. With an ax."

"No, I mean something else. Has Tom said anything?"

"Just that Ernest is"—Olivia paused—"very determined."

"No, I mean about that reporter. There's something going on there."

"Like what? What makes you say that?"

"It's just a feeling. I think they're messing around. Where does he go off to?"

"Don't you think he's just getting a break from here?"

"I don't know anything for sure, but I've walked in on him ending phone conversations a couple of times and Ernest doesn't talk to anyone on the phone."

Olivia's dark eyes burned. "If he's pulling any fishy shit, I will kill him, he knows that. But honestly, I don't think anything's happening. He's entitled to go a little crazy right now, with this situation. You have to give him that."

"I don't even tell him the worst of what's going on. I don't complain because then he tries to fix it. He's a micromanager. I should eat the right foods, drink the right potions, read things that only make me feel good, get some fresh air, close the window, wear a sweater, and on and on and on. Sometimes I just snap at him, 'Stop managing me.' He doesn't realize he's doing it."

What Cynthia didn't realize: Alison was in the downstairs bathroom, quiet while she read a magazine, waiting for her face mask to dry. Now that she'd heard so much, she was stuck in the bathroom and unable to move around, lest she signal her eavesdropping. Shit. Maybe the eerie blue mask would dry on her face permanently and then the aliens would let her into the spaceship. *Her dad was cheating.* What the hell was that about? Was her mom just being paranoid? Alison's stomach lurched with the knowledge that her mother was never paranoid about anything, not without reason. *Her dad was cheating.* Luckily, Cherice started to loudly fuss, giving Alison an opening. She rushed out of the bathroom and positioned herself at the bottom of the stairs, as if she'd just walked down.

Her mother startled at the sight of her. "Alison, I didn't know you were here. When did you get home?"

"I've been upstairs the whole time."

"You were upstairs?" Her mother squinted at her. "How long have you had that face mask on? It's all cracked."

Alison patted her dried-out cheek. "I fell asleep and forgot to wash it off."

Her mom gave her a pointed look, and so did Olivia holding Cherice. Was she imagining it or was there some sort of three-way communication between them, her mother and Olivia warning her not to acknowledge what she'd heard?

Cherice, irritated by their silence, let out a garbled call.

"I'm going to go wash this off." Alison turned and ran up the stairs.

32

After forcing down two hard-boiled eggs for breakfast, Cynthia stepped outside. Her eyelids were paralyzed, then fluttered, startled by the blaze of white that lay before her. White. White. White. A clean sheet of snow had fallen in secret in the middle of the January night, softening every detail of the suburb. Sharp rooftops were blunted like the folds of a fancy dinner napkin; the divisions erased between sidewalk, lawn, and street. She put on her sunglasses, her eyes relaxing in the cover.

Her goal was to traverse the northern half of the suburb, despite the weakness in her limbs, her lungs, but she only made it as far as Aurora Park. The snow across the expansive lawn hadn't been trampled yet, except for the small twisting tracks of an animal that had raced across. Cynthia clambered after its prints until she was marooned in the middle.

Will this be the last time I walk this park? Before she could answer herself, she flopped onto her back in the snow. Lately she'd fallen prey to "last time" thoughts: *the last time I eat cooked carrots; the last time I see Gabe struggling to read the assigned novel from his English class; the last time I make small talk with Mrs. Chang about the new parking permits.* She flung her arms and legs out, the burn of the cold penetrating through her pants. Then she flapped her arms and legs in synchronized motion, the crunch and shush of the snow breaking and then spreading close to her ears. Beneath her, the snow angel she made didn't feel all that ethereal, but she kept on. She flapped faster until a fragment of snow kicked up and dropped into her open mouth, immediately melting from the heat. She churned until snow flew through the air, hitting her face, chest, and arms.

A voice from above: "Ma'am, are you all right?"

She looked up. A figure bundled in an official brown coat and pants hovered over her, blocking the sky. Someone from the gas company again, like she'd seen a few months ago. He was holding another box, a device for testing or sampling. Everyone was so interested in testing and sampling all of sudden. "Are you all right?" he asked again.

She laughed at the absurdity of that question, at least as it pertained to her. "Of course I'm all right."

"What are you doing?"

"Making a snow angel," she said, standing up slowly.

"You shouldn't be playing around in this park, lying in the snow like that."

She sputtered in offense. "Excuse me?"

"I'm telling you this for your own good."

"OK," she said. "What do you mean 'for my own good'?"

"Never mind what I mean. You're too old to be playing in the snow anyway. You'll catch a cold."

"You have no idea . . ." she mocked.

He peered at her strangely. Was there a kind of recognition coming on in his eyes? Did she know him from somewhere? Then he clomped off.

"You look older than me," she yelled after him. He didn't turn around.

She didn't know it at the time, but the snow would paint a white stripe through her life. Before the snow: sick but still walking, talking, angling for a way back to health. After the snow: surrender. The prickly bitch of a disease responded to blasts of radiation and chemotherapy with vengeance: it spread deeper into her brain. Yet another tumor was found, smushed against the speech center of her mind, blobbing out her short-term memory. Not that her long-term memories fared much better in their fuzzy form. The present moment consisted of disparate scraps of time, jittery jump cuts from one second to the next. She was always confused now, at least a little bit. She couldn't locate her own history; her memories had fallen behind the dresser like earrings, only to be found during the next big move. Ernest tried to help her, but he couldn't stop the erasure of her mind. Her body shut down too. The cancer traveled by blood, finding new soft parts to land. By February, she was bedridden, unable to remember what had happened five minutes prior and dependent on her family to feed and bathe her.

Before her mother's cancer, Alison had never spent a single minute thinking about scented talcum powder. Now it lingered everywhere with its cloying odor. Baby powder, never gritty but always suspiciously smooth between the fingers, dusted every surface of the sunroom, now Cynthia's bedroom and palliative center. The hospital-style bed rented from a hospice-care service hulked in the middle; in the corner, a small TV flashed with sitcoms, ads, and news reports from Rwanda, Bosnia, or the South Side of Chicago but with the volume at a low murmur. Alison was preparing her mother for bed with a sponge bath.

"Raise your arm, Mom."

Cynthia lifted her arm and feebly laid it to the side of her head. Alison shook a cloud of baby powder onto her mom's freshly washed underarm. Every other day, Ernest and Alison gave Cynthia a bath before bedtime. On the other days, they had a nurse come for a few hours—that's all they could afford right now. Gabe sometimes helped, but for the most part, he disappeared when bath time came. He always found a way to be out of the house. Seeing his mother's exposed and ravaged body was just too much, and for now, Ernest and Alison didn't push it.

"You can put your arm back down now," her daughter said. Cynthia had forgotten she left it up there. Looking down near her feet, there was the cat, who lounged on Cynthia's electric blanket nearly all hours of the day and night, a vision of health with her shiny coat. Sometimes Cynthia would reach for the cat while slipping in and out of a dream that had several passages of pain, lucidity, and shadowy, half-grasped realizations that would land with clarity—*The TV is on. It is night. The cat is here*—and then dissipate again.

When her mother didn't put her arm back down, Alison moved the limb for her, tucking it under the blanket. From the kitchen, she caught fragments of her father's voice, tense and rapid. Something about Earth Day, some paper he'd forgotten to file.

"Surely we can get them to waive the penalty fees," she heard him saying.

Alison put the baby powder back on the dresser, where her mother's arsenal of aids and salves—wet wipes, several prescription medication bottles, first-aid ointment, and two other bottles of baby powder, unopened—were coated in the factory-made pollen. Every time Ernest or Alison changed Cynthia's diaper—yes, she had lost control of her bowel functions—they powdered her crotch before wrapping another cloth diaper around her. Like a baby, she could get a rash if her skin was left wet. Alison stopped short of re-diapering her mother tonight, though she was well practiced by now. She waited for her father to get off the phone, but then she got bored.

"I'll be right back, Mom."

Upstairs, in Gabe's bedroom, he hushed her and pointed to the shortwave radio. The voice of the woman from *The Book of Connections* was in full flow:

"Male elephants in rut have a gland on their foreheads that leaks a substance into their eyes; when it reaches a critical point, the elephant goes mad, strains at chains, and attacks the female elephants. Fury takes over for lust. I learned all this while visiting Cambodia. At Angkor Wat, I saw *The Churning of the Ocean of Milk*, the bas-reliefs that depict the stirring of the cosmic ocean. Some say it's really about sex and the violence of the orgasm, depending on who you're asking."

"This is kind of pervy," Alison said.

From his bed, her brother flapped his hand at her dismissively. "You wish."

"Where do you think she's from? I can hear just a trace of an accent but I can't ever pin it down."

"I don't know," Gabe said. "She could be anywhere. That's what I like about it."

From downstairs, Ernest called Alison's name.

"Guess I have to go back down there."

Gabe nodded, not looking in her direction.

"Maybe you should come down too?"

"Gotta listen to this, maybe later."

After she left, Gabe looked out the window at the spaceship, a half-globe in the dark, the glass dome impenetrable to the eye, saying nothing of who or what was inside, the way a country on a map told nothing about its residents. Whatever was inside, Gabe didn't much care at the moment. He wasn't in the mood. His mother was dying, and all the spaceship could do was mooch electricity. It had no special powers beyond telepathically plugging in an extension cord. Really, was that all there was?

33

They didn't quite know it yet, but Alison and Aubrey, two vagabonds in thrift-shop fake furs, were about to stage a production of secret theater—or was it protest?—at the Winter Parade at the Prairie Park mall.

As they approached the crowd, Alison inhaled a last time from the passed joint and nervously chewed at her lip gloss, the kind applied with a fuzzy wand. The Winter Parade was an annual slow saunter through the main artery of the mall, and unwittingly entertainment for stoned teenagers. There was standard civic pride: floats representing various community organizations, schoolchildren waving flags, and puttering vehicles carrying town hall officials. But the Snow Queen was the real draw, and what made the Winter Parade, frankly, kind of weird.

The local tradition of the Snow Queen dated back to the nineteenth century and was somewhat like Groundhog Day. The Snow Queen, if you were lucky, predicted the future. You could ask her questions about how much longer the winter would be and if it would be particularly harsh; would you find love in the spring, or would you have to wait until summer. You could shout your question from the crowd, and if she heard it or someone relayed it to her, she'd answer back. But the better strategy was to get close enough to ask her a question directly and then she'd respond in more detail. Alison had heard that the Snow Queen worked as a secretary in one of the grade schools a few suburbs west. She seemed pretty normal for an older lady. But for the Winter Parade, she was transformed—a foul-tempered soothsayer in a white satin dress, carried on top of a roughly made litter decorated with cotton puffs painted sparkly white.

They slipped further into the crowd of mostly parents with small kids on their shoulders, walking next to the Snow Queen. Some of them eyed Alison and Aubrey suspiciously, profiling her campy faux mink and black eyeliner. A father scowled at them as Alison tried to get closer. Cutting through the crowd, she jostled a little girl. A mom muttered, "Watch it." She apologized but kept walking.

Young guys in mock-military red coats held up the doddering madam. Alison recognized them as seniors at her high school, all of them jocks who mostly ignored the freshman girls. One of them— she thought of him as Nice Jock—sometimes smiled at her in the hallways. Alison

was close enough to ask a question, but then a little girl cut in front of her.

"Will this winter be the worst ever?" the girl asked in a squeaky voice that Alison tried hard not to loathe.

Lame question, but Alison enjoyed watching the Snow Queen process it, her etched-on eyebrows furrowing and then releasing under a coat of white makeup. "This is the center of the country, the heart," she said, her red mouth enunciating each word. "We are protected from earthquakes and hurricanes. We have no mountains or oceans, but we have *weather*. A violent system of weather. And yet it gives our great city its *personality*. Our weather rages: tempestuous, moody, blackhearted. OK, occasionally it's sunny, but even then, a wind will lick away your papers, mess up your hair, blow off your favorite cap. In other words, it is not simple. It does not care about you, but it will never give us what we can't handle."

By the end the child was confused, along with most of the adults, but Alison felt her face, numbed by the pot, smiling. The Snow Queen was a secret subversive. How had she never noticed this before? She was a wacked-out vessel of poetic riddles that held no easy answers. She reminded Alison of *The Book of Connections* lady if she were possibly drunk and totally unhinged.

Nice Jock raised his hand up to the Snow Queen and pointed at Alison. "You've got a question here."

Propped up on a pile of pillows, the Snow Queen turned, her eyes slowly blinking under heavy coats of mascara and fake lashes, her hand momentarily flying up to check on the tiara anchored in the cottony nest of her hair. Alison recognized the Snow Queen's white dress as one of the perennial window displays in the mall's costume shop. She had some kind of leather satchel tucked under her body; Alison could see a can of Diet Coke in there.

The Snow Queen offered her a white-gloved hand. "What is it, child?"

Before she could stop herself, she asked, "Will my mother die of cancer?" Alison blurted it out loudly, loudly enough that a discernible hush immediately radiated around her. You weren't supposed to ask the Snow Queen such heavy questions. Alison was torn between enjoying the shock on Nice Jock's and the Snow Queen's faces, and worrying that maybe somebody would pull her away, yell at her for asking such an inappropriate question. But of course nobody did. She looked back at Aubrey, who was gravely impressed and let her know by raising one eyebrow. The parents who had initially pegged her as a troublemaker now wore troubled looks on their faces. The aged Snow Queen fumbled for her answer.

"What a question." She brought her face down near Alison's and whispered, as though just between the two of them, "Let me think."

The Snow Queen closed her eyes, laid back, and reached her hands into the air, flapped them around like bickering pigeons for two very confusing minutes. Alison decided to do the same thing. She felt a hundred pairs of eyes on her. She felt Aubrey's eyes. Then the Snow Queen shot up and leaned back toward her. "I can only tell you that the winter is long and harsh, but there is always a spring. There is always resurrection, though it might be on some other plane."

This wasn't a satisfying answer. "Are you saying my mom is going to come back?"

The Snow Queen pursed her lips.

"What exact plane are you talking about?"

The Snow Queen cast her eyes around, but nobody else was offering her a question.

"You're a phony!" Alison yelled. The crowd gasped. The Nice Jock gently pushed her back and told his cohorts to pick it up.

"Heretic!" the Snow Queen said, pointing at her with a straw from a fast-food restaurant.

"What kind of psychic drinks Diet Coke from a can?" Alison yelled after them.

"A diabetic one, you dummy," the Snow Queen hissed back as the crowd finally moved on, shuffling around Alison with anxious side-glances.

Aubrey wanted to walk her home, but she told him she needed some space and headed back alone. Was there another plane? A real one apart from this one? The Snow Queen's answer was a set of words that only curled back in on itself, worse than a fortune cookie aphorism. She kept thinking about a family dinner a month after her mom's diagnosis at the House of Two Cranes, their favorite Chinese restaurant, regal and run-down, with the cumbersome menus bound with frayed tasseled cords. At the end of dinner, her mother had cracked open her fortune cookie and held the slip between her fingers. They went around the table, Gabe reading his fortune ("Adventure can be real happiness"), Alison hers ("A hunch of creativity is trying to tell you something"), Ernest his ("If certainty were truth, we would never be wrong"), and then they got to Cynthia, who shrugged and laughed. "There's nothing on mine." She pulled down her lavender cap.

"That happens?" Gabe asked.

"A misprint at the fortune cookie factory," Ernest said. "Funny!" Then he picked up the bill and engrossed himself with checking all the charges.

But it wasn't funny to Alison, who took it as a harbinger of doom. White. Blank. Blankness. Empty. How had the factory done that? Was it even a factory? Maybe it was just a man back there in the kitchen, pressing each crescent closed with his fingers, rushing through a big order. He hadn't noticed that this sheet was blank. It was just an accident, an oversight.

"You should get another cookie," Gabe said.

"Oh, please," Cynthia answered. "I don't like the taste of these anyway."

It was true: her mother never ate the cookie parts of fortune cookies. Maybe, Alison thought with some relief, that meant that nothing about the fortune would come true anyway, including when the fortune itself was an absence of one, an absence of life to predict upon. Impulsively, she reached across the table and snatched half her mother's cookie and popped it into her mouth.

"Wow, hungry still?" Cynthia asked.

"Starving!" Alison said brightly, and the table laughed.

Then her brother grabbed the other half and popped it into his mouth, maybe so he could get a laugh out of his parents too. It didn't matter what his motives were; Alison loved him for it. Sometimes her brother did something so perfect, so exactly what she wanted him to do that she hadn't even thought of it yet herself. They were young and strong; of course they were the ones who could swallow this empty fortune for their mother. They were the ones who could bear this prediction of white blankness because it was clear they were heading into a life of something else, whatever it was. Alison stuck out her tongue, coated in pasty almond dust, at her brother. He laughed and wagged his golden tongue back at her.

34

THE ACTIVITIES OF THE UNWELCOME VISITORS
FROM JUPITER: AN ALLEN FAMILY LOG

February 5: *I know a lot has been going on for the family, but this log has been neglected as of late. It's more important than ever that we fill out these reports, that we're mounting a case of evidence. We must keep up all surveillance and documentation, in case the situation clarifies itself.* —*EA*

February 5: *Looked up all instances of the spaceship dumping fluids onto the lawn. Cross-referenced them with phases of the moon to see if the ship timed its dumps in any way with the lunar calendar. No correlations could be ascertained. Can we start charting exact times for dumps, nightly system checks, etc., as I asked several weeks ago?* —*EA*

February 5: *Sure, Dad. That all sounds great. Meanwhile, back on planet Earth, Mom has developed another sty on her left eye. I looked for the meds you said to use but they're not there.* —*GA*

February 5: *Gabe, I left you a note to pick up the drugs at the pharmacy. Did you not see it? This journal isn't for keeping records about Mom's illness. It needs to stay limited to the spaceship's activities, unless you think some turn in Mom's illness is related to the spaceship. Is that the case?* —*EA*

February 5: *No, that's not what I was saying. As far as the spaceship goes, it's been pretty quiet lately. Tonight's systems check, or whatever it's doing, started at 9:40 p.m. (I didn't verify the exact second because I'm not a robot, sorry!) and could barely be heard inside the house. I had to stand outside in the freezing snow to do my observational duties. Speaking of outside, when's the last time you stepped into the great outdoors, Dad? Besides for*

Earth Day meetings or visits to the super-fun hazardous waste facility? Possibly related question: Have you ever seen The Shining? —GA

February 5: *Thanks for your concern about my interaction outside, but it's important right now that I keep close tabs on the spaceship, as well as your mother. I've called the Suburban Analytics Lab about the soil samples and they say they will have the results in a week. If anything problematic is found, we will have a family meeting to discuss our options. —EA*

February 6: *Dad, when you say anything problematic, what exactly do you mean? I thought you said nothing came up in the first test. Then you had those guys from Analytics come and dig all those holes in the yard. By the way, it's been a couple of weeks and you still haven't filled the holes. Isn't it kind of weird to have big graves just sitting there in the backyard? —AA*

February 6: *At 7:45 a.m., the ship dumped out 7.65 gallons of liquid. Fluid: slightly cloudy, chartreuse color. Light chemical scent. Weight: 83.4 pounds. Sample taken. Rest of the fluid disposed of at the hazardous waste facility. —EA*

February 6: *Can you answer my question, Dad? —AA*

February 6: *I really can't say more until those test results are in, but I'm leaving the holes open in case the lab needs to dig deeper. Please, once again, guys, where are the entries about the spaceship's activities? I can't watch it 100 percent of the time myself. —EA*

35

Ross didn't want to get into it on the phone, but he asked Ernest if they could talk before the official start of the Earth Day meeting. In the back of the Aurora Park field house, he broke his news while his wife, Marcy, arranged croissants and coffee cups across the room, her face a study of contained stress. A malignant tumor had been found in Ross's prostate, but fortunately the doctor had ranked it as not very aggressive. Ross plowed through Ernest's stunned silence with reassurances.

"Ernest, I don't want you to think this means I won't be around. I have every intention of keeping up my work with the committee. We're so close to game time, I'm not going anywhere. I'm excited to pull off the best festival this town's ever seen. Still working on that Joni Mitchell thing, by the way. Her people are going to talk to some other people; you know how it goes. Jesus, don't look so worried! We've got a killer lineup with or without Ms. Fancy Folksinger."

"That's not what I'm worried about."

Marcy, stacking paper napkins, barely disguised her eaves-dropping. Ross said, "Listen, I know your own situation makes this especially hard to hear."

"But that's just it, Ross," Ernest said as Jean and a few more organizers filed in. Ernest leaned in close and whispered, "You were at our party in the fall, right?"

"Sure, but—" Ross said, slightly irritated with the question. "Ernest, if you're about to bring up that spaceship . . ."

"It could've made you sick too. Think about it."

"Oh, Ernest, I really—" Ross stopped himself to speak more calmly. "Allow me to point out that many people were at the party last fall and not everyone has a tumor."

"I'm thinking that it's not like you get automatically sick from exposure. I mean, obviously that's not the case. Like you said, many people have been around it. It's more like if you have some sort of weakness inside of you . . ."

Marcy, setting up chairs in the center of the room, looked sharply in their direction.

"I would not say weakness," Ross said.

"Sorry, not weakness, forgive me, but susceptibility. Predisposition. Like if you have some collection of not cancer exactly but precancerous cells, then the spaceship finds that and acts as a catalyst. Springs it into action."

"Tom and Olivia, the nice couple with the AIDS baby, don't they live next door to you? How is that baby doing? Last I heard, she was doing fine, as well as could be expected."

"Cherice has HIV, not full-blown AIDS. She's doing well, but I've thought about this. She's on a potent cocktail of meds, Ross. New chemicals you and I have never heard of. Maybe somehow the spaceship is thrown off the trail in that case. Maybe those meds even protect her somehow."

"Well, that's a new one. Talk about an off-label use: HIV meds can also prevent spaceship cancer. I'll tell the world."

"There's no need for sarcasm here."

"Sorry, but it just doesn't hold water, Ernest. Spaceships are all over the country. They are not flying around poisoning people."

"How can we really know that? Just because the government says so? As if this isn't the same country that makes secret nuclear reactors? That dumps mercury into water?"

"If you're so concerned your family's getting poisoned, why are you still living in your house then? Why don't you take the kids and Cynthia and go live in a hotel? Better yet, why don't you move them back out to the wilderness?"

"Because I'm not made out of money, and it'd be incredibly hard to move Cynthia right now. Besides—"

"Besides what?"

"We've already been exposed. It's too late for us. If we are going to get something, we are going to get it. I want to limit our exposure to others."

"You're a real asshole, you know that?" Ross's raised voice gained the attention of Jean and the other organizers. "You know what I think, Ernest? You care more about indulging in your sci-fi fantasies than the safety of your family."

"Everything OK?" Jean asked.

Marcy answered: "I think Ernest was just telling my husband that he's weak for getting cancer."

"That's not what I meant, Marcy," Ernest said. "I said susceptible."

"Honestly, I don't know that I can have another conversation with you about this, Ernest," Ross said.

"But I'm trying to help you. I'm trying to tell you that I know how this happened to you."

"You know nothing! The doctor said this tumor grew slowly, probably over the last few years. The spaceship's been here for six months."

Jean looked perplexed.

"By the way," Ross said to her. "I have prostate cancer. I'm going to get the tumor removed."

"I'm so sorry, Ross," Jean said.

"My prognosis is good, but Ernest here thinks the spaceship jump-started my tumor."

"Ernest," Jean said with icy professionalism, "is this the conversation we should be having right now?"

Everyone watched him, and in turn, he marveled at their ignorance. The hostility in their sour stares, the frustration barely reined in, their lack of open-mindedness about what could be possible in their very own backyards. Didn't they see any of it?

"I was just trying to help," he said.

Marcy threw her hands into the air. "You want to help? What about saying, 'I'm sorry this happened to you'? Or 'What can I do to make things easier?' Instead of always making it about you and your paranoid theories?"

"I am fucking helping! I'm keeping everything in line. I'm getting answers."

Ernest's face flamed to the roots of his hair. He wasn't talking to her, he realized. He was answering Cynthia.

A stupefied silence fell across the room.

"All right," Jean said. "Let's take five minutes to regroup."

Jean steered Ernest over to a private corner. "I was planning to present anyway on what Prairie Park is doing on advertising," she said with a smile painted on her face. "How about I just take the lead for this meeting?"

Ernest agreed, knowing it wasn't really a choice.

36

When he got home that night, he found Alison pulling out clumps of green fuzz from her wet hair. She smeared the residue onto a paper towel, adding it to the crumpled collection on the couch. The sticky substance had been blown out by the spaceship. When she'd gone outside to do laundry, some vents at the bottom, near where the waste poured out, opened and unleashed the fuzz. Clouds of it had blown all over Alison and the yard.

"Have you written any of this in the log yet?"

"Dad, it just happened."

"But the documentation—"

"I wanted to wash my hair first, not that it did much good."

Ernest left the room and returned with the notebook, sterile gloves, and a trash bag. After he snapped on his gloves with expert efficiency, he threw all the crumpled paper towels into the trash bag. He sat on the couch next to her, the silicone stretched over his knuckles as he gripped a pen. "I'll write down what you're saying. It's important that we record every detail while your memory is fresh."

"Well, I remember that the vents made a lot of racket as they were opening."

"What kind of racket?"

"It sounded like an old air conditioner turning on. Then all this neon-green fluff shot out. I dropped the laundry and ran into the garage, but the wind was already blowing it everywhere. Dad, do you want to just see it? It's all still back there."

The backyard was possessed by fluorescent dandruff—piles of it on the blanket of snow, clinging to the barren trees, the evergreen bushes, and the back fence; the rest was carried off by the wind. The color was a hydrated shade of green that looked alive, like it might crawl off somewhere—a hive of a million caterpillars or praying mantises. It was the same density as lint from the dryer. The spaceship remained clean. None of the fuzz had clung to the ship or its legs.

"I was going to clean it up, but I wasn't sure how to do it."

"No, absolutely not," Ernest said. "Don't touch it."

The laundry basket was where Alison had dropped it, most of the clothes out on the driveway, dusted in green. Alison started to put the clothes back in the basket, shaking off as much of the pollen as she could.

"Did you hear me? Don't touch it!"

"But it's already all over me."

"You shouldn't have more exposure. We should get rid of all of those clothes."

"But, Dad, this is some of my favorite stuff."

"I'm sorry, Alison. I need to take it to hazardous waste. And you need to take a shower!"

"Dad, no way," Alison said. "These are my things. I wear this cardigan, like, every other day. Look, the dress Mom gave me last fall, when she could still shop. You're going to make me get rid of this? I can just put it in the wash."

"We don't know what this green fuzz is, how it'll affect us."

"I don't care. I'm obviously fine."

"No, you're not. You're scared." He yanked the laundry basket away from her and started toward the garage.

A loud clang from the spaceship startled them. A small shriek leaped out of Alison. Underneath the spaceship, a heap of filters dropped onto the ground, along with the usual pool of neon-green slurry. They'd never seen it in action before, but presumably a bigger slot had opened to allow for the screens to pass. The panel hummed to a close, and Ernest and Alison were left alone again. Ernest inspected the densely netted screens fitted in silver frames, coated in thick sheets of the same sticky pollen clinging to the yard. He counted fifteen filters.

"Why would they throw these away?" Ernest asked.

"Maybe they don't work anymore," Alison said. "Maybe it spewed out all that crap because these filters were overloaded. They can't filter out the junk in our air anymore so they're blasting it all out."

Ernest wasn't so sure his daughter was right. According to Alison's theory, the ship had gotten rid of the filters because they were overloaded and doing a poor job of keeping pollutants *out*. But maybe the filters had been keeping the pollutants *in*. The pollutants that caused illness. Now that the filters had been ejected, were they getting a full blast of an outer space cancer catalyst?

"You got it all out of your hair?"

"Yeah," Alison said.

Her father scrutinized her, held up a lock with his gloved hand and cocked his head at it. His inspector's eye was grim and calculating. "We've got to cut it off."

Alison snatched her hair back, tucked it into her collar. "No way, Dad." She backed away from him. "Take my clothes if you have to, but you are not touching my hair. I'll go take a shower now."

"Listen to me: it's stuck on every single strand of your hair."

"You're not taking my hair."

"It's sticky, it's not going to wash out."

"Yes, it will. Not my hair, Dad." Alison was ducking her head, as if shrinking could detour her fate.

"I don't want it to penetrate your scalp or neck. Do you know what could happen then? You could get brain damage."

"Dad, you're being crazy." She swallowed and tried a different tack. "If you touch my hair, I'll tell everyone you're having an affair."

For a moment, her father's expression shocked back to its old self, astute and skeptical. "Where did you get that info?"

"I figured it out." Alison wasn't about to give away her source. She watched her dad carefully. She had caught him off guard, so much so that he hadn't even tried to deny to it. So it was true.

Ernest shook his head, gathering himself. "There's nothing happening, Alison. But thanks for the accusation; that makes a man feel real good. Seriously, how could you say something like that?"

"Because you are. You and the reporter. I saw how you looked at her at the party."

Her father glared at her. Now she had pissed him off on top of everything else. What recourse did she have left? She tried triggering his pity. "OK, sorry! You're not having an affair. I'll wash it again," she said, panic shaking her voice. "Please, Dad, please. I'd rather wash it forty times than cut it all off."

"It's got to go, Alison. Look, it's *stuck* in your hair. It's not coming out no matter how much you wash it. Think of it this way: you'll be in solidarity with your mother."

She burst into tears as she faced the inevitable. "I hope an alien comes out of the stupid spaceship and kills you, Dad."

"Careful what you wish for." Ernest looked at the spaceship. "I'm afraid they don't have to come out of the spaceship to pull that off, Alison."

"In your sleep," she blurted out, turning and running inside.

THE ACTIVITIES OF THE UNWELCOME VISITORS FROM JUPITER: AN ALLEN FAMILY LOG

February 9: *As I already said this morning but will repeat for absolute clarity, DO NOT go into the backyard while the hazmat guys are here. They're cleaning up the spaceship pollution. It's not safe for either of you to be back there. Also, I'm paying them a lot of money to clean and have that crap tested and don't want a single thing compromised. Do you kids copy? —EA*

February 9: *Copy loud and clear. I never want to see the backyard again. Or the spaceship. Or even this house, or really, to be honest, any of you people. I look like a troll. Anyone know where Mom put that wig? —AA*

February 9: *Dad, Sinead O'Connor and I fully copy. What I really want to know is: Can the hazmat guys carry out this task with a straight face? Pretty sure cotton candy is more harmful than that fuzz. —GA*

February 9: *I have news: New World is finally admitting that our little cancer saucer is in some kind of distress. Yes, you read that right. I called them about the fuzz and they "examined our file" and concluded that this, combined with the grievous thievery of electricity for months now, points*

toward "serious distress." Of course they didn't say it was dangerous—
they never do—but tomorrow, at 7 p.m., I'm calling a mandatory family
meeting to discuss our options. REPEAT: MANDATORY. —EA

37

Ernest and Alison were changing Cynthia's diaper and bathing her for the night, which included applying Band-Aids to the bedsores festering on her back. For the fiftieth time that day, Alison rubbed her hand over her stubbled head. Every time she touched it, shock stabbed her anew. She had ditched school again, not ready to show her prickly visage after barely forty-eight hours of living with it herself.

Gabe, as usual, wasn't available to help. Ernest wondered if Gabe would show up for the mandatory family meeting in an hour. If not, he'd have to reschedule it, the very idea infuriating him as he pulled a washcloth over each of Cynthia's fingers.

In the last few weeks the house had become trip-wired with Ernest's tensions and fears. His fixation with wasted resources fueled his most radical home project yet. In the name of energy efficiency, he spent a day skulking around with a caulk gun, filling every minute crack in the wall until most of the rooms were spider-veined. Then he coated the windows in a plastic film that was supposed to further insulate. By the time he was finished, each pane of glass was cloudy with plastic that let in limited light.

The rest of the house was in shambles: stacks of dirty dishes in the kitchen; the dining table loaded with bills, unopened correspondence, and piles of magazines reporting on climatological change, chemical spills, drifting trash islands, the piebald ozone layer, deforestation. Ernest had canceled the weekly service with the Polish cleaning lady, to save money and to cut down on chemicals (he kept catching her using harsh bleaches). He also didn't want anyone in the house, outside of Olivia and Tom.

The house was sealing up around him. There were the responsibilities to Cynthia's failing health but also to the mounting suspicion that if he left the house, he might be carrying whatever poison from the ship to some other untainted place. Sometimes it was unavoidable—Cynthia's illness required a constant restocking of supplies—and he'd have to spend a few minutes in his car rationalizing to himself that he wasn't carrying anything in him or on him. He'd stare at his hands, holding them up in front of the windshield, trying hard to see anything clinging to the skin. The whites of his eyes still looked clear, his tongue healthy and pink, but he wondered if something was slowly shifting in his blood. There was nowhere to go from these thoughts but to yank himself back, to insist that, at least for now, he was fine. He wasn't delivering anything to the world that wasn't already simmering in the air on the particulate level. He'd start the car, aware that he'd beaten back the paranoia for only a little bit.

"I need you to push her up on the left side," Ernest directed Alison.

Opening a bandage in the sunroom, Ernest noticed those thoughts humming along in the background, uneasy with how they flowed through him, a ticker tape of panic and dread. He needed to concentrate on Cynthia. He needed to care for her on this very basic level. The medicated bandage, recommended by Olivia, was for the bedsore on Cynthia's back. Thin as saran wrap but very sticky, Olivia referred to the bandages as "second skin." The idea was to prop Cynthia on her side and he'd apply the second skin to the two sores that flanked her spine. Alison would have to keep Cynthia up on her side.

As Alison clumsily pushed against her mother's back and buttocks, Cynthia groaned. Alison fought repulsion every time she had to touch her mother this way. Cynthia's skin was so thin, Alison was sure she could have pulled it off with her fingers, like gobs of cold cream. She bent over at the waist, keeping one of her flattened palms pressed into the back of her mother's white thigh, which had become exposed when Cynthia's hospital gown had slipped away. Her father held Cynthia in place from the other side with his hands around her back and shoulders, a deep moan emanating from somewhere inside her.

"I'm going to let her go and come around to your side, so make sure you keep her up," Ernest said. He removed his hands and instantly Cynthia slipped back a bit. "Alison."

"I have her, Dad," Alison said through gritted teeth, holding her breath.

"Keep pushing against her." Ernest walked around, taking care not to have the medicated side get stuck to his fingers. He lowered himself beside Alison, creeping toward Cynthia's back.

Just as he got close to applying, Alison let her mother slide back again.

"Alison!" Ernest barked as one of the bandages folded on itself, his fingers catching most of the medicine.

Gabe slunk into the house and watched from the doorway. No one acknowledged him. Finally, after a few tries, Alison managed to get her mother up again.

"You've got to have a firm grip on her," Ernest said. "You've got to hold her up."

"I do," Alison growled.

They tried again: new bandage, new push, but Alison didn't apply enough pressure to keep her mom up and Ernest blew through another expensive piece of second skin. Cynthia, on her back again, groaned from exhaustion.

"What the hell's wrong with you? And what about you?" He pointed at Gabe. "You didn't notice that we needed your help?"

Both kids silently fumed.

"Fine. Shall we have the meeting now?"

They followed him into the kitchen. Alison's eyebrows crushed down, her arms folded against her chest. Gabe eyed the doors and windows.

"I can't take all this attitude anymore," Ernest said. "I can't help that this is happening to you guys."

"Wait, I think we should be logging the spaceship right now instead of having this special family conversation," Gabe said.

"You can make fun of the log all you want, but it might be the thing that saves us," Ernest said. "I've got a plan."

The kids exchanged a knowing look. They were used to Ernest's plans.

"We should face the fact that we'll probably need to abandon the house. New World confirmed the ship's in distress mode—what does that really mean? For a while now, I've operated under the belief that we've already been exposed and that the best thing was to stay put and not contaminate anybody else. I told myself you guys are young and healthy and that would be enough for you two, but I'm done kidding myself. Now with the ship in distress, releasing even more toxins, we can't take the chance. I'm thinking we can go back to living in the woods, like we did when you guys were babies. You don't remember it and not everything was perfect, but it'll work better this time. I learned from the first experience. We'll get away from the spaceship, leave all our possessions behind, and start over. But I don't want to just run away and leave this thing to kill whoever is around, I want to spread the word. I want to prevent it from happening again. The log that we've been keeping will be the basis of a book that tells about our time with the spaceship. The effects of it. I'll write chapters around the notes we already have. We can publish it so that everyone knows the effects of these spaceships, that they're not innocent fun but actually dangerous, toxic warships of some kind. That's all going to take time, I know, but we can be a part of something bigger than just ourselves." Ernest rummaged through a cupboard. "I bought these in the meantime. We can start wearing them around the house."

A jumbo box of five hundred cotton face masks, the kind with the elastic strap for holding the cup to your mouth. Ernest opened the box and held out one, but neither of the kids took it.

"Dad, this is scary," Alison said.

"I know it is, but I have a plan of action."

"No, what you're saying is crazy. You're talking about running away from our home and starting some kind of conspiracy about the spaceships and living as cult weirdos in the woods. No way I'm doing that."

"Alison, you admitted yourself that it's creepy. Did the spaceship not blow some sort of toxic pollen all over you?"

"If it's toxic, why am I not dead? Gabe, say something."

Gabe said in a flat voice, "This is ridiculous. I don't even know what to say."

"Think of something," Alison said.

"Dad, the ship landed and Mom happened to get sick. She would have gotten sick anyway. Two different things. Nobody but you has ever thought the spaceship poisoned her."

"You're not saying anything I haven't heard a million times now. From the Earth Day crew, from you guys, from Tom and Olivia—"

"But everyone is right!" Gabe said. "I mean, listen to yourself. Like, I don't even know whose kitchen I'm standing in anymore. Is this my family? Have we all gone crazy? Look at Alison's marine-girl hair. Look at Mom. Look at all this!" Gabe swept his hand out to the room, where every corner contained an elaborate mess. "Like, what is going on here?" Gabe walked up to the vacuum by the back door. "What is this project?"

"I've been vacuuming by the back door every day," Ernest said.

"I'm keeping out the weird pollen that's probably mutating our DNA, is what I'm doing."

"Are you listening to yourself?"

"Yes, and you can thank me later!"

"So what does Marilyn think about your moving to the woods?" Alison's voice was low and strange. Gabe stared at his sister.

"Alison," her father warned.

"What are you talking about?" Gabe demanded a little frantically. "Who's Marilyn?"

"Dad's cheating on Mom with a reporter, but he keeps saying he's not."

Gabe's face screwed into outrage and disgust. "Is this true?"

Ernest glared with fire. "No, it isn't. I'm not having an affair. What the hell makes you think you even have a right to ask me that?"

"She's my mom!"

"This may shock you two, but you don't own your parents' lives. You don't get to know everything."

"See, it's true," Alison said. "You're a liar."

"I'm not a liar. I'm not having an affair. And I'm not saying it again."

Gabe came closer and stood eye to eye with his dad. "You've got to realize that you've totally gone off the deep end! The spaceship isn't poisoning us. It isn't poisoning Mom. You just can't control it, and that's what's driving you batshit. Mom's going to die and there's nothing you can fucking do, you crazy asshole!"

Ernest's body slammed forward with speed. He took Gabe by the collar and pushed him against the wall. Alison screamed.

"What's it like to have zero respect for anyone or anything?" Ernest thrashed him against the wall, Gabe's head jerking with the motion, his stunned expression blank, registering nothing.

"Dad, what are you doing?" Alison shouted. "Stop!"

"Stop," a voice called out from the other room. "Stop it."

Alison ran back into the sunroom to find Cynthia hoisted up in bed, her gaze fixed with remarkable awareness.

"Mom," Alison said, "what do I do? They're fighting really bad."

Just as quickly as the awareness presented, it blew out again. Her mother looked at her with cold seagull eyes. A cry rose in Alison's chest, but there wasn't time. She grabbed the closest weapon she could find.

She ran back into the kitchen with the bottle of baby powder in her hands, ready to launch. She ran up to them—her father still thrashing Gabe—and shouted, "Stop it! Stop fighting!" and gave the bottle a violent squeeze. Ernest dropped Gabe to the floor as Alison shot a flurry at both of them. Then the top popped off and she flung out a heap. Gabe mostly dodged out of the way, but the powder clouded her father's face and his hair. He coughed and flapped one of his hands, and after a moment when he couldn't recover, he bent over, hacking with force. Retching like a sick dog, he crumpled to his knees, the powder from his hair dropping to the floor. Gabe ran to the faucet and poured his father a glass of water. Ernest's coughs subsided enough for him to take a few gulps that splashed down his chin and onto the ground, mixing with the powder. Ernest gulped in air, watery spit, and talcum from his lips. Once he recovered, he stood to look at his daughter with red-rimmed eyes, his skin chalky white.

"Get out. Get out right now and go. Take a walk. Think about the things you've said."

"Me? I should get out?"

Ernest nodded between coughs.

"Goddamn, Alison," her brother said.

"I just wanted you both to calm down," Alison said. "I thought you were going to seriously hurt each other. But you know what? Do what you want, guys. I don't care anymore. Kill each other please!"

As Ernest heard the tumbler click and her sneakers scraping down the stairs, he coughed again, thinking about miners who breathed in iron ore dust. Repeated exposure to such fine metallic particles gummed up the cilia, the tiny hairs in the lungs that did nothing but sweep out impurities—until one day when the torrent overwhelmed the system. Maybe his cancer would take root first in his lungs.

———————

Aubrey's house was a squat bungalow with extinguished Christmas lights twined around the porch ledge. Inside, it was practically a sauna in comparison to the Allen house. A fluorescent bulb glowed above the kitchen sink; the dishwasher churned on the downbeat. Aubrey told her to take off her coat. She reluctantly slid it onto the back of a chair, all the more aware of her baldness without it. She sat at the island counter.

"Holy shit. So that's a certain kind of look."

"Yeah, well, it looks like yours now."

"Is that what you wanted?"

"No."

"I'm not saying it's bad." He cracked a smile. "You look like a she-warrior."

"I look like a girl with a psychotic father."

"Oh, seriously? He did that to you?"

"Never mind, it's a long story." Alison suddenly noticed the quiet of Aubrey's house. "Is everyone asleep?" she whispered.

"They're upstairs watching TV," he said, and then offered her soup.

She wasn't that hungry, but she didn't want to refuse. Aubrey opened the fridge, the condiments rattling on the door shelves, the tiny internal light splashing on his skin. The door was covered in a mash of photos, drawings, magnets with dentists' phone numbers, and some of the same stickers her father had affixed to theirs: the

WWF panda with black blotches for eyes and the Greenpeace logo of a white dove carrying a branch. Aubrey pulled a soup pot out and placed it on the stove as quietly as possible. He kept throwing her reassuring looks as he reheated the dish. In a navy-blue bowl, he ladled corn chowder flecked with black beans and red pepper flakes. She'd never seen her brother so confident in the kitchen.

As Alison took her first bite, the flavors mingled on her tongue—soft and tart, hearty and sweet. Aubrey squeezed a cut of lime into her bowl, explaining that the soup was made with coconut milk, so the lime would taste good. She tasted the citrus, picturing some sort of spiky green sea creature dissolving in her mouth. Except for the coconut milk, the soup was made out of ingredients Alison had consumed before, but it tasted better than anything Alison had eaten in a while. No one was cooking beautiful meals at the Allen household these days. No one sat down and ate together anymore. She and Aubrey chatted casually over a shared meal, like her family used to do.

"I learn something different about you every time I see you, Aubrey," she said. "You're also a good cook?"

"It's what I do when I'm bored."

"I recognize that voice. How do you like it, Alison?" Aubrey's mother stole into the kitchen, wearing slippers but otherwise still dressed for the day in purple denim and a white blouse. Tiny gold hoops glinted in her earlobes.

"It's amazing, Mrs. Banks."

Now that Aubrey's mother had a full look at her, she stopped at Alison's hair, or lack thereof. Alison watched her swallow any commentary.

"It's vegetarian too. That's how we eat around here," Mrs. Banks said with a brilliant smile. But then she closed her eyes and rubbed them, stifling a yawn.

"I'm sorry I'm here so late," Alison said, but Mrs. Banks waved her off before handing Alison a shaker of sea salt.

"Aubrey, can't believe you didn't give her that. This is the finishing touch."

Mrs. Banks waited until Alison used the salt, then she went about putting things away in the kitchen. She didn't look anything like Cynthia. She was tall and lean, no extra weight on her frame. Her face was defined by sharper bones than her mother's, her smell a waxier herbal fullness instead of Cynthia's spritz of grapefruit oil from the health-food store. And she was stylish in a way that Cynthia would never understand, let alone attempt.

"Could I stay the night here?"

Mrs. Banks turned around. Aubrey's eyebrows were high on his forehead.

"I mean," Alison continued, "on the couch downstairs. Could I sleep here, just for tonight?"

"You can, but I'd have to call your dad." When Alison didn't say anything, Aubrey's mom peered at her and asked, "Is everything OK?"

"Yeah, fine," Alison said.

"Alison, I have to say: the haircut is throwing me. That's a bold move for a young woman. Are you sure everything's all right?"

"It wasn't voluntary, the haircut."

"What do you mean?"

"You know what? Never mind. I should go back home. Thanks for the delicious soup." Alison attempted a comforting smile.

"I'll walk you back," Aubrey said, trying to seem useful.

Aubrey's mom nodded. "Well, if you change your mind, just let me know. I'll be upstairs."

When Mrs. Banks said good night, giving Alison a quick squeeze on her shoulder as she left them in the kitchen, there was a little part of Alison that wondered if it'd be weird to ask for a hug. She decided yes and stayed seated with her empty soup bowl at the counter island. It was enough to hear Aubrey's mother ascending the stairs with perfect, healthy steps. A moment later, she was sitting on the couch in the living room with Aubrey. Everyone in bed, the household truly quiet. Finally, Aubrey leaned in to kiss her. They tried it out, lost in the novelty of each other's lips, but the kiss dwindled, stopped.

They kissed three times, but something was lacking. It didn't make any sense. Shouldn't they be attracted to each other? Alison wanted to be, thought she might be, but then some line didn't connect all the way. She'd made out with other boys before, but with him she held back. Her warm feelings for him all spilled out in a pool; they weren't pointed, sexual. They spent all this time together; they understood each other. Why didn't it feel sexual?

"I don't know why," Aubrey started, "but I can't do this."

Alison nodded. She snuck a glance at him and he looked sad. Beyond what he should. She couldn't tell what he was thinking about.

"Is everything OK?" she asked.

"Yeah, it's totally OK."

But it wasn't OK, not totally at least. He wanted something or someone else, she realized. But had he pulled away only because he recognized her hesitancy? Why had she hesitated? He was one of the very few people she knew at school who had seen her really sick mother, who'd seen this pain in her life. Did she see his? One time he'd dropped by and she let him in because she was so happy to see him, but she tried to steer him away from the sunroom, away from all signs of her mother dying. Why? Because it would make their jokes stop cold and it'd be so hard to start up again. When he'd marched in anyway, following the cat who was a big white bush with mismatched eyes, he halted as soon as he saw the woman with a hospital gown bagged around her figure.

Cynthia noted his presence with mild interest, pushing herself up in her bed. "Hello."

"Hello, Mrs. Allen."

"Who are you?" Friendly, oblivious.

"I'm Aubrey." Alison started to drag him out. "Bye now. Nice to see you, Mrs. Allen."

Alison ran up the stairs, checking to see if Aubrey followed. He looked up at her, shocked, but kept up with her manic path to her bedroom.

"I didn't know your mom was that sick."

"Yeah," Alison said, not knowing what else to add.

"You never talk about it."

"Yeah," Alison said, and started to cry as she sank onto her bed. She turned on a Dinosaur Jr. record so that no one could hear her outside the room. Aubrey extended his arms and wrapped them around her while the tears came, only able to say, "It's OK, it's OK, it's OK," and weirdly petting her hair in a way she wanted to swat at, but that was enough, that was more than anyone else had done for her in months.

Several hours after Aubrey walked her home, after she hugged him tightly and then ran inside without looking back at him, Alison awoke to a warm hand pressed over her mouth. Her cloudy eyes focused on the familiar face above her bed.

"Shh!" Gabe warned, and slowly lifted his hand. He brought her to the window. Outside, the spaceship spun in drowsy, uneven circles, like the last few spins of a coin before it rests on the table. Blue light, not the standard green, poured through the cold glass, outlining her brother's profile. There was something choppy about the motion, like a shot animal staggering before it collapsed. Its cord was still plugged into the garage, twirling with the rotations, as the kids watched with sleepy fascination.

Eventually the ship slowed down and stopped completely, snuffing out the blue lights and then lighting them again in customary green. With the same four tentacles emerging from its underside, it repierced the ground. All of its motions were slower, weaker, defeated.

"We can't put that in the log," Alison whispered. "That's another distress signal, right? Imagine what Dad might do if he reads that."

"I think we should log it," Gabe said. "It wasn't a distress signal."

"What was it then?"

"It was trying to leave."

"Was it? We don't really know. You want to feed Dad's paranoia?"

"He's leaving early tomorrow for some photo session for Earth Day. He won't read it till he gets home."

"So what? Eventually he'll read it and freak out."

"Maybe that's better. He can call them and they can tell him that this little spinning show means that it's leaving soon. And then he'll finally shut up about it."

"We're not taking that chance. Look at me, Gabe." Alison pointed to her buzz cut. "Do you want to live in a fucking tree house till you're eighteen?"

THE ACTIVITIES OF THE UNWELCOME VISITORS FROM JUPITER: AN ALLEN FAMILY LOG

February 11: *9:37 a.m., the spaceship is quiet in the backyard, doing nothing special outside of its continued use of electricity. Dad, I see that you put the bucket underneath the spaceship before you left this morning. So far, nothing. —GA*

38

Ernest pushed open the carved oak doors at the Montana, the grandest hotel in Prairie Park, and breathed in the rejuvenating power of people. It was a relief to escape the cloistered sects of his own mind, to see tourists in the lobby on shantung couches, thumbing their guidebooks; staff zipping around with luggage on carts; everyone with a place and a purpose that wasn't sad or perfunctory like the people he saw at the pharmacy or the hazardous waste dump, his two most frequent stops these days.

He found Marilyn and the photographer, a handsome guy named Doug, in the hotel's private party room with the mural of Prairie Park in its olden days lavished across the back wall. Bright and folksy, it depicted an aerial view of a charming town with its first rows of houses lining the main streets, afloat in a sea of prairie, the shades of the native grass light green and golden.

"There's my block." Ernest pointed. "I guess that's Aurora Park, this cluster of trees."

They shot him posed in front of the mural smiling proudly. Then Marilyn directed him to stop smiling, to look solemn. Doug complimented Ernest tirelessly, as well as the natural light of the room, until they were done, and Doug excused himself.

Ernest walked with Marilyn to a back elevator without asking where they were going, but of course he knew. "You're staying here?"

"Well, I've got tons of work right now, and I can't always concentrate at home."

"Still," Ernest said, "this place can't be cheap."

"The manager is an old friend."

Her room was, more accurately, a two-room suite. In the front, a living room with a couch, a TV, and a formidable writing desk. Papers cluttered the surface, a fan of them across the center. In the bedroom lining the wall, three overstuffed pieces of luggage.

"Marilyn," he said, "that's enough for months. What's going on?"

She plunked down on the bed. "How to put this? OK, we've separated. I moved out. And it's hard to be at the paper right now because, I don't know if you remember, but he's there too."

"He's a copy editor, right?"

"The biggest nitpicker of the whole bunch."

"I'm sorry, Marilyn. What are you going to do now?"

"Write all my stories longhand? Go in after his shift and type them into the computer?" She threw up her hands. "At least they have great room service here, right? Want a Bloody Mary?"

"It's barely noon."

As if Ernest's response had been an emphatic yes, Marilyn picked up the phone and ordered two, familiar and gabby with the kitchen staff.

"You'll want one once you taste mine," she said after hanging up.

It occurred to Ernest that whatever freaky business his mind was peddling—anxiety like hot ashes, an overlay of self-consciousness in which he couldn't stop watching himself as if he were a bad supporting character on TV—it wasn't going to be caught by Marilyn right now. She was too involved in her own distress. This had the net effect of relaxing him, despite everything.

"Well, so what's going on with you and the spaceship? Did you get the results of the tests?"

"I just got all of the results this morning. More of the same. A little bit of tar creosote in the ground, but not that much."

"So wait," she said, "even when you went deep, only a little tar creosote came up?"

"Not enough to warrant real suspicion."

"Too bad," she said, frowning.

"Well, no, it's good that it isn't there poisoning us, but I don't know." He paced in front of her. "It's the same thing with the green fuzz that the spaceship blew out a few days ago. It's a complete wash. At this point, I've sunk so much money into that lab that they agreed to do a super rush on it, but still, it came out as a big fat zero. Negative. Nothing toxic at all. The whole situation is screwed. My children hate me, I mean more than they usually do. They know about us, Marilyn.

I'm also a destitute jackass. I mean, in total confidence, I've lost so much money—"

"What is Cynthia saying about it?"

"She put most of it in trust funds for the kids a few weeks ago. It was right before she took this latest bad turn. What was I going to do, argue with her about setting aside money for our kids while she's puking from chemo? I just let it go. I'm happy for them to have the money, but things are tight now. Real tight."

"It's odd she doesn't trust you to manage that after she's gone." Marilyn, ever encouraging, lobbied for the silver lining. "Well, you've got Earth Day coming up and it'll be a hit. You'll be swamped with jobs after that."

Ernest nodded. The Bloody Marys arrived and he ended up slurping his down. He sank down next to her on the bed, letting his leg be just a touch away.

"The thing is, neither the tests nor the money is the worst part of all this. I don't want to freak you out, but I can't draw the line anymore. My thoughts are this kind of drumbeat, pushing me. They never stop but they also don't feel right. *I* don't feel right. I feel crazy chasing after the spaceship, but then I convince myself that being a crazy obsessive is good. I mean, who else will pursue this? Don't I have to pursue this?" He inhaled a long stream of tomato red, suddenly remembering an obscure line of literature about drinking. "'Down the red lane you go,'" he said, laughing.

Marilyn didn't understand but she raised her glass for a toast. "To pursuing all paths with gusto, even divorce," she said.

"To pursuing another drink with gusto, yes," he countered.

She laughed. "You're all right, Ernest."

Despite the momentary cheer, it didn't take long to slip back into their collective misery. The force of it met above their heads: two volatile weather patterns, crisscrossing and singeing the air.

Marilyn put her hand on his face. He grasped her hand and leaned in to kiss her. Right away, the sensation was too powerful to stop. They fell onto the crisply professional bed, the starchy fabrics announcing every seductive move they made. She got up to close the drapes, but he stopped her. It wasn't so much her beauty he wanted to see, but her evident good health. As she returned to him, and he reached for her, Ernest realized he was aching to touch that, to feel that, more than anything else. Her health. Her well-being.

◆

While she went to shower, he wandered around her suite in his underwear, eyes carelessly scanning the papers on her desk, not wanting to look but emboldened by some proprietary sense now that they'd finally fully consummated the relationship. Was this the start of a relationship? His heart winced. Soon, given how things were going with Cynthia, it could be. His eyes snagged on the words "tar creosote."

He picked up a yellow sheet of paper and read the collection of words over and over again. It was an internal memo from the parks and recreation department of Prairie Park, describing how Aurora Park tested positive for "problematic levels" of tar creosote. Hearing the shower stop, he quickly pulled on his pants and shirt, knowing this conversation would require more dignity than his underwear imparted.

"Marilyn, what is this?"

She stood in the door of the bathroom with wet hair but fully dressed.

"Why do you have this?"

A hint of a smile. Her fingers nervously pinched off fabric from her blouse and lifted it from her steamed skin. She'd gotten dressed too fast. "You were snooping."

"I didn't mean to."

"It's OK," she said. "The paper's about to publish an article that I've been working on for months."

"What is this?"

"Look, I'm just going to say it: Aurora Park is seriously contaminated."

Ernest opened his mouth, but she waved her hand at him before he could speak.

"It has nothing to do with the spaceship. There's coal tar creosote everywhere in the soil, plus a mixture of god-knows-how-many chemicals—hydrocarbons, tar acids, sulfurous materials. Not anything you'd want to breathe or touch, much less have your kids play in. It's a mess, and it might go really deep in the soil. They're still testing."

"My god, how did that happen?"

"It's left over from a coal-burning plant in the thirties. No one ever properly cleaned it up because no one really knew. After the plant was no longer in use, Illinois Gas tore it down and donated the land to Prairie Park. And Prairie Park, after about ten years or so of not paying attention to the land, built a park on the grounds, Aurora Park. They had no idea that they were slapping a bunch of sod over a chemical sludge."

"They must've had some idea."

"It was the early sixties," Marilyn said, "even the Jell-O salads were experiments in chemical living. No one thought to care."

"I can't believe this." Ernest shook his head, staring back at the paper in his hands. "I'm there all the time. The Earth Day meetings, the plans."

Marilyn sighed heavily. "They're closing down the park this week. Mandatory."

"For how long?"

"They're estimating two years for the cleanup. But, Ernest, there's more to it. Something I haven't told you before. Because I wasn't sure and it's—well, I'm still not sure how it affects you, if at all. Some neighbors close to the park"—she hesitated, drew in a little breath, still with that hint of a smile lurking—"there's been some incidence of cancer, the kind that's usually associated with some sort of pollutant or toxin in the environment. Five people from the area surrounding the park have presented with cancer. They've all reported to Chicago Metro hospital in the last six months. They were all put on a list as having tumors that may be environmentally caused, and then cross-referenced as being from the same neighborhood. It's been kept quiet until I started nosing around."

Ernest stared at his lover. On the park's walkways, he saw his wife in her bundle of fleece taking her morning walk. Always scanning the environment. She'd fished balls out of the grass, people's keys, notes from high school kids, the broken necklace with the magnifying glass still hanging on a peg in the kitchen. That brownish goo that was smeared on it—was that tar creosote? Had she touched it that first time and then immediately touched her eyes, her mouth?

"Five people. And one of them is Cynthia, I take it?"

"I don't have any names," she said. "It's all ages and statistics, but I bet you could find out." Her voice crested on an enthusiastic note, which Ernest found a little strange. "One of the patients *was* age thirty-nine, breast cancer."

Ernest took a step back, rubbed at his forehead. "So are you telling me that Cynthia's cancer might've been caused by the park? That humans are to blame for this?"

"It's possible, but I don't know. Ernest, humans are to blame for the spaceship too, you know? I hope you realize that. Humans negotiated the deal to allow them here. Humans run the company that facilitates their visits."

For a moment he closed his eyes. He saw the landscape of Cynthia's body and the nodes of her cancer as red splotches, as though his eyes were a heat-seeking camera. One scarlet mass in her brain, both of her breasts, and under her arms where the lymph nodes were secreted away. The questions bubbled up fast: What parts of the park had the highest concentration of tar creosote? Did it grow through the grass? Was he thinking of the most important questions first?

"I need to sit down."

Marilyn followed him to the bed and allowed him to study the basic physical facts of her face: the tidy glint of her eyes, the few broken capillaries on one side of her nose. She blinked at him, her posture erect, her eyes giddy with expectation.

"Why didn't you tell me about the park till now, Marilyn?"

"I didn't have anything conclusive. I didn't want to give you any false information."

"But you still don't have any conclusive evidence. You said you don't know if the park caused her cancer."

She measured her words carefully: "The evidence possibly points in a certain direction. Do *you* think it does?"

"So all that time when I was wondering if the spaceship was giving my wife cancer, you didn't ever think to say, 'Maybe, but there's this super-polluted park right nearby'?"

A playful smile broke fully on her face. "I couldn't have told you that, Ernest. I can't just blurt out sensitive information to the man who's flirting with me."

"Don't try to shame me," Ernest said, gesturing to the half-messy, half-pristine bed. "Not after this."

"I'm not. In fact I'm sorry for it. Sorry I've dragged you into my mess."

"The mess being?"

"My life," she said. "My marriage."

"I'm not asking for an apology for that, but there's something about this park news, Marilyn. The timing."

"I couldn't have said anything. I couldn't risk the news getting out, stirring up a hornet's nest of local environmentalists. It would have shut down my sources. Who knows what you would've done? I mean, all along you've been searching for a cause for your wife's cancer and getting nowhere with the spaceship angle. But a polluted park right next door is a pretty big smoking gun. You must feel furious right about now. You must feel like you were betrayed by your own community."

"Smoking gun? But I thought you said the evidence is inconclusive."

"It is, but I imagine you have to be wondering if there isn't more to it."

"Is there more to it? You would know."

"Oh," she said, leaning back a little, "I don't think I can say decisively, but do you think there is? I mean, this has to undermine your sense of security."

Ernest kept calm. "Why don't you just tell me the quote you want me to say for your story?"

"What? Ernest, no," she said, laughing.

"If you were worried about how I'd react, then why are you telling me now?"

"Because you found a paper on my desk!"

Ernest saw Marilyn clearly now. He understood. His mounting anger was somehow satisfying. After months of doubt, here was something he could be sure of: "You *left* a paper on your desk for me to see! And now you're shopping for a reaction. What do you want me to deliver, Marilyn? A protest? A campaign for answers? What would make the readers excited?"

He popped up, getting the full view of the bed; it embarrassed him now, the telltale sheets, once so crisp, now molded into ragged patterns. He snatched a sheet and yanked it clean off the bed.

"Oh, for fuck's sake, Ernest," Marilyn said. "Let me ask you something: If I wanted your reaction, why wouldn't I have just interviewed you?"

"Oh, I don't know. Because it's probably pretty sketchy, journalistically speaking, to interview someone you're planning to screw, but if he just happens to find something and he gets really angry and blustery about it and he starts knocking on doors immediately, demanding answers, then he's just part of the story on his own and you'd be remiss not to report it."

She blinked, not refuting his version. Ernest collected his things around the room.

"No Earth Day story, right? No profile on me? I mean, what's there to tell if Earth Day might not even happen now? Jesus, no wonder you wanted me to look somber. It would've looked so good with an investigative report. The wronged man on the hunt for justice."

"Never mind all that," she said irritably, but still not disowning it. After a moment, she asked in a more tender tone, "Where are you going?"

"I have no idea, but I don't think I can think clearly about this in front of you."

"Ernest," she started.

"It's OK, Marilyn. A part of me admires your ambition, your follow-through. I don't know if I'm so great at that myself."

"You are seeing this story the wrong way. This is an opportunity."

He laughed uproariously, and she recoiled a bit on the bed. He had his hand on the door and took one last look at her, the scrubbed-clean face bearing earnest intentions. The crumpled sheet on the floor.

"One thing: Did you ever believe for a minute that the spaceship might be toxic?"

She shrugged. "It was a long shot."

He nodded and let the door close behind him.

———◆———

In the hotel parking lot, he sat still, his fingers wrapped around the key in the ignition. Then he drew them back and sat up straight. The windshield bore a thin layer of ice that he was attempting to melt off by blowing the defroster at full blast. Typically he'd get out and scrape it off, but the cocoon of the car—the defroster's white noise, the plainness of the snow-crusted shrub he was parked in front of— made for a good place to collect his thoughts. He had to prepare himself for returning home. In the glove compartment, he found two ancient but still usable wet-naps from the Chinese restaurant. He tore them open and wiped his forehead, his cheeks, and his mouth and then crumpled them into a ball, disgusted with himself. Wiping off sex juices with leftover wet-naps was about as low as it could go, he thought, even if he had stopped short of swabbing off his penis. There was some part of him that wouldn't mind just nodding off in the car and dying, just like that, quickly and quietly, the news of his anonymous dead body reduced to a line or two in the police blotter. But that wasn't going to happen, so instead he let out all the names he had for himself: liar, cheater, pawn, idiot, blowhard. Those were slightly better, maybe, than calling himself a piece of shit.

———◆———

He'd barely closed the back door when Olivia paced in.

"Jean stopped by. She wants you to call her right away." Taking in his shell-shocked expression, Olivia asked, "What happened to you?"

"I'm fine, OK?"

"Oh, well, sorry to ask," Olivia snapped. "Let's be honest: Things are not really fine in this scenario, are they?"

After his morning with Marilyn, Ernest had zero patience for whatever Olivia was trying to get at. He gave her a hard glare in his slovenly kitchen, which prompted her real concern.

She cocked her head. "I don't know what's going on, Ernest, but we've got a situation on our hands."

While Ernest was gone, Olivia recounted, Cynthia had clenched her teeth so hard that Olivia heard it from across the room and rushed to her friend's side. Olivia then watched Cynthia's fists clench and her eyes revolve into the back of her head, the misplaced electricity of a seizure running up the sides of her body so that her neck muscles bowed out like two handles on a pot.

"She was having what's called a grand mal, Ernest, the worst kind," and all Olivia could do was make her more comfortable, make sure she didn't bite her tongue by wedging a plastic lid between her teeth. The minute passed, Olivia pinning her at the shoulders, absorbing the violent shakes and quivers into the roots of her arms. At the end, Cynthia whimpered and stared out, bewildered.

"You've had a seizure," Olivia explained to her. "But you're going to be OK." She ran a wet washcloth over Cynthia's sweat-prickled forehead and then lifted the back of her head so Olivia could cool the nape of her neck.

"She needs daily professional care, Ernest," Olivia said. "Not just a nurse who shows up for a couple of hours a few days a week. It can't be me, the kids, and you anymore. The kids—they shouldn't even be so involved at this stage."

Ernest nodded, taking a seat at the kitchen table. The tide of troubling images; something had to be done to stem them. Pinching both temples with his fingers did little to alleviate the raw jump cuts—from the dead bloom of the bedsheet on the hotel floor to the sight of Cynthia's rigid jaw pulsing at the joints, her fingernails digging bloodless crescents into her palms. He imagined sweeping everything, including himself and Cynthia, into the graves he'd dug in their backyard and a backhoe finally filling them in. That way, Gabe and Alison could start from scratch.

"Ernest? Are you listening to me?"

Before Olivia could stop him, he ran to Cynthia, finding her in deep sleep, her jaw now slack but her fingers in a knot that seemed almost impossible to undo—a frozen position of aggravation, like she'd been holding something with many loose parts. He slowly spread her fingers out so that he could hold her hand, and then he laid his head on her stomach. The rumble of the cat purring near her side made it sound like her body was an old engine chugging diesel fuel. His head rose and fell with her long, drawn-out breaths. He looked up the plane of her body, between her breasts to the bottom of her chin, seeing the tip of her nose beyond. He still knew this body better than any other. From any angle, it was known.

In the other room, the phone rang, but he waited for Olivia to get it.

Within ten minutes, Jean was standing on his stoop in alpine weather gear, her close-cropped hair hidden underneath an ergonomic swirl of wool.

"Let's go for a walk," she said.

He had barely dispensed with a jittery greeting when she cut him off.

"Ernest, let me get right to it. We're thinking the Earth Day committee should be headed up by someone else. We're in crunch time and you have so much going on with Cynthia's illness. There's no sense right now in making all these demands on you."

Was he supposed to believe he was getting fired for his own good, to reserve his strengths? The idea was ridiculous, but for a minute, he'd play along.

"I appreciate your consideration, but they don't feel like demands. I'm happy to do it."

Jean sharply drew in her breath, held it for a moment, and then spoke again. "It's the best thing for the group and Earth Day right now if you're no longer in charge. This is my decision, Ernest."

"You're taking away one of the few joys in my life right now."

"We need someone who can devote the proper time and resources."

"Jean," he said, stopping in the middle of the sidewalk, "what is this really about? I've done nothing but clear time from the start.

You're laying off the guy whose wife has cancer? Who looks forward to the meetings every week?"

Allowing her face to soften a bit, Jean began again: "I didn't want to get into this, but your conversations lately with certain members of the group have made some people uncomfortable. It's clear from what you've been talking about lately that you're under a lot of pressure. That you're not totally yourself."

"Is it wrong for me to confide in people I think of as friends?"

"It's not, but you've been pretty extreme about your ideas, especially regarding the spaceship. Maybe you don't realize how extreme."

"I'm working my way out of it. I admit, I let it get to me."

"It's been weeks of you bringing it up, totally out of the blue, for no reason other than to stoke paranoia and fear."

"So I won't say another word about it," Ernest said. "Look, I'm sorry. It's true that I've got a lot going on, but I've invested everything I got into Earth Day. I want to be there, I want to be part of it, Jean. This has been the most rewarding position of my career. I know I made mistakes, but there's nothing you're telling me that isn't fixable."

Jean sighed and shook her head. "Maybe, but I've got other reasons to doubt your judgment."

"Like what?"

"Do you remember having a conversation with Diane Albero? She said you tried to milk a favor from her, Ernest."

"Diane Albero told you to fire me?"

"No, she actually felt sorry for you, OK? She thought you were a nice guy pushed to your limits. She asked if you're seeing a therapist. And I hope that you are. But to my thinking, you're a liability at this point."

They'd been having this whole conversation on the sidewalk, not bothering to execute the formality of walking any longer. Now he just wanted the take-away so he could crawl back to his depressing hovel.

"So, what does all this mean? What will it look like week to week until Earth Day?"

"You'll be turning over all the paperwork and contacts to me immediately. No meetings either. Get some peace and quiet. Get well."

He couldn't stand to look at her. Did she not understand what she was taking from him?

"The park," he said, finally looking her back in the eye, "is horribly polluted. It'll close in a matter of days. Earth Day might not even happen, unless you start making plans now to have it elsewhere."

She squinted at him, bewildered and then angry and then pitying, but she managed to smooth it all back into a poker face, effective for showing a desperate person. "Is this a rumor? A conspiracy? What?"

"I'm not making this up, but I can't tell you right now how I know it. You might want to call me when the story breaks."

She stared at him with efficient sympathy. "Get some rest, Ernest. You'll survive this."

That night Ernest took care of his wife in the manner he'd grown accustomed to—preparing her dinner, setting her up in bed with magazines and the remote control within reach—but his thoughts were consumed by the day's triad of horrible firsts. One: He'd never been fired before. Two: Or slept with another woman. Two and a half: Or had that woman so quickly reveal that he was a puppet she could manipulate at will. Three: His wife had never had a seizure— certainly never while he was gone, fucking some other woman who thought he was a puppet. Worst of all, he'd launched all of this foulness into his atmosphere himself, with perhaps the exception of the seizure, but because he hadn't been there to help her, he blamed himself for that too.

He blended a protein shake for her with peanut butter and strawberries, her favorite. Dropping the fruit into the whirl of kefir, he thought about how in the past, he'd encountered these personal failings but in a much milder form. He could wave them off. He'd say to himself, Flirting was a favorite pastime, but so what? He never actually did anything. As far as being an environmental firebrand, well . . . it didn't always win him popularity contests, but that was the price for conviction, wasn't it?

He plated a plain turkey patty, yams, and sautéed spinach, sawing everything up so she could easily eat. Along with the shake and a small dish of pills, her dinner tray was set. He carried it to her and sat nearby, watching her summon energy for the onerous task of feeding herself. "Cute," she said, and nodded at the two dandelions he'd dropped in a small vase. (He always included something sweet—flowers, a little note, a colorful rock, an old photo from the shambles of them in his desk drawer.) Her appreciation made his guilt only flare brighter. What had he really done for Cynthia, her sickness, in these last few months? What had he really accomplished with his obsessions? This time, he couldn't rationalize his actions as the abrasive but valiant efforts of a moral man. He'd tipped over into delusion, all the more unbearable when paired with righteousness. He couldn't blame Jean's snobbery or the group's lack of dedication to the cause; he had to think about himself. The tenacity of his convictions had flipped over to obsession, and he'd made the mistake of not recognizing the transition.

Whatever mistakes he was beginning to reckon with, Ernest couldn't free himself from a wretched sense of guilt, disappointment, and horror at the self that sent his stomach dipping low and then pinned it there for several minutes, as if someone were trying to drown a small struggling animal. Eventually it would crawl back up but not quite to its old secure place. The images kept sending the stomach scurrying down—the memory of Marilyn, the specific hormonal cocktail of her skin, was still so fresh that he could almost conjure her in front of him. Instead, he focused on washing Cynthia's pale face with a warm washcloth, her eyes closed, taking in the pleasure of wiping away the day's grime. He helped her brush her teeth (she spat into the little bowl he held under her chin) and handed her the remote so that she'd turn off the TV before she fell asleep, knowing he'd come back in later to turn it off for her. He left a spread of magazines on the tray table as well. He kissed her good night on her papery cheek.

If he ever planned on sleeping again, every memory of the day had to be locked in deep storage, at least temporarily. Around ten at night, he wandered the house. He built a fire to soothe himself. The kids were upstairs—for the last few days, they'd passed him in prickly silence. He employed a trick: whenever an unwanted picture or sensation came into his mind, he'd do anything disruptive or distracting to chase it away. At one point, he plunged his face into the freezer, eye to eye with an ancient bag of peas. Next to it, a frozen container of homemade marinara sauce and a box of baking powder. The little diorama of freezer life was no place for a live head with such ugly visions. When he heard Cynthia calling from her makeshift room, he shut the door, the rubber seal of the freezer sucking onto the cold plastic of the refrigerator, blocking out the roar of the inner world.

When she saw Ernest, Cynthia pointed to a magazine dropped on the floor.

"Please?"

She didn't talk much anymore, because of the pain medication and the brain tumor. Monosyllables and directives sputtered out where whole sentences had once flowed. After he handed the magazine back to her, she browsed through it slowly with flat eyes, like she was passing time in a waiting room. In a way, she was waiting. The radiation and chemo had run its course a while ago; no new treatments were coming.

"Cynthia, can you hear me?"

She nodded pleasantly, tired and devoid of engagement.

"I love you," he said, and received a foggy flickering of the eyes, no real acknowledgment. Sleep was thickening her glance, and her eyelids slowly folded over. He sat there waiting until the calm spread through her entire form, and then waiting more, as if he could stay fixed here for the whole night, as if he could force the sun back up because he wanted a new day. But a new day wouldn't clear him anyway; it'd still carry the tarnish of his mistakes.

The Allen family log was at its station on the kitchen counter, all fifty pages nearly filled with the varying scrawls of the family. Cynthia's smooth cursive had died off somewhere in the middle. With scissors, he severed the string that attached the notebook to the telephone cord.

At the window, he observed the spaceship. The moonlight's pink aura tinged the spaceship's silver. The contraption was singular but also part of an unseen fleet of many more like it. After a few minutes of Ernest watching it, one of the spaceship's headlights burned out. The green light slowly dwindled down in strength until there was barely color, just a faint golden smear, and then darkness. The ship lightly rattled and gave off one anemic pop. Paranoia stirred in Ernest's gut but he resisted it. The spaceship seemed so weak.

Instead of tracking the spaceship's last few movements, Ernest carefully removed the notebook's metal coil for recycling. Then he rolled the notebook into a log and tossed it into the living room fireplace, where the flames took their time encircling and singeing the paper. Cynthia remained asleep in the sunroom; he could see the mound of her legs covered in a purple blanket. When all the pages of the notebook had blackened, curled, and smoked to ash, he walked into the next room where the air was better.

PART THREE:
MYSTERIUM TREMENDUM ET FASCINANS

39

Lydia, a hospice nurse, was hired to ensure a smooth passageway into death. Behind her large plastic frames, Lydia's brown eyes projected wisdom gained from a close proximity to suffering. She had the kind of soulfulness once-battered dogs possess. Her job entailed giving Cynthia painkillers, dabbing her sweaty brow, changing diapers, and informing the family about the progression of Cynthia's decline. First, Cynthia would need these painkillers more and more: large yellow capsules kept in a fist-size pill bottle. Eventually her breathing would become labored and shallow, but that was not now, not yet. She was at some other stage.

"Miss?"

Alison and Gabe looked away from the TV; it took Alison a moment to realize her mother was talking to her. She and Gabe snickered; it was too ridiculous, their mother calling her as if she were a waitress at a diner. Cynthia shook a plastic water cup back and forth with a questioning face. In a kindly tone, she asked, "Water?"

Alison got up and refilled her mother's cup from the small pitcher that was also on the bedside tray over Cynthia's lap. Despite the cup now being full, Cynthia looked disappointed.

"Do you want something else?"

Cynthia pointed to a packet of vitamin powder on her nightstand that could be mixed with water. Alison stirred it into the cup.

"Better?"

"Yes," her mother whispered, and then asked for a straw. The striped tube of plastic was plunged into the cup, but Cynthia couldn't seem to grasp it. The weightless tube kept slipping from her fingers. Alison helped her mother center the floating straw on her lips and watched as the liquid was sucked up. After a few sips, her mother put it down.

"Mom, do you know my name?" Alison asked in a neutral, friendly voice.

The TV chattered on, but Gabe wasn't watching it anymore. Cynthia looked at the girl and smiled apologetically.

"I," she started, and shrugged. Sheepish, she took another sip.

"Do you know his name?" Alison pointed at her brother, slumped in a chair near Cynthia's bed.

Gabe offered a short wave. "Hi, Mom." To his sister: "OK, she doesn't know, Alison."

Cynthia stared at him with kindly bewilderment. She looked back and forth at both before losing focus. The TV provided a comforting distraction and she focused on watching. Gabe followed suit.

Loudly, over the TV, Alison yelled, "I'm Alison and that's Gabe. I'm your daughter and he's your son."

"What are you doing?" Gabe yelled back at her.

"I just want her to recognize us. Sometimes she does and then other times—"

"Exactly," her brother said. "She can't help it."

***

At night, passing by Gabe's room, Ernest heard a few lines of *The Book of Connections* filtering through the door: "Some of the stars have Arabic names because they were the foremost astronomers of the world. In the constellation of Orion, there's Betelgeuse, which means 'the giant's shoulder,' and Saiph, which means 'sword,' and Rigel, which is 'foot.'"

His senses prickled at the mention of anything from space. Suspicious thoughts started to mobilize. Was *The Book of Connections* a broadcast somehow controlled or sponsored by the spaceship? Ernest plucked this thought out of the din, revolved it slowly in the light for examination, as Marilyn had generously told him to do, in a moment when she wasn't manipulating him. He could identify these thoughts as pulses from the madness that lived sequestered in his brain, dying off but still sending transmissions. He needed to head off the messages before they took root.

It had been only six days since he'd burned the Allen Family Log. He was still working on building a way back to sanity and rational thought, the acceptance that no one thing or one person was at fault. Ernest was testing the first few steps and finding them secure, even as temptation called him back.

◆

Later, as Alison passed by her father's bedroom, she saw him sitting on his bed, cross-legged and eyes closed, through a gap in the door. He sat for several minutes, his lips sometimes moving a bit. She could see the muscles in his arms flexing, the eyelids straining to keep shut. Then he got up and seemed OK, if a little flustered. He met her eyes at the door.

"What are you doing?"

"Meditating," he said. "Emptying out."

"Looked like you were simmering, is more like it."

He held the doorknob, waiting to close it.

"Are we . . ." Alison began. "The log, I couldn't find it."

"I burned it. I told Gabe, but I guess I forgot to tell you."

"I thought you were going to publish it. Not that I agreed with that plan."

"I tossed that plan into the fire too."

"Did you make a secret copy?"

"No, the log is over. You are relieved of your duties."

"Does this mean we're not going to go live in the woods?"

"Maybe at some point, but not right now." Her dad bid her good night and shut the door.

◆

At the kitchen table, Alison and Ernest picked at ragtag breakfasts they'd assembled themselves. She waited for her father to break the unnerving silence. She wondered if she should just say, "OK, you're having an affair and I don't really care," but she wasn't sure that was true. Instead, Gabe walked into the kitchen and announced, "Something's wrong with the spaceship."

Their father didn't seem to acknowledge the statement, and Alison continued to stare at him, waiting for some kind of response.

"Hello? Anybody hear me?"

"What's wrong with it?" Alison asked finally.

"It's been turned off or something. Did you do something to it?"

Ernest put down his fork with a deliberate motion. "Do something to it? I haven't been thinking about it at all."

"Wait, what? This thing that you thought was an instrument of the apocalypse a week ago is now not even registering in your thoughts?"

"I told you: I burned the log," Ernest said. "I'm dismissing the spaceship as a harmful factor and downgrading it to merely a parasite. I've retired my fixation. I'm ready to let it all go."

"You're ready to let it all go? Now it's just an annoying parasite? It's not even harmful?"

"That's right."

Gabe tossed up his hands. "It might be even more annoying to be all insane about something one minute and then a week later be like, 'Oh, la-di-da, what was I saying about toxic warships from space?'"

Ernest shrugged. "That's the way it is. Isn't that what you wanted? For me to lay off?"

Gabe scrutinized his father. The panic that had taken residence within him for months had vacated. "Bliss" was too generous of a word, but his father looked distinctly unbothered.

"There's something going on," Gabe said. "You did something to it."

"Really? What did I do?"

"You put it to sleep, like an old dog."

Ernest laughed.

"So you did do something!"

"I wish! If I had known how to put that thing to sleep, I would've done it a long time ago."

"But you haven't noticed that it's not made a sound or a movement in the last day and a half? No pops, no searchlights, no rattling or anything. Total silence. You haven't noticed?"

The three of them ventured into the backyard. The spaceship was still there of course—larger than ever, in fact—but without vitality. No energy, no hum, no ticking, no lights. Even the metal appeared dull, lackluster. The extension cord wasn't plugged into the garage socket either; it lay on the ground a few feet away. As always, the windows were dark and opaque, but there seemed to be a distinct absence.

"Wow," Alison said. "It really feels like they're gone."

"Looks like they forgot something then," Ernest muttered, eyeing the flying saucer tiredly.

"How is it possible that they're gone? Why would they leave?" Gabe asked. "*How* could they leave?"

"Don't look at me."

"But I am looking at you. There's no reason you'd be so peaceful unless you finally managed to kill this thing."

"That's another option to consider. They're dead inside."

Alison shuddered and took a few steps back, arms crossed over her chest. Gabe glared at his father from under his bangs.

"Honestly, Gabe," Ernest said. "For the last time, I didn't do anything. I don't know why you'd even think that, after all this time. It's been in 'serious distress,' remember? The company was supposed to send somebody but they haven't yet. I guess this is what happens in the end. It didn't fly away; it died."

"You killed it," Gabe hissed, "by being an asshole. You polluted its mental environment."Gabe swiped away a few tears that streaked down his cheek.

"I'm sorry, Gabe," Ernest said gently. "But it doesn't work that way." He tried to put an arm around Gabe but was shrugged off.

"Get off," he said. "You make no sense to me."

"We should put flowers on it or something," Alison quickly offered. "Some kind of ceremony."

"It's not a coffin," Gabe said.

"Maybe it'll still wake up?"

Gabe shook his head. Alison didn't believe what she'd said either.

"Look," Ernest said, "I haven't even been paying attention lately, but maybe you guys noticed something, some signal that it was about to go. Did you notice anything unusual?"

"Well," Alison said, "we weren't going to tell you this before, in case it drove you more loony, but the other night it started spinning around and then shining these blue lights. Totally different lights, never seen them before. It spun around for maybe five minutes, really quietly, like a top or something, and then it stopped."

"And you didn't put that in the log?"

"You burned the log, Dad," Gabe said. "*Why* did you do that?"

"But I read the last entries before I burned it. I would've remembered that."

Gabe was back to crying again. "You didn't have to go that far, you know. There was no reason to burn it. It would've been cool to look back on later. It's a record that something actually happened around here."

Ernest let out a short, bitter laugh. "I don't think any of us will ever forget what's happened around here."

The log had to be burned. As a sacrifice. He had to be carrying nothing on him as he crossed the ragged footbridge from paranoiac to a rational, discerning mind, the mind he possessed before. Stepping back into the rational was to re-center; it also meant burning out the obsession, all of it. He did not want to transfer his paranoia to Aurora Park, though it'd be so easy to do. He did not want to eradicate one source of blame for his wife's cancer only to shift it to another.

But his paranoia had another plan. It probed for the critical detail that would reveal that the park's pollution had caused Cynthia's cancer. When Ernest was involved with minute tasks, in the moments when a brain could slip away and think its thoughts, he would ask himself: Wasn't it Aurora Park? Didn't that make more sense than the spaceship ever had? The poisonous dirt was only a block away; Cynthia walked in it every day. But he sifted through what Marilyn had told him and he knew the problem: that even if an oily pool of tar creosote was discovered fifty feet below the ground, it wouldn't prove anything. There would never be hard proof. He'd already lost so much time that way—hunting for a reason for the unreasonable. He wanted to be done with obsession.

Meditation had always been an occasional hobby, but now he was practicing every morning, sometimes for hours. After he made peace with every twinge, itch, and ache in his body, he settled into the space where some sort of strength was illuminated in the pitch dark.

There he tried to locate permanently as he repeated the following mantras to himself:

I have no control.

It's not my fault.

It wasn't the spaceship.

It wasn't the park.

The cancer just came, struck into action by some errant DNA code. After a week, the acceptance was starting to sink in. He was fighting to make it take.

40

Two days later, Gabe approached Ernest at the kitchen table with some papers. At the top, two red-inked Japanese characters that Ernest rubbed with his fingers.

"Fancy," Ernest said. "What is this?"

Gabe nervously shuffled in his spot. "It's an application to live in Japan for the next school year."

Ernest twisted in his chair to look up at him. "For you? Why?"

"For the experience. What other reason would there be?"

"It's just so far away."

"I'll be home for Christmas. I'll be living with a nice family and learning the language. What's so bad about any of that?"

"Nothing, it's just across the planet." He was trying to be more patient, which for the most part meant he said the same things he would normally say but a little bit slower and more evenly. "Have you looked at how long the plane ride is? Probably fourteen hours. God knows how expensive . . ."

Gabe looked crestfallen. "So you won't do it?"

"I didn't say that. What are your chances of getting in?"

"Well, the counselor says I have a decent shot, especially because my photography shows that I'm seriously devoted to something."

"I need to look over the materials. Let me think about this, OK?"

"OK, but the deadline is coming up fast, Dad."

"You know that Japan won't stop being utterly foreign the whole time you're there, right? Even if you get homesick?"

"Homesick," Gabe said, like it was a bad taste. "I know it'll stay foreign. That's what I want."

"For example, there won't be any American food—maybe hamburgers, but they will still be different."

"Dad, I'm not an idiot. Are you trying to punish me?"

"Punish you for what? The spaceship is dead. I thought you blamed *me*."

"No, you've said it before. It's my fault."

They sized each other up. The truth was Ernest did blame him a little bit: For ordering the spaceship that ruined the last months of his marriage. For bringing this force into their lives that couldn't be understood. For exposing all that Ernest didn't know and would never know but had compensated for with an obsession that took down everything he had.

Ernest hesitated. He tried to say something good, but it was too late. Gabe left the room, grabbing the air with him, leaving Ernest feeling the sad, wasted space.

Marilyn's story in the Sunday paper appeared on the front page, with a luminous picture of the park from last summer, the lawn a patchwork of families spread out on picnic blankets. Ernest remembered his birthday, the look on Cynthia's face when she'd asked him to stay and not clean up the spill. She had begged him and he had turned away.

The headline: "Aurora Park Contaminated with Tar Creosote." The subhead: "Park to close today; possible link to cancer cases in the neighborhood investigated."

Ernest read the story but found nothing new, only the bitter reminder that Marilyn was an ambitious journalist. There was no foothold for his paranoia, no purchase for any conspiracy theory that wanted to gel around the park. The facts of the case illuminated a larger problem: the world's runoff that had nowhere to go but within. The planet was a rag soaking up spills. He pulled away from the thought. Right now his attentions were needed elsewhere.

41

The family was gathered around Cynthia's bed, had been since morning. The TV burbled softly in the corner of the room but no one listened; it was on for distraction. Better than fixating on her gasps. Each one sent them into a panic, grabbing for her hands or freezing them in place in their chairs, breath sucked in. But then it would pass and she would be breathing again, thick draws of air as if through a straw. It wasn't time yet.

Lydia got up and loosened the morphine drip that she had planted into Cynthia's vein last night. The plinking of the liquid increased, leaking into Cynthia's wrist.

"Making her more comfortable now." Lydia had been translating her actions for the family in a low murmur. Ernest, who sat at Cynthia's side in a chair dusted with baby powder, nodded with some mix of appreciation and approval. It wasn't time yet.

The minutes passed with stubborn slowness and a herky-jerky skipping. After hours of waiting, Alison got up to take a break. In the guest bathroom downstairs, the one that she used so infrequently it didn't quite feel like part of her house, she avoided looking in the mirror. Today would be historical to her life, and she didn't want to mentally photograph her own face. It would be scary to look, like being a kid again and daring yourself to say "Bloody Mary" three times into the reflection. She sat on the toilet lid, below the mirror's reach. Hanging off the wooden rack to the side were the towels she remembered picking out with her mom a few years ago.

"I don't want a beach theme," Cynthia had said when Alison held up the coral-colored terry cloth with satiny seashells stitched into them. "We're not anywhere near the ocean and Lake Michigan is a polluted mess that I don't particularly want to celebrate."

"But we can pretend we're near the ocean like rich people in Malibu," Alison said. "It'll be a fantasy."

"Malibu," Cynthia snorted. "You've been watching too much TV."

"OK, how about somewhere else in California? Big Sur?"

Alison had never been to the West Coast, but she knew enough to play on her mother's childhood memories. California: a place that her mother sometimes called the "Wild End." Cynthia contemplated with a hint of a smile. "Big Sur," she said. "We liked to call it Big Madam when we were kids." She tossed the towels into the cart.

The fantasy towels were still in use, but the stitching on the shells had frayed. The coral terry cloth had long ago faded to a spotty orange. The rest of the room bore out the beach theme but broken and dull. The tiled floor with seashells looked grimy, ever since her father had dismissed the cleaning woman. The glass over the photograph of a seagull on the beach had a long crack in it; she'd never noticed before. Why hadn't her parents gotten it reframed? Why was the floor so dirty? Why had he let everything go to shit? A dish of beach rocks, which she had scavenged on a Florida vacation, was on the toilet tank coated in a layer of dust. Impulsively, she grabbed the rocks, hurled them down the toilet and flushed them away. She drew her hand to her mouth, wincing as the rocks clattered around the bowl and were swept out to the sewer. She could hear her dad say, "Nothing but paper ever goes down here, OK?" The urge to destroy everything in the bathroom piece by piece—flushing, tearing, smashing—tightened every muscle in her body, but she waited it out until the tension released. The toilet refilled and she let herself out of the bathroom.

They waited some more. The day melted off into night.

Cynthia let out a hushed stream of syllables, disconnected from any apparent meaning. Ernest leaned over to see if he could make something out, but he got little more than her pungent breath. He asked her to say it again and with exertion she whispered, cracking her eyes open to two red-rimmed slivers. This time he heard the word "love," or that's what he decided to hear, and he smiled at her. He would walk her to the next place with all the quiet joy he could find. Ernest set his hand on her shoulder, bent in, and kissed her on the cheek. Her eyes closed. Ernest grabbed her hand, and Gabe and Alison shared her other hand, leaning into each other, scared to ever break contact. She shuddered with her last breath. Then her chest stilled. The stillness crept over all of her body. It kept sinking in deeper, from her skin to the muscle to the blood. They watched as her face settled into an expression of painless light. She looked like a carving. Her forehead was smooth stone. Her lips parted slightly, a hint of playfulness. She was about to amuse them with one last parting thought.

42

Gabe searched for *The Book of Connections* a few hours after her death, a few hours into the numb territory of existing without the one person in the world who, above and beyond everything else, is programmed to love you. He tried to learn the laws of this new place, but so far, he could not disentangle himself from shock. Crossing his ankles or some other casual gesture was a sheer, clumsy miracle of life, one his mother could no longer enjoy. Or hate, or not notice. She had ceased, which he understood and then didn't. Ceasing, when she had existed for years, creating him, creating his sister, then slowly, patiently helping them along every day as they grew. How could she not be here if he still was? The contradiction of it zapped him repeatedly, but without any sign that he'd ever get used to it.

He kept searching for *The Book of Connections* but it eluded him, or, worse, it had gone off air. He rolled over the station for half an hour, but there was nothing. Occasionally she skipped a night, but why did it have to be tonight? He didn't want to be alone. He could walk into Alison's room or his dad's, and maybe he would, but he wanted to hear another voice that wasn't as devastated as his, that knew more than anyone he knew. But she was taking a night off or she was gone forever, finally surrendered to the slippage, the missed connection.

He found something else. The ferocious static rose up and then parted like a curtain, revealing the voice of the Russian woman repeating the names: "Anna? Nikolai? Ivan? Tatyana? Roman?" She sounded so far away tonight—not just measured in oceans or continents, but in time, like she was calling from another era, maybe from the bitterest cold of the Cold War, not the lukewarm melting off that Gabe knew from the late 1980s.

"Anna? Nikolai? Ivan? Tatyana? Roman?"

He kept listening to her tone. Was it possible that she sounded hopeful? He'd always heard it as mournful, but in the very gesture of her constantly looking, of never giving up, there was a grain of hope he heard in her voice now, socked in by the fog of bygone eras, but there.

"Anna? Nikolai? Ivan? Tatyana? Roman?

"Anna? Nikolai?"

"I'm right here," Gabe whispered into the dark, half expecting his response to halt her search. She kept going, but he felt just a tiny bit better, knowing he'd said something.

43

The next night.

Cynthia's body was gone and the house felt desolate, even with all the foot traffic coming through: Tom, Olivia, Aubrey and his mom, even Mrs. Chang with a chicken and rice dish.

The sleep Ernest backed into was more like an endless twilight consciousness. While there, he wandered some ghost structure built by his grief. Layers of scaffolding, floor upon floor of empty rooms. Chasing a specific sense that he was always about to run into her or walk into some passage that would reset his life to a year ago, or to a deliriously happy time that he clambered for but never reached. He drifted for hours through the deserted halls, taking staircases down to sublevels, crashing through memories that colored his sleep in joy, regret, sorrow: a tinge of her laughter; the memory of her breath exhausting itself for the final time. The roaming and cycling would last for hours, repeat and repeat and repeat. He'd get to know this structure well. In the day, it receded to the background, but at night it sealed him in.

In the daylight, he wandered around the spaceship. The backyard still bore its visitor, a silent and swooping hunk of dead metal. No penetrating lights, no nightly pops or tremors for days now. New World was stumped—never had it encountered an instance where one of the spaceships had simply died on the spot. In an unprecedented display of concern, they offered to send a technician to check it out. Ernest said soon, but not now. His wife's body had just been taken out on a gurney, her face covered in black plastic. This other dead being in his presence wasn't a priority, though he fantasized about all the different ways it too could be taken: decompose or wilt, get swallowed into the ground or sucked back into the sky. But it stood as it had all along, now serving as a reminder of another time, when Cynthia was alive and still ostensibly healthy. When he had searched and scrutinized it in hopes that his meticulousness would surely be awarded with truth or knowledge. The end of mystery. Or better yet, Cynthia, exactly as she was.

———◆———

Six days later: Gabe and Alison, wired awake, camped out on Gabe's bed late at night. Stacks of family photos fanned around them. Ernest had asked them to create the front cover of the funeral program. Maybe Alison could include one of her drawings, if she wouldn't fuss over it too much. Ernest had already taken care of the inside, the order of the eulogies and the readings. The funeral was the day after tomorrow.

"What about this one?"

"That has to go in," Alison said.

Gabe held up a photo of Cynthia, her face poking out of an enormous yellow submarine costume so big the edges of the sea vessel didn't fit in the picture. Next to her, Ernest as Ringo Starr, with a mustache, paisley pants, and drumsticks clutched in his raised fist. Gabe and Alison could recite the lore about this picture—a friend who was ambitious with the sewing machine; a Halloween party themed after 1960s bands. Cynthia and Ernest had won the costume contest. The kids weren't in the photo, which is why Alison liked it. Her parents seemed younger and almost, sort of, sexy. When saddled with kids, they looked like most parents: old mules laboring on the parenthood farm.

At 4 A.M., Alison and Gabe finished a thickly taped photo collage ready for the printer. In one corner, Alison had included a sketch of her mother playing in the ocean. Working from a photo, she captured the mouth open in elation, the sun on her mom's skin. Cynthia wore a multicolored floral 1970s bikini, the pink in it nearly fluorescent—a far cry from the black one-pieces she'd favored at the end. The end, she thought, rubbing at her graphite-stained palm: a stain on her childhood too. She wondered if it was time to leave, to go back to her room. As if hearing her thoughts, Gabe said, "You should just sleep in here tonight."

She nodded, relieved the decision was made for her. Nights were difficult, sleep nearly impossible. Compulsively, her mind re-created her mother's face over and over again, zooming in closer and closer as if the precision of the vision would mean Cynthia was still alive or somehow close. If she couldn't fill in some detail about her mother's face, she'd start over again, angry with herself for already forgetting.

They settled into his bed together and, at nearly the same time, flipped away so that they lay back to back. Her body wasn't touching Gabe's, but sensing him so near made her wonder if this was how it felt to have a husband, a constant shadow-self in the bed, matching his breath to yours.

"You know what I've noticed?" she said quietly.

"What?"

"Athena's going in the backyard again. And bird shit's piling up on the ship."

"Huh."

"What do you think about that?"

"I don't know."

As Gabe heard his sister's breathing deepen, he fought away the persistent sense of absence that was cloaked around him. Still, a kind of shock—that he was alive and moving—followed his every action. He refluffed his pillow, rearranged the akimbo of his legs, and listened to the house. His dad had gone to bed; the stillness of the night was now complete. If his sister slept next to him that meant he wouldn't cry himself to sleep. But sometime after he drifted off, he must've done it anyway. In the morning, the pillow was wet.

The paper, from being out on the table for more than a week, had already taken on a slightly yellow tinge, a barely perceptible shift toward its eventual dissolve. The article about the park's pollution kept coming up whenever Ernest answered the phone or called to let people know about Cynthia's funeral. Have you heard about the tar creosote that's ruined Aurora Park? He'd say yes, but otherwise he tried to dodge the subject, not ready to speak about it in objective terms that weren't clouded by grief or his ties to Marilyn, whom he hadn't spoken with since the day at the hotel.

Now, Tom stood in Ernest's kitchen, a dark suit clinging to him like an ill-fitting superhero costume.

"You've read this, right?" Tom flapped the paper up from the table where Ernest sat, also in a suit bought on deep discount at the mall's department store.

"Many times."

"How disgusted are you?"

"When you really think about it, it's all too common. Every generation deals with the chemical aftermath of the last."

"But this cancer link, Ernest. I think it's worth exploring. How Cynthia went, how aggressive her cancer was, it's suspicious."

"That's what I said for months."

"But you had the wrong target." Tom pointed at the dead ship.

"Still absorbing the whole matter," Ernest said.

"Olivia and I are thinking about it ourselves. What if it's jeopardized Cherice somehow? What about me? What will I come down with in ten years?"

"Look, we are both in our suits," Ernest said, "and I can barely bend my arm at the elbow. Let's talk about it later."

"I know now's not the time, but let me just plant a seed in your mind. Some of the locals are talking about getting a lawyer to pursue this. Maybe you'd be interested."

"Seed planted," Ernest said, standing up. He grabbed the box of funeral programs from the printer's. The Robert Hass poem was badly spaced, but otherwise the program fit his specifications.

"Ready?" Tom asked, clasping a hand on his friend's shoulder.

"Not at all," Ernest answered.

44

Ernest, Alison, and Gabe sat stiffly in the perfumed oak pew, listening to the organist pound out a traditional hymn. The church was full of people, and Alison wondered how she should act as one of the principal mourners on display. The high school therapist she'd snuck off to a couple of times would call this technique "intellectualizing." Or was it "distancing"? She couldn't remember. As Aubrey walked down the aisle near her pew, she didn't know whether she should look at him or look straight ahead. She decided to give him a little nod. He smiled back in relief, peacocking just a teeny bit in a navy velvet jacket.

Crying, Alison had decided before she'd even sat down, wasn't an activity she wanted to share with the crowd, partially because she didn't think she'd be able to stop. But then her brother started crying. To shield everyone from his sobs, he cupped his hand to the side of his face but left the side facing her exposed. Tears and snot collected in the slight stubble on his cheeks and upper lip. Her father placed one cool hand on Gabe's knee and she squeezed in closer to him. She couldn't quite afford to wrap her arms around him or then she'd fall apart too. Gabe seemed to understand, and after a few minutes, a mournful tranquillity settled into his spent form.

Ernest's wife was lowered into the ground by six ropes; Stephen, Tom, Ross, and other men helped to ease her casket down. The coffin, made from thin pine, was guaranteed to biodegrade quickly. Its flimsy construction was making Ernest worry that the top would pop open. But the box was latched shut. There was no escape for Cynthia. Inside, she was wrapped in a linen shroud, her face covered.

As the minister intoned the final prayers, Ernest comforted himself with thoughts of returning her to the earth. Hours later, lying in bed, he could even picture her decomposition in a soothing stop-motion film, like the ones from his college biology classes where a red flower bulb twitched and then unfurled under the pearl moonlight.

Over time Cynthia's cheeks would sag, her lips would splay away from her teeth, and her eyeballs would sink into the chamber of her eroding flesh. By the time the pine box rotted away, there'd be nothing left of her but bones. The dirt would host her, slowly eating away at her calcium. She could last fifty or a thousand years, maybe more, depending on the temperature, acidity, bacteria, and other factors. There was one thing that wouldn't ever decompose: her gold wedding ring. It would stay intact, elemental, shining down in the depths of the soil. He had hesitated, but Gabe and Alison said she should be buried with it.

"You don't want it?" Ernest had asked Alison.

"It's hers," Alison said.

The thought of someone one day, far off into the future, digging up the dirt and only finding a wedding ring seemed like a trick, like some sort of magical illusion where the only clue of a body was the one symbol of its attachment to another. Ernest decided he'd get buried with his too.

45

Aurora Park's destruction began on a Monday. All the young oak trees were cut down and carted out on a flatbed truck. A massive white tent was erected to cover the entire park and obscure the brutalizing activities of a backhoe. The luscious grass was scraped off by a bucket claw. Sometimes the machine sheared it off in one long ribbon; other times the claw snagged on a root or lump in the grass and it'd break apart into rags. No matter the state, the backhoe cranked away, hoarding the grass in corners of the tent. The claw plunged deeper, tearing out the first couple of levels of soil: the dark and rich topsoil packed with rotting and alive creatures, the difference between the two sometimes negligible. Insects, spiders, worms, centipedes, mites, fungi, and thousands of microbes all threading around one another, the filigree of secret life, thriving in the densely packed dirt-suburbs. These creatures had been stepping around patches of brackish creosote their entire lifetime; they had adapted to it. The bucket claw ripped out more, cracking through rock, still miles from Earth's fiery core, but to the workers operating the machinery, the throbbing ring the claw made striking rock sounded close enough.

Heaps of dirt and rubble. Piles of rock as large as cars. Everything sifted, sorted, and tested by white uniforms at a makeshift lab in the back of the tent, for expediency and discretion, their faces protected in plastic bubbles, their hands with cotton gloves and then another layer of plastic. Still more holes were dug all over Aurora Park, to test how much the gas plant had left behind. The deepest hole went down sixty feet. Underneath, precisely where the playground's swing sets had been, the levels of tar creosote were the highest.

46

"How did you know?"

Early April. Jean was back at his door. Ernest tried not to let a triumphant smile crack his stern visage.

"The means of knowledge are unsavory in this case," he said. "I can't share."

"How unsavory?" Jean said. "Are we talking illegal?"

"I wouldn't worry about it," Ernest said coolly. "I don't work for you anymore."

"I'm genuinely curious, not suspicious," Jean said, approximating something like warmth. "No one's judging you here."

"Judging me? You fired *me*, remember?"

Jean sucked in her breath and asked if she could come in. Ernest toyed with saying no, but curiosity won over. Inside his living room, she admitted that Earth Day was a disaster. In total disarray. The committee had moved it to Franklin Park, on the other side of town closer to the city, but "we have to change the footprint, hire more security, apply for new parking permits. The list goes on and on," Jean said, making no effort to cover up her exhaustion.

"Sounds like a ton of work," Ernest said. "Too bad you're down a director."

Jean resumed her strength. "We'll get it sorted. You, of all people, should know how good the team is."

Ernest blinked at her. "You know," he said, "I didn't realize this conversation was going to be all about rubbing my nose in my own failures. I should probably return to grieving my dead wife and figuring out what I'm doing for money these days."

Jean sighed and wiped her hand in front of her like an eraser. "This has gotten off on a bad foot. Let me start again: Ernest, I know you're mad at me, but I want you to come to our meeting tomorrow night."

"Why?"

"Because we want you there. It's not exactly an Earth Day meeting," she said. "It's more about Aurora Park, and I think you'd be interested in what we're discussing."

"The lawsuit."

"That's right. Tom has told you?"

"He has but, Jean, I'm not so sure I'm up for that right now."

"Just come to the meeting. No one's asking you to do anything right now."

"I'm tired, Jean."

"I know you are," she said, "but we could use your fire for so many things. And, Ernest, I do want you back on the Earth Day team. We could use your help."

"You'll make it without me." Ernest hoped she'd beg a bit more, but Jean was too savvy for that.

"Look, I'll understand if you don't want to come back to the committee, but at least come to the meeting for Aurora Park. As soon as Earth Day ends, that will be the new mission. You might be tired now, but I know your fire is still burning in there; I know that it is. We'll be talking about the connection between cancer cases in the neighborhood and Aurora Park. We'll be talking about Cynthia, Ernest. There's no way you can sit back and just let the situation stand."

"The situation has already happened. The park was polluted years ago."

"But the cleanup, Ernest."

"There is nothing but cycles of pollution and supposed cleanup," he said. "And how are you going to get Prairie Park to do anything when you work for them? Won't that be a little uncomfortable for you?"

They sat in pregnant silence.

"OK, so this information can't leave this room," Jean said. "After Earth Day is over, I'll be resigning my post. This way I can fight for the best cleanup. I am disgusted with their lack of responsibility so far."

"So when did you find out?" Ernest said.

"Only a week before you told me."

In the garage, Ernest squatted, searching for a screwdriver on a lower shelf of his workbench, when he turned toward the spaceship. He'd never observed the spaceship from this strange vantage before, and he noticed something almost immediately—a piece of paper?—stuck to the top of one of its legs. He jumped up, paused for a moment, and hurried outside. Reaching up, he yanked off an envelope that was Scotch-taped there. He tore it open. At the top of the letter, a stationery crest from the Best Western of Wheaton, Illinois. He recognized Cynthia's handwriting immediately:

Dear Ernest,

While I'm still of relatively sound body and mind, I want to write to you and say that I love you. I don't plan to stop any time soon, no matter what form I take next. We built a beautiful life together, and the thought of leaving it now is enough to make me scream in this hotel room, not that it does any good (but that's what I'm doing). I'll probably get kicked out of here any minute. I don't think that I'll ever show you this note, and I'm hoping I won't need to. But just in case, I want you to know that everything about you, your passion and idealism and just the look in your eyes when you talk about what you love, inspires me. You're a born fighter, Ernest. You have your own uncompromising way of doing things. You insist on what you believe in and don't take shit from anyone, not even me. (OK, maybe you take a little. Let's be real.) I know things are about to change for this family, change in ways I can't and don't want to see right now, but I hope your strength never wavers. The kids will need this from you. I will too. Be there for me, and for them, even when I can't.

All of my love,
Cynthia

By the time he finished her note, Ernest's eyes were blurred with tears. He didn't have a clue as to how the letter managed to get up there, or stay up there all this time without being noticed, or how or when Cynthia was screaming inside a Best Western, but when he looked at the spaceship again, he felt for the first time what Gabe must've known all along: a rush of awe, nearly paralyzing in its bewilderment, and an unexpected sense of gratitude. He'd ask the kids later to be sure—"Did one of you leave a message on the spaceship for me?"—but they didn't know what he was talking about. They didn't leave anything for him. Somehow the spaceship had delivered this message from his wife, written while she was still fully *here*. One dead thing transferring the thoughts of another. As he read the note again, he heard her voice in his head, almost like she was standing there, still alive. This—whatever *this* was— he cried to himself, was so much better than moving an extension cord.

At the meeting, the usual Earth Day crew had joined forces with Stephen, Tom, Olivia, and a few other spark plugs Ernest knew from the local environmentalist community. Also some friends who'd attended the spaceship party a distant few months ago: Camille Banks, Aubrey's mother, and Julia Sauma, another lawyer in Cynthia's practice. In Jean's elegant living room with Persian rugs and photos of her family in sterling frames on top of the ink- black piano, Ernest's chair was positioned slightly back from the enthusiastic circle. He tried hard not to fume about Stephen's hand in his wife's end-of-life financial plans as his strapping competition passed out Xeroxed sheets with makeshift charts on Aurora Park's pollution.

"Polyaromatic hydrocarbons, the worst one being coal tar creosote, have been detected as deep as sixty feet in some places in the park. Now what does this mean? It means the pollution is deeper than the gas company thought. Original tests had the coal tar only as deep as three feet—this is obviously an enormous difference. It also gives our lawsuit better leverage; if the toxicity is that rampant, how can they dismiss five cases of cancer in the neighborhood?"

Ernest looked over at Ross, who kept his eyes trained on Stephen. Ross's determined expression suggested he was ready to fight.

"Tonight, here in this room, we have either the cancer victims themselves or their spouses. I'd like to go around and introduce them."

Stephen briefly pointed out each person and the cancer he suffered from: Ross (prostate), Michael (lung), Doug (brain), and Ethan (his wife, Karen, was currently battling breast cancer). For Ernest, he added more of a personal touch.

"Ernest is here. He's the husband of Cynthia, who recently died from breast cancer. Cynthia was my dear friend who I worked with for twelve years. She was not only a dedicated lawyer, but an incredibly wise and loyal friend. I greatly admired her diplomatic and unflappable spirit. I miss her tremendously."

The room let the weight of his words sink into the floor. Stephen and Ernest, brotherly enemies, shared a look; mourning, jealousy, and empathy impossibly fused.

"The next step," Stephen continued, "is to press the gas company to test our own lawns. It's reasonable to think that the contamination spread; the former gas plant took up a few area blocks. Regardless of whether individual property is found to be contaminated, I think we have a case. Do each of you agree? Are you interested in pursuing this lawsuit no matter what?"

They went around the room and all the parties nodded, including Ross. But Ernest refrained.

"Ernest?" Stephen said. "What do you think?"

"I'd be interested in the testing, but I'm not sure I'm interested in pursuing a lawsuit 'no matter what.' I don't think it'll achieve the results I'd want."

"What about holding the gas company accountable?"

"You and I both know how the gas company will play it. They will throw way more money into fighting down that lawsuit than we have; we will end up settling out of court. It won't teach them any lesson— only that their tactic of paying people hush money works best."

"It isn't hush money; it's the only means we have of punishing them. What other punishment does a corporation understand?"

"Well, I'm not motivated by money. I'm not looking for a payout to keep my mouth shut."

Murmurs rippled around the room. "Neither am I," Ross said forcefully. Ethan, the man with the wife with breast cancer, looked appalled. Jean shook her head.

"Hold on here. Are you saying that we shouldn't fight the gas company because it won't change anything? But how would sitting back change anything?"

"What's there to change about what already happened? Listen, the bottom line is that *nobody knew*. Nobody understood that they were leaving behind carcinogens. But you know what we are all aware of, right now? The dirt—that it's all toxic. So where is it going? Where will they take it?"

No one said anything, but Ernest saw a few faces genuinely considering the question.

"I ask again: What about the dirt? Why can't we be just as concerned about that? Isn't our biggest duty to prevent it from polluting some other community?"

"Don't you think our first duty is to our own community?" Marcy interrupted. "I'm feeling like this concern with the dirt and where it'll go next is too abstract, too far off in the future."

"It's not abstract at all. You can see tar creosote in the dirt. It's a greenish-black sludge. You can see it and touch it. That isn't abstract."

Stephen seized control: "To answer your question as far as the dirt goes, I have heard some early plans—"

"From who?"

"Marilyn Fournier. I've been speaking with her pretty regularly about this situation."

"Right, yes." Ernest responded too fast. "She's a good source."

"She said the dirt might be moved downstate using the railroad lines off the expressway. They're going to set up tracks going from the park to those railway lines heading downstate."

"Downstate where?"

"A sparsely populated area."

"But still populated. Probably with poor people. Most likely poor people of color who will have no means to fight it. Look, I understand the case's merit. I know that the idea of holding them accountable sounds really powerful right now. But they're just going to deny that they knew anything. But you know as well as I do that at some point, they did know something. This isn't the first case of a natural gas plant leaving residue. They could've looked at their records and highlighted Aurora Park as a potential calamity zone.

"Look, all I'm saying is that we have one element in this case that we are able to influence *now*—where all that dirt goes. This is what we should be preventing; this should be the focus of our next steps. We can actually change that situation if we fight hard enough."

"But isn't that for them to fight, Ernest?" Jean asked.

"*Them* meaning whoever's downstate and just as ignorant as we were a few weeks ago?"

Jean pursed for lips.

"And fight with what? They won't have law degrees and summer homes, Jean."

"You might be surprised what they have," Camille Banks interjected. "But I agree with Ernest that the issue bears out more research."

Jean prompted the meeting to a close before anything could be agreed on. A collective exhaustion had already sapped the room. Soon, Ernest and Tom were walking home in the gloaming, taking a zigzag route back to their block.

"Ernest, let me ask you something: You were willing to destroy the spaceship when you thought it was causing Cynthia's cancer, right? Why don't you want to do the same to the gas company?"

"Because the spaceship was right here. I actually *could* have destroyed it, or at least that's how I felt. But at best, we'll take a tiny nibble out of the gas company's ankle. They could not care less."

"But the spaceship was part of a bigger thing too."

"What's the bigger thing?"

"The intergalactic tourism complex? Fuck, I don't know. Is it crass for me to point out that a nibble off the gas company's ankle might be enough for you to live on for years?" Tom looked at him hard. "I know you have debt, Ernest."

"But they'll make me sign my life away for that. I'll never be allowed to publicly speak of it again. I want to keep my voice. I want to always keep my voice."

"So you wouldn't take the money?"

"I don't know," Ernest said.

They shuffled side by side in the night, the houses a dim collection of shapes. Tom was quiet with his own thoughts until he said, "For all this talk about your voice, it sounds an awful lot like 'fuck it' to me."

"Seriously, that's what you hear? Fuck it?"

"You sound like you've given up. Like you used all the battle on the spaceship and now that this other thing has come along, you don't have the energy for it."

Ernest stopped on the sidewalk to face him. "I want to spend my energy on the battle that's actually going to make a difference now. Instead of seeing the cycle of pollution and cleanup extended, I want to stop the cycle cold."

"I'm not sure it's possible to stop the cycle," Tom said with a surrendering sigh. "How do you clean poisoned dirt?"

Neither of them wagered an answer.

47

Late on a bright afternoon, a sizable truck pulled into the Allens' driveway, behind the truck Ernest had just rented to haul Earth Day supplies. Even with his contrarian behavior at the meeting, Jean had pestered him until he'd agreed to help, but only with back-end support where he wouldn't have to talk to anyone or organize much of anything. He desperately needed the money, but he didn't want to be seen doing anything like his old job, and he certainly didn't want to explain himself to anyone.

The truck was unmarked and huge, better suited to water main repairs than spaceship maintenance. A man around Ernest's age emerged from the truck with a smooth, analytical air about him and introduced himself as Martín. His tool belt jangled with screwdrivers and various measuring devices. On the side of the truck, a few coiled hoses, some consuls of buttons, and digital screens guarded by plastic shields. Martín was an independent contractor hired by New World Enterprises, and he stepped nimbly around the backyard's still-gaping holes from Suburban Analytics' tests. He held up a couple of measurement devices, one after another. The last one looked like an EMF meter but much more complicated. It pulsed at the low end of its screen.

"Yep, there's nothing going on," Martín said. "When they're active, I usually get a good frequency off of the spaceships, and I'm getting next to nothing."

"So where are they?" Ernest asked. "What's happening?"

"I don't know," Martín said. "There are a couple different possibilities here. One, they can't get the energy source they need to properly function, so they've powered down to reserve energy. The fact that they plugged into your grid for a while suggests they encountered some sort of problem or issue."

"But why did they unplug from my power supply? See the cord just lying there right by the outlet?"

"Well, it's not like the meager juice they could pull from your house could actually power any of their systems for long; whatever it was they were doing with your power, it wasn't anything serious." Martín nodded thoughtfully. "The other possibility is that they're shutting down because of some sort of toxicity nearby. And if that's the case, your outlet isn't going to do them any good either." Martín looked around. "It doesn't seem like it, but are there any industrial plants or chemical plants nearby?"

"No, but there's a polluted park just a block away. They've ripped it apart to test the dirt."

Martín nodded. "They are very sensitive to what's airborne. If they land in a spot that becomes compromised, they will shut down in order to protect themselves. They don't want their ships getting contaminated. Eventually, they'll reject it if it's polluted."

"So you're telling me that the saucer can fly through outer space, but can't handle the pollution on our planet?"

Martín nodded. "They shut down to avoid taking in the chemicals, or because of the chemicals."

"You'd think it would be tougher."

"The spaceship is sensitive. It's why you rarely see these ships land in cities, especially ones with toxicity issues, landfills nearby, that kind of thing."

"So those sweepstakes are rigged? To make sure the saucers only go to 'clean' places?"

Martín smiled wryly. "I guess you could say that."

"So we poisoned the spaceship? With tar creosote?"

"It appears that way, yes."

Ernest looked down at the threadbare grass and then up at the spaceship again. An absurd combination of guilt and relief struck him, an odd sense of responsibility. How manic he'd been for months that it had poisoned Cynthia and maybe the rest of them too; he'd never once considered the reverse. Not quite the canary in the coal mine but something close. The spaceship, responding to the tiniest fragment of toxin, died because of it. Yet, the same amount was tolerable for humans. He shook his head; what they didn't know when they landed—what none of them knew.

"How long will it stay here?"

Martín smiled at him with pity and amusement. "There's no telling. Months, maybe years. Once they go into this mode, they don't typically come out of it. New World will pay for its timely removal, of course. Plus, you'll be compensated for your time and trouble. You'll have a phone call directly from New World about that, so don't quote me on it."

"Has this happened before?"

"Rarely. Only a few times as far as I know. I heard about one dying out in the Southern California desert and now it's a New Age spot. They have drum circles, rain dances, all that hippie-dippie stuff," Martín said, and immediately looked sorry for it, given Ernest's thick cords and dolphin T-shirt.

"Is there anything I can do to get it to leave without having it removed?"

"If you're willing, we can try something that has worked in a couple other cases like yours. Basically we hook the power supply from my truck up to the bottom of the spaceship and try to trick its memory. We have to make it think more time has passed."

Seeing Ernest's blank expression, Martín continued: "It has to think it's time to go. They have their own internal sensor that tells them how long they're supposed to stay, and we have no way of knowing exactly what that time frame is, but it's never been longer than nine, nine and a half months. We'll stimulate its time sensors, and if we just happen to strike on the right time, it'll leave."

"What are the odds of that?"

"Next to zero. And it will take a lot of water. I'll have to tap into the hydrant out front." Martín explained that water raining over the ship would be interpreted as a signal of passing time, a type of seasonal cycle. Almost like spring, if you'd never experienced a spring on Earth before.

"For it to really work," Ernest said, "wouldn't you need to simulate day and night too, over and over again?"

Martín smiled and said with a touch of braggadocio, "That's what my paddles will do."

From the truck, Martín carried two large, thin rubber circles, like basketballs ironed out. Attached to the vehicle's side by two long tubes, he walked them over to the dirt and carefully laid the paddles down. Ernest peeked at them while Martín busied himself in the truck's cab: as thin-skinned as lily pads, the upturned paddles were covered in tiny suckers and prickles. He watched them move in infinitesimal quivers toward the sun.

When Martín returned, Ernest asked, "How do these work?"

"They deliver large jolts of power and information. I can't explain it much more than that."

Martín positioned one pad at a time on the spaceship's undercarriage. Once he had them in the right spot, both sealed to the skin of the spaceship with a kind of rippling motion. When Martín stepped away, two large patches of green clung to each side of the panel that dribbled waste.

Now, Martín instructed, it was time to run water over the ship. He tapped into the main water line. From the truck, an apparatus that was half-sprinkler, half-crane extended out and was positioned above the unsuspecting spaceship. Ernest didn't love wasting gallons of water. Why did the spaceship require so many resources? Even to declare it fully dead—abandoned?—required a last-ditch resource drain.

Sheets of water poured from the truck's contraption, coating the thick glass top of the spaceship. The water swirled in eddies at the dip underneath its windows and then slid off the metal and dripped over the rim, plinking into the grass, soaking into the holes. Mists rose and dispersed in the air, moistening Ernest's face and clothes. They were creating a fake environment replete with weather, humidity. Underneath, the paddles attached to the bottom rippled occasionally, letting out tiny seepages of purple-tinged UV light.

After an hour or so, Alison wandered into the backyard. Standing on the back stairs with a mug of coffee, still groggy, she lost herself in watching the water flow over the metal.

"We're trying to give the spaceship a jump," Ernest yelled to her, once they'd turned off the hoses.

"That's gonna work?"

"Martín here says it'll either work right away or not at all."

They waited for several minutes. Ernest and Alison were stationed on the stairs, out of the way, in case the spaceship sprung loose into the sky, in case it leaped up with so much force that they would need the quick shelter of the house. But it refused to loosen from the ground. It stood ghostly, an eggshell drained of its yolk. Martín finally peeled off the paddles and carried them back to the truck. Ernest followed him.

Martín shrugged. "Sorry, Ernest."

"There's nothing else to try?"

Martín shook his head. "I wish there was more I could do for you."

"Can we pry back the panel and get inside?"

"You won't get anywhere. You'll never get inside. No one ever has. And even if you did, sensors would alert New World and you would be arrested. Tampering is a federal offense."

"So we're stuck."

"Like I said, New World will pay for its removal and you and your family can take a trip to Hawaii or something."

"How would they remove it? Where would it go?"

"They'd lift it by crane and take it away. It's quite a production, but New World handles all of it, including putting you up in a hotel if you want to avoid the noise."

"Where would it go? Wouldn't Jupiter want it back?"

"It can't get back on its own, and it has no value to them either. What happens exactly, though, where it goes—that's confidential. Word is there's an agreement that we can't touch the ships, go inside them, do any research on them. They go into some sort of protected landfill."

Alison had eased over to stand next to the men. Now she asked: "So are they dead too? Inside?"

Martín looked uncomfortable. "I don't know."

Alison, confused, tried again. "Wasn't someone, more than one, living in there?"

"We don't really know. We don't have access to that information. No one knows that, except the top brass at New World and the government, of course."

"Dad," Alison said, "if they're in there, we can't just send them away. That wouldn't be right."

For all the grief it had caused him, Ernest didn't want to see the spaceship as more junk in a landfill either. For one thing, it would never break down, the metal glinting in the sun endlessly, useful to no one. He imagined taking it to a recycling center for it to be melted down like one giant intergalactic Coke can. In a landfill, even a protected one, it would be the odd machine out, huge, with unknown technology, sitting among the copiers, fax machines, pagers, phones, stereos, and TVs all marbled together, everybody refusing to pass, or be absorbed, or break down.

Alison said, "It's part of the family now. It went through everything with us."

"But what will we do with it?"

"We'll figure it out," she said. "But it has to stay here. It didn't ask to get poisoned. We can't abandon it. We can't turn our back on it now."

Ernest rubbed his eyes with a thumb and forefinger. Alison forged ahead.

"It's tied to Mom. I know it is."

Two people brutalized by loss. Three people, when he added in Gabe. Four, including Cynthia. He thought about the letter that had been taped to the spaceship, how it seemed like the spaceship had delivered it. They would cling to this one last remnant of the time when she lived. If it was too ineffable to understand, at least it was there. A monument to their lives.

Ernest turned to Martín. "We're keeping it. It's not going."

Alison yelped in victory. Her grin was all Ernest needed to know he was making the right choice.

"Really? You sure about that?"

"If they can't tell me exactly where it's going, I'm not letting it go. It's not right."

Martín shook his head in disbelief, and Ernest smiled, the first pure smile he'd had in a while.

Ernest already saw it. If the ship stayed with them, it would be eclipsed, as much as possible, by the wildest jungle he could get away with in a suburban backyard. He'd surround it with a ring of trees and foliage, the kind of kudzu that suckered onto anything, climbing up, twisting, choking around the legs. He'd try to bury the contraption in nature. Always there would be one metal spaceship in the center, but it would become, over time, a secret. A spaceship sunken into a wooded grave. One day, after the Allens moved away and the trees around it grew big enough, a gang of neighborhood kids would discover the silver skeleton underneath all the green.

48

Outside, Gabe, Ernest, and Alison stood next to the ladder propped against the spaceship. Gabe was confused; the spaceship was dead, but here forever. Or the spaceship was still alive, but winding down. Wait, no, the spaceship was just dead, and they were staring at a corpse. They looked up at the blue sky, the raggedy clouds pinned in place. Ernest had agreed, now that the ship wasn't going anywhere, that they could crawl on top of it. Carefully. Spotting one another. Taking the proper precautions. Not being idiots about the whole thing, OK? Gabe gripped the sides of the ladder, ready to vault up by enthusiasm alone.

"I'd say ladies first," Gabe said, "but I really, really want to go."

"I'd rather you scout it out anyway," Alison said. "Go for it."

Gabe rapidly ascended the rungs, never looking down.

"Go up there with him," Ernest mumbled once Gabe was out of earshot. "Make sure he doesn't do anything stupid."

"Seriously?"

"Yes."

With measured movements, she climbed the steps, looking up in time to see her brother's holey sneakers kicking off as he shimmied onto the top of the ship. Looking down, she saw her father on the ground, smaller and gripping the ladder. He nodded at her to keep going.

"Be careful," she said to her brother, less as a warning and more as an announcement of her presence on the top deck. Her brother was on his hands and knees, stable on the sleek metal stitched together in concentric rings. Blocking the sun with his hand, Gabe peered into the wraparound window of the spaceship's globed top. Nothing could be seen through the dark glass. He tried to stare through it and the material only gave back itself, densely and resolutely. When he knocked on it, the sound dropped into the material and didn't echo or travel. It was like knocking on a pillow.

Still, despite seeing nothing, he felt like he was staring at a person, or some kind of self. Like the feeling of closing his eyes and staring at his own eyelids, the slips of tissue and blood filling in for his interior, the part of himself that he'd never see the whole of. But here was another self, a distinct presence. Had the spaceship always seemed like another being? When it was active, it felt like an object *and* a presence. Now, stripped of all its rambunctious energy, the presence overwhelmed all sense of the physical.

He gave one more knock. "Hello?"

"What are you doing?" Alison said.

"Something is there!"

"*In* there? You can see it?"

"No, but I can feel it, more than I used to."

"Let me see."

Slowly, because his purchase was more tenuous than he had let on, Gabe crawled back over to the ladder. Behind Alison, a tangle of tree branches and the slats on the side of Tom's house, the horizon at a cockeyed angle.

"Alison, seriously, be careful while you're up there. It's a little freaky."

From his perch below, Ernest couldn't hear anything they were saying, but he saw Alison and Gabe switch places at the top of the ladder, a risky shift of limbs that he wouldn't have recommended, but he was powerless to stop them. Instead, he reinforced his grip.

Once Alison had inched her way up the incline of the slippery metal, she hovered close to the glass and peered in. The levers and the shadowy figure she sometimes spotted from a certain angle on the ground weren't visible this close. She tried to lean back to see if she saw more from a distance, but she couldn't get far enough away.

"Knock on the glass," her brother yelled from the top of the ladder.

She rapped a few times, but there was barely a sound. Still, she understood why Gabe told her to do it. An attention had shifted to her.

"No way!" she said quietly.

"Say something to them," Gabe hissed.

"I'm Alison," she said into the glass loud enough for Gabe to hear. "I forgive you for blowing weird green pollen on me." She giggled a little and then fell silent, noting the impenetrable reflection that contained a perfect replica of herself shining back.

"Tell me a secret," she whispered. "What will happen five years from now?"

The spaceship didn't reveal anything, lousy oracle that it was. But the attention warmed and spooled around her. Would she always be protected, even through cataclysm? No reason, no proof stepped forward to answer, but there was a sense that staring into her own reflection would always ground her. That she was a familiar and a stranger, tapping into layers—slowly, over a life—that she didn't know she possessed until she ran aground of them. No matter her family, her friends, whom she thought she knew, there was only herself in the end to connect with, and only so much of herself to access at any given time. That last fading smile her mother had left behind as she died—it somehow made sense now.

She backed her way down till she got to the ladder, where her brother looked rejuvenated.

"A little freaky, right?" He posed the question with one of his giddy smiles that got Alison revved up too.

"It's just *here*," she said. "Alien and friendly at the same time."

By the time they scrambled down to the ground, their excitement jumped to Ernest.

"What happened?" Ernest said. "They invite you over for dinner?"

"Dad," Alison said, "it's an experience. It feels like you're being watched and protected by a really friendly dog, but maybe if the dog was as ginormous as the sun."

"You have to knock on the glass," Gabe added. "Then you'll feel it."

"All right, guys, stay down at the bottom and hold the ladder."

Ernest marched till he reached the top. Unlike the last time he was up here, his perspective was clear. He was open to anything. On his knees, he crossed sheet after sheet of cool silver. His hands were sweaty enough to create a little tack as he advanced closer to the glass. Behind him, Alison had risen to the top of the ladder. He didn't bother to tell her to go back down.

Once at the glass dome, he crouched at the lip, his knees close to his chest. If he could stand up here, he'd be a little taller than the globe's top, but at this height, he felt a touch of vertigo. He stayed down and rubbed his hand across the glass, seeing faint moisture that immediately evaporated. He folded his fingers into a fist, laughing a little, and knocked as advised. Was he trapped inside a parable? Some religious riddle that coiled back on itself? "Whoever knocks on the door, the son of God will answer." Wasn't that a line his father would quote in the occasional churchy mood?

Nothing happened, so Ernest tried again: two strikes delivered officiously, urgently, as if he were a census taker at the door.

Still no answer, no sense of whatever the kids had alluded to. This time he knocked louder, all knuckle and sharp, three times.

"Apologize!" Alison hissed, "for taking an ax to it!"

Ernest shook his head ruefully; he wasn't about to say anything out loud. But the truth was he was sorry. For a lot of things.

Then it happened. Eyes leveled on him from a deep-seated place. An embracing attention. Was it coming from inside the spaceship? From outside? The glass beamed back his reflection and nothing more. He twisted back and forth in his position, to see if he could shake the eyes, distance himself or confuse them, but with any movement, they followed. He was held in their vision, peacefully watched. The sensation was closest to how he felt when he met Cynthia in a dream and she looked at him fully, talking to him, it didn't matter about what, but then there was another level: those were his eyes, watching him. He was watching himself. But the self that was watching was big and blown out, the sea and the sky, a titanic but dissipated weight. Unfathomable. Where terror could've so easily flowed in, serenity poured in instead. He wasn't in harm's way. *Never could he be,* the eyes said. *Safety. Patience. Openness. Protection.* The eyes stretched the feeling out around him like a sheet and folded him into it. Then he laughed to see if it would laugh too. It did, in its own way.

"Dad? What the hell happened? Did you knock?" Gabe asked.

"Oh, he knocked a bunch of times," Alison said, "and he laughed a bunch, like a crazy person."

"So you felt it," Gabe said. "It's alive, right?"

Ernest shook his head, the solid ground beneath him still a thing to get used to. "I'm not sure what happened."

"Did you have some kind of hallucination up there?"

"No, it was real."

"So you felt it? The presence?" Gabe's electric smile again.

Ernest nodded. "I wasn't prepared. You're right; it's watching. Something."

"We should go up there all the time. I want to feel that again. It feels good to be watched!"

"I don't think so," said Ernest. "That's not to be trifled with. We're going to surround this thing in a ring of trees. It will be a secret."

"What? Why would you cut us off from that?"

Ernest smiled. "I'm not. I want you to feel it again and again, but not here. You should go to Japan, Gabe. Go to Japan, but do one thing for me: visit Jōmon Sugi, one of the oldest trees in the world. It's two thousand years old, but some say it's as old as five thousand years."

Gabe was bursting; finally, his dad seemed to be seeing him. Alison enviously witnessed his glee.

"What about me?" she said. "What do I get to do? Look at new trees here?"

"I don't know," her dad said, "but we will figure it out. You, me, and the spaceship."

Later, Gabe helped Ernest plant the little saplings he had picked up at the nursery, tucking each root ball into the ground. They weren't talking much, but the silence was less prickly than it had been in months.

"You know, Dad, for all your talk about the big, badass glory of mother nature, I still feel like I've never seen it," Gabe said. "I've seen some dumpy-ass woods in Wisconsin, but where is it? Where is this big, bad Mama Earth?"

"Everywhere," Ernest said. "Right here. But you're going to really feel it with that old tree. Imagine, a tree that has seen two thousand years of time, weather, sitting still and fixed in place."

After a minute, Gabe said, "I'll go to Japan and I'll see that tree. But honestly, I'm more interested in Tokyo than anything else. I saw a picture of Tokyo and it just doesn't stop—all the buildings, all that glass and metal and silver. That is the real place of wonder to me. I mean, we made that, humans."

"You'll have to take lots of pictures," Ernest said.

They continued to plant the trees for the rest of the afternoon as well as the next day. Mere stick figures with a flush of leaves, they ringed the spaceship like children at a ceremonial altar, waiting for their time to step forward.

49

"Dad, I have something to talk to you about," Alison said.

She'd found him in the garage, his arms submerged in the washing machine.

"What are you doing?" she asked.

"These sheets have twisted around the middle so much that the machine has stopped. Just give me a second."

He lifted the twist of sopping sheet out of the soapy water and rearranged it so that it wouldn't stop the machine. Lowering the lid slowly, Ernest clicked it shut, and the machine sprung back into action.

"I'm getting good at laundry."

She smiled weakly back, her eyes worried.

"What's going on, honey? You want to go in the kitchen?"

She followed him into the house. They sat down at the table across from each other. Her father folded his hands, wet and red from the wash. The formality of the gesture made Alison more nervous. She dove into her story before she could think otherwise.

"I did something in the park and I'm worried that—that I might be infected now with something. It was raining, like this violent downpour, and that's just where we ended up. It was the end of last summer, so I didn't know anything about the park yet. If I had known, I would've stayed in his car or something. But we thought it'd be fun to slosh around in the mud and . . ." Alison trailed off.

"Whoa, slow down. Was this guy your age?"

"A couple of grades older," she said. "It was raining, and he lifted up my shirt. My back was completely in the mud—that stuff probably soaked into my skin. I've been thinking for the last few weeks about it, and I'm worried that I might have something wrong with me."

Ernest tried to piece together what his daughter might be telling him. She said she felt infected. Did she have sex with this guy? Did she now have the symptoms of an STD? He took a deep inhale. How he wished Cynthia could roll in right now, saying the right words in her even way. But she wasn't.

"OK, for starters, I'm glad you're telling me about this and not any other adult in your life."

"Who would I tell?"

"Olivia, or, god forbid, some teacher who'd have to relay this information to me in a very awkward school meeting."

"I would never tell a teacher anything like this."

"OK, so what kind of symptoms do you have?"

"It's hard to explain. It's more like a bunch of feelings."

"I don't totally understand. I'm going to ask you something and you can tell me the truth, OK? I won't be mad. No matter what you tell me."

"OK."

"Did you have sex with this guy?"

"No, Dad," she answered irritably. "He just went up my shirt."

"So you're not—" Ernest paused, to summon delicacy. "There're no physical symptoms? Nothing uncomfortable?"

She blinked at him. "Dad, I don't have an STD. I know all about those. I'm worried about being contaminated by the park."

"But, OK, you didn't have sex with *this* guy, but have you had sex with someone else?"

"Dad, you're totally missing the point of my story!"

"I know you take these very informative sex-ed classes, but I just want to make sure you're not missing anything or overlooking a symptom or otherwise—"

"I don't have herpes or anything else. Look at my lips." She puckered them up and then pointed at them. "Never even had a cold sore. But what I think I have is a brain tumor."

"Why?"

"Because I rolled around in the mud like that, in that polluted mud! And, Dad, I have thoughts sometimes. Like what if everything around me dies? What if it's Gabe next and then you? Or only you? Already people stare at me in the hallways. No one knows what to say to a kid with a brand-new dead mom. I'm like some untouchable warrior-orphan."

"You're not an orphan, you have me. Any headaches?"

"No, but you don't have a medical degree."

"That you know of. Any blurred vision?"

"No."

"Loss of memory?"

"Not exactly, but I'm forgetting things about Mom, very little but specific things. But, Dad, I rolled around in that mud, that poison mud."

"It doesn't work like that. You'd have to get so much more exposure."

"You mean take walks in there every day?"

"Never mind," he said. "I feel certain that you don't have cancer, Alison."

"Are you sure?"

"Yes!"

She was quiet for a few moments. "So now are you sitting here thinking that I'm some sort of slut or something?"

Ernest winced. Alison knew she had gone too far using that word.

"No," Ernest said. "There's nothing you could ever tell me that would make me think that way about you."

"So, to you, there's nothing wrong with some guy sticking his hand up my shirt."

"Alison, I hope you're being careful, that's what I can say."

She nodded. "I'm careful, but this guy was sort of an asshole."

"Why? What did he do?"

"Made out with me and then pretended he didn't really know me the next day at school."

"Does Gabe know about any of this?"

Alison gave him a look as if he were a three-headed cat.

That meant the confession was all the more meaningful. He considered doing the same to her. Telling her that he'd slept with Marilyn while her mother was clinging to the last few fragments of life. That he'd lied about having an affair, even if it was only an emotional one for the most part. Save for that one time. That one time. He could tell her and explain it in all the ways he had rationalized to himself—that he'd needed comfort, that he wasn't proud of himself but he'd been true to Cynthia the entire time of their marriage, that

Cynthia maybe would've understood herself. Upon his confession, Alison would understand that adults aren't always in full control. She'd lean over, squeeze his hand, and say, "It's OK, Dad. I get it."

Tears traveled down his face in streaks.

"Dad? I don't understand."

The ability to control himself couldn't be located. For a brief time, he surrendered. A few sobs hacked their way out before he put his hand over his eyes, preventing himself from seeing her or her from seeing him, he wasn't sure. Minutes passed while he cried, his face crumpled and red, his glasses held away in one hand.

"What's wrong, Dad?" she said softly.

"Your mother, your brother," he said. Out from his guts a long sigh escaped. "I didn't do everything right."

A confession, half of one. She wanted to hate him, so she tried on the hate. Didn't he deserve at least a little of it? A flash of anger, one that would surely return, but in the moment she couldn't sustain it, couldn't act on it. She'd never seen him cry, not like this anyway. An alarming occurrence, but then again, it was in keeping with the rhythm of chaos she'd come to expect. She tried to comfort him.

"He'll be back, Dad. He's coming back for Christmas, for one thing."

He nodded and blew out a resigned breath. Of course he knew she was right to keep it contained to Gabe. She couldn't be the one to absolve his guilt over the affair. She didn't know how, and it wouldn't work anyway. They couldn't talk about it, not yet.

"I'm sorry," he said. "I meant to comfort you, not the other way around."

"Maybe this is the way it will have to be for a while, Dad."

Ernest nodded. "Tell me some good news, Alison. Tell me something that you're excited about."

She thought for a moment. A smile crept up. "I'm going to start a sneaker-illustrating business for real. Make it official instead of just doing freebies for kids at school. Spaceship sneakers. Or whatever they want, but the spaceship design will be my specialty."

"Alison," Ernest interrupted, grabbing her hand, "promise me you'll start that business. I can see it: you'll go far in retail. I want to help you."

"How?"

"I don't know. I can't draw at all, but let me be your business manager."

"Aubrey's going to be my business partner, but you can be our consultant. All right, Dad?"

"You've got a deal."

They high-fived at the kitchen table, imagining the next year together, the only two left for now.

50

On their way to Franklin Park for Earth Day, the Allen family passed Aurora Park. They didn't have to, but it was a natural drift. Ernest led them on the sidewalk covered in gingko leaves, Cynthia's favorite tree. Alison teased Ernest about his outfit: he wore an old Earth Day shirt, from one of the first celebrations he had ever attended. The planet on his chest was a faded glob of blue, continents and islands in cracked white paint.

"Who's going to save that sorry-ass planet on your shirt?" Alison said. She was going to ream him about his braided belt too, but she stopped; it was a notch tighter than before, to accommodate his new lowered weight. On some days he didn't eat very much at all, when the grief kept him hemmed in.

Aurora Park bore no signs of being a neighborhood park anymore. Instead, it was a disaster site. The white plastic tent looked ceremonial, as if for a wedding, but there weren't folding tables with sterling settings or floral arrangements or a catering team bustling around. Just the plastic that glowed like a saccharine moon. They stood and looked at it, their hands jammed in their jacket pockets.

"How long will it look like this?" Alison asked.

"The estimate is two years, but it'll take longer than that. Now that it's been ripped apart, it's going to sit like this for months, while the gas company and Prairie Park bicker over who's going to pay for all the work."

"Dad, are we going to move away from here? From this?" Gabe asked.

"The house is worth nothing now," Ernest said. "No one will buy a house a block away from this mess. We'll have to wait it out."

Taking in the meandering multitudes at Franklin Park, it was easy to forget about Aurora Park's own destruction. Here, the suburban dream still thrived. And yet, despite its apparent vitality, Ernest wondered about the grass under his feet, wondered if it didn't have secrets too. In the spirit of the day, he decided to temporarily suspend worry. In the spirit of so many days, this state of acceptance would have to do.

Considering the last-minute upheaval, the festival appeared like it had been planned for this spot all along. The park was packed with chatty, inquisitive families; kids screaming and giving chase; lone denizens of Prairie Park weaving around the sidewalks lined with tents. Some booths sold wares: artisanal jams, lavender soaps, amber jewelry, blown-glass vases, hemp and raw cotton clothes. At one booth, a woman braided friendship bracelets on a homemade loom while a crowd of preteen girls watched and ordered specific combinations. At another booth, a little girl squirmed while a volunteer painted little strawberries with white flowers on her flushed cheek. The smell of fresh food steamed through the air— corn dogs, tamales, barbecue skewers, and kettle corn. Kids scrambled by with hunks of watermelon, dropping seeds on the walks. Ernest noticed that the educational tents, marooned from the main thoroughfare on their own separate walkway, were slightly less populated than the food and wares booths, but that was to be expected. He had to admit that the Demeter booth was constantly packed with people buying bamboo bags, manuka honey, Ghanian coffee, and all the rest. He cut through the crowd and headed for educational row.

On his way, he nearly collided with Olivia, who was holding a squirming Cherice. In the sun, she jostled Cherice, who was almost too big to be held now.

"Have you seen Tom? I lost him somewhere."

"No, what's going on?"

"I just need to use the bathroom, and it's too hard with her."

"Do you want me to take her for a while?" Ernest asked.

Olivia studied him carefully. "Really?"

"Of course. After the bathroom, you can look around for a while. I'll be right around here."

Her face loosened in relief. "Thanks, Ernest."

Olivia launched into directions about what to do if Cherice fussed, but Ernest cut her off: "I've been to this rodeo before, you know."

Cherice knew Ernest well enough to accept the transition into his arms with good humor. She stared at him with luminous brown orbs, flecks of sand in the dark irises. Her sundress and diaper mashed against the crook of his arm. He mustered his most amazed face and said, "Hello! Let's see the sights, shall we?"

His pace was different with a baby. One step. Two. Three steps, each with more weight and a growing sense of mutual astonishment at the world. He took it a step further: he turned her around so that she faced forward as well. They would see the same things at the same time. Their double vision simultaneously locked on the cloud booth. A chunky man with unruly eyebrows sat behind a table. Behind him, a drawn black curtain. Ernest heard the muffled sounds of storms and rain, many types crossing into a thunder of confusion.

"Are you Vince, the cloud magician?"

The man heartily pumped Ernest's hand and spoke in a pool of words: "Gabe's dad, yeah. Hi, how are you doing? It's great to be here, glad to do this. Sorry about your loss, your wife. I didn't know her but I recognized her from the mall, from around town." Once Ernest nodded obligatorily, Vince immediately launched into "Would you like to experience fifty types of clouds?"

"There are that many?"

Vince sheepishly explained that strictly speaking, no, but he could make the argument that each cloud was unique. Hence, fifty types. He'd filmed some of them from his roof during the last year or so; others he clipped from documentaries. He brought Ernest and Cherice into the curtained area.

"Enjoy the show," he said as he raked the fabric shut.

Surrounding them were three walls of TVs, small ones for the most part, but a few living room eyesores as well. Each TV screened an image of a cloud. Some were swollen and mottled gray with sheets of slanted rain falling from their whispery undersides. Others were sharp and shadowy—white meringue puffs with dense dark slashes. One was barely there, just a few isolated trails stitching across the sky. Another vista was all cloud, ripples of starch and wool that hung in a mass. Ernest and Cherice slowly rotated, taking them all in. On the baby's eyes a series of days were replayed—days she had experienced once and was now experiencing again, though just a sliver of it. The sky of any given day was one in a million precise details her brain had recorded and lost. But here it was again, collapsed into one moment.

In the middle of the crackle, Ernest could hear it: *t-t-t-t-t-t-t-t-t-t-t-t-t-t-t-t-t-t*, his old friend. As soon as he recognized it, it slipped away through the flooring of his mind. He could see only its tail, too late to catch it.

When he emerged, Olivia and Tom were waiting.

"I knew you'd be in there," Tom said. He began to scoop Cherice out of Ernest's arms, but Ernest ducked away.

"Not yet," he said, "I need her."

"That's right, Cherice," Tom said to his girl, "soften this old crabapple. Do the Lord's work."

"Oh, I've been softened all right," Ernest replied. "Into mush."

He saw Ross and Marcy a few yards away. Ross appeared withered but almost holy, walking in beige hemp. Marcy gripped his arm to steer him away, but Ross staggered straight for Ernest. Cherice bucked a little at the sight of him, squirming to change her view.

"You were right, Ernest."

Ernest accepted his fish bone of a hand, noticed the pink scarring from that rash last year, and held it expectantly.

"Earth Day," Ross continued. "It should be more serious." He looked around with faint disgust at the milling crowds. "I don't know if people are really hearing the lessons."

Lessons? A cue hung in the air. Ernest was expected to pontificate on said lessons, to rail against the sleeping sheep closing their eyes to the inevitable destruction. But he couldn't bring himself to perform the old dance. The sheep were awake and could see the destruction, if they wanted to. What was even the point of saying so?

"Come on, it's great," Ernest said. "I haven't made it over to the stage yet, but live music? What a brilliant idea, with or without Ms. Folksinger."

"The issues, Ernest, that's all that matters. So we don't have another Aurora Park again. Have you been to Stephen's booth yet?"

"Ross, let's get you out of this sun," Marcy said. Her gritted smile instructed them all to let Ross's words drop.

Ernest wanted to say, "There will be another one, and another one, and another one," but that would've been cruel. True, but torturous to an obsessed mind and a cancerous body. Instead, he rocked on his heels, a weird way of gaining equilibrium, and said good-bye. He promised Ross they'd talk in more detail sometime soon.

After giving Cherice back—and instantly he was bereft without her—he hunted for his own children. But he hung back once he spotted them in the crowd. Gabe was waiting in line for sushi, and Alison and Aubrey crowded around an older woman with a head of hair too thick and lustrous for her age. Must've been a wig. When he watched his daughter talk, he could almost believe that she was speaking to her mother; the same caring but annoyed expressions crossed her face.

He spotted Diane Albero a few feet away, incorrectly dressed for the occasion. Her black top bagged around her middle, and her business slacks were hiked up, revealing her white ankles swimming in varicose veins. Ernest prepared to ignore her and to be ignored in turn, but she lit up right when she saw him.

"Hi," she said with a big smile.

"Hi," he answered back, noticing that she didn't say his name. Did she think he was somebody else?

"I'm sorry we couldn't help you with that spaceship," she said, removing her sunglasses. Sweat had smeared her eyeliner around her eyes, but she looked sincere. "Is it still there?"

"It is, but it's . . ." Ernest hesitated. He didn't want to tell her it was dead. He still wanted her to feel a little guilty.

"Never mind," she said. "It'll go away eventually, but I want you to meet someone. My dear old aunt Catharine Montagna is here, painting portraits and landscapes. And they're beautiful, so special, you should really get one for your living room."

Diane grabbed his arm and led him to a booth a few steps away. He wanted to be irritated, but he couldn't help but be charmed by Diane's prideful sales tactic. She'd remembered just enough about him—the man who had a spaceship in his backyard—to approach him with her pitch. It worked. Here he was standing in Catharine Montagna's booth, an area of trampled-on grass that was packed with paintings of all sizes on easels and laid out on folding tables. The artist perched on a stool, putting the finishing touches on a landscape dominated by wiry, electrified brushstrokes. Her long legs, outfitted in a paisley pantsuit, were spread-eagled, her ankles hooked on the bottom rung of her stool. Her hair was swept up in a high bun, and she had large yellow flowers clutching to her baggy earlobes. She had to be well into her eighties, but her hazel eyes were sharp and puckish.

"I'm happy to meet you," she said loudly. "What's your name?"

"Ernest," he said loudly in return, noticing how she tilted her ear, outfitted with a thumb-size hearing aid, in his direction. "I'm happy to meet you. I've already got one of your paintings."

"You don't say. Which one?"

Diane looked on in surprise as he explained. "It's an older one. A portrait of a woman, her face made out of all sorts of natural things—wood for lips, leaves for hair. We call her the Earth Mama."

"Oh yeah," Catharine answered. "That was the original series I did, way back in the seventies. And you have one? That is great to hear. Have a seat, Ernest."

He joined her on another paint-splattered stool. For some reason, this strange coincidence seemed apt and not so strange at all.

"Auntie," Diane interjected, "I told you about Ernest. He's the fellow who has a spaceship in his backyard." To Ernest: "I can't believe you have one of her paintings!"

"Oh, that's you!" Catharine exclaimed. "I always wanted to go knock on your door and ask to see it."

"You could've done that. Everyone else did."

"Well, I don't like to intrude."

Diane slipped back into the crowd, leaving them alone.

"It's still there, if you ever want to come by."

"It is? I just might do that. Where are you?"

"Right by Aurora Park," he said. "Hey, I think you might've known my wife a little bit." He pulled a picture out of his wallet.

"I know her. She's a fellow walker, goes real fast, that one. We've chatted many a time. How is she?"

Ernest paused. "She died of breast cancer not too long ago."

Catharine's face broke from enthusiasm to bewilderment. "What, this young lady? I am sorry to hear that. I am deeply sorry."

Every once in a while when someone expressed their condolences, it would actually get to him. The sincerity of her words threatened to unloose everything he'd carefully tied together at the start of this day. But he forced himself to scatter the encroaching tears and break into a bright smile. "Thanks, yes," Ernest said. "So you can see why I'm in special need of a portrait."

"Yes, you are," Catharine said. "What are you thinking? Do you want a painting of her?"

"No, I already have that. Your other painting is her."

"Yes." Catharine's eyes lit up. "I painted her, and I just didn't know it yet."

They contemplated for a minute.

"Your painting has to involve that spaceship," she said.

He laughed. "You know what? Put me on that spaceship, flying through the air, and attach a cartoon bubble to my mouth saying, 'Get me off of this planet!'"

Her floral reading glasses, cheapies from the drugstore, nearly fell off her head as she laughed. "That's a crazy idea! I love an idea like that. But you know what? I'm going to paint that and really, what's happening is that you're flying *back* to her. Not yet in real life—you need to stay here—but just in this painting. You and I will know that."

He nodded. For a few minutes, she busied herself with getting a new piece of canvas set up and a system of brushes and paints. She fanned her fingers over the handles, thinking through something.

"I'm not going to finish this today, Ernest, but I will get a good study down. I want to get your essence first. Can you do something for me? Can you indulge this old hippie with a little meditation exercise?"

"I've been meditating every day lately," he said. "I'm primed."

51

"All right. Close your eyes. Sit there on that stool and imagine yourself rooted into the ground. Picture yourself with a pole going through the top of your head, all the way through your center, out through your pelvis, and then into the ground, and all the way to the center of the hot, fiery earth."

She paused to let him sink into it. His lower half was tingling; the pole inserted itself into some mysterious dead-center space in his guts, the soft tissue and organs folding around it like a root. Clean metal, a baton, that could pass familiarly through blood, muscle, tissue, and bone. It exited out of him and shot rigidly into the ground, striking through the trampled grass, the loose dirt and insects, the clumpy topsoil laced with worms and perlite fertilizer balls, then deeper to the sheets of rock, packed tighter and tighter toward the center where the magma roiled. The pole connected him to the earth, but it was also one and the same material.

"Now take that pole and imagine it going up out of your head, through the trees, out into the sky, into the clouds, and as far as you can take it. Into the layers of atmosphere, past the airplanes to where the air is thin and it is dark."

Ernest followed the pole into the upper reaches of the planet's atmosphere, rising through the clouds, touching the place where the air evaporates into chill and fiber, dust and black.

"Now come back here, Ernest. Right at this moment. This ground, your home."

When she said the word "home," he took it literally, but he also imagined a kind of future. The future, or a fantasy. Both. He stood in the backyard, near the spaceship, surveying the spread around him. Paper birches and weeping willows repeated outward as far as his eyes could see. Over the spaceship, the trees formed a canopy, the sun streaking through and dappling the metal with light. The weeping willows and their frond fingers rustled in the wind. He walked away from the spaceship into the cover of forest. Through the trees, he saw her—a whip of her hair, a catch of fabric from her old floral swimsuit—between the brown trunks. Ernest hurried toward her, defining the landscape with every step, trying to catch up to her. Underneath him, the world was being fabricated for the first time, blooming and rotting simultaneously. Behind him, everything that had gone before. If he were to turn back and look at it, he was afraid of what he might see for the last time. The world: traffic and birds and flashing lights in iodine blue, blood-beating red, nocturnal green. As he raced ahead, the woman in the trees, his wife, finally turned around to see him.

ACKNOWLEDGMENTS

Neon Green came together during a six-year period that in retrospect seems like a blur of café nights, early-morning writing before work, desert retreats, and notes scribbled in a series of black sketchbooks that eventually coalesced into a novel. It would not exist today without the community of people who believed in it, nurtured it, and advocated for it at every turn, even when my spirit flagged.

Thank you to Chris Heiser at Unnamed Press for his thoughtful and scrutinizing notes, which greatly improved this book. To J. Ryan Stradal, who led this book to its rightful home at Unnamed Press, I am grateful for years of friendship, close readings, and belly laughs. Thanks to Olivia Taylor Smith as well for her dedicated efforts to get this book out in the world.

I interviewed a few friends and loved ones who had experiences, professional and personal, that were useful to this book. Thank you to Adam Stolorow, Robert Baron, and especially my naturalist brother, David Wappler, the most impassioned conservationist I know, for shedding light on various environmental issues. David's quasi-religious experience in the California hot springs provided the foundation for the scene with Ernest in the Sierra Nevada. Dave, thank you for being you, and feel free to recycle this book after you've read it.

Many loved ones read drafts, came out for readings, and asked me key questions, such as "What the hell is happening in this part?" The following people read partial or full drafts and provided incisive notes: Amanda Yates, Lauren Strasnick, Joe Meno, Shawn Vandor, Taffy Brodesser-Akner, Benjamin Weissman, Edan Lepucki (also the best boss lady I've ever had), and my uncle Eugene Garber, who was the first person in my life who gave me the dangerous idea that being a writer was not only possible, but a sane and beautiful life choice. It's all your fault, Gene.

A few times I flung myself out to Joshua Tree for intense writing bouts as a wannabe desert hobo. Thank you to Janet Sarbanes and Ken Ehrlich for opening their home to me, and also to David Dodge for offering warm shelter.

To my agent, the fiery yet deadly cool Erin Hosier, I send immense rays of gratitude. You saw straight into the crazy soul of this book and never lost faith.

There are two people whose fingerprints are all over *Neon Green*:

Jade Chang, whom I sat across from while writing the first drafts of this book, thank you for being my partner in eating substandard sandwiches, for exhaustively tracking which cafés had electrical outlets (and beer), and, most of all, for dreaming of another way with me. Your enthusiasm and steady balance kept me seeing straight through several stages of the story.

And to my husband, David, my favorite fellow alien walking this planet. Thank you for love and encouragement. For caring about this book like it was your own. For arguing with me about what a character would do with utter passion and conviction. For donating metaphorical kidneys to make sure this book wouldn't die before it had a chance to live in the world. I'm so glad to be floating in this particular patch of space with you.

ADDITIONAL THANKS

The following sources were instrumental to the shape of this book: *Flying Saucers: A Modern Myth of Things Seen in the Skies* by Carl Jung; *Lonely Planets: The Natural Philosophy of Alien Life* by David Grinspoon; *Radio Territories*, edited by Erik Granly Jensen and Brandon LaBelle, especially the chapter from the radio collective LIGNA; and the article "Inside the Russian Short Wave Radio Enigma" by Peter Savodnik, published by *Wired* on September 27, 2011. Also, the environmental reporting from *Wednesday Journal* (especially the tenacious work of Katharine Grayson) and the *Chicago Tribune* on the Barrie Park cleanup in my hometown of Oak Park, Illinois, one of the most expensive environmental disasters in the state's history. I couldn't have imagined certain parts of *Neon Green* without these invaluable texts.

ABOUT THE AUTHOR

Margaret Wappler has written about the arts and pop culture for the *Los Angeles Times, Rolling Stone, Elle, Cosmo, The New York Times*, and several other publications. *Neon Green* is her first novel. She lives in Los Angeles and can be heard weekly on the pop culture podcast, Pop Rocket.

PRAISE FOR *NEON*

"Funny, sad, weird, timely: in *Neon Green*, Wappler mixes up her own distinct cocktail of these into a substantive and affecting debut." **–Aimee Bender, author of *The Color Master***

"Part historical novel, part alternative history, *Neon Green* captures the suburban-American experience at the cusp of the Internet Age, and asks its readers to consider what unites— and what threatens— a family. Strange yet accessible, goofy yet also, somehow, heartbreaking, this wonderfully original novel made me see everything around me in a new beguiling light: from my own family to the big unknowable sky above me. A debut to be reckoned with." **–Edan Lepucki, author of *California***

"*Neon Green* is an extraordinary, inventive literary triumph. Margaret Wappler's breakthrough novel of a family coming to terms with modern life is deftly written, uniquely hilarious, and unexpectedly heartbreaking. Evoking the imaginative pleasures of Lydia Davis, Aimee Bender, and Don DeLillo, *Neon Green* depicts family life, environmentalism, marriage, illness, and spaceships with ingenuity and sophistication."
–Joe Meno, author of *The Great Perhaps*

"The story of an American family's confusion, pain, and joy is given an ingenious new form in Wappler's assured debut. Deeply moving, unsentimentally nostalgic, surreal, and hilarious, her alternate 1990s unravels the curiosities and sufferings that reveal our character and transform our souls."
–J. Ryan Stradal, author of *Kitchens of the Great Midwest*

"*Neon Green* is a time capsule: it captures a moment, a slice of recent history, a feeling, a way of life. Wappler writes with humor, warmth, and intelligence. Filled with jewel-like sentences and insights that add up to a rewarding and deeply affecting novel." **–Charles Yu, author of *How to Live Safely in a Science Fiction Universe***

The Unnamed Press
P.O. Box 411272
Los Angeles, CA 90041

Published in North America by The Unnamed Press.

1 3 5 7 9 10 8 6 4 2

Copyright © 2016 by Margaret Wappler

ISBN: 978-1-939419-71-2

Library of Congress Control Number: 2016943619

This book is distributed by Publishers Group West

Cover design by Scott Arany
Jacket Design & Typeset by Jaya Nicely